She'd start running as soon as she got off the bus, as did he, from the opposite direction. They'd collide, breathless, holding on to each other for support, gulping air until they'd recovered sufficiently to essay that first kiss – as thrilling, each time, as their very first kiss – and they'd kiss all the way along Rita's front path and through the hall and up the stairs and into the scullery.

It was north-facing, the scullery, chilly even in the summer. But it wasn't the cold that caused her to tremble, rather that she shivered with anticipation.

He'd joke, as he covered her with kisses, allege that she'd led him astray, that, until her own appetite had awakened his, he'd been an innocent.

She was three years his senior. 'Does it matter?' she'd asked worriedly.

He'd taken her hand and played 'This little piggy' with her fingers. 'It might do,' he said, 'when I'm a hundred and you're a hundred and three.'

After the war was over.

KATE NORTH

Land of My Dreams

VISTA

First published in Great Britain 1997
by Victor Gollancz as a Vista Paperback Original

Vista is an imprint of the Cassell Group
Wellington House, 125 Strand, London WC2R 0BB

A catalogue record for this book is
available from the British Library.

ISBN 0 575 60385 2

Typeset by Rowland Phototypesetting Ltd,
Bury St Edmunds, Suffolk
Printed and bound in Great Britain by
Caledonian International Book Manufacturing Ltd, Glasgow

97 98 99   5 4 3 2 1

With thanks to Lavinia Trevor for her
continuing encouragement and support

For Timothy,

with love

There's a long, long trail a-winding
Into the land of my dreams,
Where the nightingales are singing
And a white moon beams:
There's a long, long night of waiting
Until my dreams all come true;
Till the day when I'll be going down
That long long trail with you.

First World War song

Chapter One

April 2nd, 1993.

Last night I dreamt I went to . . . Maisie wrote, in unconscious imitation of one of the more famous opening lines in popular English fiction. On reading it back and recognizing the provenance of the quotation, she supposed she'd been influenced by the Daphne du Maurier – although it was a different Daphne du Maurier – that she'd begun the previous night. Yesterday, returning from the library with her books, she'd encountered the woman who'd just moved in next door. She was carrying her belongings from her car to the house and she'd paused at the gate, this woman, her arms full, and introduced herself, apologizing for the fact that she had no free hand to offer in greeting, talking rapidly and breathlessly as shy people do when attempting to draw out persons even shyer than themselves. Faltering eventually, she noticed the title of the novel, *I'll Never Be Young Again*, that was faintly discernible through the triangular webbing of Maisie's string bag. 'Oh,' she said, 'I've just finished reading a biography of her. It seems she was a lesbian, or *wanted* to be . . .'

The woman had then paused and coloured up. 'As if anyone really cares,' she went on.

She's probably wondering if I'm a lesbian and therefore deeply offended, Maisie thought as the woman fled towards her front door.

Maisie wasn't a lesbian, had never wanted to be, but could

identify with that kind of foot-in-the-mouth nervousness, being painfully subject to it herself on occasion.

Last night I dreamt I went to ... Maisie had written, although her destination had been infinitely more sinister than Manderley; her destination had been the culmination of what she thought of as her Black Dream, the one that had polluted her sleep, on an irregularly recurrent basis, since childhood.

Months could go by without any manifestation and then – for no good (or at least no apparent) reason – she'd be plagued by it for half a dozen nights at a stretch: Mother would be dragging her, a tiny child in her woollen bonnet and buttoned gaiters, through the decayed tenements of some soot-blackened, smoke-shrouded city. Dank, besmirched lines of washing flapped about their faces, ragged urchins called abusive names in their wake, the streets grew narrower and meaner and the children dirtier and the women who lounged in the crumbling doorways more blank-eyed and slatternly and Mother's pace quickened until she was practically running and Maisie running, perforce, after her, her arm almost yanked from its socket. Finally they'd turn a corner into a square and there, opposite, loomed the gauntest, blackest building of all. A flight of steps led up to its portico. They were so steep that her little legs could scarcely stretch to climb them. At the top she had to pause in order to get her breath back. She'd puff and pant and raise her eyes to the triangular stone pediment above the lintel upon which, in letters cut so deep that it was impossible to believe that any passage of time, however vast, could bring about their erosion, were inscribed the words: *Lock Hospital.*

Last night I dreamt I went to that place again, wrote Maisie and closed the book and put the top back on her Biro. She'd write up today's entry later. She'd kept a diary since childhood on an almost daily basis, even though some days had been entirely lacking in significant event.

She could hear Timmy wailing below, knew that she ought to get up and let him out so that he could perform his morning bowel movement somewhere amid the garden's lush and rampant overgrowth. She'd furnished him with a litter-tray but, being old and weak-bladdered, he'd already have piddled in that and she knew that an innate delicacy (so at odds with his thoroughly plebeian appearance) prevented him from treading upon the waste matter of one bodily function in order to exercise another.

But she lingered, bed being such an unaccustomed luxury. After the onset of her mother's strangeness, Maisie had taken to sleeping downstairs on the sofa. Cat-napping. Towards the end she'd even stopped changing into her night clothes in case she had to venture outdoors in pursuit. She always hid the key after locking the front door and made a point of varying the hiding places – but Mother had an uncanny knack of locating it.

The howls of feline protest grew louder. She pulled on her dressing-gown and made her way downstairs. Descending, her heart sank, as it always did. Because downstairs was still, three months after her death, Mother-permeated, despite Maisie's determined attempts to erase all traces of the sickroom: the pill bottles, half empty, their contents gone powdery, that crowded on to every available surface, the commode in one corner of the sitting-room, in the other the camp-bed with its ruined mattress. Maisie had filled binbags, made bonfires, swept and polished with a manic zeal, flung windows wide open so that successive volumes of fresh air might displace the stale and stagnant exhalations of imminent mortality. But, beneath the eye-watering aromas of bleach and Lysol and air-freshener, something sadly persistent lingered yet.

While Timmy gobbled down his breakfast with an urgency that suggested, quite erroneously, that the provenance of his next meal was in doubt, she inspected his latest wound. Though surgically emasculated long since, he still demonstrated a level of aggression that argued against any diminution of the relevant hormone. Perhaps, she thought, he was just naturally belligerent. Old combat wounds had frilled the edges of his ears and to stroke his fur was to be made aware of his entire pugilistic history: a snapped rib that had knitted up crookedly, a broken nose that now conferred a Roman profile. His fur was rather long for a common or garden tabby cat. She wondered if he had aristocratic antecedents, knew nothing about them. He had appeared one morning on her doorstep and levelled at her a challenging stare. By the time he condescended to sample a saucer of milk her heart, so long starved of sustenance, was entirely forfeit.

The doorbell rang before she'd had the chance to wash herself, let alone get properly dressed. 'Another of the Morecambe people, I'll bet,' she said to Timmy. He raised his face from his dish, morsels of meat dribbling from between the partial dentition of his gums, and shared with her what she interpreted as a glance of commiseration.

They called them the caring professions, that vast body of doctors and nurses and counsellors and social workers; she lumped them all together under the umbrella title of *the Morecambe people*. This was because, after Mother's death, their chief concern seemed to be that she should have a change of scenery. 'When did you last have a holiday?' they'd said sternly. 'A proper holiday?' Well, she'd told them, before Mother became really ill they'd sometimes had a week or so in a boarding-house in Prestatyn, together with other holidaymakers who also returned yearly to the same location: the Carpenters, she remembered, who had tried, with overpowering bonhomie, to persuade them into joining trips, purchasing theatre tickets, playing clock golf; the Maysons, who organized card games and then cheated . . . Mother had advised her to rebuff all such advances. 'We keep ourselves to ourselves,' she'd said. It had been the guiding principle of her life.

Long before that, there'd been a childhood holiday. She remembered digging for crabs on the beach at Filey under the supervision of an older boy, wonderfully glamorous in a bright yellow bathing-suit. Had it been '20 or '21? She couldn't exactly recall. Mother had still been in black, that much she remembered.

Anyway, they'd booked her in at some place in Morecambe,

these caring people, despite her repeated assertions that she wasn't much of a one for holidays. But when the time came she'd experienced a bit of a funny turn so the expedition had had to be cancelled. Postponed, *they* called it, and refused to let the matter drop.

'Thank goodness!' said Miss Miles, insinuating her foot into the door's slight and unwelcoming aperture. 'I was beginning to worry. You really ought to let us have a key.'

She'd said this often before. And Maisie, who'd asked why just as often, repeated the query.

'In case,' said Miss Miles. It was her catchphrase. She used it as indiscriminately as Mother had used hers, which was 'For fear.'

Miss Miles came from the Social Services. She could be referred to as 'my social worker', Maisie realized; she had heard the unmarried mothers in the queue at the post office talking of 'my social worker' as though this fundamentally impersonal connection had the same authenticity as a natural relationship.

Miss Miles appeared to be in a permanent state of dermal irritation. On her previous visit her upper lip had shown evidence of a cold sore just about to erupt; now it had properly made its debut. She picked at it covertly as she talked of holidays and heating allowances. Maisie averted her eyes and then closed them as the voice of professional concern recited the list of welfare benefits to which she might be entitled. Too little, she thought, too late.

'Oh, and I've arranged a visit for you from Dr Owen,' said Miss Miles, shuffling the papers in triplicate to which Maisie had obligingly affixed her signature. 'He's new at the practice. Very enthusiastic. I take it that you're still getting the pains?'

'Now and then,' said Maisie. She'd mentioned them once before, tentatively, to Dr Morrison who was old at the practice and had since retired. 'What's the trouble – apart from age and decay?' he'd said, ungallantly. 'I get this – sort of pulsating sensation when I lie on my left side,' she'd replied. 'Well, if I were you,' had been his response, 'I'd lie on my right.'

'Well, Maisie,' said Miss Miles, snapping her briefcase shut with a professional finality. 'I'll be back to see you as soon as the level of your Income Support has been decided. And do please give some more thought to having help in the house. It's nothing to be ashamed of, you know.'

Maisie's surname was Carruthers. She was not overfond of it, suggestive as it was of crusty retired coloneldom, but neither did she care for what she considered to be over-familiarity. They all called her Maisie: Miss Miles, the ladies from the WRVS when, during the last days of Mother's illness, they'd carried in their unsolicited and undesired cooling dishes of meat and two veg, the nurses who'd powdered her sores and sponged her sour flesh, the vicar who made such a point of not being religious.

They'd call her Maisie and, on their way out, they'd pick up that old photograph that stood on the hall table and they'd say, 'Is this you when you were a girl? Weren't you pretty?' She never disabused them of this notion. In fact, it was a photograph of her mother. Perhaps they didn't look closely enough. For if they had done they'd have seen that the photograph had once included two figures: a fact made obvious by the evidence of the man's hand resting on Mother's shoulder; if they hadn't been, collectively, blind as bats and thick as short planks, they'd have observed that – in terms of symmetry – the photograph was distinctly lop-sided.

It was Mother who'd cut Pa's likeness off that picture and then thrown it into the fire grate, along with other pictures: the wedding photograph, a studio portrait of Pa in his uniform, dated 1915, just before he left for France. All the time she was doing it – cutting the studies in sepia into smaller and smaller pieces, consigning them to the flames, watching the varnish melt from the paper which then curled and blackened and collapsed into ash – the tears had streamed down her face and dripped from her chin. Maisie had heard them hissing on the coals.

Tears on the coals. Water under the bridge. She breathed on the glass of the photograph frame and buffed it on her sleeve but the photograph itself was fading fast. Decay. Degradation. Change. It was inescapable. All around. This had been a quiet neighbourhood, an elderly neighbourhood; tenancies were surrendered and sale boards sprouted in accordance with the announcements in the obituary column. But everything was altering: as the fixed-rent tenants were carted off, feet first, so the un-modernization was beginning: hardboard and chipboard and vinyl and veneer were being torn away to the accompaniment of cries of delight as beading and cornicing and quarry tiles were revealed; the cheap, grant-aided softwood casements were being re-replaced by Victorian sashes and Georgian stiles, butlers' sinks reclaimed from the salvage yards whence they had found their way when the landlords had installed stainless-steel units, might even be returned – at exorbitant cost – to the very houses from which they'd been ripped.

It was happening next door: hammering and banging, lifting and shifting, to-ing and fro-ing. The Kandinskys, in residence when Maisie and her mother moved in, had once made tentative overtures of friendship but had been frozen out so determinedly that they'd soon taken the hint and, being quiet people of reticent disposition, had scarcely impinged thereafter. When they died the house had been put up for sale but it had been on the market for so long that Maisie had almost come to believe that it would remain forever unsold.

She heard a car drawing up at the front and then the crunch of footsteps along next-door's path which was currently covered in gravel but would doubtless soon be stripped down to the original encaustic tiles which lay beneath. Next-door's knocker (an ersatz brass lion's head purchased from B & Q and proudly affixed by Mr Kandinsky during one of his *House Beautiful* phases) rose and fell upon next-door's (authentic) Victorian front door.

After a while Maisie's doorbell rang. She hadn't heard the footsteps receding, so presumably the visitor had, impolitely, vaulted the low iron railings that separated the two driveways.

She'd have let the bell ring, except that she knew she could be seen through the glass of the door: an elderly lady in her dressing-gown hunched on the bottom step of the stairs. Whoever it was, glimpsing her thus, might fear the worst and call for assistance. Once, not long after Mother's funeral, a too-prolonged ignoring of the bell-ringing and door-thumping of the More-cambe people had led to a visit from the local constabulary: a pink-faced young policeman who'd at least had the courtesy to address her as Madam while delivering his kindly admonition.

A large woman stood on the doorstep. She wore a great deal of heavy ethnic jewellery and a crystal, dependent from a leather thong, which nestled within her canyonesque cleavage and rotated gently as her chest rose and fell, each of its facets suffused alternately with colours reflected from the door's stained glass panel: rose, gold, acid-green. The effect was quite hypnotic. Maisie had to blink vigorously and avert her attention from it as the woman enquired of her whether she knew when Mrs Williams would be back.

'Clare,' the woman said. 'Next door? She's expecting me. Oh God, don't say I've got the wrong day?'

'I really don't know,' Maisie was starting to say and then they both heard the sound of a car decelerating and screeching to a halt and a door slamming before the person in question came running down her path, calling, 'I'm *so* sorry, Lizzie, I got stuck behind the shopper from hell in Sainsbury's – first she queried every item on the bill and then she found she'd forgotten her card and didn't have enough cash to settle it . . . Oh, hello,' she said, on glimpsing Maisie, and left it at that, probably remembering Daphne du Maurier.

'No sweat,' the woman said, striding back over the railings. 'Only I've arranged to meet That Prick at two-thirty.'

Later, Maisie wrote in her diary: *I have a new neighbour. Her name is Clare Williams. She is slight and pretty with dark hair and a startled expression. Her friend – a big woman, in every sense of the word – came to visit. And then in the evening, when I was*

18

letting Timmy out, I saw a man leaving. He kissed her at the door.
For a moment, I was reminded of Bob – not that this man looked
anything like Bob, it was just the way he kissed her, as though it
might be for the last time. It was like that for us. During the war
when you kissed it was for ever, for eternity, Maisie wrote faintly
and fainter still because her Biro was running out. *I remember*
... Maisie wrote, but then the pen gave up the ghost completely
so she put the diary away and went to the pantry for the bottle
of Bailey's Irish Cream that was kept there. She'd bought her first
one in the supermarket soon after Mother died – there'd been a
special offer. It had come as a delightful surprise to discover that
these days alcoholic drinks were formulated for those who didn't
care for the taste of alcohol. Now she swallowed it nightly, savour-
ing its sweetness, grateful for its sedative effect, wondering, as
she became tipsily tranquil, meltingly mellow, whether she might
dare to sample, so late in the day, other such unfamiliar treats.

Chapter Two

'Next door? Granny Clampett?' Lizzie said, searching vigorously
– and in vain – among the tea chests for a corkscrew. 'What's
the score?'

'You won't find it in there,' said Clare, replacing items scattered
in the course of this frantic quest. 'If there is one it'll be somewhere in the kitchen boxes, the ones marked with the green dots
– but I have a funny feeling that it wasn't packed.'

'Time you got your priorities right,' Lizzie said. 'What are you
afraid of: the neighbours talking? "She drinks, you know." Well,
I *need* a drink. I must have a drink. I can't do it sober. We'll just
have to do a Clint Eastwood. Watch yourself!' And she took the
bottle to the sink and smacked the slenderest part of it smartly
against the porcelain. 'Quick! Glasses!' she cried as the wine began
to gush from its severed neck. Clare obliged, but said, 'I'm not
terribly sure that I fancy Château Ground Glass.'

'Don't be such a wimp. It was a clean cut. *Salute!*' said Lizzie,
quaffing mightily. 'So,' she said, 'next door. What *is* the word?'

Clare shrugged. 'Haven't a clue. We didn't get beyond names.
Hers is Maisie. Maisie Carruthers. Miss.'

'Maisie Carruthers! How marvellous. Sounds like a character
out of *White Mischief.*' Lizzie refilled her glass and ran her fingers
through her hair until it framed her face as luxuriantly as that
of some Pre-Raphaelite heroine. Unfortunately her face was out
of a different picture altogether, being not pale and interesting
but broad and high-coloured and bearing – at this moment –

20

a somewhat bellicose expression. She said, 'How do I look?'

'Perfectly fine.'

'I don't want to look perfectly fine. I want to look either desperately wronged or else absolutely knock-out, drop-dead gorgeous, look-what-you've-passed-up, you twenty-four carat twat.'

'What time did you say your appointment was?' said Clare. She shivered. The pallid early-spring sunshine had disappeared behind a cloud and the kitchen – bare, apart from the basic essentials – seemed dismal and unwelcoming. The removal had originally been planned for February but a critical link in a vendor's chain (for months she had thought only in terms of vendors and mortgagees and bridging loans) had proved intransigent and they'd had to postpone until April. April 1st. 'How inauspicious,' she had said, but Lizzie, more sanguine, and besides involved only at a remove, had replied, 'Crap! You know what your trouble is? You *look* for trouble.'

Now she said, 'Half-two. It'll be a waste of time though, I know it. There's no way he'll ever admit to being even marginally, *peripherally*, in the wrong – and I presume that that's what the whole business is about: owning up to your marital shortcomings? He'll sit there, looking alternately smug and hard-done-by and I'll just want to hit him.'

'You did,' Clare said. 'On several occasions.'

'You know, I always used to think: Marriage Guidance, Relate, call it what you will – silly buggers,' Lizzie said, tipping the bottle, but it was drained too thoroughly to yield anything but a few drops, crimson as blood. She retrieved them with her tongue from the bottom of the glass. 'And now, here I go, about to join up.'

Clare twirled her glass by its stem. She said, 'Do you remember, that night in Hall when we had the ouija board and you asked it about your future and it told you that you'd be happily married with four kids by the time you were thirty?'

'I rather thought that that was what it told *you*. Make-up!' said

Lizzie, producing a somewhat grubby bag of the same. 'Less or more?' It was necessary to deflect Clare when she started do-you-remembering. Invariably, to proceed in that direction was tantamount to following Auden's crack in the tea cup; it opened up if not a lane to the land of the dead, then certainly one to the regions of lost opportunity and unsignposted ways.

'That depends on the impression you want to make.'

'One that says, "You'd better not fuck me about, you adulterous creep." That would do for starters.'

'Oh, Lizzie! It's meant to be a process of reconciliation. If you just want to fight with him, then what's the point?'

'Maybe I miss fighting.'

She put down her glass, wobbled a bit and said, 'Perhaps I ought to eat something before I go. I don't want them thinking I'm pissed.'

Clare made coffee and sandwiches. It took longer than usual because of the unfamiliar surroundings. She kept going to a cutlery drawer which – here – did not exist. It was the cutlery drawer in the kitchen of the old house. It would be months, she knew, before that stopped happening.

They ate perched on the edge of the kitchen table, its matching chairs having apparently dematerialized somewhere in transit. There was scarcely space to put a foot between the chests and boxes ranged around them. The stuff you acquired! The pots and the pans and the books and the records, all the pictures and plant pots, mirrors and magazine racks, pepper mills and fondue sets and nail scissors – and that not even taking Gwyn's belongings into account.

Lizzie intercepted her glance. She said, 'I'll come round tomorrow. Give you a hand. I'm due a day off. Incidentally, has Whatshisname had the pleasure yet?'

'He came last night.'

'Did he by Jove!'

Lizzie swept crumbs from her person, disentangled an earring from a tumbling tendril of hair. She said, '*He* bought me these.

For our wedding anniversary. He'd seen me admiring them in the shop. I suppose he does have the *odd* nice trait.'

For a second an expression akin to fondness appeared on her face and then she remembered herself and said, 'Gwyn'll be back soon to lend you a hand anyway. When did you say he breaks up?'

'The week after next,' Clare said. He was coming home from boarding-school, for good. It was a prospect to which she had looked forward with great eagerness for a long time.

'Incidentally, have you given any more thought to the party?' said Lizzie, belting herself into her trenchcoat, stiffening her sinews and summoning up her blood — at least, she had a fairly hectic flush, if that was anything to go by. 'If it was here,' she said, 'you could combine it with a house-warming.'

Their birthdays were in the same year on adjacent days. So much for astrology, Clare had often thought. She had been happy to ignore this approaching milestone: their respective fortieths; Lizzie, unfalteringly gregarious, had other plans.

Now she reached into her bag for her cigarettes, remembered that she had given up smoking some six months before and settled instead for a gruesome old bit of chewing-gum that reposed, half-wrapped and gathering fluff, at the bottom. 'What do you bet,' she said indistinctly, as she attempted to chew some flexibility into this fossil, 'that she looks like Virginia Bottomley?'

'Who?' said Clare, who was visualizing — should the house be in a fit state by mid-July to accommodate such a gathering — an elegant soirée: lights flickering among the trees, tables on the terrace covered with starched white cloths, bottles of wine nestling among ice, Gwyn handing round canapés with a suavity that belied his years . . . Perhaps Theo would come. She preferred not to dwell upon the grim reality of Lizzie's previous parties: divorces had been known to occur in the aftermath of Lizzie's parties, lifelong friendships irrevocably severed, true sexual orientations belatedly discovered . . .

'Virginia Bottomley,' Lizzie was saying, 'this counsellor,

mediator, whatever she calls herself . . . I expect I shall detest her on sight. Right,' she said, straightening her shoulders, 'Michael Twist, Michael *Cyril* Twist, here I come. So reconcile me.'

'Is that really his name? Cyril?'

'Yes. It rather suits him, don't you think? Well, aren't you going to wish me luck?'

But luck didn't come into it. Relations between Michael and Elizabeth Twist were, as far as Clare could tell, as ritualized as a courtly dance: they converged, they parted, they circled one another, they linked up with different partners, they were reunited. They had been performing the same steps in much the same sequence ever since they'd married, resplendent on the town hall steps in, respectively, boa and thigh-high boots, and kipper tie, velvet jacket and loon pants. Clare had taken too many tearful telephone calls, sat up until four in the morning commiserating; had offered refuge, consolation, even advice, had listened, rapt, as bloodcurdling anecdotes were related: pyjama-clad pursuits into the night armed with kitchen knives, telephone handsets torn from their sockets and hurled through the double-glazing, movements monitored, pockets searched, showdowns carefully choreographed. She had made apprehensive contact on innumerable mornings-after only to discover that domestic harmony once more prevailed. In short, she was fairly inured to it. And even though, among all the comings and goings, the flights and the fights, the rights and wrongs of it all, there had been bitter tears shed, she had never been quite convinced that any of Lizzie's afflictions produced a pain comparable to her own. This was a fault in her nature, she supposed, an only-child, centre-of-the-universe sort of fault. Possibly Gwyn suffered from it too.

A proud-mother image of him flashed into her mind: his dark eyes, dark curls, smooth complexion. He was well-grown too, tall and strong; strong enough to be of assistance with the manifold chores that lay ahead. Taming the garden, for instance. She stood looking through the window for a long time after Lizzie had left. It was a smaller garden than they'd had before; everything here

24

was smaller than they'd had before. Though, considering its over-grown state, that was probably all to the good. Next door was even worse: pygmies could have lived incognito amid the grass next door; nettles towered, five feet high, thrusting towards the light, brambles proliferated, ground-elder and bindweed advanced steadily, colonizing the uncultivated earth. Neglected next-door gardens meant, Clare knew, that an offensive must be mounted on all fronts, but presently all that she saw was her own patch of Eden, as it would be: a white garden, glimmering at twilight, crammed with roses and gypsophila and Miss Wilmot's Ghost. 'Your own little Sissinghurst,' Theo had said the night before as they surveyed the wilderness. 'Why stop there? What about a gazebo? An avenue of pleached limes? A temple of Venus?'

At length, she turned her attention from what possibly could be to what indubitably was and began to unpack the first of the green-spotted packing cases that lay in her path. There still seemed to be a fair amount of junk, despite the massive clear-out that had taken place before she left the old house; she'd dispensed largesse to jumble sales and Oxfam and the Little Sisters of the Poor with an almost careless abandon, as if a new house, a new life, demanded that she rid herself of all those things that connec-ted her to and reminded her of the old one.

But of course caution had eventually prevailed: you couldn't discard perfectly good sheets simply because you'd lain upon them with your late ex-husband. And the usefulness of a clock that kept good time cancelled out any connotations suggested by the chip on its case where it had collided with the doorpost; she had aimed it, inaccurately, at his head.

She worked steadily all through the afternoon, arranging her possessions inside cupboards and upon shelves, vacuuming the fluff from the newly laid carpets, banging the dust out of books, sorting through records and discovering among them a couple of cuckoos in the nest: Miles Davis, Thelonious Monk – Huw's, overlooked in his headlong flight to extra-marital bliss; she dis-liked modern jazz almost as fervently as he had detested the piano music, Schumann and Rachmaninov and Lizst, of which she was fond.

She inspected those records in their tattered covers, thinking of how far they'd travelled since her parents had bought them, together with the Dansette record-player, for her seventeenth birthday. Shortly afterwards they had died: he of kidney failure, she ostensibly of leukaemia, though sheer inability to carry on might have been an equally appropriate diagnosis. An aunt – sole close relative – had been morally obliged to accept guardianship. There was no love lost between them. Clare remembered the huge, dank house crammed with Victorian furniture: escritoires, chiffoniers, pier-glasses, jardinières and chaises-longues, monumental, cold to the touch. She remembered the cast-iron bath with its stained enamel surface into which she had been permitted to submerge herself on one evening per week, remembered being too embarrassed to ask about the disposal of sanitary towels. At home they'd been burned; Aunt Winifred managed with the occasional three-bar electric fire, of which only one bar was allowed to radiate its feeble glow amid the encircling gloom. She remembered too, most vividly, her last visit to the family home for the purpose of collecting the cat. But the cat had scratched her face and sprung from her arms and disappeared into the night. Just as well perhaps, she had thought, since Aunt Winifred would most surely have had it put down. After a half-hearted search in the shrubbery, she'd abandoned it to its own devices and called at the house of a neighbour to collect a skirt that had been ordered from her catalogue. She'd carried the parcel back to Aunt Winifred's and there, among the tasselled chenille and the plush, she'd unpacked it. She'd tried it on and waited to be delighted, knowing even as she did so that there was no consolation to be had: her parents were dead and her aunt was a loveless woman as cold as her house, and the most beautiful skirt in the world could not begin to compensate.

She hadn't cried then; the tears came later. And then she'd cried for weeks, every night, soaking her lumpy flock pillow.

She'd cried all the time that she was completing her Advanced Level examination papers. So it came as something of a surprise to discover that she'd actually performed well enough to win a university scholarship.

She'd cried too at first at college. And then she'd met Lizzie. 'Cheer up,' Lizzie had said. 'It might never happen.' Lizzie was large and confident. She ate raw garlic and wore a scruffy Afghan coat that smelled of recently dead wild animal. They first encountered each other in the communal kitchen where Clare was struggling with the water-heater. 'Not like that, you chump,' Lizzie had said, but not unkindly. 'Don't they have electricity where you come from?' Only just, Clare had wanted to say, and even so Aunt Winifred gets the meter-man to change the bulbs. 'So where are you off to tonight?' Lizzie had said, lighting a Disque Bleu as they waited for the kettle to boil.

'Well, it's the Freshers' Ball . . .'

And Lizzie had laughed with such energetic scorn that she'd swallowed smoke and almost choked herself. When she'd recovered she said, 'The Freshers' Ball? Are you deranged? Unless you really *like* being fumbled by pustulent youths, that is? Everybody goes to the Downbeat Club in town on a Friday. That's if you're interested in meeting gorgeous men?'

She'd left the question dangling, as though there was the faint possibility that Clare might reply, 'Well, actually, I prefer pustulent youths.' 'Want one?' she then said, offering her cigarette packet. Clare had accepted, but she'd had scant opportunity to practise smoking and blew when she ought to have sucked so that ignition repeatedly failed to occur. In the end Lizzie had lit the cigarette for her. 'You need taking in hand,' she'd said.

In hand. It had sounded such a safe place to be. She'd stopped crying, quite soon afterwards.

Gwyn had not cried when told of his father's death, at least not within her hearing. His upper lip had remained disquietingly stiff. She'd waited for him in the headmaster's study, ashamed that she was accepting condolences under false pretences – the

27

news of Huw's death had produced nothing more than a quiver of shock. Gwyn had been summoned from an art class. He was good at art. At one time she'd pinned up drawings he'd done, pointing them out proudly to visitors, until his blushes had made her realize that this was yet another way she'd found of embarrassing him beyond measure.

She smoothed the quilt on his bed, arranged his books on the shelves, his tapes in a drawer. Perhaps they were books and tapes that should have been donated to the jumble sale. Perhaps he'd say, 'Why have you brought that old rubbish?' in a way which suggested that every false move she made was not by accident but design.

It was a difficult age, everyone said so. But all the same she was counting the days until he came home.

Chapter Three

MY DIARY

PRIVATE AND CONFIDENTIAL

January 8th, 1925.

My name is Margaret Alice Carruthers, Maisie for short – but not for long, Pa used to say, and today is my ninth birthday. Grandma has sent me this diary as a present. She lives with Grandpa in the country which is where I was born and lived when I was a little child. Now I live at number 32, Grenfell Crescent in rooms that we rent from Mrs Mendelssohn. (I had to ask her how to spell her name and at first she teased me and answered in a strange language called Double-Dutch. She also speaks Yiddish which I believe is what Jewish people speak as a change from Hebrew or English. She says I am a little mensch, *and when I asked Miss Marriott what it meant, she said man, so I am none the wiser.)*

This is the fourth address we have had since we left the Dales. First there was number 94, Strawberry Avenue, but Mother said we had to leave there because of bugs, then number 9, Danube View, but the landlady there was forever poking her nose into what didn't concern her. After that we moved to Mossop Avenue but Mother said the drains were bad and gave you dip (it is diphtheria that she meant, Miss Marriott said).

I am in the Fourth Grade and Miss Marriott is my teacher. She

29

is very tall and thin and I think she is remarkably pretty. Once she gave me a humbug when we were walking home because I came top in the test. She said, 'Keep it under your hat,'. I didn't know what she meant because I didn't have a hat on. We don't wear hats at Howarth Road School, except for the girls with nits, they wear scarves. I shall wear a hat if I get to the Grammar School, but that is a very big if, Mother says, even though I usually come top in the tests. It is either me or Peggy Hudson. Up until I was seven I was kept back with the tots which wasn't fair because all they do is learn to button their boots and tell the time. I have been able to tell the time for years. Miss Marriott told Mother that they thought I was slow but then they found out it was because I couldn't see the blackboard. As soon as I got the glasses I raced ahead. Mother needs glasses too because of doing such close work but she says want must be her master.

I hope we stay here with Mrs Mendelssohn. It's a very nice house and we have two large rooms overlooking the park. On Saturday, which in Jewish is called Shabbas, Mother lights the gas for Mrs Mendelssohn and ties her shoelaces because Jewish people are not supposed to do anything on this day. Which I think must be very boring.

I intend to continue this diary and fill in every page. I have written to Grandma to say thank you and ask her to give a kiss from me to Beauty and Daisy and Clover (cows), Shep the dog, all the lambs when they get born and the hens and the cockerel too which nips your ankle though he doesn't really mean it. I said to Mother, can't we ever go back to the Dales? It's very nice here but the farm was lovely and I miss Grandma and Grandpa. She said, Finish up your porridge like a good girl and don't ask so many questions, it gets on my nerves . . .

'Is this where you get the pain?' Dr Owen said, prodding vigorously in and around her ribcage. 'Here? Or here?'

'Yes,' Maisie said obligingly, in answer to each prod. She was itching to get her blouse back on. She'd have been more particular about her underwear if she'd known he was coming but he'd turned up unannounced: an incredibly young man wearing a leather jacket and jeans; at first she'd taken him for the window-cleaner and had said, as she always did when they came canvassing, 'No thank you. We do them ourselves.'

'We'd better get you checked out,' he said. 'Just to be on the safe side. I'll make you an appointment to see Mr Haydn-Jones at the hospital.'

She'd started to protest, to say, 'But I can't leave Mother . . .' and then remembered.

'I'll mark it urgent,' he said, 'but don't hold your breath.'

He wrote something on his pad and then sat clicking the top of his pen in and out, asking one question after another. How was she coping? Had she access to a day centre? Did she have a home help?

'No,' she replied. 'Not any more.'

Not for a long time. They wouldn't stay. On account of Mother.

At last he got up to leave. At the front door she said, 'I don't know what all the fuss is about. I've never ailed a thing.'

Though that was not strictly true, could not have been strictly true. Or else why those visits to the hospital when she was a tiny girl? Because the Black Dream was not merely a recurrent nightmare; the Black Dream had its basis in reality and sometimes she remembered those visits of over seventy years ago with a startling clarity: the square that opened out from the maze of narrow streets, the steps, the great door and the impassive expression on the face of the nurse who opened it. Inside, everything had been drab and ugly: the green distempered walls and the dark brown varnished doors and the nurses in their rigidly starched caps that shielded their eyes like vizors and – worst of all – the women who lay in the beds that they glimpsed through the open doors of the wards. Once, there had been one who turned to look at them and where her nose should have been there was only a gaping hole.

Maisie had screamed then and continued to scream when the

doctor came, because although he had a pleasant face beneath the alarming black whiskers and patted her on the head and called her Little Dolly Daydream, this was merely to catch her off guard so that he could stick needles into her arm.

She couldn't remember exactly how many visits they'd made: it could have been many or only a few. But she did remember how, after each visit, her mother would weep inconsolably, tears more copious and bitter, it seemed to Maisie, than those she'd shed after her father had died of the Spanish flu.

After the doctor had left she went upstairs to search out the underclothes that had once formed part of her bottom drawer, but later had been redesignated as appropriate for just such an eventuality as this one. Located, they smelled musty – she'd have to rinse them through – almost as musty as Mother's trousseau which lay beneath them, still wrapped in its original tissue, yellow as butter: the nightdress with the faggoting at the neck and the hem, the petticoats trimmed with Nottingham lace, the blouse with the sailor collar and the gloves of finest ivory kid. And suddenly Maisie wept as she inhaled these old familiar scents, wept with the total lack of restraint of those who weep alone. What she wouldn't have given, just then, to lift the net curtain and see Mother, half-clad, shuffling along the path, her eyes fixed on the ground before her, pausing at intervals to pick up the rubber bands that the postman had discarded when he undid his bundles of letters, pick them up, stuff them into her pockets and, later, into her mouth.

'A blessed release,' they'd said, just one of the clichés that had been recited after the funeral by the district nurse, the health visitor, the vicar, who obviously knew nothing about the strength of mutual need.

Eventually she wiped her eyes on the vests and knickers, closed the drawer and turned to go downstairs. As she passed the landing window, a movement in the garden next door caught her eye. It was the woman with the same man that she'd seen the other night. They stood together, their hands barely touching, a contact so slight yet so evidently deliberate that it suggested previous contact of a much closer variety. It took Maisie a second or two to recognize what she saw in their faces and then she remembered: it was the slightly dazed expression of replete sexuality.

They made a handsome couple. Like, of course, went to like, as a general rule. She thought of her mother and her father, and her grandparents: pretty women, good-looking men. She thought about them more and more often these days, closed her eyes and conjured up visions of Grandpa showing her how you took the cows' teats that belonged to Beauty and Clover and Daisy and squeezed them rhythmically in order to induce the gushes of warm frothy milk to spurt into the galvanized bucket; of sitting beside him in the governess cart when he shook up Punch into a trot to take them to the station where they'd deliver a parcel or collect a soldier on home leave, fresh from the trenches. Once one of them gave her a foreign coin. It was called a franc, Grandpa said. She'd determined to keep it for ever but it had eventually got lost, somewhere in transit.

She'd see Grandma who, having completed the long day's final task, which was to scatter tea leaves on the stone-flagged floor before sweeping it, would then offer her lap and open the picture-book: Snow White biting into the poisoned apple, Rapunzel letting down her golden hair, Rumpelstiltskin dancing himself to death. 'So you *can* read, Maisie,' they'd said later, at school, when they'd diagnosed her as being severely myopic. Until then they had merely humoured her scarlet-faced assertion, as she strove to identify the blurred marks on the board or the slate, that she had indeed been able to read – once. In fact, they'd said, Grandma and Grandpa, that she was smart. It was only since moving to the town that she seemed to have become stupid.

'Town? Town?' Mrs Mendelssohn had said. 'Why, this is practically the countryside.' And she'd made an expansive gesture that included the harsh-smelling privet that separated each pebble-dashed villa from its neighbour, the few soot-spangled bushes planted in the garden's thin soil, the trampled recreation ground and the dusty park and the cinder path beside the canal. Maisie's countryside had been the beck running shallow across the sparkling stones, glow-worms like lanterns in the hedgerows at dusk, the lambkins rejected by their mothers that had to be brought beside the fire and fed with titty-bottles of warm milk, the bullocks being led down the lane, frisky if there was thunder in the air, liable to bolt. Maisie's countryside had been waking to smell the effluent from the cows rather than that of the gasworks.

But Mrs Mendelssohn was kind. And besides, she and Mother had something in common – apart from the fact of their widowhood. Before he died, Mr Mendelssohn had been in the garment trade and this was the work which Mother now undertook to earn her living. This, she said, was the reason for moving to the town: there were precious few clothing factories to be found in the Dales. But Maisie suspected that there was another reason, one that was never made explicit. Once, when Grandma came to visit, she'd said, 'Come home, Rose. No good ever came of running away and hiding. For the child's sake at least. She'll never thrive here.' But Mother had shaken her head furiously and said she wasn't going to give the tongues any more cause to wag. She'd rather take poison.

Thriving was one thing; like Mrs Mendelssohn, Maisie was a stranger in a strange land, taunted by the other children because she spoke with a country accent, because she was short-sighted, because she was slow and then because she was smart.

There were other outsiders, of course: girls with squints or legs bowed by rickets. 'Aren't they lucky!' one of them had said wistfully – a girl with a harelip – as they watched the pretty, popular girls being dressed up as fairies for the school pageant. The girl seemed friendly, but pride had prevented Maisie from accepting her friendship; she belonged with the fairies, not the harelips, the birthmarks, the calipers.

And anyway, Mother wasn't keen on her bringing home girls from school.

Mother hadn't stayed long at the sewing factory. They were

34

such a nosy lot, she said – and so dreadfully common. Instead she advertised her private tailoring services, bought herself a second-hand treadle machine and sat at it all day long and often into the night, expertly turning revers and pinning on facings, smocking yokes and binding hems, letting out and turning up and cutting down. Maisie became accustomed to the sight of ladies standing on the table in their underwear while her mother measured their relevant dimensions. Generally they were ladies from the crescents and the drives at the other side of the park. They referred to Maisie's mother, between themselves, as 'that little woman who runs up my summer frocks'. Some of them were a bit snooty, condescending, but others, shedding formality with their clothes, were inclined to chat, tried to draw Maisie's mother out. She, though unfailingly polite, retreated into herself as fast as they advanced. 'We don't want people poking their noses in, do we?' she said to Maisie. 'We're quite happy as we are.'

And perhaps, on balance, they were. Certainly Mrs Mendelssohn was their nicest landlady. Even Mother thawed somewhat in the glow of Mrs Mendelssohn's exuberant physicality. Mrs M laughed without restraint, fell to her knees and gave thanks for the slightest stroke of good fortune, screamed with temper when the geyser played up or the damper stuck, kissed and hugged without needing much of a reason or an excuse. Maisie had been apprehensive to start with: she looked so fierce and strange with her sallow skin and black boot-button eyes that darted hither and thither, and her funny un-hair-like hair, as dusty and black as a dead crow's wing – it was a wig, Mother said, said that Jewish ladies shaved off all their hair when they married and thenceforward covered their bald pates with wigs.

But, despite her strangeness, Mrs Mendelssohn had proved to be approachable in a way that Mother was not, became, in time, more motherly than Mother, ever ready with an embrace, an encouraging comment, an endearment: 'Come, see, *schatzie*, what I have for you' – a thick slice of dark bread sprinkled with poppy seeds as big as mouse droppings, a little *gefilte* fish on a spotted plate, a nut and a tangerine and a peg-dolly stuffed into her stocking on their Gentile Christmas morning. It was Mrs M who spooned *lokshen* soup into her mouth when she had the measles and was obliged to lie in bed with the curtains closed for fear of blindness, Mrs M who cried, 'Genius!' when she got a gold star, and comforted her when the bullies lay in wait on the way home from school. They had done the same to her Sammy, she said: chased him, calling: 'Jew Boy, Jew Boy, who killed Christ?' And Sammy had cried too. But look at him now, Mrs M said, training to be a doctor in London while his tormentors – what should they do but pick rags or sweep the streets, like the *schmucks* and *schlemiels* that they were?

'Your time will come too, *liebchen*,' Mrs M had said. 'It will come.'

Maisie roused herself from reverie. (It was, of course, the classic symptom of old age: this ability to recall the events of a lifetime ago more clearly than those of yesterday.) She rinsed her underwear and took it outside and began to peg it out on the line. She didn't want to go to hospital. Perhaps, she thought, she could simply ignore the summons when it arrived. But she knew that she was fooling herself because *they*, the state-appointed guardians of her welfare, would make sure that she attended. Mother might have been able to keep the world at arm's length but things were different now. Impingement was unavoidable, even here in her own back garden where she could see that her new next-door neighbour and the man were still contemplating the wilderness before them.

The woman acknowledged her presence with a smile. 'Terrible, isn't it?' she called, and then perhaps realizing that this criticism implicated Maisie's garden too and was therefore somewhat tactless, continued rapidly, 'We're just dreaming of how it will be.'

She spoke the phrase tenderly, as though it encompassed much more than the mere landscaping of a garden. *He* said nothing, just placed a hand lightly but with unmistakably proprietorial intent on his companion's shoulder and smiled. He was an attractive man and it was a most engaging smile. This time she realized just why he reminded her of Bob. 'With a smile like that, you could get away with murder,' her friend Rita used to say. Though this advantage had been of no use to Bob whose nature was as sweet as his smile. 'Poor Maisie,' she'd once overheard someone say, the implication being: poor Maisie, with her terrible mother and her impoverished, desiccated, spinster life. Which just went to show what little they knew.

Chapter Four

Lizzie whisked them off, herself and Clare, to the ballet. She had complimentary tickets. Her job – in public relations – guaranteed her a regular supply of freebies. 'You deserve a break,' she said. 'So do I, come to that – slaving away all yesterday.'

Slaving was putting it a bit strongly; Lizzie had been too full of her matrimonial affairs to be capable of devoting much attention to hanging curtains or unpacking plates. She'd transferred her bottom from one horizontal surface to the next: kitchen table, window-seat, Gwyn's bed, while she related her Relate experience. 'I have a one-word response,' she said, 'to that pious sentiment expressed by counsellors and their like that men never stray unless there's something wrong at home, and that is: Bollocks!'

It was a one-word response that served her on many an occasion, whether her succinct opinion was required or not.

'You of all people,' Lizzie said, 'should know what a facile generalization *that* is. I mean, it wasn't down to you, was it, when Huw started flying his kite?'

'I don't know,' Clare said. 'I honestly don't know.'

She was gradually coming to the conclusion that, in terms of consequence, nobody was blameless. The fact that this was a conclusion that excused her own behaviour was by the by.

Lizzie, refuelling herself with coffee at regular intervals, had flicked the odd duster, attached a few curtain rings, been prevailed upon to lend assistance when a wardrobe needed to be moved or a picture hung, but mostly had devoted herself to expounding upon the duplicity of her husband and the uselessness of the conciliation services. 'She's called Valerie, incidentally, this counsellor – and actually she's more Gillian Shephard than V. Bottomley – and she sat there nodding away while he came out with this stomach-turning garbage to do with all we'd been through together and how he couldn't bear to throw it away. He omitted to tell her that he wants to come back because the tart's chucked him out.'

Nevertheless they had agreed to a trial period of rapprochement, which was to consist, at first, of meetings of brief duration: morning coffees, afternoon teas, walks in the park. 'A bit like those schedules for the sexually dysfunctional,' Lizzie said, 'you know – for the first week you must do nothing more than hold hands, then you're allowed to kiss; it's months before they give you permission to swing from the chandelier . . .'

Meanwhile, ordinary life went on.

'It's *Swan Lake*,' Lizzie had said. And when they got to the theatre she made for the bar to order drinks for the interval. 'Intervals, actually,' she said, 'in the plural, it being *Swan Lake*, which goes on for ever. Therefore I think drinks plural too, don't you?' People parted obediently to let her past. It wasn't just that she was tall and imposing; it was her air of authority. She'd always had it, had been able to convince college porters that she had permission to stay out all night, landladies that the man sharing her room was her brother, tutors that consistently late essays were due to the decease of a grandparent.

They had good seats, in the middle of the third row of the front stalls. Every muscular ripple of each dancer's torso was clearly visible. The man dancing Prince Siegfried was gloriously handsome. 'What I couldn't do to him!' Lizzie murmured behind her programme.

She continued to extol his charms in this vein throughout the interval: speculating upon his fitness, asserting that she could eat him for breakfast – lunch and dinner too. Clare, eventually wearying of this somewhat puerile monologue, said, 'Oh do shut

39

up. You're beginning to sound like Julian and Sandy – "Vada the lallies", "bona queen", sort of thing.'

'Who are Julian and Sandy?' Lizzie asked, waving to someone she knew at the opposite side of the bar.

'*Round the Horne*,' Clare said. 'Kenneth Williams and – I forget. Sunday lunchtime. Don't you remember?'

But Lizzie had been educated at a convent boarding-school where *Round the Horne* had not featured, during Sunday lunch or at any other time. 'We used to listen to Luxembourg on our transistors under the covers after lights out,' she said helpfully.

The excellence of their view also meant that every svelte inch of the ballerina's figure was displayed in magnificent close-up before their envious gaze. Afterwards, in the Chinese restaurant, Lizzie announced herself inspired – or possibly shamed – into embarking upon another diet.

'What's the point?' Clare said, gazing about her at their fellow diners, just as she'd gazed around the third-row stalls and the bar and the theatre foyer. Gazing had become a way of life. But unlike Lizzie, who did so in the hope of recognizing people, Clare's scrutiny was a covert affair. Theo had, undoubtedly, a social life, patronized theatres, dined out with friends. Sometimes there was a heart-stopping moment when she thought she saw him – a tall fair man with a pale complexion and a disconcertingly direct regard, wearing a black coat, his hair just beginning to curl over its collar ... But always, thankfully yet at the same time disappointingly, it turned out to be a different tall fair man.

'What d'you mean: what's the point?' Lizzie said crossly, as she gnawed at the first of many barbecued spare ribs.

'Well – ballet dancers,' Clare said. 'They're different. There's no way in the world ...'

'It's all right for *you*,' Lizzie said sourly. '*You've* got one of those racing metabolisms. You can eat what you want.'

'I actually eat less than you.'

'Only proportionately.'

'But if I have a racing metabolism and you haven't, then obviously your proportions are wrong . . .'

'Oh don't go *on*,' Lizzie said. 'You know, you could go on for England.'

Maybe it was true. Huw had often said so. Gwyn too. Heaven forbid that Theo should ever be given the opportunity to comment.

'I'm going to give it a go anyway,' said Lizzie, making very short work of a skewered portion of chicken.

'Oh yeah? As soon as this pub closes . . .'

'You may mock.'

In college it had been Ryvitas and cottage cheese – interspersed, when she became ravenous, with Mars bars and bags of chips. Later on there had been the F Plan, the Hip and Thigh Diet, the Cambridge Diet, the Hay Plan, the eat-nothing-but-pineapple diet and even, once, standing in line behind a queue of bulging polyester shell-suits at Slimmers' World. None of these had resulted in any significant weight loss. Anyway Lizzie was intended, genotypically, to be Junoesque. She looked good large; reduced, she'd look like a scraggy thin woman who was meant to be a good-looking large one.

Clare toyed with a morsel of duck flesh. It was true what they said about love diminishing your appetite. Perhaps that might be Lizzie's solution. But when Lizzie talked of love – and at one time they'd talked of little else: '*Gorgeous* man! I could *die*!': the rugby captain, boots slung nonchalantly over one shoulder, gloriously aloof; the music tutor with a profile that resembled the young Tennyson's, the Rhodes scholar with his Paul Newman eyes and his Rochefoucauld wit and his rower's muscles and his fiancée back home in Ohio – Clare had always felt that she meant something different, something infinitely less blissful, or harrowing – at least if her recovery rate was anything to go by.

'I'll show you,' Lizzie said, bravely forgoing the last pancake. 'I mean, if I don't do it *now*, it'll be menopause next oh-my-God

41

and it's put on weight if you take HRT and put on weight if you don't . . .'

'Try helping me to hump a few more wardrobes,' Clare said. 'That should shift a few pounds. I still think Gwyn's room looks wrong somehow.'

'It'll be wrong anyway,' Lizzie said, lacking experience in this area but nonetheless infinitely wise. 'Whatever you do will be wrong. And I'd rather hump Nijinsky back there. Oh,' she said, 'those thighs! How old, d'you think?'

'Not old enough. Not for you.'

'Oh, I don't know. It beats Prozac. Anyway,' Lizzie said, 'I have a better idea. I'll send Pauline over to give you a hand. She might as well hump wardrobes; she's always telling me she's out of the game as far as anything else is concerned.'

Pauline was Lizzie's twice-weekly woman. Years ago Lizzie had declared that for one person to occupy a position of servitude vis-à-vis another, whether in receipt of recompense or not, was unspeakably iniquitous.

'She might as well. I don't really need her twice a week any more. Not since I redecorated.'

Lizzie had recently gone minimal. Exceedingly so. Presumably in reaction to the over-abundance of chintz and swags and stencils that had characterized the flat in its previous incarnation. Not long ago dado rails and cornices had been the thing, faux this, that and the other – there hadn't been a salvage yard within miles safe from Lizzie's depredations. Now one was confronted with great parchment-coloured expanses and a few distorted twigs arranged within the severe contours of opaque glass vases, low-line calico-covered sofas and a fiercely streamlined stainless-steel kitchen that resembled something off the set of *Star Trek*.

'I've only let her keep the hours because she's skint.'

'I don't think I should really,' Clare said. It wasn't so much a matter of principle as the fact that Pauline was a young woman with a catalogue of social problems and a propensity to discuss them at length.

'She's fine,' Lizzie said, 'once she gets going. On second thoughts though, maybe she ought to give the heavy lifting a miss. She's got one of these womb things. They want her to have a hysterectomy but she's worried about leaving the kids, not to mention the boyfriend . . . I'll send her round on Friday. It'll suit her better anyway, being nearer home.'

Lizzie lived in mansion flat splendour whereas Clare's neighbourhood included, at its furthest boundary, possibly one of the worst council estates known to man and/or social historians.

'Why don't you get lover-boy to help you,' Lizzie said, 'with the humping? If you'll pardon the expression.'

'He has a name.'

'I know,' Lizzie said, 'but I am reluctant to dignify him by making use of it.'

She didn't know him, had never met him, was expressing disapproval solely on the basis of his marital status. Which was rich, considering that Lizzie hadn't been averse to another woman's husband or two in her time. That was different, she said, because she'd been married as well – there was a kind of freemasonry between married couples; she said that Clare's situation might be appropriate for a twenty-two-year-old, or somebody who wore Christian Lacroix and lived on the Avenue Montaigne, otherwise it was just plain tacky.

'He isn't at all,' Clare had said, in defence of Theo. 'If you'd met him, you'd know.' But it was too early in their relationship to risk such a meeting and, thus far, she had succeeded (more by good luck than good management, given his inability to provide her with much advance warning of his visits) in keeping them apart.

No one else had met him, not as a connection of hers – neither friend nor mutual acquaintance; not even Gwyn. Especially not Gwyn.

'Describe!' Lizzie had said, when she began to pick up on the continual use of his name. And Clare had attempted to do so: '. . . one of those faces where all the features seem to relate to each other quite perfectly. It's not really to do with handsomeness – though he *is*; it's something more – a kind of familiarity: you feel as though you're re-recognizing someone you once knew.'

She could hardly believe that she'd met him as recently as four months ago: just before Christmas, during the halcyon days of late December. *Jours heureux*, the French called them, *jours de bonheur*.

'Who does he look like?' Lizzie had said, expecting, presumably, a comparison to some current icon.

'He looks like himself,' she had replied. And so he did; that was the point.

'And?' Lizzie had said. 'And?'

Well, he was forty-nine years old, which meant that the ten years between them was less of an age gap than the fifteen that had separated her from Huw. Lizzie said that perhaps, little by little, she was growing out of her father fixation.

And, well, his face bore a habitually solemn expression that was totally at variance with his eyes which sparkled with light and laughter and suggested that he might risk that which he oughtn't for the sake of novelty, or entertainment, or adventure. She'd forgotten, but it was exactly this combination of solemnity and sparkle that had attracted her to all the others: the boys, the young men, and eventually Huw, who had sparked her interest, ignited her emotions, excited her loins.

'What's he do?' Lizzie had asked, knowing that she was unlikely to be surprised by the answer; Clare wasn't the sort to get intimately acquainted with the man who mended her car or filled her teeth or sat at the next table in the pub. Clare's men must come along in the course of her work, which was to assist in the editing of a scientific society's monthly journal. Mostly they didn't come along at all, not because she was unattractive in either looks or personality but because she had never embraced the philosophy which stated that, in the absence of the one you loved, you might as well endeavour to love the one you were with.

'He works for Kriess-Rettingen. Marketing. D'you remember,

they sponsored that prize for the best piece of original research in the field of cognitive therapy?'

'Well I don't, actually,' Lizzie had said, the implication being that she considered cognitive therapy but one step removed from casting the runes. At university, Clare had prudently embarked upon a combined degree in Psychology and English, whereas Lizzie, whose ambition had been the Great Novel or, at the very least, some highly regarded slim volume, had looked upon such bet-hedging as the unacceptable face of compromise.

The presentation of the award they'd sponsored had been made at a soirée in the Institute. The heating always seemed to be going full-blast at the Institute. That, coupled with two glasses of Bulgarian Cabernet Sauvignon, and Clare had begun to feel uncomfortably warm. The man who turned out to be Theo, rising to introduce the Chairman, who duly presented the recipient with a cheque and an indeterminate piece of sculpture, had looked so cool and collected, as though neither blood vessels nor sweat glands would dare to disobey a perfectly modulated temperature control, that she had felt herself instinctively drawn to him. Perhaps he didn't have blood in his veins at all, but ichor, like the gods. His profile, at any event, she considered to be distinctly god-like.

She'd been introduced to him earlier among a welter of introductions, and had wondered if her impression that his gaze had lingered upon her marginally longer than was strictly necessary had been mere wishful thinking. But even if interest had been shown, she couldn't have pushed herself; she wasn't the type. She'd have to wait for his approach, anticipating the same outcome as on so many previous occasions: an attractive man glimpsed and the evening over and nothing come of it.

But for some reason, this time her silent plea had not gone unanswered. Smoothly, gracefully, he had woven his way through the crowd to where she stood, her glass misted within her moist grasp. Someone jolted her in passing and a few drops of red wine splashed on to her blouse. 'Perhaps I should spill white on it

45

now. It works for tablecloths. Or is that soda-water?' she had said, gabbling in her nervousness. He'd put a shielding arm about her, not quite touching her shoulder-blades. 'Isn't that just an old wives' tale?' he'd said.

'Is it?'

'I've really no idea. Perhaps we ought to find an old wife and ask her.'

She was aware of the beat of blood in her ears. Too ridiculous, she thought. Her birth certificate might put her age at thirty-nine, but really she'd never got beyond seventeen: stomach in turmoil at the sight of the handsome boy on the other side of the dance floor, as she noted his appreciative wink and debonair approach – but it was usually directed at the girl standing next to her.

They'd chatted inconsequentially. I must think of something memorable to say to him, she thought wildly, remembering how, when she first met Huw, she used to rehearse clever and light-hearted remarks. Now all that she could manage to dredge up was some silly, smart-arsed comment about the presentational sculpture. Oh Christ, she thought, immediately afterwards, he probably commissioned it personally.

'Pretty ghastly, isn't it?' he said quietly. 'Produced by the Chairman's nephew. For those who like that sort of thing . . .'

'. . . that is the sort of thing they like,' she finished for him, delighted to discover, as she did so, that he too was obviously aware of the quotation's source.

And then, oh sudden and unmitigated disaster, there was a hand on his shoulder, a stubby, hairy, almost Neanderthal hand that was not fit to touch the hem of his garment, let alone that impeccable, finely striped serge suiting: 'Theo, I'd like you to meet . . .' An apology and he was gone, leaving her bereft in her wine-spattered blouse.

She could see him across the room, embedded within a circle of important people. She was not important enough to consider infiltrating it. That's that then, she thought, and put down her glass and went to the cloakroom where others of her colleagues,

46

equally lacking in clout or consequence, were gathering together their coats and bags. 'We thought we might try that Indian round the corner,' someone said, including her in this invitation. She remembered nodding vaguely in assent but when she got into the lift and somebody else said, 'Hold it!' in order to wait for a late-coming passenger and the passenger turned out to be him, so immaculate and discreetly cologned among the press of crumpled suits and eye-watering aftershaves, she forgot about that intention entirely.

And God looked down and was good because when they emerged it was into a rainstorm, the downpour ricocheting off the pavement and not a taxi in sight. He said, 'Can I give you a lift?' And she offered up thanks for the provision of the Bulgarian Cabernet Sauvignon, which meant that she'd left her car at home.

'And?' Lizzie had said. 'And?'

And he had driven her home and she had been so overwhelmed by his exhilarating proximity that she couldn't remember anything of what they'd talked about, except that the conversation had flowed easily and unforcedly and they'd reached her house all too soon. 'Oh,' he had said, as the *For Sale* sign in the front garden hove into view, 'you're on the move?'

And this had given her the opportunity to provide a little relevant biographical detail: the death of her ex-husband and the need to move to a smaller house because there would no longer be any maintenance forthcoming and she'd thought to use the profit from the sale to keep her son at boarding-school, except that her son had announced in no uncertain terms that he wanted to leave.

Short of sticking a label across her forehead that said: 'I am available', she could scarcely have told him more.

He said, 'We moved last year. It was hell. They do say that it's one of life's more traumatic experiences, third only to divorce and bereavement. Sorry,' he said, looking at her sideways, 'that was pretty tactless of me.'

But she was still trying to assimilate her disappointment on

47

hearing that first person plural – no less keen for all that she'd prepared herself for it.

'And?' Lizzie had said. And then had answered her own question: 'And he's married.'

He had rung her at the office the next day, using as a pretext some fairly irrelevant detail concerning his firm's continuing sponsorship of the award. She could have told him that this was hardly her territory, that she was merely a minion who chased up copy, appointed referees, edited papers. She could have said that in the decision-making hierarchy her position was among the lowly, this being due to lack of gumption rather than opportunity or gender.

But of course she didn't. She waited, phone in hand, eventually identifying a long-forgotten feeling as that of rising excitement, and praying that he wouldn't trot out some antiquated gambit that would unwillingly lower him in her estimation, but he just said, straight out, 'Tell me to get lost if I'm reading things wrong, but I really would like to see you again.'

She knew, of course, just how bad a hand she was dealing herself and, familiar with her own nature, was aware that there would be no question of keeping it light, or drawing back, or calling a halt, but it was such a long time since anyone had set her pulse racing and she was so hard to please that she succeeded in convincing herself that this was knowledge that could be ignored, as could the inevitable ending-in-tears, so far distant, at this golden moment, as to be safely over the furthest horizon.

Chapter Five

April 27th, 1926.

   Mrs Gradwell's daughter Diana has invited me to a party. Mrs Gradwell is a lady Mother makes petticoats for. I got back from school yesterday just as she was leaving. 'Well, Maisie,' she said, 'shall we be seeing you next week? Your mother did tell you, didn't she? About Diana's party?' When she'd gone, Mother went red and said she'd forgotten all about it and anyway I'd feel out of place. 'They're not our sort,' she said. While I was wondering what 'our sort' was, Mrs M came in for the rent. 'A party?' she said. 'Wonderful! Of course she must go. She will make nice new friends.' Mother said, 'That's as maybe. And what on earth is she to wear?' and Mrs M replied, 'What is she to wear? What kind of a question is that? You, the dressmaker! The kind of dress you can make for her, she will be the belle of the ball. Sometimes!' Mrs M said, and hit the side of her head with the flat of her hand. 'Oy vey,' Mrs M said (if that's how you spell it).

   So we have been to the market this morning to pick out material: organdie and taffeta, pink and white. The man on the stall smiled and teased me and said, 'You shall go to the ball, Cinderella,' but I'm not sure I really want to go to this party. Mrs Gradwell lives in one of the posh houses by the park. Mrs M said they have maids galore and a shuvver for the Bentley. She pushed her nose up in the air with her finger and said, 'Snobs. Twopence to talk to them.' Then she said, 'Only my joke, liebchen. You will have a lovely time. I will lend you the silk gardenia for your hair which I wore when

Mr Mendelssohn took me on honeymoon.' Then she told me about her honeymoon with Mr Mendelssohn in the kosher guest-house in Bridlington, which she has told me a hundred times before, but because I am fond of her, I pretended to listen and just let my mind wander to the book I'm reading at present which is Kidnapped. *Kosher means suitable, when the rabbi has made sure that the animal has been killed properly, and no part of the pig is allowed because they are considered unclean. A horrible man used to come to kill the pigs on the farm. He had a face exactly like Uncle Ebenezer Balfour in the illustration in* Kidnapped. *It is the best story that I have ever read. I don't want it to end. I borrow as many books as they will let me have from the public library. The lady behind the desk calls me a bookworm and says, 'We can hardly keep up with you. You'll have to bring your bed in here.' It's such a marvellous exciting feeling: just the smell of all those books together and the way, when you start to read the stories, you forget about everything else, about being bashed on the way home from school and not being picked for the pageant and feeling a bit nervous about Diana Gradwell's party.*

We met Miss Marriott on the way back from the market. All week long she has been collecting for the families of the striking miners, rattling her box right in people's faces. Some of them tell her that she, and the miners, should be ashamed of themselves. But now it's the weekend, she's having a break and meeting with her hiking chums for a day on the fells. I started to ask her whether they'd be going anywhere near to Bligh's Farm at Low Rigg and if they were to say hello to everybody for me, but Mother hushed me as she always does. I don't think she wants anybody to know that she used to live at Low Rigg . . .

Once, in the vicinity of the black hospital, Mother saw someone she knew. She attempted to hurry on by as though she hadn't noticed this woman, but the woman – the wife of a neighbouring farmer – wasn't about to let herself go unnoticed. She was a long, lean lady with a big stride and she'd caught up with them in no time at all. 'Now then, lass, where's tha bound?' she enquired. She was wearing a dark red coat and Maisie's mother's face had flushed up until it was the same colour as that coat. She'd gripped Maisie's hand so tightly that Maisie gave a little cry and the woman said, 'What's the matter with the bairn?' and bent down to fuss her, presumably forgetting in the process that she hadn't received an answer to her question. She remarked upon the lowness of the neighbourhood in which they found themselves. She was here to see after little Annie, their maid, who had come back home when her mother was laid up with the white leg after she'd had the new baby.

'Are you going for the tram?' the woman had asked and Mother had told a lie and said they weren't and so the woman had gone off in one direction while they took another, which involved a long and wearisome walk. Mother had talked aloud as they walked, talking to herself rather than Maisie. 'That woman has the widest mouth in the Dales,' she'd said. And, 'She'll ferret it out. She's a terror. She knows when a lass is in the family way before the lass knows it herself.'

That was their last visit to the hospital. And when, shortly afterwards, they attended the Harvest Home in the village hall, Mother made sure they sat well away from that woman and her family.

But, after that, it wasn't so much a question of Mother distancing herself from others, as that the distancing became reciprocal. 'I'm being avoided,' Maisie remembered her saying. She'd been to chapel, come home and sat holding her hat in her lap, twisting and twisting the veiling that swathed its brim until she'd frayed the edge of it. 'Nay,' Grandma had said. 'You're imagining it.'

And then, Christmas having come and gone, it was Maisie's birthday and there was talk of a party. She'd not had a party before; she'd have been too little to appreciate it. Besides, so soon after Pa dying, it would have been unseemly. But this time, apparently, past omission was to be remedied in a big way: all week Grandma had been making jellies and blancmanges, placing them to wobble themselves cool on the slate shelves of the larder, baking buns and tarts and a magnificent iced cake that was to be adorned with five pink wax candles that Maisie would be called upon to extinguish with one large breath while the assembled company sang, 'Happy birthday to you.' Games were to be organized: Hunt the Thimble, Grandmother's Footsteps, Ring o' Roses, and there was to be a paper poke of spice for each child to take home at the end of the afternoon.

Excitement had woken Maisie early. She remembered seeing Jack Frost on the inside of the window and feeling the floorboards cold beneath her bare feet. She'd run downstairs in her nightdress and Grandpa, coming in from the fields, snow on his boots, breath steaming, had caught hold of her and lifted her up and whirled her round, calling her his birthday girl and Grandma had admonished her, telling her she'd catch her death of cold before shooing her towards the warmth of the range where there was a bowl of porridge oats waiting, a golden syrup-filled crater in the centre of it and a speckled egg specially laid by Flossie, her favourite bantam and, best of all and wrapped in fancy paper, her birthday presents: a new picture-book, a game of diabolo, a red ribbon for her hair and a rag-doll with yellow woollen curls and a pretty smiling face: big blue eyes and a rosebud mouth, embroidered by Mother who was quick with her needle.

All day the excitement had mounted. She kept going to the parlour door to peep in at the table which was decorated with streamers and in the centre of which reposed her cake in all its frosted splendour. She saw herself blowing out its candles, heard the singing and the applause.

Invitations had been issued instructing the guests to arrive at three o'clock. They'd come in carts or on foot across the frozen fields, clad in clean pinafores and blouses, their boots shining, their faces rosy, the girls' hair freshly curled, that of the boys combed rigorously flat, children she hardly knew, given the isolation of the farm, but she'd get to know them and, when she started school, she'd get to know them better, as well, perhaps,

52

as she knew the children in her picture-books: Snow White, Hansel and Gretel, the babes in the wood.

At half-past three Mother was pacing the yard, up and down, up and down, scanning the horizon. 'Get in here!' Grandma called. 'Or at least put on your shawl.' At four o'clock she came back inside, sank down on to the settle and put her head in her hands. Grandma said, 'Mayhap you put the wrong date on the cards?' She kept winding and unwinding a skein of wool round her hand. Mother had looked up. Her shoulders were hunched practically to her chin. Her eyes, which were large and blue, as brilliantly blue as those of the rag-doll, had no light in them whatsoever. She said, in a voice devoid of emotion, 'We're being shunned. They want nothing to do with us.'

At four-thirty Grandpa came in from the milking and said, 'To the devil with them all. We'll have our own party.' And he made everyone put on the paper hats that were left from the Christmas crackers and they ate jelly and blancmange and cut the cake and sang, 'Happy birthday,' as Maisie blew out the candles. They even played Grandmother's Footsteps and the Farmer's in His Den, and Grandma and Grandpa were as deliberately jolly as could be, but of course it wasn't the same.

Soon afterwards, during the worst spell of winter, when Grandpa dug out overwintering sheep from the top fell and Grandma had to break a plug of ice on top of the rain barrel before she could wash Maisie's hair, they had packed their suitcases and taken the trap to the railway station, where there had been such a to-do of tears and huggings on the platform and then Grandma had said, 'You're making a big mistake. Don't go, Rose, please don't go.'

But go they did. And, ever since, it was as though Mother had progressively withdrawn them from anything but the most essential of social contacts. So, given this aversion to company, Maisie knew that, had it not been for Mrs Mendelssohn's intervention, there would have been no party, no lengths of organdie and taffeta to be cut and pinned and tucked, smocked and frilled and be-ribboned to a degree of gorgeousness fit for Diana Gradwell herself. 'A dream!' Mrs M had exclaimed, patting and tweaking and smoothing and finally kissing Maisie fulsomely on both cheeks. 'Wear it in health!' she had cried. Maisie had stood on her tiptoes to see her reflection in the looking-glass. The dress was indeed a dream, a confection, a sugar-plum of a dress, and her hair had been put into rags the previous night so that now tight ringlets bounced from her skull, but still, intercepting what she interpreted as her mother's dissatisfied glance, she wondered if, party frock and bobbing curls notwithstanding, she was, would ever be, pretty enough.

She'd wondered also, apprehensively, if this party would make up for that other that never was, would somehow be the means of her transformation into a popular social being, that these children – more gently reared than her schoolfellows – would accept her into their midst without prejudice. But there had been misgivings even before she stood so definitively alone, isolated among the acres of polished parquet that comprised the Gradwells' hall.

Hers was indeed the prettiest dress. But that was the only consolation.

Diana Gradwell, a fat, rather scowly child, had accepted Maisie's present with lukewarm thanks. While she was still expressing this half-hearted gratitude, a big bony girl had pushed herself between them, prodded Maisie in the chest and said something that sounded like: 'Ick ick pah boo.'

She repeated this peculiar phrase, her rising inflection suggesting that it took the form of a question. 'Pardon?' said Maisie politely.

'Ick ick pah boo,' the girl said again, emphasizing each syllable with an increasingly painful prod. With her other hand she pointed to her chest. Pinned to the smocking of her dress was a blue badge. 'Gugnuncs,' she said. 'You know: Pip, Squeak and Wilfred? Go on – say it!'

'Say what?' implored a mystified Maisie. As far as she knew,

Pip, Squeak and Wilfred were the medals, bronze and silver discs on bright striped ribbons, worn by old soldiers at the war memorial on Remembrance Day.

'Goo goo pah nunc, of course. Aren't you a Gugnunc?'

Blue badges proliferated. It became apparent that she was the only non-Gugnunc – whatever that might be – among a roomful of them. Eventually Mrs Gradwell, rather languidly, enlightened her via an address to the assembled company: 'Perhaps Maisie doesn't follow the cartoon – it's a club that they have, dear, with all these silly words and signs. Perhaps Maisie doesn't read the comic papers.'

There had been some old *Chicks' Own*, Maisie remembered, that Grandma used to save for her: Ally Sloper, round as an egg . . . But that had been in another life, a life that still contained the possibility of pleasant social interaction.

The only comfort that she had been able to draw upon during the rest of that terrible afternoon was the knowledge that eventually one must wake from even the most ghastly of dreams. Once a nasty boy with black hair sleeked down so that his head resembled a billiard ball, pinched the back of her arm quite viciously because she had been too slow in passing the parcel to him, but that was merely physical misery; far far worse was to be ignored: they picked teams and at the end only she remained, unchosen. 'Now come on, children,' Mrs Gradwell had said, testily, 'you can't have uneven teams, can you? Go to the blue side, Maisie, and make up the numbers.'

The entire occasion was Gugnuncery, pure and unequivocal. She didn't know the rules of any of the games, stood foolishly, holding a ball or a hoop or an orange, while the rest of them screamed at her: 'Throw it!' or 'Pass it!' or 'Roll it backwards between your legs!' Vanity had brought her out without her glasses so she couldn't read the clues for the treasure hunt, and when they dispersed for Sardines, the soles of their dancing pumps squeaking on the waxed floors, she wandered off uncertainly and found herself – as if drawn there by some latent instinct of humility – in the house's nether regions. A maid brought her back upstairs, urging her forward with an ungentle hand in the small of her back. 'Found her in the scullery, madam,' she told Mrs Gradwell, as though Maisie's intention had been to plunder the pots and pans.

And then there was the conjuror and he wanted a child to assist him with his trick and they all put up their hands, shouting 'Me! Me!' but she knew, with an awful certainty, even before his eye alighted upon her that she would be chosen, and she was, and nervousness paralysed her brain to the extent that she couldn't get the hang of it. He got quite tetchy and then – humiliation upon humiliation – as she stood there, clumsily failing to follow his instructions with regard to boxes and scarves, she suddenly felt the involuntary relaxation of the sphincter of her bladder, and urine gushed through the gusset of her matching satin drawers and down her leg and splashed – could be heard to splash – upon the parquet.

'Too much excitement,' was how Mrs Gradwell explained it to Mother when she arrived to collect Maisie. 'I've put her underthings to be washed and I'll send the girl round with them when they're ironed.' Distaste still oozed from her every pore as it had done when she'd sent for a servant with a mop and then raced Maisie upstairs, ordered her to step out of the dripping drawers and provided her with a substitute pair of Diana's.

I will never need to see these children again, Maisie kept telling herself as, freshly girded, she took her place at the festive board. She kept her eyes fixed on her plate upon which appeared, at intervals, delicacies of the most mouth-watering kind, which might have been sawdust for all the appetite they aroused. Eventually she stopped trying to eat. To be sick would be the final indignity.

Mother made no comment about her accident, other than to say, as soon as they got home, 'Take off those knickers and I'll rinse them through. Nice cake,' she said later, unwrapping the portion that had been prepared for Maisie to carry home, together with a bag of sugared almonds and a streamer and a jumping jack. Tucking her up in bed that night, she'd hugged her close. 'I only want you to be safe, my pet,' she'd said. 'That's all that matters to me.'

Maisie closed the book. Lately she'd taken to re-reading bits of her diaries, dipping into them here and there; it was hard to believe that they'd been her own thoughts; it was as though she was reading about someone else's life.

She heard a commotion in the garden and went to investigate. Blackbirds had recently built a nest among the tangled briars that grew against the fence and deposited within it four speckly blue-green eggs. Now they had hatched and although Timmy was too old and well-fed to have any inclination to hunt, another cat sometimes came into the garden and it was this creature, a thin striped tabby with avid eyes, that was responsible for the disturbance. As Maisie watched, the cock bird, squawking loudly, flew down from the fence and straight at the predator. The cat ran for the cover of the bushes. This happened several times, each time the bird squawking louder, flying closer, flapping its wings more belligerently, the cat retreating further into the undergrowth until finally it abandoned its quest and fled.

Parental instinct to protect its young was, Maisie thought, powerful to behold.

A woman came out of the house next door, carrying cardboard boxes to the bin – a different woman. This one had dyed blonde hair and wore a very short, tight skirt. She stood, arms akimbo, listening to the birds' clamour. 'Noisy beggars,' she said. 'I could hear them above the radio.'

Through the open back door Maisie could also hear the radio which was transmitting the usual ear-splitting cacophony that passed for music. On the evening that the other woman had stood outside with her male companion, music of a different sort had drifted through the french windows, violin music: swooping, soaring sounds, up and down the scale, strung together to produce a melody that had brought the tears, involuntarily, to her eyes.

'Grand day,' the woman said, her meagre chest rising and falling as she inhaled the scents of burgeoning spring: a clump of bluebells beside the grid, a few straggly daffodils that had pushed through the brambles. She then reached into the pocket of her skirt and brought out a packet of Benson and Hedges and a box of matches. 'Ciggie?' she said, approaching the fence.

Maisie shook her head. The woman lit up and flicked the spent match into the bushes and then stood smoking and yawning. She said, 'Can't have a fag inside anywhere these days. It gets up your nose.'

Maisie was tempted to reply: perhaps that's because it gets up other, non-smoking noses. But she rarely said what she was tempted to say. Entire intricate conversations took place, but only inside her head while, at the same time, she'd nod and smile and say yes and no and please and thank you very much.

'Just helping out,' said the woman, jerking her head in the direction of the house. 'She's a friend of Mrs Twist that I clean for regular. Crossing my fingers she decides to keep me on. I could do with a few more hours. I don't know where the money goes these days and my fellow's not been in work for months. She says she's got her son coming back home from school next week, so she might want somebody – seeing as she goes out to work. She's divorced. Though who isn't nowadays? Twice, me. That's why I won't marry Terry. Too much hassle if it all goes wrong. And while you just live together you can always order them out. When you've got kids that's a big consideration.'

The woman talked – and smoked – furiously, the stream of her conversation interrupted only by the necessity to place the cigarette between her lips.

'Oh well,' she said eventually, 'better get back to it. She's got some lovely things though, nicer – well I think so anyway – than Mrs Twist's. She *used* to have it beautiful: embossed wallpaper and velvet curtains and that, but now she's gone all modern, all steel and chrome and what have you. It's not to my taste. If you ask me, she's got more money than sense. Still – she's all right, is Mrs Twist. She's a good laugh. I'm hoping that me and this Clare are going to get along. She's on the quiet side, isn't she?'

Perhaps, Maisie thought, as the woman went inside and closed the door behind her, it was because she didn't get the chance for a word in edgeways. She racked her brains to try to bring to mind who it was that the woman reminded her of and when she remembered, why, Nancy, of course, she wondered how she could possibly have forgotten: Nancy, with her cocky stance and bold blue eyes, Nancy who could talk the hind leg off a donkey, who could screw up her cheeky butcher boy's face to produce every rude noise under the sun, who gave not one tuppenny toss for anyone.

It must have been '28 when they came to Mrs Mendelssohn's: Gertie and Nina and Nancy. The landlady of the theatrical digs where they usually stayed had died – 'She finally poisoned herself with that bloomin' greasy old stock-pot,' Nancy said, and then she said, 'Toss-pot,' and stuck out her tongue and the other two girls tittered with horrified glee. They had come for the panto: *Jack and the Beanstalk* at the Empire; they did panto every year, Madame B's Dancing Babes. Madame B was actually an Armenian gentleman with sad eyes and a Ramsay MacDonald moustache whom Nancy referred to as Dirty Dickie, his name, she said, being Dikram Something Absolutely Unpronounceable in Armenian. 'Tries to touch you up,' she said, 'in the wings. He's harmless enough though, poor old sod. Is there any more of that honey cake?' she asked Mrs Mendelssohn who stood speechless for once, astonished by this little girl's *chutzpah* – and her appetite. 'The grub's good here, isn't it?' Nancy said. 'It's starvation rations where we usually stay – bread and scrape and tea like weasel's water – and we're growing girls!'

They had arrived two weeks before Christmas, after special pleading on the part of the theatre management: Mrs Mendelssohn didn't normally do short-term lets, least of all to theatricals, but Rena Rubin, wife of the manager, was also some exceedingly distant, way-back-in-the-Moldavian-mists relation of Mrs M's, so she finally capitulated.

They had arrived in a blur and a bustle: Maisie, leaning over the banister, saw fur hats worn at an angle and snowflakes spangling the curls that escaped from beneath them, red cheeks, tiny little high-heeled boots – and heard noise, such noise, of laughing and quarrelling and the stamping of feet.

But despite the noise, the giggling and tittering and exclaiming, Gertie and Nina were essentially sober, biddable girls who hung their clothes neatly over the backs of chairs and said their prayers and sucked Fulnana cachous 'for the breath' and gave Miss Aldridge, their matron, a glum lady who wore a felt cloche adorned with the dustiest, least iridescent examples of birds' plumage, no trouble at all. Nancy was a different matter. Nancy was an imp, a clown, a puller of faces and tongues, a user of bad language, a pert little madam and a thoroughly disruptive influence. She'd have been kicked out long ago, except that she could out-perform all the others. She did the speciality spots: the toe-work and acrobatic dancing. The day after they arrived, Maisie had come out of her bedroom to look over the banisters in the hope of spotting their new guests and found that the banisters were already occupied by Nancy who hung from them, upside down, apparently careless of the precipitous drop that yawned below. Maisie had stared entranced at the effortlessness of the pose, at the sturdy dancer's limbs, the muscular strength that defied gravity. And then Mrs M had appeared at the bottom of the stairwell and screamed: 'Down! Down! You will be killed! In *mein* house!' And Nancy, insolent, had hung there for a few moments longer before slowly righting herself, curling first one leg and then the other over the banister rail. Maisie was reminded of the cavortings of the sad little monkey in the red jacket who swung from the organ-grinder's shoulder. He played *Tipperary*, the organ-grinder, and *There's a Long, Long Trail a-Winding* and *Le Rêve Passe*. Mother would flap dusters out of the window at him. 'Move on!'

she'd shout. 'Go away with your racket!' Mother hated anything to do with the Great War; she always refused to observe the two minutes' silence, just kept treadling away as normal.

Eventually Nancy had hauled herself into upright mode and sat on the banister, kicking her heels against the spindles. 'Do you live here all the time?' she asked. Maisie nodded. 'I'd go spare,' Nancy said, 'if I had to live anywhere all the time. We're on tour. We've been to Cardiff and Portsmouth and Birmingham and Norwich and Sheffield and Hull.' She counted off the towns on her fingers. 'But we always come here for the panto. Is she your grandmother?' Nancy asked, gesturing down to the hall where Mrs Mendelssohn was welcoming her friends Sadie and Golda with whom she played halma on Sunday nights. Maisie shook her head. 'I didn't think she was,' Nancy said. 'She's Jewish, isn't she? Solly Rubin at the theatre' (she pronounced it 'theayter'), 'he's a Jew. He has those things hanging on his door.' '*Mezuzah*,' Maisie said. Mrs M had them too. 'But I've seen him with a pork chop,' Nancy continued. 'You're clever, aren't you?' she said, looking into Maisie's face as though signs of cleverness were there to be read if only one's scrutiny was powerful enough.

And Maisie had been quite prepared to be ashamed. The assurances of Miss Marriott notwithstanding, her cleverness had always seemed to her to be something of a burden, an attribute that set her apart as definitively as her accent and her tin spectacles.

But Nancy, peering ever more fiercely, said, 'Aren't you the lucky one! I'm not clever. Though only because I wouldn't go to school. If I'd have gone, I'd probably be as clever as you. But school don't pay the rent. And we need the money. My dad copped it at Vimy Ridge and my step-dad can't work because of the wet-lung. Cough, cough, cough all night long. Doctor says he should have sea air. Not much of that in Clapton. How old are you?' she said abruptly and apropos of nothing. 'Twelve,' replied Maisie, 'going on thirteen.'

'How old d'you think I am?'

She could have been any age. If she'd said thirty-five it wouldn't have surprised Maisie. 'Sixteen?' she hazarded.

'Nah!' Nancy exclaimed scornfully. 'I'm twelve, same as you. Have you started your monthlies yet?'

The rushing blood crimsoned Maisie's cheeks. To speak of such things! If it had to be done, then it must be done behind the hand, in hushed whispers. It was Mrs M who'd wiped away her tears when she'd stared horrified at her stained bedsheet, because Mother had neglected to prepare her for such an eventuality, Mrs M who'd torn up an old pillowcase to make pads. But even she had indicated that it was a shameful state of affairs.

She could only nod.

'I have too,' Nancy said. 'Ages ago. Those two haven't though: Gertie Gitana and Nina Thingummy-Whatsit – she's a Russian, you know. Dickie calls her Olga-the-beautiful-spy – and they're older than me. You have to tell me to shut up,' she said, as she scrambled down on to the landing. 'Otherwise I just go on. I have the gift of the gab, you see. My ma says I was born talking.'

That was what the woman next door said, the cleaning woman – her name was Pauline – when she came knocking at the back door later that day. 'If she's got sugar anywhere, then I'm blowed if I can find it. You wouldn't mind, would you? Just a couple of spoons. Now, *tea*, I don't mind *that* without, but coffee – I've got to have my sugar. Oh,' she'd said, poking her head round the door, 'so this is what it'd have looked like before the new kitchen was fitted. *Lovely* new kitchen. Well, I say lovely, but I can't pretend I like all this battered stuff. I said to her this morning, "Do you know all your cupboard doors have got bashed? You want to ring them up and complain." She tells me they're meant to look like that – distressed, it's called. Barmy, I'd call it. Ooh thanks, lovey, you've saved me life. Heck, is that the time? That's me, going on. I've got the gift of the gab. Me mum says I was born talking.'

And, for one hallucinated moment, it was as though Maisie was hearing Nancy's voice; she looked at this woman, prepared to see Nancy's face: her stubborn chin and stare-you-out eyes, prepared to believe that perhaps she was some relation: her daughter, or even her granddaughter, but then of course she remembered that there never could have been a daughter, or a granddaughter, not for Nancy.

Chapter Six

Clare found Pauline's monologues oddly relaxing. For the first few days after Lizzie had released her, gallantly waiving the transfer fee: 'Oh, have it on me, until you decide whether or not you want to make it a permanent arrangement,' they worked together most compatibly: unpacking boxes, deciding on the disposition of their contents, stepping back from putative arrangements, picture hook between teeth, hammer in hand, 'Up a bit, do you think? Slightly to the right?' They folded blankets and slid cushions into covers and emptied coffee beans and spaghetti and cereal into storage jars. 'My Kerry goes mad on this,' Pauline said, funnelling muesli, 'but I generally get the own-brand stuff from Kwiksave. Does your lad like it?'

Well, Pauline, he used to do, when he was younger, Clare thought. But then he used to like plotting the passage of the Perseids and learning how to tie granny knots; he used to like memorizing the flags of all nations and building infinitely complicated structures out of Lego bricks. I like to think that I knew exactly what he liked, Pauline, but that was long ago and in a different kitchen.

Pauline had four children: Kerry and Lorraine and Michelle and Damien, ranging in age from fourteen down to five. 'You must have been very young when you had the eldest,' Clare said. Pauline, though she looked considerably older, was only thirty-two. 'No,' said Pauline, 'I were seventeen.

'Mind you,' she said, 'I first fell at fifteen. Before I knew what it was all about.' They'd taken that one from her and put it up for adoption. She was determined that they wouldn't have the next, so when she fell again, she married Jimmy, even though she knew what a gamble it was. It wasn't so bad at first because he was away in the army, but then he got chucked out for insubordination and after that he was just hanging about the house all day, skint and looking for trouble. Eventually he found it: started nicking. When they caught him, as they invariably did, they'd put him on probation. They gave him every chance. 'We've given you every chance, James McMahon,' the beak said, before sending him down. She'd met Tommy by then, so she put in for a divorce.

All this Clare learned as they filled bookshelves or washed glasses, handing each one gingerly to the other to be polished; as they sorted through a mixed bunch of documents: ancient receipts for long-forgotten services, antiquated gas bills, Gwyn's prep-school reports: 'This boy has tremendous ability and his prospects are excellent . . .' Pauline prattled on and Clare found it almost hypnotically soothing: 'Did you just want the one kiddie, then? I never intended on four, but you know how it is?' Nothing had worked for Pauline, neither coils nor pills nor condoms. After Damien, they'd sterilized her. She'd been furious. It wasn't natural. They said she'd signed a form, and maybe she had, but she hadn't *read* it. Who the hell read forms? 'My fiancé,' she'd told them, 'wanted a family, more kids of his own.' She called Terry her fiancé although in actual fact she was still married to Tommy. In fact, she confided, she'd never have taken up with Terry if Tommy hadn't left her. He'd been a smashing bloke. But his trouble was that he liked the ladies too much. 'You know what I mean?' Pauline said. 'Oh, absolutely,' Clare had replied.

Anyway there wouldn't be any more kids. She was waiting to be called in for her operation. In a way, she said, she wouldn't be sorry to lose it; it had been nothing but a damn nuisance from the word go.

'D'you know, you're not supposed to lift so much as a kettleful of water after the op,' Pauline said. 'Some chance! The kids'll have to go to me sister's. I've told our Carol she's to keep an eye on Kerry, make sure she doesn't bunk off school. Though Carol's eldest does it too. They all do. God knows what the teachers have to complain about: there's hardly ever any of them there to need teaching, as far as I can see.

'Of course, it'll be different,' Pauline said authoritatively, 'with your lad.'

The lad who'd once had tremendous ability and excellent prospects.

'Perhaps he might be better suited to one of your local sixth form colleges,' his headmaster had said. 'That's if he has any serious intention of working for his A Levels.' He had been brusque; his patience had run out long since. Gwyn's reports now said: 'Consistently hard work will be required if he is to realize his potential,' and 'He will need to adopt a much more mature and responsible attitude if he is to derive benefit from his education.'

'It isn't that he's a bad lad,' the headmaster had said, 'but he has an unfortunate knack of putting everybody's back up.'

'Well,' Pauline said, 'he's got a smashing room to come back to. You've done it out a treat.'

She herself had done up Kerry's room nice out of the catalogue, she told Clare: quilt and curtains to match and frilled cushions and a little portable telly that cost something shocking even over forty weeks; but one day the telly was gone, together with the ghetto-blaster and the microwave. Terry reckoned there'd been a break-in, break-ins being as common as lawful entries in their block, but she'd had her doubts.

It really was a most attractive room, Clare thought, surveying her handiwork with pride. She'd painted it in rich, opulent colours. She'd gilded finials and burnished knobs and crackle-glazed the furniture. She'd draped the bed and stencilled the floorboards with heraldic motifs until it resembled the chamber of some Renaissance princeling. She'd provided it with television and video and hi-fi, justifying the expense to herself by thinking of the school fees that would be saved over the next couple of years by his entry into the state system. She'd never wanted him to go away to school in the first place. That had been Huw's decision. 'If you think I'm letting him go to that sink school down the road,' Huw had said, 'you can think again.'

'We'll move,' she'd said desperately, 'to where there's a better one.'

Money wasn't all that plentiful; Huw was still supporting a first wife and two other children who never seemed to grow any older in terms of no longer needing school fees, only larger in the matter of requiring clothes and shoes and ever-more-esoteric forms of sports equipment. 'Why can't that cow remarry?' Huw used to say. Clare thought that his insistence on boarding-school for Gwyn was something to do with showing that cow; so much of his behaviour seemed to have been predicated on that principle.

Well, Huw no longer had any say in the decision-making. Huw was dead. Felled at fifty-five by a massive stroke. Huw was dead, and bad school reports were a thing of the past. Gwyn would settle into this lovely room and get back on track: Cambridge, perhaps, and medicine, as had once been his intention. Or even the newly elevated former polytechnic of some inner city would do, and one of those strange catch-all degree courses, 'Studies', they called them: Urban Studies, Media Studies, Community Studies. As your children grew older and less malleable, so you moderated your vicarious ambitions.

'You do think it's all right, this room?' she'd asked Theo. 'Not too much?'

'Well, I don't know Gwyn, do I?' Theo had said, with unarguable logic. 'But it's certainly very striking.'

He himself lived in some splendour. Once, despising herself thoroughly, but unable to help herself, she'd driven out of town to the village where he lived. It had been a fairly futile expedition: the house was barely visible at the end of a winding driveway; she could see only a few chimneys, a gable-end, and a hint of cast-iron scrollwork at the apex of a conservatory.

'Am I to meet him?' Theo had said, turning to present her directly with this question. He was one of the few people she knew who actually looked straight at you. He must have shaved just before coming to see her: there was a speck of lint on his jaw. She felt her hand rising, of its own volition, as though she'd been hypnotized, for the purpose of removing it, for the excuse to touch his skin, for the electric-shock delight of even the slightest contact. His very proximity made her tremble with lust, his kiss sent her reeling.

At length she'd controlled herself. ('I can't stay, my darling,' he'd said, groaning. 'I'm due at a meeting.' Well at least he doesn't visit me purely for sex, she'd thought. She found herself justifying him all the time, as though to some shadowy sitting jury, though – apart from Lizzie – there was no one else requiring any such justification.)

She said, in reply to his question, 'Well, it's rather up to you.' Though that was not so: Gwyn, at home, would be hard to avoid. There had been a couple of men since Huw left, but she had managed to limit their visits to term-time. Anyway she had never felt that these relationships were likely to endure, had known really from the occasion of the first drink, the first meaningful glance, that whatever might develop would be on their terms and not hers. Whereas this time: oh, this time . . .

'I'll get gone then, Clare,' Pauline was calling from the hall. 'I've got to pick up our Damien from school.'

From the bedroom window, Clare watched her walking down the road, struggling with carrier bags. She walked like a woman who had had four children and whose womb was playing up. But she was also a woman going home to a resident partner and even though the said resident partner sounded as unattractive as could be, Clare felt a brief pang of an emotion that could only have been interpreted as envy. Theo was not only a married man, Theo was a married man with two young children; the likelihood of him abandoning home and family for her sake was bound to be remote. In all probability she had sentenced herself to a future of lonely Christmases and solitary Bank Holidays – for as long as the affair ran its course. Better perhaps to renounce it before he became ingrained in her to the extent that the pain would grow extreme, unbearable. If only she could. If only she could weigh the pros and cons and force herself to make the rational, the moral decision. Perhaps she was one of those women doomed to seek out men who could never provide for their needs. (For hadn't she known, when agreeing to marry Huw, that the light in his eye which shone so luminously for her had done so before for others and would probably do so again? But apart from Lizzie – 'He's too old for you and he's got lechers' earlobes.' 'What are lechers' earlobes, Lizzie?' 'That's just it: they don't have any!' – there had been nobody to advise her; Aunt Winifred wouldn't have objected to her marrying the rag-man, as long as it meant the termination of her responsibility.)

Lizzie reckoned that people began affairs only when they were bored or dissatisfied. 'Take up Scottish dancing,' Lizzie said. 'Travel to exotic places. Change your job. You've been talking about it for long enough.'

But she owed meeting Theo to her job. God worked in mysterious ways. Sometimes she'd stop whatever she was doing in order to devote all her attention to remembering, recapitulating every detail of their earliest meetings: the tentative approaches and retreats, the diffidence and the boldness, the mutual delight in acknowledging a hum of desire that increased in velocity by the minute. 'I've fallen for you,' he'd said. And she'd thought how accurately that described the feeling; it was a falling: headlong, precipitous, without benefit of safety-net. 'I've fallen for you too,' she'd replied. She could scarcely breathe. 'Hyperventilation,' Lizzie said. 'Find somebody who's actually available,' Lizzie said. 'They can't *all* be awful. I worry for you,' Lizzie said.

The Telecom engineer arrived to install the phone. He obviously intended to make this his last job of the day. She was obliged to conduct him from room to room, indicating where she wanted the extensions to be put, while she listened to him talking, on and on, about the low moral standards exhibited by politicians, about the crying scandal of the bonuses awarded to the bosses of privatized utilities, about the lunacy of European directives and the diabolical price of season tickets for the football. He emphasized each opinion expressed with a gesture of his crimping tool. Get on, get on! she cried to herself, mad with impatience – she wanted Theo to be able to ring her, to be the first. The phone did ring once, but it was only the exchange.

He held his tea cup towards her for replenishment. 'What I say is,' he said, pliers aloft, 'with regard to the international money markets, what I say is—'

And then they heard a rumpus in the street below and, resigning herself to the fact that she'd never know what he had to say concerning the international money markets, she joined him at the window.

A group of girls had surrounded her next-door neighbour, were jostling her, subjecting her to serious harassment, if not downright mugging. 'Little sods!' cried the telephone man, struggling with the window latch – to no avail because Clare, overloading her paintbrush, had succeeded in sealing it shut. He ran downstairs, Clare behind him. 'Damn little wasters,' he shouted as he ran. 'Want your arses smacking, the bloody lot of you. Want to go back where you belong.' And other such politically incorrect sentiments.

By the time he burst out of the front door they were in retreat and the old lady, Maisie Carruthers, Miss, was attempting to lever herself upright. Her beret had been knocked sideways and books were scattered all around.

Clare bent down and helped her to her feet. The woman had shown absolutely no inclination thus far to be sociable, but obviously she had no option now other than to accept the proffered hospitality. Clare ushered her inside, went to put on the kettle once again.

'Nice one!' the engineer said, arriving back panting, having failed to catch up with the miscreants. 'Two sugars please. Are you all right, Grandma? Not nicked your purse or anything, have they?'

The woman shook her head, sat on the very edge of the chair, trying to control her trembling as Clare placed a cup of tea, heavily sugared, within her grasp.

'If it was up to me,' the phone man said, 'I'd bring back corporal punishment. Nothing like a few strokes of the birch to get them back into line. Look at the Isle of Man – no problem with mugging there. I *say* look at the Isle of Man, but even they've gone soft. Corporal punishment, that's what's needed – that and compulsory repatriation. If it was up to me . . .'

'Has it happened before?' asked Clare, and she saw a look pass, fleetingly, across the woman's face, as much as to say, what do you think? Then she made the sort of non-committal gesture that could have meant: no, never before, or yes, a dozen times a day, or simply: what's the use of discussing it?

She was a sweet-faced old lady but attempting to engage her in social chit-chat was quite an uphill struggle – 'Have you lived here long?' 'Since the war.' 'Is it a nice neighbourhood?' 'It's changing.' 'Would you like me to drive you to the hospital so that they can take a look at your hand?' A magnificent bruise was appearing on the woman's wrist. 'Oh no, no thank you, I'll be fine.' Clare felt that she was talking to someone whose conversational powers had grown rusty through lack of exercise. As soon as she decently could, the woman finished her tea, gathered up her books and, expressing her gratitude, left.

Later, Lizzie rang. 'You're connected then?' she asked, unnecessarily. Clare let out her breath in a long sigh of disappointment, knowing that this would be the pattern from now on: the sound of the bell, the rush to answer it, the subsequent let-down. 'We've had a bit of a drama this afternoon,' she said, and related to Lizzie the turn of events. But Lizzie had her own news to impart. 'I've got free airline tickets,' she said. 'I thought I might as well make use of them before everywhere gets booked up. A long weekend in Lisbon,' she said. 'And see where we go from there.'

'You mean *he's* going with you?'

'On strictly agreed terms,' Lizzie said. 'Separate rooms and no funny business. Otherwise the deal's off.'

After Theo left her, always too soon, Clare was wont to indulge a fantasy: one that involved a trip undertaken together, somewhere hugely atmospheric: terraces, wine, a carved bed, heavily curtained, the faint strains of music across the water, time together with no limit . . . 'Well you've a hope,' Lizzie said. 'He's a married man, isn't he? With married men, it's usually the flat of some bachelor friend who's none too particular about changing the sheets, or else a special offer in one of those commercial hotels in Manchester. Or Bradford. Or Leeds.'

Chapter Seven

Nancy hurled herself at the boys who taunted Maisie and proved herself to be mistress of an entire lexicon of insulting epithets: 'Oy! You! You pox-ridden, louse-bound, parish-reared tripe-hound!' she'd shout at the biggest, most impudent lout. 'I'll 'ave yer goolies for blood ollies. And don't think I daresn't.'

They'd trade jibes at first but eventually they'd run, just as the cat ran from the cock blackbird in the garden. And Nancy would raise her fingers in a rude gesture to encourage their retreat, adjust her little fur Cossack's cap, smooth down her curls and regain her composure. 'You don't want to let little snot-noses like that upset you,' she'd say. And when, eventually, Maisie gathered the courage to relate to her an expurgated account of the events of the afternoon of the Gugnuncs, Nancy had stared at her as though she was severely wanting. 'Getting worked up over *that*,' she'd snorted. 'And I'll bet you there wasn't another one there as clever as what you are. If you lived round our way,' Nancy said, 'you'd soon learn to deal with the likes of them.'

Though she and her family – her mother and her little brothers and sisters and her endlessly coughing stepfather – wouldn't be living round their way much longer. When Nancy became a big star they'd all move out to a posh house like that: and she'd point towards one of the imposing villas of the Gradwell sort that edged the park where they walked sometimes in the afternoons when Nancy didn't have a matinée. 'Only, by the sea,' she said. 'Frinton. Ma went to Frinton once and said it was ever so lah-di-dah.

We're all going to have a bedroom each,' Nancy said, 'and mine's going to have a pink bed shaped like a shell like Norma Talmadge in that film. It'll cost a lot of money, but I'm going to make a lot of money, I am,' said Nancy. 'They've given me another spot, you know, opening after the interval. Before the brokers' men. They're rubbish. I wouldn't give you tuppence for them. And that Billy Burnham – the fat one – he drinks, stinks of the booze something desperate! Did I tell you about the time he fell on his *tuch*?'

She had learned *tuch* from Solly Rubin. Once she said it in front of Mrs Mendelssohn and Mrs M had cried aloud, saying, 'Dirty little girl, wash out your mouth!' But Nancy, sniggering, had confided to Maisie that she knew better swear words than that, the majority of which, apparently, had been learned at her mother's knee.

'You, girl, should learn some respect,' Mrs Mendelssohn would say, slapping Nancy lightly on both cheeks. She called for the washing out of mouths with soap, screamed with vexation when Nancy helped herself to unauthorized second helpings, shook her head slowly from side to side saying '*Meshugine*' when Nancy demonstrated the splits on the parlour table or tonged her curls so enthusiastically that the scent of singed hair could be detected all over the house, but Maisie got the impression that her disapproval was really a sham, that Mrs M found Nancy's naughty ways somehow quite endearing.

Mother's disapproval was genuine, and total. Nancy was a foul-mouth, a bad lot, a degenerate. Nancy, Mother said, would come to a thoroughly bad end. Maisie was to have nothing to do with her. But Mother was too busy to exercise a constant vigilance, and during the afternoons, when Nancy didn't have a matinée, they'd walk in the park, cuddle together against the cold inside the deserted bandstand and share a kaline sucker. 'Who's your favourite,' Nancy would say, breathing hard down her nose and spraying sherbet in all directions, 'Norma Talmadge, Greta Garbo or Gloria Swanson?' Sometimes they had tiger nuts or the long strips of everlasting toffee that had to be chewed so vigorously that it gave you jaw-ache. 'Who's your favourite,' Nancy would say, 'John Gilbert or Douglas Fairbanks or Ramon Novarro?' And then her eyes would start from her head when Maisie was forced to confess her ignorance. What! Maisie had never been to the movies? Never been to the flickers? The tuppenny rush? The laugh and scratch?

'You've never been to the *pictures*?' Nancy said. Sometimes she'd pretend to be astonished for effect. But this was genuine. Her mouth was agape. She was chewing on a piece of liquorice so her teeth were stained black. She flashed them in a gruesome grin. 'The Colgate Kiddie,' she said. And then she repeated: 'Never? Not ever? Not once?'

Never, not ever, not once. Neither to the cinema, nor the theatre, nor even the music hall.

Later, while they waited for the great geyser in the bathroom to heat up and disgorge its contents into the tub, Nancy sang: '*Maisie, you're driving me crazy*. It's *Daisy*, really.' Then she said, 'Won't you be coming to see me then? It's a real good show, you know – well, most of it – and I'm brilliant, simply brilliant.'

'I'm not allowed.'

'I'll wangle you a ticket for a matinée,' Nancy said. 'It'll be a good seat: front row of the dress circle, or the stalls. Better be the stalls for you, speccy-four-eyes, or you'll not see a thing.'

Maisie felt herself sweating. This was due to embarrassment as much as the bathroom's steamy heat. She said, 'Mother won't take me. I asked her. She said that that sort of thing only gives you ideas.'

'Well go by yourself then,' said Nancy. 'You're a big girl now. Just jump on the tram – I'll lend you the penny – and get off at the theatre and go round to the stage door.'

She'd never told Mother a lie before. '*Toot-toot-tootsie, good-bye*,' sang Nancy, executing a perfect handstand on the edge of the bath. Her petticoat fell down over her face. '*Toot-toot-tootsie, don't cry-y*.'

'Oh Nancy, how do you *do* that?'

She righted herself, dipped a toe in the water and started to take off her drawers. 'Kid,' she said, 'you ain't seen nothing yet.'

January 3rd, 1929.

Nancy was simply brilliant. When she ran down at the end to take her curtain call, wearing a frilly ballet frock covered in gold-coloured lace, she got more applause than anybody, more than Jack, more even than the Principal Boy, and Nancy says she's somebody who's really famous in the legit theatre – whatever that may be. Nancy had an act where she did cartwheels across the stage and handstands and the can-can and the splits, and after each of these the audience applauded madly, banging their heels on the floor. Once, when she was holding a pose – an arabesque, she said it was called, at the front of the stage – she winked at me, a really big, obvious wink. I nearly died with embarrassment.

Though I can't say that I understood the story all that well: they kept stopping it to have dancing and singing: once the Dancing Babes were dressed as Chinees, and I don't know how that was supposed to fit into the English countryside. But the songs and the dances were lovely, and the brokers' men were hilarious. Nancy had said beforehand: 'You'll be able to smell the booze off of them from where you're sitting. And for heaven's sake don't light a match.' But I couldn't. All I could smell was the plushy warmth and the greasepaint and the ju-jubes which a lady sitting at the end of my row kept passing to me, saying, 'Go on, be a devil, take two.'

I'd gone to the stage door, as Nancy had said, and at first I couldn't get the doorman to notice me and when he finally did, he wasn't going to let me in, but then I said, 'Miss Ballantyne is expecting me,' as she'd also told me to say, though it sounded so silly, calling Nancy Miss Ballantyne, as though she was a grown-up instead of a girl my age who's mad on sherbet and gets told off for picking her nose. At any rate it worked because she was sent for and came running, wearing this old rag of a dressing-gown, her face painted in all these tremendously bright colours – which, neverthe-

less, *looked really natural when she was up on the stage – and she led me through corridors and up and down flights of stairs until we emerged through a door in the auditorium and she showed me to my seat.*

When the Giant came on we all had to boo and hiss. He was enormous but Nancy said he was just an ordinary man on stilts. We'd been told to call out to Jack to warn him. We had to shout: 'He's behind you.' And Jack would look the wrong way and then say, 'Oh no he isn't.' And we had to shout back: 'Oh yes he is!' The little boy sitting next to me was shouting and jumping up and down until he was red in the face and laughing and crying all at the same time. 'Calm down, Gordon,' the lady with the ju-jubes said, 'or you'll wet yourself.' But the way she said it – laughingly – didn't make you think that to have done so would be the worst thing in the world.

It was just wonderful, all of it: the huge hairy Giant staggering on his stilts and the green-faced Demon King making his entrance through the trap-door with firecrackers going off and clouds of smoke and the Principal Boy, so handsome, slapping her thigh and inviting children on to the stage to join her in the singing, all the noise and the colour and the sweet smells of powder and paint and knowing that everyone was happy and laughing and friendly, just how people ought to be. It was the best time I've ever had.

Afterwards I waited at the stage door for Nancy to come out and we linked arms and travelled back together on the tram and on the way we sang the songs from the show, It's a Bright, Bright Day *and* Roll Along, *really loudly and we kept shouting* Fee, Fi, Fo, Fum *over and over again until the nice conductor, the one who always says, 'Are you a penny scholar?' when he sells you your ticket, said, 'A little less noise, if you please, young ladies. A modicum of quiet, please, there at the back.'*

She'd hidden her diary. She always did. Varying its hiding place every so often. Not that there had been, before her pantomime visit, much to conceal; it was simply that she needed some part of herself that was not laid open for Mother's avid scrutiny.

But it wasn't the diary that gave her away. It was one of Mother's customers who had been sitting two rows behind Maisie and who had said, all unwitting, when she came in for the final fitting of her tea-gown, 'Did your little girl enjoy the pantomime?'

Mother had had a mouth full of pins. She'd removed them, very slowly and deliberately, one by one. 'Go into the other room, Maisie,' she'd said, in a very calm voice, without ever once taking her eyes off the woman's bust-darts.

'Did she give you a belting?' Nancy asked later. They communicated in whispers from one landing to the next. Mother was treadling and Mrs M was out at the shops, but it was fraught all the same. They were in disgrace. Gertie and Nina came tittuping past, noses in the air; they'd been instructed not to have anything to do with them. Nancy made a gesture with her longest finger. 'One word to the pair of you,' she said.

'Did she wallop you?' Nancy asked.

A walloping might have been easier to bear. But that was not Mother's way. Mother's way was the long, silent, reproachful stare, and then the verdict: 'You've let me down, Maisie,' delivered with a tremble in her voice that denoted unplumbable depths of sorrow and induced within Maisie an almost unendurable pang of guilt.

'I've told you before,' Mother had said, 'we keep ourselves to ourselves. We don't want to be getting involved with other people, being led astray.'

'But why not? Why not?' Maisie had cried in a sudden passion. 'What's wrong with other people? I only went to see the pantomime . . .'

'You *only* went to that party,' Mother said, 'against my advice.'

And it was as if her shameful lapse had occurred only yesterday; her whole being burned hot and bright as she re-experienced the ignominy of it.

'I don't want *ever* to have to tell you again,' Mother said. And there was no support forthcoming from Mrs M's direction.

Defiance and deceit were deplorable at the best of times; to defy and deceive one's own mother was deserving of the coldest of shoulders. She sent Maisie to Coventry and cut Nancy's rations to the bone.

'Well sucks to her,' Nancy said on the stairs. 'We're off next week anyway. We'll have a jolly good feed when Ma gets my wages. *Proper* grub,' she said, raising her voice. 'Not this kosher muck. Only fit for pigs,' said Nancy, emboldened by bravado and hunger.

Maisie had stopped listening. Her future was visibly shrinking until it appeared as nothing more than a pin-hole of light at the end of a long black featureless tunnel. She knew, of course, had known from the start, that Nancy's stay could not outlast the pantomime's run.

'We've a fortnight off and then it's up to Glasgow,' Nancy said. 'That's if I don't get a film offer first. Then Dirty Dickie can stick his contract where the monkey put his nuts. What's up, kid?' Nancy whispered. She clambered over the banisters and came to sit next to Maisie. 'I'll miss you,' Maisie said. Overcome with shyness, she stared hard at her knees. 'Will you?' said Nancy; she sounded quite surprised. Perhaps because most people sighed with relief at the prospect of her departure. She pondered this unusual reaction for a while and then she reached behind her to unclasp the beads that she wore. 'You can have these,' she said, 'to remember me by. They're ever so valuable.'

They were green, made of glass, translucent, pretty. Maisie kept them for years but then they got mislaid, along with the French franc.

'I've nothing to give you in exchange.'

'That's all right,' Nancy said. 'When I'm a big star and you're — ' she racked her brains for an area in which Maisie might be expected to excel, 'and you're a professor or something like that, we'll meet up. Honest. At one of the posh hotels. The Ritz. Dead swanky. You know the Ritz? Down Piccadilly?'

Maisie shook her head helplessly. 'Oh you'll find it,' Nancy said with the easy confidence that might, in time, have proved to be contagious. 'Pals?' Nancy said. 'Cross your heart and hope to die?' And, spitting upon her index finger, she drew it across her throat to the accompaniment of a profusion of gagging and choking noises. 'I'll send you a postcard,' Nancy said.

The following Christmas, Mrs Mendelssohn met Miss Aldridge, matron of the Dancing Babes, and asked after that cheeky little baggage she'd put up the previous winter, and Miss Aldridge had stopped looking lugubrious due to harassment and looked instead simply sad. 'Did you not know?' she'd said. 'Have you not heard? Poor little Nancy. I'm afraid she had to go into the sanatorium not long after she left here. Poor little Nancy,' Miss Aldridge had said.

'Dead! Within the year!' Mrs M had cried, and then she'd set to and scrubbed the house from top to bottom, just as though, had there been any lurking TB germs, they wouldn't have manifested themselves well and truly by then. Once Maisie caught her wiping her eye with a dishrag as she knelt before the bucket of steaming carbolic. 'I cry,' she admitted, 'for that little crazy one. I cannot help it. You too, her friend, maybe?'

But Maisie had shed all her tears crouched behind a letterbox that would never yield anything more, ever again, after that solitary postcard, which had borne the message, written in misspelt scrawl: *My cousin Nellie, that had the rickets, they called it the Glasgow Leg and I know why now. It's always dark here, never see daylight. I've been coughing away like a good 'un, they are making me spit in a jar. Don't forget the Ritz!! Your pal, Nancy.*

There'd be deeper sorrow, longer-lasting grief, but she'd never cry as violently as that again, tears falling until the postcard's ink ran and *Your pal, Nancy* became totally illegible.

Another postcard had arrived for her this morning, sixty-four years later. It contained a request for her to present herself, in a fortnight's time, at the local hospital in order to be scanned. She remembered when Mother had been scanned. She'd had a lumbar puncture too. Her screams had echoed through the hospital corridors, though by then she'd scream if you so much as attempted to change her nightie.

It was an appointment that had been arranged after she'd begun to wander and to eat all kinds of inappropriate substances: rubber bands, the contents of the dustbin, her own dirt, and Maisie had been obliged, despite repeated cries of 'No doctors! No doctors!' to call one in. He'd asked all manner of silly questions, such as what day was it and who was the Prime Minister, questions to which Mother had replied with a mere supercilious curl of the lip because by that stage she was past knowing who was a doctor and how distraught she'd once been at the idea of coming into contact with one.

When they got the results of the tests, a specialist had asked to see Maisie. 'Your mother has a bacterial infection, undoubtedly of very long standing,' he'd said. 'It's probably the reason for her strange behaviour. The good news is that she can be treated so that she doesn't deteriorate any further.'

But she had done: giggling hysterically for no reason at all, touching herself lewdly, developing a malevolent slyness that quite confounded Maisie's attempts at confinement. By the time she died there was scarcely anything of her original personality left to inhabit the withered frame that Maisie cleaned and washed so conscientiously and kept communion with throughout the long nights.

She became aware that someone was banging on Clare's front door. And then her own doorbell rang. And after that someone who – like the large lady before him – had obviously vaulted the railings began to beat a tattoo on the glass so peremptorily that it was impossible to ignore. She opened up to be confronted by a youth with beads in his hair and holes in his jeans who wore a frayed T-shirt that sported the legend: *King-Size Asshole*. She shrank from him as she shrank from most of those of his age and general appearance in case they bore her ill-will, although he didn't look in any way threatening. But then neither had those girls the other day who'd sidled up to her and insinuated themselves with smiles, before shoving her to the ground and delving – to no avail, as it turned out – into her coat pockets. However, when she looked more closely at this boy, she could see that, obscured though it was by the beads and the locks and the scrubby, irregular bits of facial hair, his resemblance to Clare was unmistakable.

'Hi there,' he said, shifting from foot to foot, leaning negligently against the doorpost, straightening up again to flick back a braid – a fidgety sort of boy, evidently. 'My mum,' he said. 'She ain't in. Not left a key with you, by any chance?'

All his late twentieth-century accoutrements seemed somehow out of keeping; his was a face from a statelier age: wide-browed with high cheekbones and a long straight nose, a face from a colour plate in an art book: a Medici prince; a Venetian duke. It was quite enchanting. She sought for the name that she'd heard Pauline mention: something Celtic: Wyn? Glyn? *Gwyn*! and repeated it aloud.

He moved his head in a brief gesture midway between assent and denial. 'Joe,' he said. 'Pleased to meet you.' And then, 'Thought she might have bunged you a key. No? Don't know where she's gone at all? That's a pain. Got all my stuff here. Couldn't leave it with you, could I, while I search her out? Or – look, d'you have a ladder? I could get in the kitchen window, no probs.'

'I've some steps.'

They had come with the house. 'They'll be useful,' Mother had said. 'We'll be able to clean our own windows.' Soon after, Maisie had found her standing bewilderedly atop them, having forgotten entirely the purpose of her ascent in the time it took to accomplish it.

'Ye-e-ah,' the boy said, stabbing his fist triumphantly at the air and following her into the kitchen.

'I'm not sure,' she said worriedly when the steps were located.

The rubber studs on the feet were missing and they wobbled alarmingly.

'They'll be fine,' he said, striding back through the house, carrying them aloft. 'You can hold on to the bottom if you like though, to stabilize them, in case I have to jump on to the window sill.'

He did have to jump. She'd watched, her foot on the bottom tread and her heart in her mouth, as he leapt upward and gained a precarious foothold on the meagre jut of the sill. He'd begged a chisel off her too but she didn't have one so he'd had to settle for a screwdriver which he now manoeuvred between the bottom of the casement and the frame.

By dint of balancing on one foot and holding himself at arm's length from the window while he levered away, he managed to free the catch. Open, the aperture seemed scarcely large enough to allow entry to a very small child, let alone a large youth, but he wriggled his shoulders and contorted his limbs, bending each long leg carefully, edging his feet gingerly through the gap. 'Geronimo!' he shouted as he swung his backside across the sill, and then there was a muffled crash, followed by the breaking of glass and he yelled again, but this time presumably as a result of pain and then could be heard to say, 'Oh shit!' and, 'Oh shit!' again.

She climbed the steps until she could see into the kitchen. 'Are you all right?' she called as she climbed. 'Me bleedin' ankle's wasted, I think,' he replied. He was sitting on the floor, clutching the joint in question. Around and about him lay shards of pottery and slivers of glass. 'Broke it, I reckon,' he said, massaging the top of his boot and screwing up his features into various grimaces indicative of agony. 'Oh dear,' she said; she'd have wrung her hands, except that she needed to cling on to the window sill. 'What can I do?' She had no telephone and the nearest public call box was at the bottom of the hill.

He swung himself upright, putting all his weight on the uninjured leg and then, tentatively, attempted to transfer it to the other one. 'Jesus!' he said. And, 'What did she want to leave

83

all that stuff on the sink for? She should have washed up before she went out,' he said self-righteously.

'Can't you walk at all?' she called.

'I might be able just to hobble,' he said hopefully and, suiting action to words, began to inch his way across the kitchen.

'If you could manage to open the door,' she called, 'I could take a look at it.'

As she waited, she noticed his belongings which were strewn across the grass. There was a large rucksack with various slogans stencilled on its surface, superimposed upon each other: she could make out *Butthole* something or other and above that *Massive Attack*. There was a holdall and a studded leather jacket and a guitar and, tied together by their laces, a pair of shoes of a kind that seemed somehow familiar and then she remembered that Nancy had had shoes like that: with steel caps on the soles and the heels. 'For my tap numbers,' she had explained and demonstrated vigorously on the lino'd landing, much to Mrs Mendelssohn's annoyance. Nancy's had been red and about size three; these were black patent and proportionately larger.

At length the door was opened. He'd grabbed an umbrella for use as a crutch. He looked extremely woebegone. 'I think,' he said, wincing extravagantly, 'that it might be a compound fracture.'

But if it was it made a remarkably rapid recovery. She'd unlaced his boot and unpeeled his sock – which gave off the aroma of a sock that has clothed an adolescent male foot for a day too long – and soaked a towel under the cold tap and applied this compress to his ankle that showed only the slightest of swellings – slighter, in fact, than that on her own wrist – and, after he'd stopped yelling, asked him if he could waggle his foot. She remembered reading somewhere that if you were able to move a limb quite freely then it couldn't be broken.

He waggled away uninhibitedly as though impressed by his ability to perform this feat. And then either the pain subsided or else he grew tired of being an invalid because he suddenly jumped up, declaring that he was starving and began to ransack the fridge and the cupboards. 'Hey, thanks,' he said, as he carved thick slices from a loaf and even thicker slices from a wedge of cheese and proceeded to sandwich them together in layers. 'Thanks for the first-aid and that. I didn't catch your name . . .'

'Miss Carruthers,' she started to say, as she unfolded the towel and spread it over a radiator to dry. And then she changed her mind and said instead, 'Maisie. If you like.'

For some reason, in this case, she felt no misgivings about familiarity breeding contempt.

Chapter Eight

Clare was always bemused when she read about women who ran off with their best friends' husbands, never having had a best friend for whose husband she'd felt any attraction whatsoever. Somehow, their status as such automatically rendered them off limits. And Michael Twist was no exception.

She bumped into him at the delicatessen counter in Sainsbury's. Had she seen him first, she'd have put into effect the most strenuous of avoidance tactics, but they were practically trolley to trolley when he hailed her. His contained a single portion, boil-in-the-bag lasagne, a six-pack of lager and a packet of muffins with ten pence off because they had reached their sell-by date. 'Tomorrow's dinner,' he said, indicating this unappetizing fare. She knew that he expected her to feel sorry for him because he was a lone male having to forage for himself. She remembered him as a student, holding forth on some subject (any subject: he was an authority on everything) in bar or bedsit. He was a not terribly bright young man with inordinate self-confidence, the sort of man who expounded, who talked through your responses and smiled patronizingly if you hazarded an opinion that conflicted with his own. She couldn't understand why Lizzie had married him, any more than Lizzie could understand why she had married Huw.

'Back to self-catering,' he said ruefully, obliging her to enquire about the Portuguese weekend. Lizzie hadn't yet been in touch

86

to report and Clare took this delay as symbolic of the fact that it had gone rather better than expected.

He scratched his head as though he needed to think his reply through before presenting her with it, as though he couldn't just say, as anyone else would have said, 'Fine,' or 'OK,' or 'Terrible, actually,' and then he rearranged what remained of his hair and screwed up his forehead as if in contemplation of far-distant horizons and said, eventually, 'Superb hotel, but you know Lizzie and her enthusiasms: she kept dragging me off to these *fado* houses: women in shawls, wailing. Cheeses you off after a bit. Otherwise, most satisfactory.' And he bared his teeth in a smile of smug lechery. Oh Lizzie, Clare thought, no one but Huw asked for my hand in marriage, but you had any number of proposals. Whatever possessed you to settle for a twerp like this?

'We must get together some time,' he was saying, 'now that – well, you know, Lizzie and I are starting to make a go of it again. I'll get her to fix something up . . .'

In your wildest dreams, she thought and left him requesting an individual portion of Belgian pâté and pressed on, filling her trolley with Gwyn's favourite foods. She was going to cook him paella for a homecoming treat. They'd spent their last holiday en famille in Minorca. It had not been an unqualified success: she had spent most of the time interceding between the ten-year-old Gwyn who had carelessly lost a wallet full of money, who had locked the key inside their room, who had wandered off for hours with another boy without stating his destination, and an increasingly irate Huw who seemed incapable of understanding that ten-year-olds were prone to such childish and inconsequential behaviour. But she did remember fondly Gwyn's seemingly unassuageable appetite for paella.

She was thinking of this, recalling the way that the waiters had looked on in admiring wonderment at the size of the little boy's appetite, as she reached home and put her key into the lock. Before she could turn it, the door opened and she froze, an intake of breath trapped in her lungs. 'Hi, Ma,' said this intruder – or, more accurately, since he was on his way out, extruder – and she looked more closely and saw that the dreadlocked stranger wearing a roadmender's jacket complete with fluorescent armbands was indeed her son.

He put an arm round her shoulder and hugged her. He had his guitar and a pot of yoghurt and a teaspoon in the other hand. Her breath escaped in a gasp. 'You nearly gave me heart failure,' she said. 'I wasn't expecting you until this evening. And what on earth have you done to your hair?'

'Got a lift with Toby Jamieson's folks,' he said, ignoring the second question.

'But how did you get *in*?'

He tore the top off the yoghurt carton with his teeth. 'Through the kitchen window,' he said. 'Open invitation, that. We'll have to get it sorted. I did my ankle in. I'm practically crippled.'

'And where are you going *now*?' she said, trying vainly to detain him. For a cripple he certainly moved fast.

'Tobe's. By the way, don't move any of those bits on the kitchen table. It's my amp I'm fixing. And leave that mess. I'm late. I'll clear it up when I get back. Good to see you, Ma. See you later. Bye.'

And then he paused, halfway down the path, yoghurt spoon suspended. 'Whose is the ponce's room, by the way?' he said.

'What?'

'The one with all that drapery stuff and the patterns on the floorboards.'

'Well,' she said hesitantly, 'I thought it might be yours . . .'

'Come on! What do you think I am: some kind of shirt-lifter?'

'Gwyn!'

'Don't *call* me that,' he shouted. And then, 'Catch you later.'

She called him that again, louder, but he'd already disappeared around the corner.

His rucksack and bag lay, unpacked, in the hall. She stepped over them and put her own bags down on the kitchen table between the component parts of his amplifier. She could see

88

fragments of broken pottery and glass on the floor. Closer investigation revealed that it was her favourite blue jug that had been shattered, and the wine glasses from which she and Theo had drunk the house-warming champagne that he'd brought. There was a large footprint on the draining-board and the remains of a cheese sandwich on a plate beside it.

When he was small he'd been so very loving, so touchingly dependent. 'Mother, don't leave me!' he had cried on the kindergarten steps and, Judas that she was, she had left him. Well, she thought as she unpacked the ingredients for the welcoming meal that must be postponed, now she was paying for her betrayal. She longed for those early days back again, the days of caps and blazers and gaps between his teeth and tufts of hair sticking up on the crown of his head, the days of Beatrix Potter bedtime stories, clumsily made calendars carried home proudly from school, the days of go-karts and puppet theatres and Action Men and kites and great holes dug in the garden for no reason other than that is what little boys do. Given a re-run, she'd have done it all differently, so that the hand that had once clasped hers so tightly hadn't so soon afterwards been snatched away, so that 'Mother, don't leave me,' would not have changed into an embarrassed 'It's OK. You can push off now.' It was Huw's fault for sending him away; it was Huw's fault that there had been no other children – he'd said they couldn't afford it.

There was one advantage of Gwyn's clearing off with such indecent haste: at least it left the coast clear for Theo, meant that there would be no necessity for partial explanations that carefully skirted the truth. He'd said that there was a chance that he could manage to see her for a few hours later in the evening. The most outside of chances was sufficient to propel her towards bathroom and wardrobe to undertake a rigorous regime of beautification: pampering her skin with outrageously expensive lotions and filing her nails into neat polished ovals where normally she just cut them across when they got in the way of her typing and slapped on a bit of Pond's cream.

She was growing accustomed, on evenings such as this, to charting the progress of her mood, being able to pinpoint the exact moment when hope dwindled and died and the desolate realization that he wasn't, after all, going to arrive became inescapable. Worse, that he couldn't, for whatever reason, telephone her to explain why. During the anticipatory period she found it impossible to settle to anything: picked up a book, a magazine, threw them down, turned on the television set, switched it off again. In a strange way, disappointment came as something of a relief when, at ten-thirty, she finally stopped listening for a car drawing up outside and went to put on the kettle for her bedtime cocoa.

After drinking it (disrobed of her finery, clad in her disgraceful, not-for-public-consumption dressing-gown), she must have dozed off because the peal of the doorbell woke her with a jolt. Gwyn was leaning on it with his elbow. 'Sorry,' he said, 'I should have asked you for a key,' not, 'Sorry I'm late.' It was past midnight. 'Honestly!' she said but he stepped around her, staggering a little. 'Tell me off tomorrow,' he said. He looked shattered. She relented and said, 'I've put the electric blanket in your bed if you want to go straight on up.'

He produced a yawn so vast that she could see his tonsils. 'In that faggot's room?' he said. There was the alibi smell of peppermint on his breath. He said, 'You must have gone temporarily insane when you did that. Tomorrow I'll get some white paint.'

He climbed the stairs, his boots clattering against the edges of the uncarpeted treads. From the front, they still looked rather alike, he and she, but from the back his resemblance to Huw was quite marked. Perhaps his genetic inheritance was equally balanced; with luck, she thought – hoped – he might have inherited the best from each of them: from Huw, an ebullience, a goal-directedness that shrugged off inconsequentialities, and from herself . . . ? 'You're a trusting little soul, aren't you?' Lizzie had once said, years ago. Clare hadn't been entirely sure that she'd meant it as a compliment.

*   *   *

'Somebody's been having a smashing time,' Pauline said, as she emptied the refuse bin the next morning and brushed the kitchen floor. She'd brought her two youngest children with her. 'Hope you don't mind, Clare, lovey,' she'd said on the doorstep. 'It's the school holidays, see. Terry's signing on and Lorraine's on a trip to the planetarium and our Kerry – who was supposed to look after these – just slung her hook this morning. They'll be no trouble. They've got a video. Now then!' she said and marshalled them roughly into the sitting-room where the girl, without further preamble, switched on the television set, inserted the cassette into the recorder and pressed the play button. After a moment or two prehistoric monsters appeared on the screen.

'Oh well . . .' Clare said. She'd never had a talent for putting her foot down convincingly. 'Would they like a drink or something?' They were glum, unattractive children who had not acknowledged her by look or word. 'Brought it,' Pauline said promptly, and unpacked from her bag two packets of crisps, various chocolate bars and a couple of waxed cartons stamped with virulently coloured pictures of fruit. She punched holes in these containers and then inserted drinking straws and passed them, ready primed for consumption, to each of her children. They received them silently, without taking their eyes off the screen where something resembling Hollywood's idea of a stegosaurus was engaged in ripping off a man's right arm.

With her free hand the girl secreted something into her jacket pocket. 'What've you got there?' Pauline demanded.

The girl didn't reply. When asked again, she said sullenly, 'Nish.'

At this, Pauline plunged her hand into the pocket and withdrew from it an elasticated hairband frosted with glitter. 'That's our Lorraine's scrunchie, you little robber,' she proclaimed, confiscating the article. 'And speak proper!'

The phone rang and Clare was obliged to abandon this charming domestic tableau. 'You must have thought I'd fallen off the planet,' Lizzie said. 'How's tricks?'

She sounded the way she always did when, despite all her fighting talk, she'd decided to give Michael the benefit of the doubt: uncharacteristically hesitant, vaguely embarrassed.

'Not a bad weekend,' she said. 'Although I managed to put back those three pounds I lost. Sardines, I put it down to. But quite enjoyable all the same.'

'So I gather. I met him in the supermarket. He was talking about "get-togethers".'

'A touch premature,' Lizzie said. 'But then that's Michael all over.'

'But we are envisaging a back-under-the-same-roof scenario, I take it?'

'Maybe,' Lizzie said. 'Perhaps. What's that racket?'

'It's Pauline, singing. She's brought two of her kids with her. They seem – well, not quite with us.'

'Count yourself lucky she didn't bring the boyfriend – one chromosome less and he'd have been a turnip. Is Gwyn back yet?'

'Yesterday, actually. He's still in bed.'

He descended eventually, yawning and saying, 'Oh God!' as though he'd been forcibly awakened at dawn, rather than allowed to surface gradually at one o'clock. She was ironing some shirts that she'd unpacked from his rucksack and washed.

'What are you doing?' he asked with a puzzled stare as if ironing were some ancient and outmoded practice like lacing stays or blackleading grates.

'I thought I might as well get these out of the way before your trunk arrives full of the next lot.'

He paused with the Cornflakes packet in his hand, fixed her with an eye worthy of the Ancient Mariner. 'Kindly don't ransack my belongings,' he said.

'I'm sorry, I didn't realize it contained anything private.'

'That,' he said, 'is beside the point.' And then he cocked an ear towards the hallway where, above the Hoover's drone, could be heard the strains of *Mi-i-i-i-ississ-i-ppi* as rendered flat by Pauline.

'It's Lizzie's cleaner. She's helping me out pro-tem.'

'Servants, yet!' he said. 'Aren't we coming up in the world!'

This morning his T-shirt said *Sexy Punk Boy* on the front and with it he wore a pair of ex-army combat trousers. These were not garments that she had been involved in the purchase of; she could only conclude that much of his wardrobe was acquired by a process of barter. She noticed that the holes he'd had pierced in his nose and his ear were healing. The headmaster had objected to them, as he had also objected to the matching holes that he'd punched in his overcoat. The tightly plaited locks into which his hair was braided quivered as he crunched his cereal.

'Doesn't it hurt,' she enquired, fascinated, 'to sleep in those?'

'No,' he said, staring at her as though she'd asked a completely imbecilic question.

Having finished his breakfast, he took from his pocket a tobacco tin and proceeded to roll himself a cigarette. 'Oh, Gwyn!' she said. 'If you must – not those. You'll kill yourself.'

He looked up. 'Ma, please!' he said. 'Can we get it straight: cut out all this Gwyn business?'

'But it's your *name*.'

'Only because the old man was full of that *Cymraig* crap. It makes me sound like somebody who plays on the back row for Llanelli.'

'Lack of team spirit,' one of his later reports had said. 'Absence of esprit de corps.'

'Just stick to Joe, can't you?' he pleaded. 'It's also my name, after all. It's what you called me.'

Pauline entered, dragging the vacuum cleaner behind her. She nodded at Gwyn who was in the process of lighting his roll-up. 'Here,' she said, bringing forth a packet of cigarettes from the pocket of her jeans, 'have one of these. Them sort'll ruin your chest.'

'Thanks,' he said and took one.

She continued on her way through to the utility-room where the Hoover was kept. 'Nice boy,' she said, nodding towards Gwyn as though he was a specimen in a zoo or some eye-catching object in a shop window.

'So,' he said, when she'd disposed of the vacuum cleaner and retraced her steps, 'where do I find a paint shop?'

'A paint shop?' Clare said.

'Yeah. You know – a shop where they sell paint?'

'I think there's one on the Parade. Why?'

'Told you,' he said. 'I'm going to paint my room. It gives me the creeps. It's like sleeping in the middle of the set of that Roger Corman film – what was it called? – *The Masque of the Red Death*.' He stood up. 'Could you bung us some dosh then? A tenner? What does paint cost? Maybe a score?'

'Now?' she said.

'Yeah. Why not?'

'Because,' she said, 'I've hardly clapped eyes on you since you got back and there's a lot to discuss.'

'Yeah?' he said innocently.

'Yes. Your future generally. And starting at this sixth form college in particular.'

'Well,' he said, 'I've got until September . . .'

'September?' she said. 'What do you mean?'

'September. When the year begins.'

'But what about next term?'

'In the GCSE class?' he said. 'I've *got* GCSEs. What would be the point?'

He did have GCSEs. Ten of them, all at excellent grades. Because he'd been in the express stream at school, he'd taken them early, before adolescent idiocy had him totally in its grip.

'I'll be able to give you a hand around the place,' he said, sweetly reasonable. 'You'll need a hand, won't you? Look at that grass, for a start. I could do the garden for you. Say – five pounds an hour?'

She saw that he was serious. She said, 'I didn't expect to have to pay . . .'

'Fifteen quid an hour, gardeners can charge. What d'you pay *her*, Mrs Mop?' he asked sternly.

'Well, Lizzie's still paying her. But if I decide to keep her on, I think it's five pounds.'

'You see!' he said, as if he'd just proved some particularly relevant abstruse point of logic. 'And anyway it's a hell of a lot cheaper than school fees. So, can I have the paint money?'

She took two ten-pound notes from her purse. She said, 'Won't you be bored stiff? I mean, here by yourself – all your friends away at school still?'

He shook his head. 'It'll give me a chance to practise my tap-dancing.'

Upstairs Pauline ran the hot water and flushed the loo and sang *Billie-Jean*, excruciatingly off-key. Gwyn made for the door. She thought she'd heard him say something about tap-dancing but perhaps she'd been mistaken.

She was about to call after him, to inform him that, like it or not, and sooner rather than later, he must sit down with her so that they might address themselves to the topic of his recent, appalling scholastic record and the reasons for it, when Pauline's daughter appeared in the doorway. 'Where's me mam?' she asked. She looked not at Clare but slightly past her shoulder. Perhaps she has a squint, Clare thought, giving her the benefit of the doubt.

'Upstairs in the bathroom, I think. Why, what's the matter?'

'It weren't me, it were our Damien – spilled his juice on the rug.'

Theo rang that afternoon. She recounted to him the day's events: her son walloping white emulsion all over her artistry, her pains-taking gilding and glazing and stencilling, to a background of what Gwyn said was called Techno. 'I presume you can hear that dreadful noise?' she asked him. It was totally unmelodic, just a persistent thudding that made the house vibrate: the heating pipes clanked in rhythm; the window panes trembled in their retaining putty.

'And then this wretched child spilled blackcurrant juice over my kelim, the new one, the one that Lizzie brought me back from Morocco last year . . .'

She always tried to present her doings in a witty, light-hearted fashion. Heaven forbid she should give him the impression that she wasn't on top of things. Heaven forbid she should enquire about last night. She must wait for him to bring up the subject.

'I'm sorry,' he said, 'about last night. It just wasn't possible. I'd have given anything . . . But Thursday, definitely. If that's all right with you?'

He always said that, as though she had some incredibly vibrant social life that he was loth to interrupt. And perhaps, given her determinedly bright and breezy persona, it was a reasonable assumption.

She put down the phone. I'm not like that at all, she wanted to say. I'm not bright and tough and capable. It was early days yet, but she wondered already if she'd left it too late to correct this erroneous impression. You constructed a façade and someone fell in love with it and then it fell away and so did he. It had happened before; she couldn't bear for it to happen again.

Chapter Nine

August 21st, 1929.

Last week the rain poured in through the skylight and wetted all Mrs M's Chinese carpet and left discoloured patches on the top of her very valuable mahogany sideboard that Mr Mendelssohn bought for a song at auction when Lord Somebody or other squandered his inheritance and went bankrupt. She was dancing up and down with rage but she has only herself to blame because it's been leaking for ages and, instead of getting it seen to, she's tried to save money by sealing it herself with a combination of Plasticine and sticky tape.

Anyway, this time she's had to call in a proper workman, a builder. Mr Dorricot, he's called. He went up into the loft and when he came down again he said, 'I'm afraid, madam, that there are quite a few slates too that are in need of attention.' That endeared him to her, in spite of the prospect of a bigger bill than she'd anticipated; she likes to be called Madam.

Although his job involves dust and dirt, Mr Dorricot always looks very spruce with his overalls neatly pressed and his boots dubbined. Unlike his lad, Stanley, who, as well as being gormless, looks as if he might benefit from a good scrubbing. 'Stanley,' Mr Dorricot says, 'you look like the wreck of the Hesperus.' Stanley just grins goofily and says, 'It's our mam. She's over at me gran's so we don't get no washing done.'

'Well do it yourself then, man,' Mr Dorricot says. 'You're not incapable, are you? Who do you think does mine since Mrs Dorricot

passed on? Why me, of course. You could do with a spell in the army, my boy. That'd smarten you up.'

Mr Dorricot is an ex-army man. Even if you didn't know, you could tell by his straight back and his bearing and the way that he does everything so neatly and efficiently, even unwrapping his sandwiches and setting out his billy-can when they sit on Mrs M's back step to eat their dinner.

It being the school holidays, I have taken to cultivating a bit of the garden. In the spring I planted some seeds and now we have a clump of Virginia stock, pink and white and purple, and beside them those dark blue hairy cornflowers and papery poppies like those that used to grow in the hayfield at home, yellow-eyed daisies and love-in-a-mist. 'You must have green fingers,' Mr Dorricot says, when he sees me out there with my trowel. Mother says I should be helping her but I don't like being cooped up on sunny days and Mrs M sides with me, saying that I need fresh air. (Actually, I think she's very happy for me to attend to the garden; it saves her from getting somebody in.)

Stanley usually scrounges sandwiches from Mr Dorricot who says, 'Make your own, you lazy Arab,' but he always relents before brushing the crumbs off his moustache and lighting his pipe. The other day Mother came round the side of the house to put our kitchen rubbish on the ash-midden. Usually she doesn't show herself if the workmen are still there but on that particular occasion they were later than normal on account of Mr Dorricot having to wait in the builders' yard for a delivery of four by two. 'Good afternoon, ma'am,' he said. She just nodded and kept her eyes fixed ahead of her. His eyes were fixed on her as she walked the length of the garden and back again. The next day, as he tamped the tobacco down into the bowl of his briar-pipe, he said, 'Your mother's a very bonny woman, isn't she, Maisie?' I said that I supposed she was, for her age. He threw his head back and laughed. 'For her age!' he repeated. 'And what, pray, might that be?' Well, Mother was married at seventeen and I was born the following year, so I did some mental arithmetic and said, 'She'll be thirty-two come November.' He nodded very *thoughtfully, sucking on the stem of his pipe. It had gone out but he didn't seem to notice.*

On the Monday, when he unpacked his bagging, there was a bar of Turkish delight for me and the next day a bag of bulls'-eyes. I'd always been warned not to take sweets from strangers but Mr Dorricot isn't strange; he's friendly and, I'm certain, a very nice person indeed. He has those sort of eyes that people have who can be trusted. Stanley kept begging the bulls'-eyes off me. He said, 'He's taken a shine to your ma. That's why he's buttering you up.' I told him not to be so soft, but on the Thursday when Mr Dorricot opened his bait-tin and handed me a stick of barley-sugar ('Sharley-bugger', Stanley calls it), he also gave me a letter and said would I be so kind as to pass it on to Mother as he hadn't seen her in person recently and he didn't like to presume.

I ran upstairs straightaway. Mother was threading a shuttle, her eyes screwed up with the effort of focusing. I said, 'Mr Dorricot sent this for you. He's very nice. His name's William. He has a collie dog called Shep, like our Shep at home and an allotment where he grows potatoes and beans and rhubarb.'

We had talked a lot in the last few days, Mr Dorricot and I. He had asked me how long Mother had been widowed. He had asked me if she had 'anyone special'.

'What does it say?' I asked her. She'd torn it open as though it was one of those telegrams that folk used to receive during the War and as she read it I saw that the hand that held the note was trembling.

'Does he want to take you to Dolly's Tea Rooms?' I asked. Dolly's Tea Rooms were as posh as they came, Mrs M said; the waitresses wore huge starched aprons and there were finger bowls with petals floating on the water and something called langues de chat that melted deliciously upon your tongue.

'Mind your business,' Mother said. She was trembling all over by now and her face had gone at first very pale and then brick red. She walked to the window and stood there, tapping the corner of the envelope against her teeth. Eventually she said, 'I think we could

99

do with a bit of a break, a few days out.' So on the Friday we went on the train to the market at Skipton and on Saturday to the fair on Holbeck Moor. Monday she took me to Mother Shipton's cave at Knaresborough and stood waiting for me on the river bank while I ran across to where the hokey-pokey man was selling ice-cream. I looked back. She was pulling leaves from a bush, one after the other, furiously, until the poor thing was stripped bare.

Mr Dorricot and Stanley didn't turn up on Tuesday because their work was finished. Mrs M told us he'd said 'The job's a good 'un!' and then he'd enquired after us and had looked a bit long-faced when she'd informed him that we were off enjoying ourselves. But she wasn't very concerned about that. 'See my lovely new skylight!' she said. 'And what do you know? He gave me a good discount for prompt payment!'

Maisie had enjoyed growing flowers, was indeed green-fingered, but no one would ever have guessed it, given the state of her garden now. There just hadn't been time or energy to devote to it. She'd kept the house spotless; she'd kept Mother spotless too; everything else had had to go hang.

She was startled by a sudden roaring noise in next-door's garden and, looking out of her bedroom window, saw young Joe astride a huge mowing-machine. He was cutting swathes through the undergrowth with abandon, negotiating turns and corners with a scornful disregard of caution: once he narrowly missed a collision with the garden shed and frequently mismanaged his halts, crashing into the Lombardy poplar at the bottom of the garden so often that its branches shivered in a perpetual frenzy.

She was washing her breakfast cup at the sink when she became aware of a sudden silence. A moment later the boy knocked at her door. 'Morning!' he said. 'How's it going?'

His attire intrigued her, altering as it did, quite drastically, from one day to the next. This morning the beads had disappeared and his hair was shorn as close as that of the children in the schools of Maisie's youth, prior to their heads being drenched with liquid paraffin and white ointment to dispatch any lingering louse. And he wore the sort of prison-issue shirt distributed in olden times to stone-breakers on Dartmoor, together with a pair of exceedingly tight vinyl trousers.

'How is what going?' she enquired cautiously.

('You take things too literally, Maisie,' Miss Marriott used to say.)

'*It*,' he said. 'You know, the whole damn thing: life, death, sex, drugs, rock 'n' roll? Now look, would you like me to bring the machine over here and give your garden a going over? Ma said it seemed a good idea while we've got it.' (Ma had actually said, 'See if you can persuade her to let you loose in that jungle of hers, or there's not much point in doing this side. Use your charm.' Charm he had in abundance, an attribute handed down from the paternal side.)

'Or are you actually cultivating a wildlife sanctuary?' he asked in all seriousness. 'No,' he said, waving away her demur, 'I can respect that. I think it's pretty neurotic, lawns and flower beds and stuff, but that's what my mother's about. She's going to have it all laid out with the Taj Mahal or something where that old coal-bunker is. It's for free,' he said reassuringly, 'if that's what's worrying you. We've hired it for a couple of days.'

'Thank you,' she said. 'I'd be most obliged. But you'll have to watch out for the blackbirds.' And she led him to the nest where the four down-covered chicks huddled together, their beaks pointing supplicatingly towards the sky. 'Neat,' he said, peering at them. 'I never realized the bones of their backs were all unjoined-up like that – where the feathers are coming.' 'I think it's like a baby's fontanelle,' she said, but he looked at her blankly. Perhaps he knew no more about babies than she did.

'Right then!' He rolled up his shirt-sleeves in a most business-like fashion. 'I'll go and fetch it. You wouldn't be about to put the kettle on, by any chance?'

She made him a large mug of tea but even fortified thus he

101

couldn't manage to force the machine through the grass. It bucked and reared as it encountered ancient tree roots and heaps of rubble that had probably lain undisturbed since the builders left.

Stronger measures were called for. He leapt the wall and returned, swinging a scythe. 'If I can get it down to manageable proportions,' he said, 'then I can have another go with the mower.'

It was gruelling work. He sweated freely, eventually removed his shirt and hung it on a bramble bush. His mother, leaning out of an upstairs window, called out a warning concerning sunburn. 'Sunburn?' he shouted back. 'More like frostbite.' And Maisie went out to him, guiltily aware that if this fate should befall him, it would be her fault. 'Don't be daft,' he said. 'It's just my mother doing her usual over-the-top maternal bit. Wouldn't say no to another mug of tea though.'

She made him several during the course of the morning. He worked like fury, slashing at the undergrowth with rhythmic swinging strokes, pausing only to shake the sweat out of his eyes. From a distance, Timmy watched his every movement, knowing, no doubt, exactly where he was due to uncover a series of feline latrines of varying antiquity. 'Oh!' cried Joe, from time to time, 'Cat-shit! Gross!' and stamped his besmeared boot upon clean grass or scraped the edge of it on a paving stone.

At lunchtime his mother called to him again, saying that she had prepared a meal. 'Not for me!' he cried. 'I don't eat lunch.' But later, in Maisie's kitchen, he accepted a cheese sandwich with his mug of tea.

The cat had followed him inside and fixed him with an unwavering gaze. 'Oy, you, Fang,' he said and reached forward and picked Timmy up with one hand, lifting him until their eyes were level. '*You* are a health hazard.'

Timmy usually took great exception to his dignity being compromised. And when he was eventually deposited on the floor, claimed sulking sanctuary beneath the table. But Maisie

102

noticed that, after a while, he emerged, crept gradually closer and finally, with a cry, sprang on to the boy's lap, circled it a few times and then settled down, purring steadily.

'You're highly honoured,' she said. 'Timmy doesn't take to everyone.'

Then she got out her purse and pressed upon him a five pound note. He looked at it, nonplussed. 'Take it,' she urged. 'You've worked so hard. I know the garden's in a state. I never seemed to get round to it . . .'

He recoiled from the proffered money as if from contamination. 'No,' he said, shaking his head vigorously. 'Absolutely not. No way,' and pushed the hand that held the purse away from him with some degree of force.

And then he looked around, surveying the kitchen appreciatively, appearing not to notice how old-fashioned it was, with its outmoded appliances that dated from the time they'd moved in, just after the war. Grandma and Grandpa had died and although, by then, the farm had been partly in hock to the bank, there had been a small legacy and it had enabled her and her mother to wave goodbye once and for all to rented rooms and sour-faced landladies.

'Great floor, this,' he said.

'Is it?'

It was quite an ordinary floor, its quarry tiles worn smooth by years of traffic.

'Ours is covered with that sisal stuff,' Joe said. 'This would be great for practising on.'

He tipped Timmy off his lap and stood up and essayed a few experimental steps.

'Practising what?' she said. 'My tap-dancing,' he replied, and she remembered the shoes in the garden and also remembered the Dancing Babes tapping away furiously in coordinated line at the pantomime and Nancy demonstrating the steps, steel practically striking sparks from Mrs Mendelssohn's lino: 'Look, this one's called a buck and wing.'

The boots that he wore, huge sturdy things with thick rubber soles, were not appropriate for showing off his skill. 'I'll give you a demo,' he promised as he slid squeakily to a halt, 'when I've got my proper shoes. I'm pretty good. I learned from my girl-friend, but then she had to go back home. Venezuela,' he said, looking, momentarily, quite tragic. 'Anyway,' he said, 'now I'm back I can find a class of my own.'

The dancers of Nancy's day had been small and compact, whereas he was tall and sturdily built. Still, perhaps requirements were different now; most things were different now.

March 17th, 1930.

Mrs M died last night. 'Apoplexy,' the doctor said. I feel as shocked as I did when I heard about Nancy, even though Nancy was a young girl and Mrs M had had more than her three score and ten. It was only last Monday that she was teaching me the steps of the Viennese waltz in case I ever get invited to a ball. And although I said I didn't think it likely that I'd be invited to any ball as grand as the sort where you had to do a Viennese waltz, she said, 'Maisie, think big! Live and be well and look forward.' When we stopped dancing she gave me a piece of honey cake. It was delicious; its sweetness exploded in my mouth. 'Life is sweet,' Mrs M said. 'And God is good.'

I went to look at her this morning after everyone else had been: the Rabbi and Golda and Sadie and all the others. She had on a white cap which was tied tightly under her chin and she was laid very straight on her back, and she didn't look dead at all. I kept waiting for her to open her eyes and say, 'Smile, dolly, it's a good day. Later we'll practise the valeta. For when you make your debut.' I keep remembering how she used to blow me a kiss when she saw me turning the corner on the way back from school and had big dark raisins waiting for me on a plate, and that first Christmas when she put me a peg-dolly in the toe of my stocking. Mother had bought me a new pair of boots, but Mrs M said, 'Boots are boots, but it ain't Christmas.'

I keep waiting to cry, but I haven't done yet. Crying always seems to happen much later than you'd expect.

Now we're waiting for Sammy to come back from London. When he does, Mother says, that'll be that.

Of course she did, eventually, weep for Mrs M. Mother said, 'Save your tears for yourself. We shan't find another place like this one in a hurry.'

And, sure enough, when Sammy came back, after he'd donned his yarmulka and his scarf and officially mourned his mother, a week-long process that involved much loud chanting of prayers, he asked them if they would be so kind as to look for alternative accommodation. He was most polite, gave them ample notice to quit and they were fully aware that the house must be sold. But they knew that he'd never approved of his mother renting to goyim. They had not been invited to the funeral, but Maisie went along anyway and watched from the cemetery gate the interment of the coffin into a plot among those reserved for persons of the Jewish persuasion. A man in a coat with an astrakhan collar stood beside her and handed her a cough drop. She already associated honey cake with happiness; now the astringent taste of cough candy would always bring back with a poignant urgency the memory of grief.

The month of Mrs Mendelssohn's death was also the month when Maisie officially grew up. Despite her protestations, her schooldays were over. Miss Marriott came downstairs from the Fourth Grade to say goodbye and exhorted Maisie to keep up her reading, even spoke about the possibility of night-schools, but they both knew that Maisie's chance had come and gone three years earlier when she'd had to turn down the grammar school place. 'If it's the uniform . . .' Miss Marriott had said then. The uniform was so often the stumbling block. But that hadn't been the problem; Mother could have dashed off a bottle-green barathea tunic and a blazer, blouses four, gingham dresses and double-gusseted drawers on her machine in no time at all. The problem was financial need and Maisie, seated at a grammar school desk conjugating Latin verbs or proving Pythagoras' theorem, would not be in a position to contribute.

'It'll be the sewing, I suppose?' Miss Marriott said. Sewing was, after all, what Maisie knew. From childhood she'd been surrounded by shuttles and bias-binding and bugle-beads, French chalk and fringing, bolts of taffeta and shot-silk. 'I'll be able to take on more customers,' Mother said, 'with you to lend a hand.'

She came out of the school gates for the last time, the faint and forlorn echo of Nancy's confident prediction ringing in her ears: 'When I'm a star and you're – a professor or something like that, we'll meet up. The Ritz.' It was a prediction that had proved false in all its components.

She walked on down the hill and past the station where the blind man stood with his white stick and his tray of matches. A sign propped beside him said 'Wounded on the Somme.' The coat he wore was frayed almost to transparency, his boots were patched to the extent that there was more patch than boot. She thought of the song that Mrs M used to sing:

> Oh the moon shines bright on Charlie Chaplin,
> His boots are crackin'
> For the want of blackin'
> And his little baggy trousers they want mendin'
> Before they send him to the Dardanelles.

She looked at this tattered ghost of a man and reminded herself that things might have been worse, much worse. Though she couldn't help but wonder if they might have been better if Pa hadn't died. Or would he too, by now, have been standing with a tray of matches and an appeal to the negligent conscience of the nation? She wasn't even sure of the wording of the notice that he'd have employed, whether he'd been on the Somme or at the Dardanelles or wherever. Once upon a time she'd asked Mother repeatedly for information about his wartime exploits but Mother had been no more inclined to satisfy her curiosity than she was to stand to attention on Remembrance Day in silent commemoration of that war.

She knew so little: only that he'd volunteered, joined one of the Kitchener Battalions as a shilling-a-day private, that he'd looked so very jaunty in his uniform in that studio photograph taken just before he embarked for – wherever; that Grandma once, spitting upon the smoothing-iron, had said unwarily, 'I used to use this to kill the lice in your pa's uniform when he came home on leave. All in the seams they used to lurk, the little beggars. The men themselves used to chase them with a lighted candle when they were in the trenches. What was it they called it, Rose? Chatting up?' And Mother had shot her a murderous glance and she'd changed the subject directly.

She remembered less: there was only one memory that seemed reliably authentic: he'd been lying on the sofa in the parlour with a rug over him. His breathing had sounded like an old rusted machine that was running down fast and his whiskers had shown very black against the pallor of his face. She wasn't supposed to go into the parlour because the influenza was highly infectious and had only been drawn there out of curiosity: she'd heard her mother crying and shouting and had thought it cruel of her to shout so at an ill person. 'You devil!' she'd cried. 'You filth!' And she'd rushed out, slamming the door so hard that it closed and then rebounded open again.

Maisie had hovered in the doorway, watching through the gap, watching the tears running down her father's face. He seemed to cry without effort or restraint. Eventually he caught sight of her and held out his arms towards her. 'Oh my little lass,' he said. But, alarmed at the queerness of it all, she'd run through the house and out into the yard and sat down by the fowl run, clutching a brown hen for comfort until the cockerel strutted by and nipped her ankle and then she cried too and Mother came outside and scolded her for getting hen-muck all over her pinafore.

*   *   *

The bones of the garden gradually emerged from beneath the long years of neglect. The boy slashed and chopped and mowed. He uncovered a sundial and a little illegible headstone where, presumably, some small family pet had been buried. He found a rockery and what had, obviously, in the house's palmier days, been an ornamental pool; there was even the rusted remains of some sort of fountain. He kicked at it experimentally as though expecting that, after this long desuetude, it might resume its former functioning. 'Weird, isn't it?' he said. 'This garden was once probably exactly the way my mama wants ours to be now. She reads all these poncy magazines and gets ideas.'

'Don't you agree with them?'

'Me?' he said. 'I couldn't care less one way or the other.'

Nevertheless he worked enthusiastically to bring this despised vision to fruition, vaulting from one side of the wall to the other whenever he got bored. She imagined that these fierce bursts of energy would be succeeded by periods of extreme inertia, that he'd be a creature of overwhelming but brief enthusiasms. Certainly he tap-danced as vigorously as he chopped down undergrowth. He'd turned up with his shoes the day after he finished the mowing. '*Said* I'd show you,' he'd proclaimed with such childlike pride that she could scarcely refuse. He'd also brought along a machine that played tapes and, to the background of some appropriately rhythmic music, and having enjoined Maisie to seat herself comfortably, he launched into his routine.

As he danced, she suppressed the faint, hysterical notion that his movements resembled those of her mother at the end of her life: the jerky, stiff-legged gait that the doctor had called loco-motor ataxy.

He danced with the rapt expression of one who is pleased to be entirely concentrated on the task in hand. And, though she was unqualified to judge whether he was good, bad or merely indifferent, he seemed to be perfectly satisfied with his performance. 'This floor's ideal,' he said, as he came to a halt with a series of extravagant gestures.

Well, he had toiled long and hard in her garden and fair exchange was no robbery. 'You're welcome to do your practising here,' she said, 'if it's suitable.'

'Ye-e-ah?' he said delightedly. 'No kidding? That'd be well-neat. I was going to use the bathroom at home but Ma's paranoid about scratching these tiles she's spent about a hundred million pounds on. That's fantastic. When I'm a star you'll be able to get one of those blue plaques put outside on the wall.'

When I'm famous ... when I'm a star ... The echo of a similarly confident assertion came ringing down the years. But at least people didn't die of TB any more. It was a scourge that had been practically wiped out, together with all those other horrors of the ancient medical textbooks: smallpox, diphtheria, typhoid – a scratch of the skin, a needleful of penicillin: a thing of the past.

Chapter Ten

Gwyn's room resembled a monastic cell. He'd ripped down the drapes and painted every surface white: the walls, the floor, the ceiling. There was paint left over. 'I could do some other rooms,' he offered, obviously keen to practise this newly discovered aptitude. Clare declined hurriedly; bad enough that her careful handiwork should have been obliterated, though she supposed he had a perfect right to demarcate his own territory. Perhaps he needed to scent-mark it too. At any event Pauline was denied access. 'I'll clean it myself,' he said. It wasn't inconceivable that he possessed other domestic skills of which she was unaware, but she doubted it.

After several fruitless attempts to pin him down, she finally succeeded one breakfast time. Even then he was hopping about like one demented as he waited for his toast to brown. She'd switched off the radio. 'Hey,' he'd protested, 'I was practising my routine to that!' 'Tough,' she'd replied. 'Now listen, Gwyn – oh, please stand *still* for a minute! You look as though you're suffering from St Vitus's dance. We really do need to talk about your plans . . .'

He'd raised his face, moustached in milk, from his cereal bowl. 'I want to dance,' he'd said, in the manner of some idiotic character in one of those a-star-is-born Hollywood biopics. She'd have suspected him of deliberate parody, except that those sort of films were before his time. Those sort of films were before *her* time, for heaven's sake.

'Well, yes,' she'd said, 'but I'm talking about your career . . .'

'Yeah,' he'd said. 'So'm I.'

To pursue the matter would have achieved nothing except a dangerously elevated level of blood pressure. She let it lie. No doubt it would pass, in common with other passions now spent: astronomy, model aircraft, science fiction.

And when she finally got round to mentioning Theo, she chickened out from the fully comprehensive explanation. He seemed quite uninterested anyway. 'Yeah?' he kept saying, prompting her onwards, just as Lizzie had said 'And?' Then he stared at her as though waiting for some astonishing disclosure: so she had a chap coming round? Wow, as he used to say when he was younger, big wow.

'Will you be in?' she enquired. All she could see of him was a pair of raised eyebrows above the copy of *Loaded*. 'Doubt it,' he said.

He wasn't, as it turned out. It was Pauline who seemed determined on playing gooseberry. She'd forgotten that Thursday was Pauline's afternoon. She'd also made a fundamental error by offering her a cup of tea. Pauline sat down and began to talk, warmed to her theme. Clare thought of glasses to be polished, aubergines to be blanched, chops to be seasoned, titivation to be embarked upon, and twitched with impatience, wondering why she couldn't just say, Drink up and go, Pauline, if you wouldn't mind, because I'm expecting a guest. She'd always believed that it was innate politeness that prevented her from being forthright, but really it was just cowardice.

Pauline's conversation wandered extravagantly from its initial subject, which had been the prevalence of the prescribing of diazepam among a certain socio-economic grouping, along many and various narrative highways and byways until it had encompassed all aspects of the human condition. Her original theme had been prompted by catching sight, while dusting Clare's desk, of the current issue of the journal she helped to edit; the lead story for the month, trailed on its cover, was a report about new research in the attempt to produce a non-addictive type of tranquillizer. 'Tranqs!' Pauline had said. Her sister Carol was on tranqs, had been for years. The whole estate was on them. They were high-rises, deck-access. You couldn't live in a deck-access high-rise without resorting to tranqs, what with the broken-down lifts and the vandalism and the piss-sodden stairways and the break-ins. Most of the adults on tranqs and half the kids on smack – Carol had had to get herself a big dog for protection. A council flat was no place for an Alsatian; everybody left the task of taking it out to somebody else, and sometimes it didn't get let out at all and then the place stank something savage – but what could you do?

And she was worried about what Kerry might get up to while staying there. Kerry was well developed for fourteen, quite a looker, and what with all this truancy business, chances were that she'd get it together with some toe-rag of a lad with time on his hands and a notion to find out what his whatsit was for and before you knew it she'd be up the spout, despite all this sex education they got at school – though the benefit of that, of course, depended upon them being there to get it.

'No,' Pauline said contemplatively, blowing across the surface of her tea, 'no, I don't like the way our Kerry's turning out.' Bad blood, she spoke of. But what could you do: get every fellow checked out before you let him buy you a drink, in case you had a kid by him? And even if you did, it would be no guarantee.

'Men, eh?' said Pauline.

Yes. Quite. Couldn't agree more. But all the same – hope having a habit of triumphing over experience – I'm expecting one of that gender to arrive any minute now. Clare held Pauline's coat towards her with the prompt attentiveness of a waiter seeing off a tardy customer and eventually the message was received and understood.

She raced through the house, trying to discharge all the last-minute tasks while maintaining an air of composure. Although an air of composure was foreign to her nature. She was prone to fluster, always had been: she burned her hand on the oven; she spilled water from a flower vase on to the table's polished surface; she'd had the vegetables on and off the gas – worried that they'd be overcooked – half a dozen times before she heard a peal of the doorbell that wasn't just a figment of neurosis.

He stood on the doorstep, her lover, so thoroughly and uniquely himself that she knew that no one else would ever do, thought of those half-glimpsed strangers with their vague resemblances – ahead of her on the street, backs turned to her in a queue – and her terrible disappointment on discovering just how vague the resemblance was.

'Would this be,' he said, in cod bog-Irish brogue, 'by any chance the address of the woman herself?' and opened his arms to her so that she could be enfolded and entirely safe, however briefly.

They hugged uninhibitedly in full view of any passer-by. Her only other previous married lover – Huw – had been well organized in terms of the clandestine: closed doors, shaded rooms, obscure car-parking arrangements; Theo was guilty of no such shabby stratagems. On the other hand, perhaps he was perfectly confident of being far enough away from home for his anonymity to be preserved.

'Is this appropriate?' he said eventually, taking a bottle of claret from his overcoat pocket and unwrapping its tissue paper. 'I didn't know what was on the menu.'

'It's spot-on,' she said, taking it from him. All his life, she imagined, he would have been effortlessly in tune with the world, rarely guilty of solecism or gaucherie or gaffe. They might have discovered that they had a great deal in common but in this respect they were chalk and cheese.

'Help yourself to a drink,' she said, 'while I see to the food.' Stupidly, she'd opted for showing off, preparing the sort of meal that required constant and finicking attention. Why she hadn't just slung everything into a casserole that could take care of itself, she couldn't imagine. (Or, rather, she could, but preferred not to.)

On her way back from the kitchen, she glimpsed him through the open door. He was sitting in the armchair by the window, one leg crossed over the other (and, oh, he was possibly the only man in the universe who could do that without exposing three pallid inches of the lower limb), an abstemious small gin, much tonic, at his elbow. His profile was outlined against the dwindling evening light as he flicked through the pages of *Granta* that had been left lying around, largely for effect. She *had* been reading it but she'd also been reading a copy of *Hello* which, though unrequested, Pauline had kindly loaned her, and she'd tidied that away all right.

This, then, was the one, the man for whom, if obliged, she might contemplate crawling over hot coals, crossing Arctic tundras, waiting in the rain beneath soot-blackened railway arches. Why him? she wondered. Why him and not another? Although the question was redundant. She had always recognized the concept of affinity, had believed in it unfalteringly, despite the fact that its pursuit had led her up not a few dead ends and blind alleys.

He had always taken her out to eat before. A meal in was categorically different, a meal in meant that he had consented, however briefly, to become part of her environment, knew where she kept her pots and pans, had used her corkscrew (she'd found it eventually in the box marked 'Loft'), had seasoned his chops with the dolphin-shaped salt-shaker that, though chipped and subject to clogging, was kept in constant use because Gwyn had bought it for her birthday when he was seven.

She talked about Gwyn as they ate, because it was desirable – and necessary – that Theo also should be primed for their meeting. 'He's just had this Borstal haircut,' she said, excusing his appearance in advance. 'It used to be dreadlocks – or as near to dreadlocks as a white boy can get. It's as though he's experimenting with every variety of persona available to him.'

'Well didn't we all,' Theo said, 'at his age?'

'And what were you?' she asked.

'I was a Mod. You remember: deckchair-striped jacket and KDs, feathered haircuts and Hush Puppies? Or was it all before your time?'

'I think I might just have caught the tail-end.'

They'd had crotch-skimming mini-skirts, she and Lizzie, and midi-length PVC macs, they'd had cheesecloth shirts and tank tops and loon pants, beads and Afros and Cuban-heeled boots. Now and then they got out the photograph albums and fell about at the depiction of these grotesque earlier versions of themselves.

'I had a James Dean phase too,' Theo was saying. 'My brother went to America and brought back some authentic Levi's and a Gibson guitar, so for a while I was quite mean and moody. Though I expect I'd have been like that anyway, with or without the jeans and the guitar.'

She wondered if Theo too had photograph albums and whether she would ever gain access to them. The desire to be acquainted with every aspect of his life, every detail of his development, was overwhelming.

And, at this early stage at least, it appeared to be mutual. 'What about you?' he was saying. 'Weren't little girls of your age in love with Paul McCartney, or whoever?'

'No. I was never in love with the entirely unattainable.'

Perhaps she ought to have been, got it out of her system at the appropriate time, instead of saving it for later.

'How sensible of you,' he said. 'With me, it was Catherine Deneuve. She used to send my hormones into overdrive. Oh, and Monica Vitti. I'd almost forgotten. Monica Vitti!' he said. 'Whatever became of her? I saw *La Notte* five times.'

'I imagine,' she said, 'that you had girlfriends galore? Real ones.'

'I don't know about galore, but I eventually cottoned on to the fact that celluloid didn't quite do the trick, that there must be more to it than that.'

Good-looking heterosexual men who married fairly late must

115

have some dreadful personality defect, she thought, a rattling skeleton in the darkest corner of the closet; either that or an absolute roll-call of ex-girlfriends. She detested them, each and every unknown one of them, for the advantage they had over her in terms of previousness.

Strangely, she felt a stronger antipathy towards them than she did for his wife. Sarah. Younger than him. Younger by almost as many years as she'd been younger than Huw. (She felt that this was, in terms of tradition, the wrong way round, that wives ought to be older than mistresses.) Sarah, mother of his two young children. 'Kids!' Lizzie had said. 'Well you *have* got a hope, haven't you?'

He mentioned her infrequently, but when he did there was never anything in his tone suggestive of hostility. On the contrary, it seemed that a good deal of fondness existed between them. Clare derived no consolation from this knowledge. A man with a bad marriage might be excused an affair; anything else was philandering. Was Theo, like Huw before him, merely an unreconstructed adulterer? She sought for resemblances between them, but could pinpoint nothing obvious: whereas Huw had been glib, Theo was delightfully fluent; the glint in Huw's eye denoted the incorrigible womanizer, that in Theo's, simply a highly refined aesthetic appreciation.

They finished the claret. She tried to entice him with dessert wine to accompany the pudding, plied him with brandy when she brought in the coffee. He resisted both these blandishments. 'I have to drive home,' he said.

And perhaps she had been conniving at his inebriation so that he would be obliged to stay. Though her attitude was ambivalent. When he took her face between his hands and began to kiss her, so sweetly and yet at the same time most purposefully, she had to deter him, telling him that her son could return at any moment and to be caught even in the preliminary stages of *flagrante* would be hideously embarrassing.

He unbuttoned her blouse, cupped a hand around her breast

and, at a deeper level, her palpitating heart. 'We could go upstairs and lock the door,' he said.

Her door had never been locked against Gwyn. And anyway the internal doors in this house were not furnished with locks.

But the hand that stroked her breast produced a steady throb of desire between her thighs. She became entirely subordinate to the singular logic of want, allowed him access to all her areas of pleasure.

Fortunately she'd had the foresight to put the bolt on the front door. It allowed them the grace to adjust their dress and permitted their heart-rates to slow down before she had to go into the hall to release it. Gwyn swayed on the doorstep. 'What's the big idea?' he almost succeeded in saying.

'I must have put it on by mistake,' she said feebly, as if anyone could put on a bolt by mistake.

But he was beyond registering her explanation. She opened the door and he almost fell inside. Of course, she thought savagely, I might have known you'd choose tonight of all nights to get plastered.

By means of feeling his way along the hall, in the manner of a partially sighted person, he arrived at the sitting-room door. 'Oh. Right. Mr Boyfriend,' he said, attempting to raise a hand in greeting but being obliged to lower it again in order to grab the edge of the door for support.

Theo proffered his hand. She felt herself flooding crimson as she performed the introductions: 'Theo, this is my son, Gwyn,' and tried not to look as Gwyn, saying, 'Joe, actually,' staggered across the carpet, his arm extended in some blurred attempt to make their grasps coincide. She felt again the humiliation she'd experienced when he'd been the only child at the swimming pool who wouldn't jump into the water, the one who climbed the steps of the slide in the playground only to turn round at the top and climb back down again. His appearance suggested that he might have fallen down on wet pavements at some stage during

117

his homeward journey: jeans ripped and filthy, a great tear in the sleeve of his hole-punched greatcoat.

Theo gave up trying to coordinate the handshake. 'Well, hello, Gwyn, or Joe, or whoever you are,' he said. 'Good to meet you.' Gwyn suddenly stood stock-still. His complexion changed colour until it might have been accurately described as conforming to that unpleasant shade known as eau de Nil. His Adam's apple moved rhythmically up and down his throat as he swallowed desperately and repeatedly. And then there was a tearing sound as he retched and suddenly lurched forward so that the prodigious disgorgings of a direly insulted stomach were vomited all over Theo's suit.

She closed her eyes. When she opened them again Gwyn was almost slumped on his knees. He seemed to fall in slow motion, finally coming to rest in a foetal position at Theo's feet.

There were no words adequate to describe the expression on Theo's face. Shuddering, he slowly removed his jacket and placed it, sick side up, next to Gwyn on the carpet, brushed away her own squeamish attempt at a helping hand. 'We'd better get him to bed,' he said brusquely, as he hauled Gwyn upright, got one of his arms around his neck and half-dragged, half-carried him upstairs and, grunting with effort, deposited him upon his bed.

He rolled him this way and that, divesting him of his overcoat. He said, 'If you could take off his shoes?' She did so, thinking of Theo's children: Max and Chloe. She imagined them variously: as Rubens cherubs, as grave, sturdy little Mabel Lucie Attwell tots, as illustrated by Arthur Rackham: pale, ethereal, exquisitely beautiful. She wondered if they would ever, in the fullness of time, come to this.

Theo pulled up the covers and Gwyn, stirring, said, 'Leave it out!' and then began to snore in the manner of one of the least refined inhabitants of a pig-sty.

'A few too many sniffs of the barmaid's apron,' Theo said. His words were uncharacteristically clipped, as though he was struggling to contain a potential volcanic explosion of disgust.

Downstairs she took custody of his beautiful, soft, dark-blue, faintly pinstriped, ever-so-expensive suit, sponged it fairly ineffectually at the sink – Gwyn's last meal had obviously included a great quantity of chilli sauce – and dared to enquire, humbly, how this state of affairs was to be explained.

He shrugged. 'Obvious, isn't it?' he said. 'A drink on the way home. Yob at the bar, stoned out of his brain. City type. Too much shampoo . . . that sort of thing. Don't worry.'

And then he must have registered her expression: a mixture of shame and sorrow and fearfulness. He put an arm briefly about her shoulders. She couldn't detect much warmth but on the other hand it wasn't as chilly as might have been expected. He said, 'If this is the worst that happens . . .'

'Your lovely suit,' she said. It almost made her cry: the spoiling of such elegance. She *thought* it was the suit, at any rate, that made her feel so sad.

Chapter Eleven

October 10th, 1930.

Grandma came over for the day. She was going to come a few weeks back but the harvest was late due to the rain. It has rained incessantly for weeks. Mr Maynard – Gerry – who lives upstairs said that it put him in mind of the flipping monsoon. He's been out East. He used to be a ship's engineer until the ship he was on struck a reef in the South Seas and went down. Most of the crew were rescued but after that, he said, he sort of lost his nerve. Now he works in a factory which, I think, must be a bit of a come-down, but he just pulled a funny face and said, 'It's an honest dollar. I don't ask for more.'

He is very handsome with curly hair and dark eyes and his skin is still tanned from all those years sailing to the tropics. 'Tanned?' Mother said, when I mentioned it to her. 'It's yellow. Malaria. He still gets bouts of it, according to Mrs Chapman.'

(Mrs Chapman, our landlady, seems to know everything about everybody. Gerry calls her the Bugle, says he has no need to buy a newspaper while he lives here.)

'You seem to be getting very pally with him,' Mother said, snapping thread between her teeth. 'Just be careful. Remember what I've told you about those sort of men.'

It's true that he's pleasant to me and always takes time to chat if we meet on the landing, and whenever I see him I get a sort of fluttery feeling in my stomach, but I don't think he's one of those sort of men (who lure away little girls, Mother says, in order to do

*something terrible to them, although what it is she won't say).
Anyway, it isn't me that Gerry is interested in; it's Mother.*

*Though I can't imagine why. Once she used to curl her hair and
I remember seeing a little pot of rouge and a papier poudre in her
handbag. (She used to use them on the sly, because the Chapel-goers
of the Dales didn't approve of titivation.) Now it's as if she's going
out of her way to try to make herself look plain. Grandma stared
hard at her and said, 'Have you been poorly?'*

*She brought fresh eggs with her and butter and cheese and a ham
and a boiling fowl, as well as bread and scones and oven-bottom
cakes. There was a jersey she'd knitted me too and several jars of
pickles and plums that she'd preserved. Her bag weighed a ton. 'A
right nice young man gave me a hand with it up the steps,' she
said. 'That's Gerry,' I told her. I like saying his name. And then I
said, very boldly – but I don't often get the chance to say what I
really think or to crack a joke, 'I believe he's a bit sweet on Mother.'*

Mother glared at me and Grandma said, very slowly, 'Is that so?'

*I suppose I must have got over-excited because I felt as though I
couldn't stop talking. 'I think he's trying to pluck up courage to ask
her out,' I said. 'Just like Mr Dorricot.'*

*(In a way, although I liked Mr Dorricot a good deal, I'm glad
Mother didn't take up with him because Gerry is even nicer. And
younger and handsomer too. He's always whistling:* To Be a
Farmer's Boy *and* Annie Laurie. *You know immediately when he's
come into the house. And he can do tricks with penny pieces and
playing cards: making them appear from behind his ear or a hand
different from the one he'd put them in originally. He says he'll
teach me how to do them.)*

*'Mr Dorricot?' Grandma said. Her face went all wrinkly, and her
mouth was pursed up as though she'd eaten rhubarb without putting
sugar on it first.*

*Mother said, 'She's romancing, as usual.' Then she rubbed her
hand over her face. 'I don't care for these rooms,' she said. 'I found
that nosy Mrs Chapman in here the other day going through the
bureau. I reckon we'll be moving on.'*

121

'Oh no!' I said. I'm tired of moving on. Just as soon as we get settled and start to make friends, it's move on, move on.

But of course nobody would dream of taking my feelings into consideration. Grandma just shrugged and said, 'If that's how you feel . . .' and continued to unpack her bag. Then she said, 'Oh, here it is! I found it when I was cleaning out the bedroom cupboards. It belonged to our Rose. I brought it for you, Maisie. Or are you too big a lass now for kiddies' games?'

She handed me a battledore and shuttlecock. It was a kind thought, I suppose. I bounced it up and down a few times. But Grandma forgets the age I am which is far too old for childish things.

'What you watching, Maisie?' Joe called, entering through the kitchen door.

'Battledore and shuttlecock,' she replied.

'What? Oh, badminton,' he said as he caught sight of the screen. '*What* did you say?'

'Battledore and shuttlecock. It's what they called it when I was young.'

'Oh right. In the olden days. Pre the invention of the wheel. Or should I say the fuse?'

He lifted Timmy from a chair and, having usurped his seat, plonked him unceremoniously on his lap and proceeded to stroke him vigorously, all the while yawning and groaning and rubbing his hand across the stubble that was his hair.

'What's the matter?' she said. 'Aren't you well?'

'Hangover,' he answered tersely and before she could open her mouth to comment, said, 'Please, save it. I've had enough GBH of the ear'ole already from my mother. Apparently I made a complete prat of myself last night and f— mucked up her romantic whatsit. God, this is boring,' he said, as the televised match proceeded. 'It'd be more exciting watching paint dry.'

But having a functioning television set was such a novelty that she was inclined to watch anything and everything: game shows, soap operas, Open University programmes about astro-physics.

They'd been given the television, she and Mother, by some charitable institution connected with the church. It was a small black and white set and quite soon after delivery it gave up the ghost. She hadn't been particularly concerned – she had her books – and Mother was past being aware of the deprivation, so she had never bothered about getting it mended, had almost forgotten its existence until the previous week when Joe had come banging at the door with some urgency.

'Can I watch your telly?' he'd said. 'Ma's out, I've forgotten my key and *Swing Time*'s on in ten minutes. I meant to tape it but I forgot.'

And then she had had to admit that this would not be possible.

'Why? What's up with it?' he'd enquired crossly.

She didn't know, she said; one day it had just stopped working.

'Did you try the plug?'

He'd had his guitar with him and from its case he'd taken out a packet of fuses. 'I always have some,' he'd explained, 'in case my amp blows.'

Quickly and sure-handedly, he'd opened the plug and substituted a fresh fuse for the blackened object that nestled within, screwed it back together, plugged it in and – '*Voilà!*' he'd said. And, 'Honestly, Maisie, you are a *case*.' And then, as the picture appeared, 'Oh come *on*, this is steam telly. Where'd you get it: *Antiques Roadshow*? It's black and white!'

So, she had pointed out, was the film.

Now she switched the set on as soon as she got up and tuned into the most interesting debates about everything under the sun: drug abuse, child abuse, transvestism. Once they showed an extract from a musical currently running in the West End: a line of young negro men wearing sparkly suits tapped their way across the screen. 'Quick!' she called to Joe who was similarly engaged in the scullery. 'Come and see!' 'Oh wow!' he'd said. 'Aren't those suits just brilliant? My mate George at the class, his mother's making him one, but mine can't thread a needle.'

After a pause, she'd said, 'Perhaps I could. Make you one, I mean.'

'Yeah?' he'd said. 'No shit? Sorry, I mean could you really?'

The machine worked as well as ever. And skills so long practised were never totally lost. 'I could,' she said, 'if you were to buy the material.'

He paid for it out of his gardening wages and now she sat, watching *Anne and Nick* and *Richard and Judy* and the Snooker World Championships while she sewed scarlet silk revers and attached to them sequins by the score, remembering all the dresses and the gowns and the pinafores, the jackets and boleros and dirndl skirts, that she had helped to make, all the shapes and sizes of womanhood that had divested themselves of their outer garments and climbed up on to the baize-covered dining-table and, while they were being measured, talked of the events and engagements and celebrations in honour of which these clothes had been commissioned, all the contingent lives . . .

June 12th, 1932.

Babs Poole helped me to choose a lipstick in Woolworth's this afternoon. I've been saving my pocket-money for ages. 'Pocket-money!' Babs said. 'Doesn't your mother pay you a proper wage?' I explained that she couldn't afford to do that, that once the rent and the household expenditure had been taken care of, there wasn't much left. 'She's exploiting you,' Babs said. Her father is a trades union activist. He talks a great deal about exploitation and the dignity of labour. He nearly blew a gasket when Babs decided to train as a Lyon's nippie, because he said, if there was an industry that thrived on exploitation, it was the catering game. Babs takes no notice of him. She likes the work. You meet all sorts, she says. It broadens your horizons.

I couldn't decide between Paradise Pink and Rose Anjou. We rubbed both on the back of my wrist and debated between them for such a long time that the assistant said, sarcastically, 'We close at six, you know.'

'I think the paler one,' Babs said at length. 'With your complexion. The other one might make you look a bit sallow.'

So that's the one I bought, even though I'll have to keep it hidden.

Afterwards, when we were having a bun and a cup of coffee in the Kardomah (inferior in every way to her place of work, Babs says, but nippies aren't allowed to patronize their own corner houses), I put on the lipstick and pressed my lips together as she had shown me. It had a lovely perfume but I found the consistency a bit jammy. 'What do you want,' Babs said, 'from Woolie's best? Now if you could have afforded Max Factor . . .'

Babs knows all about beautification, about the correct shades of lipstick and powder, and Marcel waves and how to pluck your eyebrows into perfectly semi-circular arcs and put slices of cucumber on your eyes before you go to bed to prevent bags and softening the skin on your elbows by resting them in halves of lemon. She knows the whereabouts of the pulse spots, the places which, if sprayed with perfume, can drive the boys wild.

She knows all about boys too. She has been practically engaged twice already though she's barely six months older than me. She calls me 'Sweet-sixteen-and-never-been-kissed', can't believe that I've never been out with a fellow.

That doesn't mean, though, that I've never wanted to, that I've never fallen for anyone: as well as Gerry Maynard (who, I realize now, was far too old for me; it must have been what they call puppy love), there was the curate at St James's who had a profile like Rupert Brooke, and then Mr Rogers, the civil servant who lodged above us for a while and who always used to say, 'And good morning to you, beautiful young lady,' and smile as though he was smiling just for me. And of course the man who looked like Ronald Colman and played the trombone in the silver band in the park on a Sunday. And, possibly, the delivery lad from the Maypole grocery who used to ride his bicycle no hands and whistle at me. Although his ears were big, flapped almost, whenever he had the wind behind him.

Once Mother caught me looking at him out of the window and told me to stop mooning about. She said, 'You don't want to involve *yourself in* that *sort of nonsense. You'll only regret it if you do.'* Just *as though there was something so peculiar about me that I mustn't want or have the same as other girls. So this afternoon, when we'd finished our Chorley cakes and re-lipsticked our mouths, I asked Babs, because she knows so much about making yourself attractive and about boys, whether I was, in any way, nice to look at.*

'In your opinion,' I said, 'am I, in any way, at all, nice-looking? In your opinion.'

She put her head on one side and then the other, weighing me up from all angles. After a bit, she said, 'You're not bad-looking. You've got what they call an interesting face. Now if you were to have different glasses and maybe wave your hair a bit . . .' And she took the ribbon off my plait and started fiddling about with my hair, trying different styles, using her own combs. 'A little more make-up . . .' she said, as she combed and curled.

'Mother says make-up's common,' I said. (She'd obviously forgotten her own use of it long ago.)

'Oh, Mother be blowed!' said Babs. 'Listen to her, and you'll end up an old maid.'

She'd become acquainted with Babs when she came round with her mother to Adelaide Terrace, where they were living then, in a house with a cellar-kitchen, for a fitting. Mother was making her a dress for her sixteenth birthday party: a concoction of satin and lace which reminded Maisie of the frock she'd worn to Diana Gradwell's. Though this party was to be a totally different affair: young men and girls, a gramophone, dancing . . . Babs's cheeks were hectic with excitement. 'Now then, Barbara,' her mother had said, as stolid as her daughter was febrile, 'just calm yourself down or else there'll be no party. I've had the devil's own job convincing your father. He thinks a sit-down tea would do very well. And he wants to know why you're not inviting your cousin Wilma.'

'My cousin Wilma!' Babs had said, when they met again by chance at the Co-op counter. 'She breathes through her nose like a horse with adenoids and she's got a thick black moustache and body odour. My dad's crackers.'

Babs was perhaps prone to exaggeration, Maisie discovered, when a friendship, of sorts, was struck up between them. Things were either 'perfectly divine' or else 'utterly hideous'; emotions veered between ecstasy and despair; as for young men: if they weren't John Barrymore, then they were Bela Lugosi. Maisie often lost track when it came to the current young man in favour: Leonard, Jack, George, Frank, Gilbert . . . This one had brought flowers, that one a box of fondants, a third had tried it on. 'You know, going too far?' Babs had confided in the Kardomah café, her eyes wide above the steam that rose from her cup.

'I told him: "You can cut that out right now."'

But this was an admonition that had not, apparently, always been applied. For when Babs came again to Adelaide Terrace to be measured, this time for a tailor-made, Mother saw something that made her recoil. Afterwards she trembled with disgust. 'I don't want to see that young woman here again,' she said. 'I'd rather go to the workhouse.'

'But why?' Maisie had asked, disingenuously; she wanted to find out whether Mother would actually articulate the reason for her repugnance. 'She's not a fit girl for you to mix with, that's why. And that's all I'm saying,' Mother had said, 'so don't bother asking me again.'

Maisie didn't need to ask. She had seen the offending blemishes for herself. She had seen them previously when Babs unwound the chiffon scarf from around her neck in the café, displaying the sort of marks that had caused Maisie to wonder whether someone had tried to strangle her. One of the neighbours, perhaps; Babs said they were always complaining because she played the gramophone too loud: *Tiger Rag*, *Black Bottom*, *West End Blues*.

She knew better now. 'Love-bites' they were called and when Babs stood stripped to her camisole, waiting for Mother to get out her tape measure, they became blazingly apparent: dark red weals that stigmatized her otherwise smooth pearly skin; one either side of her neck, another just above her left breast.

How far was too far? Maisie passed on Mother's message when they met each other at the tram stop. 'She's very strait-laced. She says she's not out of pocket because she hasn't bought the material yet, but she'd be pleased if you'd take your custom elsewhere . . .'

It was horribly embarrassing, but Babs didn't seem to be listening. She was very pale and she shivered, although it was quite a warm day. 'Listen,' she said. 'I'm in trouble. I haven't come on. It was Gilbert. We went dancing – he's a smashing dancer – and he persuaded me to have this drink. I wouldn't ever have, otherwise. And now he doesn't want to know. He said I was cheap. Oh Maisie,' she said, chewing all the Burnished Cherry lipstick from her lips, 'whatever am I going to do?'

There was no question of choice. She was sent, so Maisie heard, to an institution in another town where girls of her sort were obliged to scrub floors and iron endless heaps of laundry while listening to pi-jaws aimed at convincing them of the error of their ways. On Sundays they were led in a shame-faced crocodile to church and, after six weeks, were made to hand over their offspring. For adoption, if they were lucky, otherwise to the tender mercies of the orphanage.

While avoiding any explicit acknowledgement of Babs's predicament, Mother had allowed herself only one, rather cryptic comment: 'It's never anything but tears,' she said. 'Take my word.'

Maisie had dreamed about Babs the previous night: Babs, curls bobbing, arms and legs akimbo, dancing to the music of her gramophone, winding it, turning up the volume ever higher. Waking with a start, she realized that the music, rather than being a figment of her imagination, was real, came blaring through the party wall with a thudding insistence. When she was bringing her milk in later she saw Clare who blushed and said, 'I hope you weren't disturbed last night by Gwyn's awful racket? I gave him a good telling-off.'

It hadn't been so much awful as just completely pointless: there being no tune to it, nor variation in its rhythm. The music to which he tap-danced was exhilarating, whereas the strange sounds that blasted through the connecting wall seemed to bear as much relation to any formal composition as the random noise of the traffic.

'It's *dance*,' he told her, and tried patiently to explain that it was music for a different sort of dancing. 'I bet what you danced to when you were young,' he said, 'would sound just as peculiar to me.'

There hadn't been a great deal of dancing, because Grandma and Grandpa were Chapel. Pa wasn't though. Pa came from a freer, jollier kind of background. Pa had been to the music hall. Her very earliest memory was of Pa performing a silly song, rising on tiptoe, waving his arms and clicking imaginary castanets, adopting a foreign accent as he made bullfighting flourishes: '... he shall die, he shall die, he shall die – tiddley-hi-ti-ti-ti-ti! I'll raise a bunion on his Spanish onion if I catch him bending tonight. Olé!' And they'd all laughed, despite themselves and their Chapel upbringing: Grandma and Grandpa and Mother, especially Mother.

How rapidly, she thought, the change had come about: from the exuberant young man clicking his heels and twirling on the flagstone floor to the coughing shadow wrapped in blankets on the parlour sofa.

That picture came into her mind as she laid out clean clothes for her hospital visit. Joe called in as she was ironing a blouse, for a progress report on his costume. It was beginning to take shape, coming increasingly to resemble a bullfighter's suit; it would have done for Pa in the days when he sang *Alphonso the Toreador*.

'Will you be doing some more today?' Joe asked wheedlingly. He was anxious to show it off to his tap-dancing classmates. There was a girl whose name kept cropping up: 'Mickey'; she'd thought at first that he was talking about a boy. He'd said, 'Not you as well! Ma decorated this bedroom for me like I was a poofter.'

Mickey was extremely talented. Almost as talented as he was. He talked of her fondly. Maisie hoped that *she* wouldn't leave for Venezuela.

'Perhaps I'll do some when I get back,' she said. 'I've a hospital appointment.'

'Bummer!' he said, but didn't pursue it, being far too young to be interested in hospital appointments.

She caught sight of him from the window of the bus, cycling towards Mickey and the class, and wished him joy of them both. Leaving had, apparently, featured too frequently in his life already. He had once, briefly, mentioned his father's death. She gathered this was a topic that, at home, was on the prohibited list on account of his mother's tendency to rush straight into what he called 'the psychologicals'. 'She keeps waiting for me to throw a wobbler,' he said. 'I mean, I *do* miss him and that, but I never actually saw that much of him . . .'

At the hospital, Maisie was scanned, like her mother before her. Three doctors and two nurses squeezed into her cubicle, peering closely at a monitor and, as the various masses that were her internal organs swam into view, exchanged comments. 'Oh yes,' they said, and, 'No doubt about it,' and, 'Just about ready too.' They exuded an enormous satisfaction as though they'd just collectively discovered some hitherto unknown geographical feature. When they'd finished and she was dressed again and directed towards the consultant's office to be informed of what they'd found, she almost expected him to say the source of the Nile.

Instead he said that she had an aortic aneurism: a weak place in the wall of a major artery. This condition was potentially dangerous, as the pressure exerted by the circulating blood could cause the vein to rupture with subsequent internal haemorrhaging.

'However,' he said, 'not to worry. We can do something about it.' And she continued to listen but more sceptically because they'd said exactly the same thing about Mother, and the injections she'd had hadn't made a scrap of difference.

A by-pass operation, he was talking of, the introduction of an artificial piece of artery. Aneurisms were usually allowed to grow to a certain size before surgery was attempted; fortunately she would not be obliged to wait as hers, growing apace, had gone undetected for so long. As soon as a bed became available they would send for her. No problem was foreseen – above and beyond the normal risks attendant upon surgical intervention.

'As good as new,' he said. 'Better, in fact. So just go back home and take it easy until you hear from us.'

He was a big man with silvery hair brushed back, whose face bore a somewhat self-satisfied but not unapproachable expression. She drew breath deep into her lungs to ask a question, a seventy-year-old question, but even as she was inhaling he had risen to his feet and was holding out his hand: pin-striped sleeve, good-quality worsted; immaculate cuff, impeccable manicure; and she knew that she was as incapable of giving voice to it as ever she had been.

Chapter Twelve

'Are you in?' Lizzie enquired. 'I need to see you. Urgently.'

'About what?' Clare replied indolently, buttoning her dressing-gown. She was languorous after love and resented the interruption, wanting to savour her solitude so that she could relive every delicious moment. She said, 'What's wrong?'

'Not over the phone,' Lizzie said. And then, 'You are alone? Where's the boy wonder?'

'Gwyn? He's gone to his dancing-class. He's signed up for jazz-dancing now, whatever that might be—'

Lizzie cut her short. 'And lover-boy? He's not in residence?'

'No. Why are you being so cryptic?'

'I'll get a cab. Have you got anything remotely drinkable in? I don't suppose so. I'll bring my own,' Lizzie said, and rang off.

Clare had always been rather abstemious with regard to the content of her drinks cabinet, friends with children in permanent residence having warned of lightning raids by party-crazed teenage hordes. Gwyn throwing up, she knew, would be as nothing compared with the throwing up of multitudes.

Lizzie brought a bagful of ring-pull ready-mixed gin and tonics and proceeded to pull off rings with the sort of fervour that suggested a great sorrow in dire need of drowning. She was wearing a pair of large baggy jogging pants and requested a cushion to sit down upon.

'What's the matter, have you got piles?' Clare said. Piles were what you shrieked with mirth about when you were young and

132

suffered from when you got older. In fact most of the topics that were the source of so much youthful merriment exacted their revenge sooner or later.

'I should be so lucky,' Lizzie said. 'Oh God, I'm nearly forty. Wouldn't you think that by now I'd have learned sense? Oh God,' Lizzie said, shifting about in the manner of one sitting on hot coals, 'I've got two sanitary towels on – and *still* . . .'

'What are you on about?'

'Well . . .' said Lizzie, picking up a copy of the *Psychologist* and studying its contents page with unconvincingly close attention, 'you remember that trip to Lisbon?'

She spoke as though it had been aeons ago rather than a matter of two weekends.

'Yes, of course.'

'Well,' said Lizzie, 'that bastard has gone and given me something. I'm in agony.'

'But you said it was to be purely platonic—'

'Oh yes, yes,' Lizzie said irritably. 'We all *say* things. Oh God,' she continued, 'what am I going to do? I thought at first that it would go away, but it's getting worse. I hardly dare to go into work and I have to keep *spraying* myself like you do with dustbins in the hot weather . . .'

She gave off the sort of sinus-stunning aroma that Clare remembered from their college days, when they'd spent their lunchtimes in department stores, helping themselves to complimentary squirts from every perfume counter they passed.

'It'll be something he picked up from the tart,' Lizzie said. 'Oh how unutterably disgusting – the very idea of it—'

'Well don't get it out of proportion,' Clare said emolliently. 'Contagion is contagion – whether it's below-the-belt stuff or measles or chickenpox—'

Lizzie screamed, pulled off another ring. 'Don't even *say* that word,' she said. 'What do I *do*?'

Clare prepared a pot of coffee, deducing that it would be required in very large quantities before the night was through.

'Go to the doctor,' she said. 'And get in touch with Michael – if you haven't done so already. Perhaps it's just thrush.'

'No, it's *not* just thrush,' Lizzie said. 'I've had *that*. Everybody has. This is quite different. And no, I haven't been in touch with him. I never want to see or hear from him again in my entire life. And I can't go to the doctor. For God's sake, we go to the same *gym* . . .'

'Well go to the hospital then.'

Once again Lizzie shrieked. 'The clap clinic? You're joking!'

'They aren't called that any more. They haven't been called that for ages.'

'Oh, right, yes,' Lizzie said, sounding as though she was exactly contemporaneous with Gwyn, '*special* clinic, I suppose, or some other equivocation that fools nobody.'

Like many a world authority on anything you cared to mention, there were large and surprising gaps in Lizzie's knowledge.

'They're called genito-urinary clinics, and I shouldn't think anybody bats an eyelid.'

'Are you sure?' Lizzie asked, humbly, gratefully.

'Positive. Now do stop swilling gin and have some coffee.'

Comforted, if only briefly, Lizzie flicked through the *Bulletin*. She always did have a short attention span. Her eye was caught by an article. She read aloud from it: 'The Prader-Willi syndrome – it *sounds* like it should be what I've got – but actually it's a deficient gene which, if you inherit it from your father, can cause severe over-eating. If it's inherited from your mother it's called Angelman's syndrome and makes you walk funny. Gosh! Imagine if you inherited from both . . .'

Clare handed her a cup of coffee and took the magazine out of her hands. 'Never mind that,' she said. 'I've got some news for *you*.'

And if Lizzie hadn't been absorbed in her own problems to the exclusion of all else, she could surely not have failed to notice the glow of delighted anticipation in which her hostess was bathed.

'He has to go to Venice – it's a corporate entertaining thing – trolling clients around to concerts and receptions and the opera and so forth. He wants me to go too. Obviously we won't be able to spend a great deal of time together . . .'

'Venice!' Lizzie was shrieking. She seemed to be in shrieking mode this evening. Then she said, 'Who's paying?'

'Well he is, of course. There's no way I could afford it.'

'You mean he'll bung it through on exes,' Lizzie said. 'Nice one. I once had a bit of a dalliance with this chap who sold – I forget – Mediterranean villas, was it, or Mars bars? Anyway. The *restaurants* we ate in! I put on stones. And then the firm took the chopper to his expense account and he dropped me like a hot brick.'

Clare plaited the fringe on the belt of her dressing-gown. She said, 'I'm not going to let you spoil it, Lizzie.'

She wasn't going to let anybody spoil it. Not Lizzie. Not Gwyn. Certainly not work. She was due back before this proposed trip was to take place. She rang her boss and said, 'If I were to forgo the rest of this holiday entitlement and come in on Monday, could you spare me for the week starting 24th of May?'

She moved the receiver away from her ear while he hummed and hawed. He'd oblige her to beg, she knew, before agreeing to her request. She wanted to tell him to stick the job. She thought of Sarah, serene in her beautiful home, tending her two beautiful children, able to pick and choose if and when she returned to work. When I get back, she thought, I really will brace myself and look for something else. Other people, people no more intelligent or capable or dynamic than herself, had better jobs. Lizzie for one. And though Lizzie maintained that it just about beat picking oakum for a living, at least her salary made up for it.

'Will you come with me to this clinic place?' Lizzie had pleaded. She seemed uncharacteristically timid. They sat in the hospital, surrounded by out-of-date copies of *Woman's Realm* and a huge variety of people. Lizzie, wearing two pairs of thick knickers in case she were to pick up something even worse than what she had, if that was possible, speculated in whispers about the diseases which these fellow-sufferers might be harbouring. But the authorities had shown a compassionate discretion and combined two lots of patients in one waiting-room, so some of the people whom Lizzie had identified as having galloping gonorrhoea or terminal pox, when eventually called forth, actually made their way to see the ophthalmologist.

She'd been given a number but even so they called out her name when her turn came round. 'What if there's anyone here I *know*?' she hissed. Clare said, 'Well I don't suppose they'd want to publicize the fact any more than you do.'

Swabs were taken and a syringe full of blood and she was told to come back in a week's time. 'I thought they'd tell me there and then,' she wailed.

'They have to attempt to grow cultures,' Clare explained. 'Oh, *don't*,' Lizzie said and began to describe the awfulness of her ordeal, milking it for all it was worth. Clare changed the subject abruptly. 'Lizzie,' she said, 'would you do me a favour and have Gwyn to stay while I'm away?'

Gwyn had always got on well with Lizzie, principally because she wasn't a parent but also, Clare suspected, because she had never made any concession to his status as a young person. 'OK,' she said, 'but I don't think he's going to be very happy with the idea.'

He wasn't. 'Are you *totally* out of your tree?' he said. 'Have you lost it *completely*? Do you seriously imagine that I can't look after myself for a few days?'

'I thought you might welcome the change,' she said disingenuously.

'Well,' he said, 'you thought wrong.'

Lizzie would probably be relieved anyway.

Lizzie was relieved anyway on a different score. She rang up a week later to say that her problem had been identified: it wasn't some life-threatening virus after all, but a fairly innocuous little organism that went by the name of *Trichomonas Vaginalis*. She had been given a course of tablets to clear it up. 'They're called Flagyl,' she said, 'and they act like Antabuse.' It meant, she moaned, that she wouldn't be able to have a drink for the best part of a fortnight. She'd been asked whether she had a regular sexual partner and then provided with enough medication for him too, though the doctor said that the route of transmission was not necessarily sexual. 'I suppose I caught it off the toilet seat,' she'd said scornfully. 'It's rare, but possible,' the doctor had replied. 'It can also be contracted from swimming pools, especially if you stay too long in your wet swimsuit . . .'

'That gym!' Lizzie said. 'And when you think of the price of the subscription! Although it sounds like a fairly long shot to me. More likely to be that sod. Either way,' Lizzie said, 'this is the end, absolutely the last straw, finito.'

Clare wasn't sure whether she was referring to cancelling Michael or her subscription.

When she next saw Maisie, she said, 'I'd be awfully grateful if you'd keep an eye on Gwyn while I'm away. Pauline's agreed to come in and do him the odd meal, but what I'd like to be sure of is that the house is secure and he doesn't go out without turning the gas off – that sort of thing.'

Maisie was an expert on that sort of thing. She took Clare's spare key, assuring her that both eyes would be kept out for untended gas burners, unlocked doors, suspicious characters lurking; anybody, in fact, who did not qualify for right of entry. 'I expect she's asked you to change my nappies while she's away,' Joe said when he came in later. 'This is just *so* embarrassing.'

'Mothers worry,' Maisie said. 'I expect she couldn't go away with an easy mind otherwise. Is she going somewhere nice?' she asked, to distract him from what he saw as the unendurable humiliation that had been visited upon him.

'Venice,' he said, 'with the Medicine Man.'

'Who? Oh, you mean her friend. Why do you call him that?'

'Because he works for one of those pharmaceutical companies that make huge profits out of bunging chickens full of antibiotics and cows full of hormones and people full of all sorts of stuff that hasn't been properly tested, and then when they get ill or give birth to kids with no arms or two heads, wash their hands of the problem and pay out pathetic compensation, if any—'

He was getting quite heated. She said, 'Don't you like him?'

'I don't like what he *does*. Still, it's not me that's shagging him.'

'Oh Joe!' she said. 'You mustn't talk like that.'

'Why not? If it's true?'

'Because she's your mother and deserves respect.'

'Oh, respect, right,' he said, bending to lace up his boots. 'You mean the sort of respect she gives me by pillocking about asking all and sundry to spy on me?'

Clare had chosen her words with the utmost care when it came to describing her trip. And because she found it difficult to reconcile the fact that she would be enjoying herself in an exotic location while he was stuck at home – thus reversing the principle that had, for some obscure reason, embedded itself in her consciousness: sons enjoy, mothers sacrifice – she was aware that she was making it sound like a tour round the slag heaps.

'You don't mind?' she kept saying anxiously.

'Why on earth should I mind?' he'd said. 'And you can tell Thingy downstairs she doesn't need to bother coming in to cook. We do have a freezer and a microwave, in case you hadn't noticed. And I can read the instructions. It's one of the benefits of a public-school education.'

She gave Pauline this news guiltily, conscious that she'd be depriving her of income. It wasn't the best time to impart further unwelcome news. That morning Pauline had turned up for work with her eldest daughter in tow. Clare's house being situated midway between home and school, this was as much as she could do to make sure that the girl actually put in an appearance. There had been a letter, she confided, and though she normally chucked correspondence that she knew was bound to be unpleasant to the fireback – final demands, enquiries from the Social, and so on – something had prompted her to open this one, official

138

though it was. It turned out to be from the school, informing her that Kerry's absences had now reached the stage where they outnumbered the amount of time she actually spent there. Repeated warnings having been ignored, there was no option but to call in the Educational Welfare Officer.

'The truant man!' Pauline had said, waving the letter in the air. The subject of the correspondence stood sullenly staring at the floor and chewing frantically at her fingernail. She had a pert, small-featured face that still bore the traces of last night's make-up. Her hair was scooped on to the crown of her head where it exploded in a frizzy top-knot and her school skirt was hitched up to mid-thigh. She wore a pair of white high-heeled shoes and the obligatory gold rings in her ears. Jail-bait, had been Lizzie's description.

'Beyond control, that's what you are,' Pauline proclaimed.

Kerry eventually succeeded in wrenching a sliver of ragged nail from her index finger and spat it on to the floor. 'You dirty little devil,' Pauline said and grabbed hold of her hand. The girl tried to snatch it away. A bracelet rattled down her arm towards her wrist. She made an attempt to conceal it beneath her sleeve, but Pauline was on to it in a flash.

'Where'd you get this?'

'It was a present,' Kerry said.

'Who off? *Who off?*'

'Off Lisa,' the girl said, after a pause.

'Lisa!' Pauline shouted. 'Where does Lisa get that sort of money? I've seen ones like these in Ratner's window. They cost upward of twenty quid. You've nicked it, haven't you? Haven't you?'

The girl shouted back even louder. 'Don't you shame me, you sad old bag.'

And then Gwyn had come downstairs, rubbing his eyes. 'What's all this noise about?' he'd said crossly, just as if, the night before, the very foundations of the house hadn't vibrated as he'd turned up the volume on his stereo to its brain-numbing limit.

Eventually the girl took off – for school, one could but hope, and Pauline picked up her duster, but by mid-morning she had given way to tears: it wasn't just Kerry and her misdemeanours, it was everything: life on the estate, attempting to make ends meet, and Terry, out of work, getting drunk, sitting around until he was in danger of getting segs on his arse – most of all Terry. In an attempt at cheer, Clare talked of her forthcoming holiday. She had equipped herself with every travel book available: the *Blue Guide*, the *Rough Guide*, *Venice for Pleasure*, was already something of an expert on vaporetto stops and Titian ceilings.

And gradually Pauline had bucked up. Though not at the idea of Venice, about which she knew little and cared less; Pauline dreamed of winning the Pools and taking them all to Florida. As she talked of it her face shone. Florida was Pauline's Eldorado: Disney World and steaks a yard across and a hundred flavours of ice cream. Sometimes, when she was waiting for Terry to stumble in from the pub, she'd try to get off to sleep by imagining herself there with Tommy Shaughnessy: sitting in an air-conditioned cocktail bar, sipping a Tequila Sunrise, lying on the beach next to him beneath an unalterably blue sky, climbing into a four-poster bed beside him, waiting for the first electric touch of his hand.

'I'm going to get one of them brochures,' she told Clare, 'on the way back.' She was quite cheerful again. 'We can all dream,' she said.

Sometimes, very occasionally, dreams translated themselves into reality. Clare took advantage of Lizzie's free afternoon and prevailed upon her to act as fashion consultant while she trawled the shops for Venetian-holiday clothes. 'Pity you can't wait and buy them when you get there,' Lizzie said, as Clare darted in and out of cubicles and paraded herself for the elicitation of one of several responses: 'Possibly,' or 'God no, you're not sixty-five yet,' or 'God no, you're not sixteen.'

She surveyed herself dubiously in a lavender silk number which – if she could persuade herself that it made her look gorgeous –

might conceivably justify its expense. 'Chance,' she said, 'would be a fine thing. I'm spending what I shouldn't as it is.'

Lizzie, currently deprived of both sex and drink, had bought herself a box of chocolates and sat chomping through them as Clare posed and twirled before her. They were very expensive chocolates with a guide inside the box that described them in mouth-watering detail. 'Enrobed in the finest Belgian chocolate,' Lizzie said, rolling the words – and the chocolate – about her tongue. 'Enrobed! Is that not the most delightful word? Perhaps,' she said, 'he'll buy you something in Venice.'

'I'm not a tart.'

Suddenly the lavender dress made her look exactly that. She unbuttoned it hurriedly.

'And must you scoff those one after the other?'

'It's comfort-eating,' Lizzie said imperturbably. 'Really, to do the thing in style, you ought to be travelling there on the Orient Express.'

That, so far, was the only fly in the ointment. Not only were they not travelling on the Orient Express, they were not even travelling together. 'I'm sorry,' he'd said, when this fact came to light, 'I thought you'd have realized . . .'

A colleague was to accompany him. The plan was that she would follow him out the next day. He would meet her, of course, at the airport. 'It isn't a problem, is it?' he said.

'No, of course not.'

It was bravely said but she'd always been a nervous traveller, convinced that, left to her own devices, she'd board the wrong plane and end up stranded in some featureless no-man's-land on the way to nowhere. And she found herself immediately beginning to assemble a list of things that could conceivably go wrong. Stop it, she told herself sternly. She didn't need Lizzie or Gwyn or work to spoil things for her; she was supremely well qualified to do that for herself.

Chapter Thirteen

August 12th, 1934.

I met Miss Marriott this morning. I'd set out for the wholesaler's to stock up on sewing thread but found I couldn't cross the road because the police had stopped the traffic to let the Hunger Marchers from Tyneside through. Miss Marriott too was trapped on the same side of the pavement. She hailed me and we stood together while they passed: gaunt men in patched clothing with poverty seamed into their faces, they marched in step as perhaps they and others like them must have marched towards the trenches. Others like my pa. I think of him more and more these days. I found his death certificate a while back when I was looking for the rent book. Alfred Carruthers, it said. Born 3rd September, 1894. Cause of death: Pyrexia of unknown origin.

'They think the government doesn't know of their plight,' Miss Marriott was saying as we watched the procession. 'They think they have only to get down to London and everything'll be hunky-dory.'

Local organizations have prepared canteens for them and places for them to sleep. I'd have expected Miss Marriott to be involved; it was her sort of thing. But she just sounded scornful. Apparently she has other concerns: she told me she was arranging accommodation throughout the town for some Jewish refugees. She'd formed a committee to try to raise funds. I think Miss Marriott likes to be in the vanguard of social work and charitable actions. Once other people get in on the act she seems to lose interest.

'Why don't you come along, Maisie?' she said. 'We could use another pair of hands: addressing envelopes and suchlike.'

I half-nodded, but I knew I shouldn't go even when she was giving me the address. For one thing, I'm not as keen on Miss Marriott, with her rapidly changing causes, as I once was; for another, Mother would make such a song and dance about it and whereas once I might have felt justified in defying her, now I've begun to be worried. She acts so oddly sometimes . . .

And besides there are a couple of Jewish girls here already, just down the road from us.

Eva and Lieselotte – 'Lottie' – girls of her own age, the first thin and sallow and earnest, the other plump and inclined to frivolity. After they'd passed each other on the street a few times, they nodded to her and eventually the chubby one, Lottie, had smiled and said, 'Good morgen,' and the other one had nudged her and hissed, 'Morn*ing, ing*.' After that they always said, 'Good morning,' in unison.

And then she saw them in the library, whispering together and looking rather bewildered as they surveyed the somewhat forbidding stacks. They wore funny dark old-fashioned clothes and spoke German. Miss Mills, the librarian, kept looking at them sideways and suspiciously.

They were delighted to see a familiar and friendly face. 'We are trying to improve our English,' Eva said. 'At school we learned a little, but not all – useful.' She frowned with the effort of concentration. Lottie said nothing, simply stood by, smiling; it was Lottie's solution to all awkward situations, the disarming smile. Eva said that Mrs Fischbein, their landlady, was very kind but always wished to speak Yiddish, whereas they needed to become conversant with the tongue of their new country so that when *Vati* and *Mutti* (Lottie's father and mother, that was, her cousin Eva being an orphan) and the brothers arrived they would be able to interpret for them.

'It is difficult,' Eva sighed, 'when you have no teacher and you do not know which are the correct references.'

Maisie had juggled her library books, *The Mayor of Caster-*

143

bridge, *Babs the Impossible*, *Romany Rye*, and thought, with an unaccustomed rush of confidence: perhaps *I* could be their teacher. 'You were always a good scholar, Maisie,' Miss Marriott had said. She had been, she was, and, while she sat tacking together the component parts of bodices or outlining patterns in French chalk, she felt that it was all going to waste.

So she equipped herself with a basic grammar and chose from the shelves books that she thought they might find entertaining as well as instructive, and on Wednesday evening, which was the occasion for her weekly visit to the public baths, she presented herself at Mrs Fischbein's front door.

'*Where* did you say you were going?' Mother had asked. She was sorting pearl buttons into her own idiosyncratic system of classification. She'd asked that question once already.

'I told you,' Maisie said. 'The baths. It's Wednesday.'

Mother made do with strip-washes at the sink but Maisie enjoyed an indulgent soak at the Carpenter Street Baths where, for your threepence, you were provided with a scratchy towel and a bar of hard greyish soap. She always took her own – Pears, a private luxury – and a bottle of henna shampoo which, she believed, brought out the copper-coloured highlights in her otherwise unremarkably mousy hair.

She did go to the baths on that particular evening and all the subsequent Wednesday evenings, but whereas she normally lolled in the tub until the water had cooled and the bubbles evaporated, now she performed her ablutions with dispatch in order that there would be time to spare for the lessons.

She had never met persons so entirely lacking in guile. With Eva and Lottie – to use the modern idiom – what you saw was what you got. They would be waiting eagerly at the front door, ready to greet her with great ceremony: to take her coat and usher her towards the chair nearest to the fire in the front parlour. They would enquire as to her health, her comfort, her disposition. Only when they had satisfied themselves that all was as it should be would they seat themselves beside her and begin, hesitantly, to conjugate those peculiar English verbs, stumbling over the tenses: 'I eat, you eat, they have eated ... *nein? Ach!* Once more! I understand, you understand, he, she or it *understanden ...*' Or else they would read from the books with which Maisie supplied them: at first, Fan and Dan and Nurse and their dog Spot at the seaside, but gradually, as Eva became more fluent (Lottie, with her shorter attention span, would never make a prize-winning student), she introduced them to her own familiar, much-loved works of literature: '*Alice was beginning to get very tired of sitting by her sister on the bank,*' and '*I lingered round them, under that benign sky: watched the moths fluttering among the heath and hare-bells, listened to the soft wind breathing through the grass, and wondered how any one could ever imagine unquiet slumbers for the sleepers in that quiet earth,*' and '*... he spread his hands across his chest and jerked his head up as he promised himself: "To die will be an awfully big adventure!"*' They'd raise their faces from time to time, in anticipation of correction. Lottie would giggle; Eva would hush her with a stern glance. At the end of these sessions they would ply Maisie with delicacies of a sort that she hadn't tasted since Mrs Mendelssohn died: cakes rich with honey and raisins, pastries scattered with toasted almonds, tiny cups of sweet, dark, aromatic coffee. And they would jump up and throw their arms around her and kiss her so thoroughly that her cheeks would be glowing all the way home.

And when she got in, Mother would say, 'Wherever have you been? I've been half out of my mind with worry,' and all the good feelings that the evening had produced would drain away.

One day she found them in tears, jabbering away in German to each other. She tried to discover what it was that had upset them so much but in their distress they had reverted to being monolingual. It was left to Mrs Fischbein to provide enlightenment. She accompanied her explanation by spitting on the floor, dangerously close to Maisie's feet. 'Scum!' she said '*Scheisse!*' Apparently they'd run into a couple of Mosley's Blackshirts who were swaggering down the street. Jibes had been uttered, insults hurled.

'It's only Billy Wilmot and Arnold Griggs,' Maisie had said. They'd been in her class at school: stupid boys, uninterested in or incapable of learning. They'd have been unemployable in the most buoyant of economies. She'd seen them and those like them strutting along the road, chanting in time to their marching feet: 'The Yids, the Yids, we've got to get rid of the Yids . . .' They might even have been the very same taunting boys whom Nancy used to take on and trounce, single-handed. If these were of a similar calibre to Herr Hitler's followers who, so Miss Marriott warned, were not to be trusted in terms of their potential for another bout of territorial aggression, then, Maisie thought, there wasn't much to get agitated about. Louts like Billy Wilmot and Arnold Griggs might be able to frighten girls but that, surely, was the sum total of their capacity for terrorization.

Once, she'd made the mistake of passing on Miss Marriott's views about Herr Hitler to Mother: about the way he'd capitalized on the paranoia of the German people, which arose from their country's economic ills, about the political mess at the end of the war which looked as though it might have sown the seeds for another one. Mother had reacted violently: throwing the pinking shears, with which she'd been cutting a pattern from a length of blue silk-shantung, against the opposite wall, and shouting that there must never again be another filthy war. The scissors had taken a chunk out of the plaster; their landlady of the time, who was not anyway endowed with much of the milk of human kindness, had certainly played war.

'Where are you going?' Mother would say. And, 'You're not off *again*?'

But somehow Maisie made the time and found the opportunity to continue her tutoring, stayed out longer and longer, trusting that Mother would have abandoned her vigil and fallen asleep, becoming aware that, as the weeks went by, a relationship above and beyond mere teacher and pupil was developing. 'You are our friend, Maisie,' they said. 'You are our first English friend.' And they'd kiss her cheek and clasp her hand and slip an arm around her waist. She'd been deprived of close, affectionate physical contact since she'd left the farm, had often longed for the comfort of an embrace, a hug, a cuddle – Mother was an undemonstrative woman, seemed to hold back as though afraid that intimacy was in some way demeaning or dangerous. Maisie felt herself falling in love with them as an entity: Lottie-and-Eva: the one prone to sloth and inconsequentiality, the other gravely aware of her pioneering responsibilities.

But Eva was also capable of passion. She had brought her violin from Germany and sometimes, if entreated, would play for them. One piece in particular used to bring the tears to Maisie's eyes. Its name was the *Meditation* and it came from an opera called *Thaïs*. It was the same tune that she was to hear years later, wafting through the french windows the night that Clare and her gentleman friend had stood in the moonlit garden, barely touching yet closer than could be.

After these impromptu concerts, Lottie would produce her photographs, handling them lovingly, imprinting kisses upon the likenesses of her relations until their features became grubby and blurred. 'Look!' she would say, 'This is my *vater* – father. He makes the eye-glasses and the – what is it, Eva?' 'The instruments,' Eva said, as she wrapped her violin in a piece of silk before replacing it in its case. 'Uncle Solly, he made the binoculars for *der Kaiser*.' 'Little Willy,' Maisie said.

'*Comment?*' Eva said, her head on one side. Sometimes she'd inadvertently slip into French, her grasp of the language being superior to that of English.

'Little Willy,' Maisie said. 'It's what we used to call him.'

'Little *Willi*,' they choroused, 'little *Willi*,' seeming to find this soubriquet endlessly amusing.

'And look!' Lottie would say. 'Here is my *brüder*, Ernst. Next to him, Jacob and there, at the back, making the *verrückt* – the crazy face, my Rudi.'

Ernst the Talmudic scholar, Jacob who was training to be a lawyer – ah, Lottie said, her brothers had certainly got her share of the family brains. 'And Rudi?' Maisie had asked, studying the photograph. Ernst and Jacob resembled Eva: solemn, serious-minded; Rudi hailed from a different segment of the temperamental spectrum: a monkey face, brimming with glee, yet handsome, with the sort of dark good looks that had always appealed to her.

'Rudi *ist beklopft*,' Eva said. 'He was the most brilliant student of the year and Rudi wants to be . . . *ein Schauspieler* – what is it? – an actor upon the stage. He makes Uncle Solly grey hairs.'

But so handsome, so full of life and mirth.

'You them will meet,' Lottie said, 'when they *kommen* in England. There will be delight.'

Eva corrected her. 'They will be delighted. To meet our dear friend, Maisie. Because she will be their friend too. All the family.'

For months, while Eva and Lottie conjugated irregular verbs and strove to get their tongues around the many English words which looked as though they rhymed but were pronounced quite differently – 'Not "boff", Lottie, "bow".' 'But Maisie, "bough" is like "cough" and "cough" is not "cow"' – Maisie speculated on the prospect of this vicarious family life. She didn't doubt that their desire to welcome her into it was the genuine article and looked forward to the arrival of *Mutti*, *Vati* and the rest in the same way as, when she was a child, she'd looked forward to Christmas.

But Christmas morning had so often produced little more than the walnut and the tangerine – and those put there by Mrs Mendelssohn: the toys and games and frivolities once provided by her grandparents had given way to more sensible gifts: half a dozen woollen vests, a topcoat, a pair of fur gloves. And it was one Wednesday evening quite close to Christmas when Eva and Lottie met her at the door with the news that an uncle – hitherto believed lost – had turned up to claim them and offer them a home until their closer relations arrived.

'It is in Manchester, Maisie,' Eva said. 'Do you know of Manchester?'

And, oh, she knew of Manchester, all right, knew that although, geographically speaking, it was not so far away, in terms of their continuing friendship, it might just as well have been the Berlin from which they had fled.

There were farewell presents: handkerchiefs embroidered with her initial, a lavender sachet for her wardrobe, a beaded spectacle case. There were tears. 'We will write,' they promised. 'Always.' Maisie had nodded. It was what people said. It would not take so very long, she thought, before out of sight became out of mind.

But envelopes addressed in that strange spiky Germanic script continued to arrive quite regularly. 'We are making a home for our family,' Eva wrote. 'I am practising my music. Uncle thinks I may find a place at the Academy. Lottie keeps house. Her cooking, sometimes, is quite unusual ... We send our love to you, Maisie, and ask you to remember your friends, Eva and Lottie.'

And then the uncle died unexpectedly and, Lottie reported, with a spluttering nib and evident excitement: 'We are to go to a cousin in California. And Mother and Father and the boys are to join us there.'

They never did. Delays occurred: difficulty with money, with papers, with travel arrangements. Too-long delays. Auschwitz claimed them in the end: Mother and Father, Ernst and Jacob. Rudi, beautiful Rudi, with his irrepressible good spirits, managed, somehow, to escape transportation but died of fever, compounded by malnutrition, while hiding out in a sympathizer's attic.

The letter that told of these horrific events had been brief. The words did not exist that were adequate to express such pain, and no catharsis could be achieved by the mere setting down of the awful facts. Like other survivors, they closed the knowledge within themselves and lived with it, carried on living, with such a clever approximation to normality that it almost convinced. When Lottie came over to England in 1975 she looked like any other middle-aged Jewish matron; and her talk was of the Californian climate, of her large, healthy American grandchildren destined for the medical profession or the law, of bridge afternoons and gala evenings and visits to Israel, but there was something else too, something discernible only as an expression at the back of the eyes, behind her smile.

Although the envelopes had continued to arrive, supplemented during the war years by sumptuous food parcels, Maisie had wondered if their eventual meeting would prove to be anything more than a strained encounter between people who had never actually been more than acquaintances and whose lives had subsequently moved so far apart that they would now no longer have anything at all in common.

But despite the fact that Lottie was ultra rich, dripped furs and jewels and spoke with a ripe adopted accent, her embrace was as warm, her lavish kisses as affectionate.

They'd met in a suite at Lottie's hotel, which was plush almost to the point of suffocation and kept at a constantly tropical temperature. Her husband, a tall, quiet, courteous man, a corporation lawyer, Lottie said proudly, spent most of the time on the telephone. Europe could not be embarked upon, it seemed, without the maintenance of a continual connection with Los Angeles.

Lottie hadn't needed years of good living to turn her into a shape almost as wide as it was tall – her genetic destiny had been evident at seventeen; she perched her wobbling flesh on the very edge of the elegant sofa but still her feet, crammed into gleaming, hand-crafted glove leather, scarcely touched the floor. Maisie sat opposite and opened the presents that they had brought for her – beautifully packaged toiletries, a silk scarf, a writing-case of tooled leather – while Lottie repeated her invitation, the same invitation that had been issued and reissued by letter over the years. Maisie was to visit, all expenses paid, the house in the Hollywood Hills with its colonnades and its swimming pool, its multi-occupancy garage and manicured lawns, its smiling Puerto-Rican maids and its Japanese gardeners. Cousin Eva would come over from New York where she had established her music school, their sons would entertain her, take her on trips, their grand-children's Chevvies and Caddies would be entirely at her disposal.

And Maisie had spread her hands and contemplated her fingernails and said, as she'd said so often in her correspondence: 'But Mother...' She'd watched the clock's hands travelling around its dial. Mother could be left in those days, but not for very long.

'Mother!' Lottie had cried, sparks flashing from her little bejewelled hands as she gestured extravagantly. 'Bring Mother too!'

Maisie had turned both her hands over in her lap and inspected the broken lines of destiny that bisected their palms. She had always, deliberately, out of a sense of delicacy, understated the extent of Mother's queerness, the gravity of the situation.

But every letter since had continued to extend this offer of hospitality. The latest had arrived only a few days ago. What excuse did Maisie have now? Sometimes, after a few glasses of Irish Cream, the idea seemed feasible. If there *was* to be a holiday, it would certainly put Morecambe in the shade.

And then she'd wake up the next morning and realize that it was too late, that she no longer possessed either the motivation or the nerve for such an enterprise.

Chapter Fourteen

Venice. Venezia. The Queen of the Adriatic. The Bride of the
Sea. La Serenissima. 'You'll be gobsmacked,' Lizzie had said.
Apparently, Venice had featured as part of her honeymoon – the
better part, she'd hinted darkly.

Gobsmacked would hardly have been the word of Clare's
choice; enchanted would have been nearer the mark; enraptured,
even.

Always inclined to be suspicious of places with glamorous
reputations, she'd been prepared to be distinctly underwhelmed,
but from the moment when the water-taxi, having sped across
the dazzling waters of the lagoon, turned towards the mouth of
the Grand Canal, she was utterly beguiled. The originals of all
those pictures, so familiar as to have become banal, were more
ravishing than any depiction could ever hope to be: the domes
and spires and cupolas of *palazzi* and churches glittered beneath
a cobalt sky; geraniums tumbled from wrought-iron balconies,
trailed across fretted balustrades and intricately carved façades
which were painted in gorgeous hues; reflections were everywhere: shimmering gold and rose and bronze and jade upon the
sparkling water. She stood upright in the boat, avid for a glimpse
of every detail of this unfolding splendour. 'Is that the Rialto?'
she asked, pointing, like an excited child. 'Is that the Accademia?
Where is the Bridge of Sighs?'

He laughed at her, at this uncharacteristic demonstration of
spontaneous enthusiasm; he knew her, thus far, only as a wary

soul. 'Go easy,' he said. 'Take your time.' But time, she knew, was at a premium. And she knew also that she must savour each moment as it occurred rather than succumbing to her normal dismal mode of functioning, which was to store things up, together with her reaction to them, for future reference, as though they only became properly real in retrospect.

They cruised past the grand hotels. 'Ruskin stayed there,' she said, espying the Gritti Palace, 'when it was a private residence. He went by gondola to the theatre. Imagine! And, look, that little red *palazzo* over there belonged to d'Annunzio; it has the only private garden on the canal.'

'Ever thought of getting a job here as a guide?' he said. 'Given that you're so clued up and you seem to be pretty disenchanted with the one you've got.'

'Me?' she said. 'It takes me all my time to differentiate between my left hand and my right.'

She was to remember that comment later with a certain ironical amusement.

Officially, he had a room at the Danieli. Otherwise they were booked in at a small hotel at the bottom of a winding alleyway off the Campo San Bartolomeo. As they made their way towards it, he explained that their time together, for obvious reasons, would be limited; he had receptions to attend, escort duties to perform, clients to be trundled through exhibitions and shepherded to the opera but, with luck, his colleague, Duncan Fry, would cover for him some of the time.

The notion of this duality made her feel distinctly uncomfortable, but she tried to put that thought out of her mind, to concentrate upon the seductiveness of her surroundings; it wasn't possible to conduct an extra-marital affair without putting a thousand and one such thoughts out of one's mind.

They were welcomed exuberantly by the hotel manager. He and Theo conversed in Italian, mirroring each other's extravagant gestures. 'Does he know you?' she asked worriedly as they were climbing the stairs.

'Never met him before. I think he just happens to be one of those fortunate individuals who find themselves in the occupation most exactly suited to their talents.'

Lucky him, she thought, wishing she could have said the same about herself, though she wasn't exactly sure where her talents lay.

'There's no canal view,' Theo said, opening shutters on to a secluded square where pigeons pecked around a mossy fountain (here the word 'shabby' could only be complimentary), 'but the room's fine, isn't it?'

'It's delightful,' she said.

And it was, with its painted furniture and its fairground chandelier made from the coloured glass of Murano. But then any room in which they could be assured of privacy would have been delightful by definition. He closed the shutters again and took her bag out of her hand and pulled her to him. By and large, their love-making since Gwyn's return had been snatched, infrequent and nerve-racked. She was starved of him, although she realized, with a pang, that she was undoubtedly the only one of them to be suffering from sexual deprivation.

He had only to touch her for her juices to flow. He had only to kiss her eyelids, her earlobe, stroke her flank, and her body became entirely deliquescent. It was as though she was making love for the first time; all other such encounters faded into insignificance. And, looking at his rapt face, she couldn't believe that it was anything but the same for him, that he was as far from being the clichéd philandering male as it was possible to be, that he had experienced exactly the same coup de foudre as herself. It was what he professed had happened: 'That night, the presentation: I just somehow couldn't cope with the idea that you'd leave and I'd never see you again or know your name or why you looked so worried.'

'I always look worried,' she'd replied. 'All my life people have told me to cheer up, it may never happen.'

He said, 'I love you,' and so did she. Probably they were both

154

the sort that had to make this declaration to each other in order to justify their behaviour. Though what she felt for him seemed to her to be completely beyond lust. The swoon as she climaxed repeatedly and her unconditional delight in his body – its small imperfections, the appendix scar, the mole, the knob of badly knitted bone where he'd once broken a rib, as much as its pleasing contours – could only have come about as part of a wider context: a meeting of minds, a congruence of sensibilities, a belief that, in terms of everything that mattered, their views were (given the unavoidable dishonesty involved in their relationship) intrinsically in accord.

Afterwards there was the delight of showering together, of soaping and sluicing away – if only temporarily – the lather produced by their amorous exertions, of watching him dress: a disguise adopted for the strangers out there, for here, at least, only she knew the bone-naked truth of him, the vulnerability in his face at the moment of release, the thud of his heartbeat, the scald of his semen. They exchanged one last kiss, one last but one kiss, one last but one but one – 'I must *go*,' he cried, as if in pain, disengaging himself from her. They were to rendezvous later at Florian's. 'Just follow the signs,' he said. She had a map, but he said that no one yet had succeeded in producing an accurate map of Venice, said that even Marco Polo, whose house this hotel allegedly abutted, would probably have given up on that one.

She dressed unhurriedly and opened the shutters, noticing for the first time that opposite, cheek by jowl with the sequestered square, there was a shop-window and in this shop-window were displayed a number of curious items. It wasn't until she left the hotel and turned the corner and came face to face with the display that she saw what they were: joke figures, crude models of animals and human genitalia: a pig rode on the back of a giant penis, the grotesquely rendered lips of a vulva disgorged a mouse that played a drum.

Harmless enough, she supposed; amusing, even, in a crass sort

155

of way. But the sensation they evoked was akin to biting into an apple and finding a worm at its core.

She wandered cautiously, sticking to the main thoroughfares. There would be time enough to explore when accompanied. She lacked the gene for direction. Once, on a rare and memorable day's outing to the coast, she'd misread the map and they'd found themselves on some minor road that seemed to be leading, if not nowhere, then certainly inland. 'No,' he'd said, 'it isn't. The sea's this way. Trust me.'

She'd wondered then, at that early stage, whether she dared. Not that it made any difference, because by then it was too late: she was already in thrall.

Lizzie had been right about the shops. Their windows displayed goods of such chic desirability that she was motivated to translate *lire* back into sterling, and then blenched when she arrived at the approximate result. But she wasn't greedy for baubles – love took away that appetite too.

Pausing on a bridge, she wondered briefly if Gwyn was behaving himself, but it was only briefly: a young gondolier, too handsome, surely, not to be an actor dressed up for the part, tried to entice her towards his boat. '*Prego, signorina.*' It was just the Italian equivalent of blarney, of course, but so what? And anyway perhaps love, as well as diminishing all other, secondary appetites, had been the agent of her rejuvenation, had wiped the lines that betrayed her age from her face.

She turned a corner and suddenly she was in the Piazza. And she was stunned by its fidelity to all the pictures in all the picture-books. She stared around her: at the gorgeously gilded basilica, the wedding-cake decoration of the Doge's Palace, the towering campanile, the pigeons lined up like sentries along the upper colonnades of the Procuratie Vecchie. The strains of waltzes and mazurkas and Argentinian tangos issued from the cafés where competing orchestras vied for the applause of the drifting crowds. As she hesitated, a waiter ushered her to a table. Discovering too late that this was not Florian's but one of its across-the-square

156

rivals, she submitted and ordered a cappuccino and watched the passing parade to the background of a vigorous rendition of *Roses from the South*. Tourists bought corn from the vendors in order to entice the pigeons to perch on their shoulders or their out-stretched hands while their companions photographed them. Exorbitantly priced jewellery and iridescent glass glinted behind the plate-glass windows in the arcades. The violinist in the white dinner-jacket launched, with much vibrato, into *Black Eyes*. In other circumstances, anywhere else, she would have considered all this completely over the top. But here the notion of kitsch was somehow transcended, was as irrelevant as it might be in the context of a dream. There was something intensely dreamlike, unreal, about the place itself, as though it had no more substance than a stage set which, at the end of the performance, would be struck and folded neatly away, leaving only the empty lagoon, weed-clogged, mist-shrouded, with its barely submerged mudflats and its sinister Canale Orfano within whose depths were said to moan the unquiet ghosts of the drowned.

She caught sight of a telephone box in one of the arcades and wavered. 'I'll ring when I get there,' she'd told Gwyn. 'Per-lease!' he'd said.

Perhaps tomorrow.

She was watching an elderly American couple, perfectly matched in terms of their smallness and stoutness, very gravely – and with surprising elegance – performing the steps of a tango in the middle of the square. He held her as though she was as fragile as glass. They were probably seventy-five and it was obvi-ous that they still loved each other. The crowd parted admiringly to allow them through. She felt a pang of whatever was the opposite of nostalgia – would someone be holding her with such tenderness when she was seventy-five? Theo startled her, appear-ing suddenly at her elbow. 'What is this,' he said, 'separate tables? I've a drink waiting for you over there.'

He bent and embraced her, kissing her full on the lips. This time it was she who expressed caution, looking around her nervously as though the square seethed with spies. 'What about your clients?' she said.

'Safely ensconced in the Campo San Stefano, listening to Vivaldi.'

'Is that the one with the church with the crooked campanile?'

'You *have* done your homework.'

'I've been mugging Venice up ever since I knew I was coming,' she said, as they strolled across to Florian's, 'so that when I remember this, I'll be able to put it all into context.'

And she realized that, despite herself, she was busy consigning the present to a time to be cherished in the future rather than enjoying it now, for its own sake.

He lit a cigarette. He rarely smoked: perhaps half a dozen in the course of a month. She was intrigued by the singularity of an appetite that could consume with such obvious relish and yet, at the same time, be capable of monkish restraint. She'd given up smoking years ago, but knew that if she were to succumb to temptation, she'd be back on thirty a day in no time. Cautious she might be but, once committed, it tended to be a case of all or nothing at all.

'You're doing it again,' he said, watching her narrowly through an exhalation of smoke.

'Doing what?'

'Ruminating.'

'Isn't that what cows do?'

She shied away from the other, technical meaning of the word: pursuing a process of thought that chases itself around like a rat on a wheel, leading neither to development nor resolution.

'Anyway,' he said, 'what do you think of it?' indicating the Piazza and everything that lay beyond. 'Isn't it just the most marvellous place? Every time I come here I feel as though I've been given a new lease of life. Can you imagine what it must be like to *live* here? To wake up every morning and open your eyes on some incredible vista? Oh,' he said, 'if ever I'm rich beyond the dreams of avarice . . .'

His enthusiasm was almost palpable. His face had become unguarded, boyish even. She smiled and touched his cheek, not reverentially as was perhaps her usual mode of caress, but lightly, teasingly and said, 'You don't have to sell it to me. You're preaching to the converted. What I've seen of it so far, anyway.'

He caught her hand in mid-air, clasped it. 'When there's a place that you really love,' he said, 'you want to show it off to the person that you really love.'

It was the first time he'd uttered such a sentiment outside the environs of the bedroom and the words were balm to her soul. The 'I love yous' exchanged at moments of passion were as nothing compared with the conviction of a statement made in the cold light of dawn.

The warm light of evening, at any rate. They finished their drinks and strolled to a restaurant that he knew of near the theatre. The maître d' greeted him warmly, ushered them to one of his best tables. Perhaps, as Lizzie said, it was all courtesy of the expense account, but she could hardly condemn him for utilizing the perks of his job.

The lighting was discreet. She could make out only odd details from the frescoed walls: a Botticelli nymph being pursued by a satyr, draperies billowing out behind her, a shepherd asleep on a Tuscan hillside, the scales of justice dangling from a skeleton hand. The service was also discreet, as though they were used to those couples who required no more than an adequate amount of attention. Waiters hovered only briefly, leaving them in peace to feed each other with small delicacies: a peeled prawn, a morsel of *polenta*, a mouthful of *tiramisu*, to drink the pale golden wine of the region, simulating an appetite for food and drink when their only real appetite was for each other, to exchange perilous kisses above the candle's flame, to hold hands and relinquish their grasp simply for the delight of the anticipation of touching again.

Afterwards they walked through shadowed alleyways and across brightly moonlit squares, almost deserted now; at sunset the tourist hordes departed for the resorts in which they were based. They paused to lean over bridges and glimpse the reflection of their embrace in the water. A stanza of *Santa Lucia* came wafting faintly towards them as a boat drifted around a distant bend of the canal.

He said, 'We could pick up a gondola, if you like.'

'Really?'

'Why not?'

'I thought it was generally regarded with disdain. Lizzie says—'

'Who is Lizzie?' he interrupted her to ask, though she'd often mentioned Lizzie. One expected, somehow, that the beloved would savour every word that fell from the lover's lips.

Lizzie, she wanted to say, is my friend and erstwhile mentor. But now it's a bit like the blind leading the blind.

'She says that only the Japanese and blue-rinsed Yanks would be seen dead in a gondola.'

'Poor Lizzie,' he said, 'she must deprive herself of an awful lot of simple pleasure if she works on that principle.'

Their gondolier was silent and as discreet as the waiters had been. Perhaps they were like taxi-drivers. He didn't so much as glance round at them when Theo, hugging her close, said, 'Shall I sing? Well I can't sing, but I can warble,' and did a very bad impression of Pavarotti belting out *O Sole Mio*. 'Will that do?' he asked. 'It'll do,' she replied. 'It's more than adequate. You're quite different here, aren't you?' she said. She was certain that, at home, he would consider such loss of dignity as anathema.

'Well,' he said, 'it's the holiday me, isn't it?'

She tried not to dwell upon the notion that the holiday him must also exist – and more frequently – in the company of others.

Sailing slowly, Theo's arm around her shoulders, she watched as the glories of the Republic hove into view: the gorgeous palaces, the decorous Palladian outline of the Redentore and the sudden dazzle of white stone off water as they came upon the baroque magnificence of the Salute. 'Must give you a kiss,' he said at this

160

point. 'I should think it's obligatory in a gondola,' and duly obliged. She remembered Lizzie talking about dirty weekends in commercial hotels. Although, in the face of all this evidence to the contrary, Lizzie would probably only say something like: 'Don't forget, it can change from *O Sole Mio* to *Just One Cornetto* in mid-chorus.'

'How do you know when it's love?' they had asked each other so often and so earnestly when they were young. And Lizzie, wise perhaps beyond her years, had said, 'If you can't fart in front of each other without dying of embarrassment then it's all only make-believe.' Clare remembered arguing hotly that as a definition this left something to be desired.

She was reminded of Lizzie's remark later that night. Love (whatever its definition) had made her thirsty. She left his sleeping side and opened the minibar, searching for mineral water but, apart from beer and wine, there was only something called *Analcolico*. She sniffed at it dubiously, wondering if it was something along the lines of the Collis Browne's Mixture with which her mother used to dose her as a child when she had the runs. He woke as she was debating whether she ought to risk its contents and raised an eyebrow. '*Analcolico*,' she said. 'What can it mean? It smells like orangeade.'

She lifted the bottle so that he could read the label. He began to laugh, and laughed uproariously until he was weeping with mirth, burying his face in the pillow in an attempt to regain his composure.

'What's so funny?'

He moaned and wiped his eyes. '*An-alcolico*,' he said, placing the stress on the first syllable, where it belonged. 'Non-alcoholic. It *is* orangeade. What did you think it was, a remedy for flatulence or something?'

'I'm slow on the uptake,' she said. Her failure, during all those months, to recognize that Huw was betraying her had proved that.

'Those are the best sort of women,' he said. 'Those are the

women I like,' and ducked, shielding himself with his pillow, as she made as if to throw the bottle at his head.

She knew nothing about the women he liked, or whether or not she was representative of them. Other men she'd known had talked of their previous lovers (sometimes in unnecessarily precise detail). Not he. Perhaps he considered it bad form. Whenever she attempted to question him, he'd turn the conversation towards some less controversial topic with the suavity of a publican steering the discourse of his clientèle away from politics or religion.

Physically, they couldn't have been closer but she sometimes felt that the current of his real feelings, his true motives, ran as deep, and was as unfathomable to her, as the Orphan's Canal.

Perhaps Duncan Fry might be the man to enlighten her. Slow on the uptake she might be, but she realized that the instant she set eyes on him the following day.

At her request, that morning they had visited San Michele, the cemetery island. 'Diaghilev is buried there,' she'd explained, 'and Stravinsky and poor Ezra Pound.'

'Well it's not my idea of a fun time,' he'd said, looking at her quizzically. 'But, whatever lights your candle. I am here solely to indulge your whims.'

All the islands fascinated her: this one the repository for plague victims, that one for lepers, others to whose shores had been banished the tubercular, the criminal, the insane.

They'd disembarked from the vaporetto and walked between the cypresses on the island of the dead, looking for famous graves. It was a lovely place, peaceful and deserted at this time of day. But even here, she discovered, *particularly* here, the worm lay in wait: for unless you could afford to lease a plot, your bones would be dug up after ten years or so and consigned to a communal ossuary. She thought that perhaps Venice, achingly beautiful Venice, was a hard mistress, rendering as it did all the normal activities of daily life indescribably complicated: earlier they had watched a piano being winched, with extreme difficulty, into a high window, a bride almost losing her footing as she stepped from a gondola on the way to be married at the Municipio, the flotilla of black craft that was a funeral cortège sailing across the lagoon. Venice was, perhaps, like an affair: an unalloyed delight if you were happy to be just passing through, damned difficult if you wanted to make it a permanent arrangement.

(You started off believing that you'd be content with so little; you ended up wanting everything there was.)

They had re-embarked for Murano and wandered in and out of the glass shops. Some of the merchandise was hideously garish, some – more expensive – infinitely covetable. She threw caution (and the last of her funds) to the winds and bought him a figurine: a tiny, stylized depiction of the winged lion of St Mark. 'You can put it on your desk,' she said, forestalling any painful query along the lines of: 'How am I to explain this away?'

She'd felt that she needed to give him something because, earlier in the day, he had indulged another of her whims, that time more expensively.

As they were walking along the Frezzeria in search of an amazing cake shop that he recalled from a previous visit, her eye had been caught by a window displaying unusual and distinctive jewellery. 'How lovely,' she had said, indicating a pair of translucent green and gold earrings. 'Much nicer than all that sparkly stuff in the Piazza,' and prepared to pass on.

They never did find the *pasticceria*. He'd pulled her inside the shop and, having requested that the assistant bring the earrings out of the window, held them up against her face, gravely calculating the effect. As she admired them, he translated for her the conversation he'd had with the shopkeeper: 'They're Roman beads, he says. Fourth century. They are beautiful, aren't they? Let me buy them for you.'

'Oh no,' she said automatically, remembering Lizzie's cynical remark.

'As a souvenir?'

She shook her head.

'Why not? Unless of course you'd prefer a plastic gondola?'

Well, they were only beads, after all. And perhaps they weren't all that expensive.

But then she saw the huge amount of *lire* on the bill and it was obvious that he was about to part with a considerable sum of money. She tried to stay his hand, was ashamed at the half-heartedness of her gesture, at the feebleness of her integrity.

She'd substituted the earrings for those she'd been wearing originally, and had preened herself in every reflective surface that she passed during the rest of the morning, was preening still when, as they stepped off the boat on their return from Murano, a voice greeted them. 'Well, hello there,' said this voice as its owner pushed through the throng in order to waylay them. 'Fancy meeting you.'

He surveyed her, every inch of her, while Theo performed the introductions. He was smiling broadly all the while but for some reason she no longer felt like an attractive woman wearing beautiful earrings; the effect of his fierce scrutiny was to make her conscious of her every physical imperfection: the hard skin on her heels, the trace of cellulite on her thigh, the birthmark on her shoulder.

'This is Duncan Fry,' Theo said, 'my aide-de-camp and trusted right hand.'

Smiling still, Duncan Fry said, 'Who're you calling Ada?' And then, without taking his eyes off her, he said, 'And whither art thou bound, Theo old chap?'

'I'm taking Clare to Harry's Bar for a Bellini,' Theo said. 'She can't leave Venice without having a Bellini in Harry's Bar.'

'Why, Theo,' said Duncan Fry, 'you sweet old-fashioned thing!'

Steeling herself to raise her eyes to meet his, she saw that he was a stockily built man with dark curly hair and what used to be described in the women's mags as chiselled features, and a physique of that hirsute, bursting-with-testosterone sort: body hair poking out above his collar, from below his cuff, through the buttons of his shirt. His smile showed small sharp teeth of a dazzling regularity and whiteness. She was not normally a jumper-to-conclusions, but her immediate impression was that he had the face of an assassin.

Chapter Fifteen

January 16th, 1940.

Mr Maxwell was gassed at Passchendaele. Shell-shocked too, if you ask me. He shows us the pistol that he keeps in the bottom drawer of the bureau. It's a Luger, wrapped in a piece of black silk which reminds me of the silk which Eva Rosenfeldt used for protecting her violin. He took it from the body of a dead German officer in the last lot. If the Hun invades our shores then he intends to load this gun and shoot everybody: his wife Minnie, his two daughters and himself; even Spot, the dog. Better death than dishonour, he says. Better that quick finality than to be ground beneath the oppressor's heel. I don't know if we, as lodgers, are included in this intention; I didn't dare to ask.

He is quite deaf and sits with his ear pressed up against the wireless set, snorting out rejoinders to the announcements: 'You'll not stop Fritz that way,' he'll say. 'Take it from one who knows.' Sometimes he gets really aereated. 'This war is being run by a battalion of Whitehall pen-pushers,' he'll fume. And whenever there's a reference to the French, he bangs the top of the set so hard that the valves rattle. They always say that the men who saw the worst of the fighting during the Great War don't care to talk about it, but Mr Maxwell does, at length and with relish: terrible stories of how the Frogs were too damned idle to bury their dead properly so that when he and his fellow soldiers inherited their trenches they found heads and arms and feet sticking up all over the show.

I think of my poor pa, trudging, cold and wretched, through that

166

vile carnage and I think of how he must have longed for comfort and warmth.

I suppose, in the circumstances, these are the worst rooms that we could have ended up in, what with Mr Maxwell talking about nothing else but this war and the last one and Mother throwing a fit if anyone so much as mentions the subject. This morning he set about building a shelter in the back garden. All the time he was digging up Mrs Maxwell's herbaceous border and heaving bits of corrugated iron about he was whistling Mademoiselle from Armentières and Goodbye-ee. Mother was practically beside herself, made as if she was going to empty the overnight contents of the jerry on to his head. I stopped her just in the nick of time. We'd have been out on the street. But mostly it's as though she's switched off, as though she won't accept that anything has changed since Mr Chamberlain came back from Munich waving his bit of paper. This afternoon, for instance, we went to buy black-out material and coming back past the station we saw all these little children with labels pinned to their coats queuing up to board the train. Mother said, 'Where on earth are they going? And what are those boxes they've got round their necks?' I said, 'They're being evacuated to the country. I've told you before. And those are their gas masks.' She stared at me quite blankly as though I'd made it up. And I can't get her to carry her own gas mask, not for love nor money.

It's really strange nowadays: everybody waiting for something to happen; as though the whole country is holding its breath.

Maisie sorted through boxes of papers. If she was due to go into hospital then it might be prudent to locate the Co-op insurance book that contained a paid-up policy. In the event that she should come out feet first, the proceeds would at least bury her. While searching for it, she came across a couple of field postcards from the First World War that, unaccountably, had survived the slashing scourge of Mother's scissors. How pretty they were: intricately embroidered with pictures of dimple-cheeked girls bearing posies

167

of roses and lavender; no unbriefed recipient could ever have guessed from the look of them that they emanated from trenches flooded with excrement and blood, from crater-pocked tracts of land littered with the crazy jigsaw pieces of exploded soldiers, from shattered copses and shelled pill-boxes out of which men stumbled, frothing green at the mouth as the phosgene gas destroyed their lung tissue, to expire, agonizingly, of 'air-hunger'.

Each postcard bore the same printed formula in which the unwanted sentences were to be struck out: 'I am quite well,' 'I am coming home on leave,' 'I have been wounded.' Both were signed: 'With all my love, dearest, trying to keep merry and bright, your husband, Fred.'

She continued to rummage. Beneath the postcards, in the old tin box, were their ration books. 'Points,' they'd called them, to be handed across various counters in exchange for butter, sugar, eggs, and clothing. She remembered how it was then that Mother's trade had really picked up: a length of parachute silk, a bolt of cloth carried back from foreign parts by a seaman, some grandmother's wedding dress that could be unpicked and made over – sewing skills were at a premium. And although Mother acted most peculiarly on occasion, either forgetting or refusing to admit that there was a war on, for example, it was the war that brought about an upsurge in her fortunes.

Though, after a time, she worked alone: treadling away in the Maxwells' back parlour while, in the front, Mr Maxwell offered tetchy advice to what he called the powers that be on the proper conduct of warfare and Mrs Maxwell knitted balaclavas and the daughters, June and Patricia, drew lines on the back of their bare legs to simulate stocking-seams and rolled up their hair and practised jitterbugging and sneered at their father when he demanded to know why they were determined on getting a name for themselves.

'Tart' was the name he had in mind. The longer the war went on, the more the professional sort were being ousted by amateurs. Later on, it would be the Americans who were to blame; many a girl previously as white as snow had been known to succumb to a packet of Pall Mall and a flash of good dentistry.

Rita was the authority on women whose morals were looser than their knicker elastic. She was on the next machine at the factory where army uniforms were produced – other ranks only. She'd link Maisie on their way to the canteen and point out offending females: 'She goes with Yanks. And her. Ought to be ashamed.' But there was no real malicious motive involved in this identification; she was just as likely to condemn some other girl for her excessive primness. She'd say, 'Will you look at her! Miss Iron Drawers.' And she'd skip Maisie along, chanting in corresponding rhythm: 'Tight as a drum, Never been done, Never been inter*fered* with.'

Rita was a married woman of six months' standing. 'Ten days' standing, in actual fact,' she confided. Her husband had been posted on the eleventh. 'We didn't half make the most of those ten days, though,' she said. 'I could hardly walk afterwards, cocker. No kidding.'

She was coarse, Rita. And common too. She put peroxide on her hair and plastered on lipstick and pronounced aitch as haitch and said, 'Lend us your bug-rake a minute, kid,' and held her knife as though it were a pen. Mother would have been horrified. She thought the Maxwell girls were completely beyond the pale and they, at least, had office jobs and telephone voices to match.

But Mother didn't have a say. In that same factory where she had briefly operated a sewing-machine, now Maisie and her fellow-workers churned out battledress tops and forage caps. She'd tried to lay down the law but Maisie had said, announcing her intention to join its workforce, 'Well, it's either that and good money or else I'll get called up and sent heaven knows where. Take your pick.'

What she didn't tell Mother was that, like Pa all those years ago responding to Lord Kitchener's call, she too had volunteered her services for King and Country. She'd stood shivering in a curtained cubicle in the Drill Hall while the medical officer had subjected her to various tests: striking her knees and her elbows with a little rubber hammer, rapping at her chest with his knuckles and listening to its response, pulling down her lower eyelids and inspecting her fingernails.

She presumed that it was the eye-test that had let her down. 'What category were you, then?' Rita had asked. 'A1, D4, or Blind-as-a-bat?'

She could see all right, provided she wore her spectacles, with their progressively stronger lenses. She had wanted to join the WAAFs. Not only did she like the uniform, but she'd seen it as a way of escape, a chance at independence provided by the most indisputable of justifications.

And, instead, because of her previous experience, she'd been allocated to a sewing factory. 'Do you believe in fate?' she'd asked Rita.

'I believe in what I can see,' Rita said. 'Nowt else. I'll believe in this war when it happens.'

But when the raids started it was hard to recall that there had ever been that sunlit hiatus when sandbags were piled high in the parks and barbed wire stretched along the beaches and men patrolled the coastline with rifles empty of ammunition and the nation waited apprehensively and then became blasé.

'Why did I open my big mouth?' Rita said, and then she'd shout, 'Jerry, you bugger!' shaking her fist at the ceiling when the siren went just before clocking-off time. She lived over Spring Park way and she'd always try to get back there, but more often than not the wardens would order her into a shelter. It wasn't so bad if there was a handsome chap in there – made it worthwhile missing your tea. Only flirting though, she assured Maisie, said that she'd never ever do the dirty on her Geoff – principally because he'd kill her if he found out.

'Still,' she'd say, 'if you click and he's got a nice friend . . .'

Maisie had been out with a few fellows, a very few. She'd been to the pictures and the ice-skating rink, even once to that mecca of her youth, Dolly's Tea Rooms, with a young man who fancied himself and acted as though he was at home in the most sophisticated of surroundings and then let himself down, in her eyes, at any rate, by leaving the waitress an insultingly small tip.

None of these casual encounters had developed into anything more meaningful. For one thing, they had to be conducted on the sly; she wouldn't have dared to bring anyone within shouting distance of Mother for two reasons: Mother would have made her life a misery and the chap in question would, undoubtedly, have been so disconcerted by her peculiarities – suddenly stopping dead, as though hearing something that was completely inaudible to everyone else, the way she had of muttering to herself and denying it when challenged – that he'd have taken to his heels. Farewells had to take place at the corner of the street. Sometimes one of them would say, 'Why can't I walk you to your door?' And then she'd blurt out some excuse to do with her mother disapproving of her associating with boys. It had sounded extremely feeble, but she could hardly tell them the truth.

And then there was her terror of coming within miles of that place known as 'going too far'; unused to men and their ways, she was never sure how much contact could be permitted without them turning into wild animals and, invariably, she misjudged the moment when a hand ought to be pushed firmly away. 'You're a prude,' one of them had said when she'd recoiled as he'd tried to insinuate his tongue into her mouth. Better that, she'd thought, than to follow in the forlorn footsteps of Babs Poole.

And, besides, she'd never met anyone, since she was a silly mooning girl, who'd really made her feel as if she *wanted* to be courted seriously. It was as though she too, in common with England, during that phase they called the Phoney War, had been waiting . . .

But things were different now: she had a proper job, she had begun to go dancing with Rita on a Saturday night. They'd have a Welsh rarebit each (or what passed for it in those days) in the Odeon café and then they'd go to the Embassy ballroom where, though she'd never learned, properly, to dance, apart from Rita's tuition in the cloakroom during dinner breaks, sometimes a chap would trundle her round the floor. Though rarely the same one twice. 'Relax!' Rita would say. 'If you'd only relax, you'd soon get the hang of it. We'll have you championship standard yet.'

A proper job, Saturday night at the dance hall; one evening she succumbed to the cajolement of June Maxwell who was, most uncharacteristically, at a loose end, and agreed to a permanent wave. Mother might complain and sigh exaggeratedly and glare and dish out the silent treatment, but that was all she could do, and even that was just about bearable when you were out of the house for most of the day.

Sleepless nights became the norm, dragging yourself to work in the morning, yawning your head off all day. 'Direct hit last night,' Rita said, rubbing her eyes. 'That terrace on Corporation Street. Went down like a pack of cards. I was stuck in the North Road shelter with a ruddy kid wailing all night long.' She yawned and stretched. 'I ache in every limb,' she said. ' "It's agony, Ivy." '

Maisie preferred the public shelters, the alternative being the Maxwells', and when Mr Maxwell was not playing his mouth-organ and drenching you with spittle in the process, he'd insist on relating the goriest of war stories: how the officer of his platoon had had his head blown clean off his shoulders 'as close to me as you are'; how rats as big as very big dogs had bitten their extremities; how they'd used the odd moribund hand that they found sticking out of the wall of a trench as a convenient resting place for a mug of char or a plug of baccy.

It was in a public shelter that she met Bob. The one in Sebasto-pol Street. At eight minutes past nine on the evening of 14 April 1941. That night it had seemed as though there was every incendiary device known to man falling out of the sky, and no let-up at all in the bombardment. He had fallen over her: a tall young man with curly black hair springing up around his cap and legs of a length that required more space than a jam-packed shelter could reasonably provide. He'd apologized profusely, moving her foot gently back into the position from which he'd dislodged it.

172

And then he'd taken his cap off and flourished it and said, 'May I have this seat?' just as though he was asking her for the pleasure of the next waltz, but with more panache than the young men who invited her on to the Embassy dance floor.

She saw him directing covert glances at the book she was reading, *The Grapes of Wrath*. After a while, and a certain amount of throat-clearing, he said, 'It's good, that, isn't it? Have you read any others of his?'

Indeed she had. She'd read *Tortilla Flat* and *Of Mice and Men*; she only wished, as she scoured the library shelves, that Mr Steinbeck would hurry up and write some more.

They discussed *Tortilla Flat* and *Of Mice and Men*, and then they discussed Hemingway whom he liked a great deal more than she did, and Scott Fitzgerald, for whom the reverse was true. They discussed *The Good Companions* and *Tobacco Road* and *Cold Comfort Farm* and *Brave New World*. They discussed *The Stars Look Down* and *A Gun for Sale* and *Gone with the Wind*. He'd read as much and as widely – if not as indiscriminately – as she. It made a pleasant change to be engaged in intelligent conversation; normally, in the shelter, you talked of who was buying it tonight and who'd bought it last night and which shop had cigarettes under the counter.

The next morning, Rita, who'd been stuck under the stairs, averred that it had been the longest night of her life. Maisie agreed; the difference was that Rita had wanted it to end and she hadn't.

'I'm asleep on me feet,' Rita said, threading her machine with fumbling fingers. And when Maisie pointed out that she was, in fact, sitting down, said, 'On me bum then, clever clogs. Where were you all night? In the knife-box?'

She'd never been wider awake. The only part of her anatomy that felt remotely fatigued was her larynx: she'd talked so much. So much and so easily. It wasn't that the reserve between them had quickly evaporated, but that there had never been any reserve in the first place. There were people you knew all your life and the distance between you never grew less, and there were those whom you'd known scarcely any time at all and yet you *felt* as though you'd known them for ever.

He'd stretched out those long legs clad in their airforce blue and loosened his tie and looked across at her sideways and said, 'I don't often meet girls that are as well-read as you. Not in my way of life, at any rate. Usually it's just dances and film stars they want to talk about. Are you a college girl?' he said.

She'd wondered at first if he was teasing her: she was a bit long in the tooth to be mistaken for a college girl. Besides, college girls had a certain look to which she could never aspire. But he was perfectly serious, college being, ultimately, his own ambition: 'After this lot's over.'

(He was a rear-gunner. She looked at him, awed. Rear-gunners – Tail-end Charlies, they called them – were said to have shorter fighting lives than anyone.)

He'd had to leave school at fourteen, he told her, and had taken any job that came along, but he was determined to better himself. There'd been night-classes at the Mechanics' Institute, a correspondence course, and then, at the outbreak of war, he'd volunteered. The Services offered excellent opportunities for advancement – he had only narrowly failed the navigation course. He intended to keep trying. A commission might secure him a university place when he was demobbed. That was his dream.

He talked with such energy and enthusiasm that, by comparison, she felt uncomfortably aware of her own feeble-spiritedness. Especially considering that his circumstances had been so very much more adverse than her own. He'd told her that he was due leave and would be spending it at the home of a pal of his, as he had no family.

'Are they dead?' she'd asked sympathetically.

He'd bent down and pulled up his socks, each one, very precisely. 'I don't know,' he'd said. 'I couldn't say. I was a foundling.'

And then he'd looked directly at her and the look had said: And I'm not ashamed of it. Why should I be ashamed of some-

174

thing which was not of my making and over which I had absolutely no control?

'My name's Bob,' he'd said, extending his hand. 'Robert Worthington. They called me after Worthington Street where I was left in the porch of the cop-shop. And Robert after the sergeant who found me. Could have been worse,' he'd said, grinning. 'Could have been dumped in Foul Lane just round the corner.'

She remembered the curate's Rupert Brooke profile and the trombone-player's Ronald Colman moustache and the civil servant who'd had a look of Adolphe Menjou; she thought of the young men who'd tried to paw her in the cinema or pushed her across the dance floor, their sweaty hands on the small of her back. She knew now exactly why she'd been waiting and who she'd been waiting for; she knew in an instant: that it was for someone with a high forehead, dark hair, tightly curled, a mouth that curved upwards good-humouredly even when in repose, intelligent eyes, never still, a nose that could have served as a model of perfection for all other noses.

She looked at him and thought that he was beautiful beyond compare and, as such, probably completely out of her league. He was telling her about pals of his, all of whom had joined up at the same time and who, astonishingly, had returned intact from every one of their ops so far when, quite suddenly, his eyelids closed and he shifted so that his limbs were more comfortably disposed. His head, heavy on her arm, caused cramp, but she bore it stoically, even experienced something approaching pleasure, for the awful likelihood was that, after the all-clear, she would never see him again.

Joe's girl, Mickey, was also beautiful, with a cherubic face and a cascade of crinkly black hair – there was a touch of the tarbrush somewhere in there, Maisie thought. She'd sometimes wondered about Bob's parentage when she took into account his lustrous eyes, his mop of curly hair and the dark silky sheen on his skin that was observable sometimes when the light fell on it in a particular way. Perhaps his father had been a Spanish grandee or a Moroccan prince. 'And perhaps he was a Lascar seaman,' Bob had said.

Mickey tap-danced and juggled and sometimes ate fire. She performed these activities publicly in order to earn her living. She resided in a lorry, Joe said, together with other travelling players who also supplemented their dole by various means: busking, riding unicycles, drawing pictures on the pavement. He'd brought her home the minute his mother's back was turned. The day after she left, Maisie had rung Clare's doorbell and, receiving no response, had let herself in with the intention of checking, as promised, that everything was in order. She'd assumed that Joe was out but as she closed the door behind her she'd heard a scuffle at the top of the stairs and then the girl had appeared, half-clad, on the landing. 'Yeah?' she'd said challengingly. 'It's OK, Mick, it's only Maisie,' Joe had said, appearing behind her. He'd had the slightly askew appearance of one whose clothes had been hastily donned. He'd come thudding barefoot down the stairs. 'Hiya, Maisie,' he'd said. 'We both overslept, that's all. Everything's fine. Mick just crashed here last night when she missed her last bus.'

Maisie had turned and made for the door. 'Keep *stumm*, eh?' he'd said with awkward bravado. 'Ma will only think the worst and go apeshit.'

It wasn't her business. Her business was unlit gas-taps and unlocked doors.

The rest of Tuesday passed peacefully enough. And Wednesday too. She didn't attempt a return visit. If he was old enough to be courting, then he was presumably old enough to be relied upon to keep the house secure. On Wednesday afternoon she heard sounds from next-door's garden and, on looking out of her bedroom window, saw that the sudden arrival of hot weather had enticed them outdoors. The girl lay on her back on a towel on the terrace, naked except for a pair of briefs. Joe, in fluorescent

176

cycling shorts, took the hose and trained it upon her. 'Bastard!' she shouted and jumped to her feet and chased him across the recently turfed lawn down to where Clare had plans for her gazebo or belvedere or whatever it was that Joe referred to as the Taj Mahal. When she caught him she gripped his arm and bent it behind his back until be begged for mercy.

Eventually the cloud thickened and they went indoors. The tuneless thumping that passed for music started up again and once there was a crash and a shriek as though some item of furniture had collapsed, but at no time did she get the feeling that anything untoward might be about to happen, not even the next afternoon when, returning from the shops, she saw the two battered vans parked outside Clare's house.

They arrived in dribs and drabs: a succession of young men and women. With their flowing locks and patched garments, their scraggy lurchers and their musical instruments, they reminded her of that childhood rhyme: 'Hark, hark, the dogs do bark, the beggars are coming to town . . .' A very dirty girl, wearing a long, pleated chiffon dress that looked as though it might once have graced some Twenties' debutantes' ball, bore on her shoulder a little monkey in an embroidered waistcoat that was investigating itself avidly for fleas.

One by one and two by two they trudged towards the house. By mid-evening, Maisie judged that it must be bursting at the seams. And indeed people began to spill out into the garden. A tall fellow with a matted beard who was hung about with tinkling ornaments began to beat a drum; a girl whose flesh appeared to be pierced in the strangest of places blew a melancholy air from a flute. From the open windows blared the repetitive beat of what Joe had informed her was called acid-techno-rock, or was it house, or funk, or even jungle?

And then she caught sight of Joe himself, running out of the house and into the garden, confiscating bottles, picking up cigarette ends, imploring these possibly uninvited guests to be quiet, to beat it, fuming, yelling, cursing: 'Cool it, will you, for fuck's sake! If my mother finds out about this, I am in deep shit.'

How many people, Maisie wondered, constituted an acceptable number of friends? Though she knew perfectly well that this lot would far exceed Clare's definition.

Somebody lit a barbecue. Malodorous black smoke drifted across the fence. The drumming increased to a pitch of frenzy, drowning out the flute's wavering melody. What am I to do? she agonized.

The decision was taken out of her uncertain hands. Somebody called the police. There was always somebody to call the police. Arriving with a greater degree of alacrity than if they'd been tipped off about a bank job, they herded the alfresco revellers inside. One of them reached up into the poplar tree and lifted down a couple of those sort of lamps that were used to warn motorists of roadworks and which, presumably, had been placed there to provide illumination as the evening wore on.

All the various noises ceased abruptly and in the sudden quiet, individual voices were to be heard raised in protest, Joe's prominent among them. And then a van arrived, the sort that Maisie knew as a Black Maria, and into it were unceremoniously bundled a man who looked like Christ, a girl with a tambourine, three spiky-haired punks, a boy with a dove tattooed on the bald crown of his head and, protesting more vociferously than anyone, Joe. Others followed on foot, their dogs, sniffing and defecating, in their wake. The vans departed in a cloud of exhaust fumes.

She wondered if she should go in. Half a dozen times she went to the gate and turned back again. She had her hand on the latch when, to her relief, Clare's friend, Lizzie, her name was, drew up in her car.

She said, 'Hello?' not so much as a form of greeting as in the way of an apprehensive enquiry. Although there was nothing to see. The street was quiet again now, other neighbours, enticed outside by the drama, having lingered only long enough to tell one another how shocking it was and to exchange epithets such as 'Scum' and 'Parasites'.

'Why is it,' this Lizzie said, 'that I know exactly what you're going to tell me?' Then she said, 'Give us your key. We might as well know the worst.'

In the event, it wasn't nearly as bad as either of them had anticipated. There were cans scattered about and cigarette ends and a jumble of tapes and records on the floor in the sitting-room, and every plate and glass appeared to have been used and left in an unsavoury mess in the kitchen, but after they'd washed up and vacuumed and dusted, the only real damage revealed itself to be a burn mark on a coffee table and a broken chair (and Maisie had a hunch that that could be explained by the crash and the shriek that she'd heard the previous night, before ever the hordes had descended).

Lizzie said, 'I could wring that little idiot's neck.'

Maisie blamed the girl. She had undoubtedly led him astray. For one thing, she was older than he was and all that raggle-taggle bunch had obviously been friends of hers rather than his.

'I don't think Gwyn requires much leading,' Lizzie said. Not being a parent, she had never got into the habit of laying the blame for an offspring's behaviour on any or all of his friends.

He came back alone, later that night. Lizzie opened the door to him while he was still turning his key in the lock. 'Get in!' she said, and aimed a swipe at his head.

He submitted quite stoically to this abuse. He knew it could have been a good deal worse. Four of them had been done for possession; in view of his age and obvious naivety and the fact that the miscreants had been gate-crashers, they'd let him off with a smacked wrist.

'I can't believe you'd allow it to happen,' Lizzie said furiously. 'Obviously you can't be trusted an inch . . .'

He was falling asleep even as she berated him. 'Sorry,' he said, 'but I didn't invite all that mob. And it was only a bit of blow, after all.'

'Try telling that to your mother,' she said. 'I've half a mind to ring her up this very minute and put her in the picture.'

'Oh no,' Maisie said, involuntarily. His behaviour hardly warranted the interruption of an idyll, idylls, as a rule, being hard to come by and usually short-lived.

Chapter Sixteen

'Don't be such a cynic,' Theo had said to Duncan Fry the day they encountered him on the Riva degli Schiavoni. 'It's what Venice is *about*: gondolas and Bellinis and paying a fortune for a cup of coffee at Florian's. Otherwise you might as well stay at home.'

Duncan Fry had performed a sort of mock salute. 'If you say so, baas.'

The problem was that there were just too many delights to be crammed into the brief time at their disposal. The last day dawned. He curled strands of her hair around his fingers as they lay in bed, listed alternatives: 'There's Tintoretto at the Correr, Matisse at the Guggenheim. There are some lovely Carpaccios in a little church on the way to the Arsenale. There's the Arsenale itself, for that matter – if you like ships and guns, that is. You don't, do you? Oh, I'm so glad. Heavens, you haven't even been inside the cathedral yet! Or, there are the other islands, besides that to which your morbid fancies led us. There's Burano, where they make the lace, and Torcello, and there's a charming little place inhabited by Armenian monks where they show you the scourging chain removed after death from their founder's body and tell you that Byron learned Armenian there in three days flat, though I take that with a very big pinch of salt . . .'

'You choose,' she said. It would have been nothing short of sacrilege for her to suggest that she'd be as happy to stay, with him, in bed.

181

He chose Torcello. Sailing towards it, they passed little deserted islands which supported only ruined dwellings or the shell of a church. She looked at them longingly, fantasized about the two of them disembarking and never going back, was prompted to share with him this quaint, if nonsensical notion.

'Well,' he said, 'I suppose we could always swim across to that Cipriani place on Torcello whenever we felt peckish.'

Was it destined to be no more than a fantasy, she wondered, the idea of a life together? Would she always feel obliged to maintain this note of flippancy whenever she spoke of such matters, in case he might recognize demands being made of him and take to his heels? These were cold thoughts for such a warm day. She shivered as she walked beside him down the path which led from the landing stage along the bank of a sluggish, weed-choked canal. A haze of mosquitoes hovered above the water. She'd been warned about Venetian mosquitoes but these were the first she'd encountered. Perhaps bad thoughts conjured unpleasant manifestations.

'You can't be cold?' he said. He'd pulled off his sweat-shirt and draped it over his shoulders. She was unused to seeing him in mufti; clad in T-shirt and jeans, his manner was younger, more carefree than that conveyed by his normal, formally suited self. She noticed, though, that the jeans bore a Valentino label; it would have been a catastrophe of equally major proportions had Gwyn chosen to throw up even over this casual attire.

'No,' she said. 'Just a goose walking over my grave. Whatever that means.'

They crossed a stone bridge and found themselves in a tranquil piazza which was flanked by the remains of an arcaded church and a stone-shuttered cathedral. Entering the latter, she bought a candle and lit it, aware that the prayer she said to accompany this gesture probably constituted blasphemy, it being contrary to the edicts of the Roman Catholic Church to request that your lover might, one day, consider divorcing his wife so that he could marry you.

'Wow!' he said, sounding just like Gwyn, as their eyes became accustomed to the interior light and they looked up at a huge mosaic representing the Last Judgement. Some of the tortures of the damned displayed a perfectly horrid inventiveness. 'Blue demons!' Theo said. 'They look like something that might appear in the throes of one's worst hangover.'

She thought that they looked as though they would probably have some specifically hideous torment reserved for adulterous women.

On the opposite wall there was, depicted in mosaic and set upon a blazing golden background, a stylized madonna of evident Byzantine origin. 'Beautiful!' Theo said, obviously moved. She had an exotic face, with dark, slanting eyes and a sad and contemplative gaze; it was a face as different from her own, which was round and small-featured, as could be imagined. As she watched him admiring the picture – it was plain to see that, aesthetically, it had struck a chord at some deep and very personal level – she wondered, not for the first time, but this time with an intense curiosity, what Sarah looked like, whether she had almond eyes and high cheekbones and a glance that conveyed a boundless compassion.

But she didn't want to think about Sarah. Not today. Obediently, she inspected other of the cathedral's marvels: the altar screen and the Gothic crucifix and the sarcophagus containing the relics of St Somebody or other, followed him into the adjoining church to check out the guide book's assertion that it was the most elaborate work of its period in existence, admired its marble pillars and the low-slung, almost cosy dimensions of its cylindrical dome, but she felt happier when they stepped outside into the sunshine.

The stone seat in the centre of the square was called, as she knew also from her guide book perusals, the Chair of Attila and legend had it that anyone sitting there would be wed within the year. She saw it as an omen, but so many people were intent on the same purpose, queuing up to be photographed thus, that she

183

grew tired of waiting and instead walked across to join Theo who was sitting on the grass beside the church, basking in the heat. She wondered if he'd read the guide book too and perceived her motive, but he didn't comment, just raised his face to the sun and said, 'Poor old Duncan. Trundling that bunch around museums even as we speak. He certainly drew the short straw today.'

They lunched alfresco on the terrace of 'that Cipriani place', looking over a garden laid out with box hedges and pergolas over which deep red roses scrambled in vivid profusion, to charming effect. Suddenly, by comparison, white flowers glimmering at twilight seemed perhaps a mite anaemic ... 'No!' Theo said, biting off the end of a breadstick and divining her thought processes. 'You can't. It's far too late to change your mind. Anyway, I didn't think you'd be so fickle.'

She wasn't; she'd always been the one to cling on, limpet-like, long after a relationship had reached its use-by date.

A party of people entered the restaurant. Among their number was a tall woman, elegantly dressed, wearing a wide-brimmed hat that shaded her face. Her face was heavily powdered, dead white. 'Lawks!' Theo said, peering at her, but discreetly, around his menu. Surrounded by her companions, all of whom were Italian and sported shiny suntans the colour of ripe chestnuts, the pallor of her skin stood out in ghastly contrast.

They speculated, sotto voce, on the reason for her bizarre appearance: 'They've dug her up,' Theo said. 'It's some kind of Italian voodoo. Or, maybe, it's the Latin equivalent of Noh theatre.' 'She's got a horribly disfiguring disease.' 'She's trying out for the circus.' 'It's sun-screen, factor 93, with added asbestos.'

She choked on her bread. He had to resuscitate her by administering small sips of water and patting her gently between the shoulder blades. Coughing and spluttering and giggling still, she added this woman to her list of Venetian memories. 'Do you remember,' they would say, in the future, 'that funny woman who'd put half a bucket of whitewash on her face, that old couple tangoing in St Mark's Square, *Analcolico*?'

It was the mutuality of memory, as much as anything else, that kept people together. Although she knew that, in this respect, she could never hope to compete with the abundance of Sarah's experience.

They walked slowly back to the landing stage, hand in hand. The air was filled with the scents of cypress and rosemary. And then his phone rang. He grimaced as he answered it. It was a mixed blessing: she supposed that he owed his ability to sleep away from the Danieli to the invention of the mobile phone, that it allowed him to contact Sarah without necessarily being in legitimate situ. On the other hand, it also allowed her to contact him, permitted the world to intrude, informing her, only his mistress, brutally, that she didn't have, could never have, the monopoly on his time and attention.

She watched his face changing, interpreted what she saw there as the stunned look of one who has just received the most unexpected and unwelcome news. But it was only a momentary lapse, and she wondered then if he'd cultivated the reserve that was such a fundamental part of his nature, despite his superficial sociability, wondered if this kind of reserve could be considered in any way equivalent to dissimulation, if battening down the emotional hatches meant, necessarily, that only secrets of a disreputable nature were concealed.

'Trouble?' she mouthed at him. He moved away from her, saying, 'There's hardly any signal here. It's breaking up all the time. Ah, that's better . . .'

Distancing himself from her by the minute, he replied to this caller in terse, almost staccato fashion. 'Duncan,' he informed her, when their conversation was concluded.

'Oh?'

'I'm afraid there's a bit of a snag. God has just descended. The chairman, that is. He's come to see *La Traviata* at the Fenice – he's heavily into culture, with a capital K. Anyway, the upshot is that my presence is required. He's mixing pleasure with business, what he calls a debriefing.'

He looked at her with mournful eyes. 'Our last night together,' she said. She'd looked forward to meeting him later for a meal as leisurely as their mutual desire would allow, looked forward to another long night of love, to waking together the next morning and experiencing that curious, but not altogether unpleasant, light-headed, disembodied feeling that succeeds a night when sleep has been forgone in favour of passion.

He seemed uncharacteristically edgy, flicking their return tickets back and forth against his thumbnail, pulling at an earlobe, smoking a cigarette with deep and rapid inhalations. She looked out over the lagoon at the view which had earlier filled her with delighted anticipation, but now her dejection had dulled its appeal. She'd never been good at dealing with disappointment, though for his sake she tried to disguise her feelings. But he seemed too distracted to notice either her despondency or her attempt to conceal it. Perhaps, she thought, it was the prospect of the chairman's visit that made him nervous.

The boat arrived. As they were boarding it, he said, 'Don't worry. I'm not leaving you abandoned. I've arranged for Duncan to take you out to dinner.'

She wasn't at all sure that being squired by Duncan Fry would come under the heading of a pleasurable experience, but could hardly say so, felt that it was incumbent upon her to try to like him: one's married lover's close male friends often being more of a threat, in terms of the influence they wielded, than his wife.

'And what about tomorrow?' she asked, in what she was embarrassingly aware sounded perilously close to a plaintive whine.

'I don't know yet,' he said. 'We'll just have to play it by ear.'

Of all the clichés in the English language, that was the one she detested most of all.

After he'd left her (in obvious haste, with a cursory peck on the cheek, a squeeze of her hand), she washed and dressed and went down to the lounge where she waited, rather glumly, for her escort to appear. A large extended Italian family were sitting close by: they conversed vivaciously, roared with laughter, frequently embraced one another. She watched them pensively, transforming them in her mind into Theo and his unknown family: his parents, hers, their sisters and brothers, those picture-book children, Chloe and Max.

She was in mid-muse when she felt a hand on her shoulder and almost jumped a foot. 'Madame,' said Duncan Fry. 'At your service.' And then he said, 'Sorry if I startled you. I didn't realize you were so jumpy.'

His tone might have been described as jocular; she felt that she could detect a note of mockery, that, for whatever reason, he was intent on putting her at a disadvantage. When, as a last-ditch attempt to avert this meeting, she had said to Theo, 'But I thought no one was to know that I was here with you. I thought that was the reason we had to travel separately,' he'd replied, 'Oh that wasn't on account of *Duncan*. No, not at all. Duncan's quite sound.'

Why was it then that her instincts informed her otherwise, as she sat next to this Duncan, sound as he was, on the vaporetto, travelling towards a charming little restaurant in Canareggio that he knew of, well off the tourist track, and was filled with a sense of foreboding?

'Don't you have to be there then, tonight?' she asked idiotically, it being perfectly obvious that he didn't.

'Not me,' he said, offering his cigarette case: 'No? How very sensible. Oh no,' he said, lighting up and expelling smoke very elegantly through flared nostrils, 'I'm much too small fry for that, if you'll excuse the pun. It's strictly big-shot time tonight. Family and friends. You know?'

She didn't but let it pass as they had, by now, reached their destination.

It was a no-English-spoken establishment to which he'd brought her. Interrupting what she considered to be his somewhat patronizing translation of the menu on her behalf, she plumped

187

for a dish that she vaguely recognized. 'Cuttlefish?' he said, raising his eyebrows. 'Are you sure? All that black inky stuff, seeping into everything else and staining it? Ugh!'

The theatricality of the shudder he gave went some way to confirming her suspicion that he was gay. She'd had friends, good friends who were gay, but remembered that, when crossed in love, they had also been capable of exceeding malice.

But surely it wasn't this that caused her to feel such unease? It was, rather, to do with the unmistakable scent he gave off, the scent of mischief.

He looked at his watch. 'They'll just about be reaching the end of Act One,' he said. 'Everyone getting ready to sprint to the bar. And that's just the singers.'

'Aren't you sorry to be missing it?' she asked. She'd have liked to be there herself. The music of Verdi, that most melancholy of men, always cheered her up.

'Not likely,' he said. 'I'm not into tales about tarts. Though I suppose she did do the right thing in the end.'

He raised his glass to her, regarding her steadily through the wine's golden glow. His eyes too appeared golden. Cats' eyes. The eyes of a big cat, with razor-sharp teeth and claws that could rip you to shreds.

He pulled a prawn's translucent shell apart and ate its contents with relish. Inside, his mouth too was cat-like – extremely pink, with a vaulted palate, narrow and ridged. 'I say, these *are* good,' he said. 'Theo was right. I didn't even know about this place until he pointed it out. Of course, he tends to get around more than I do. He was here for Carnival. Was it you who came with him, or . . . Oh sorry. Foot in the mouth again.'

She fixed her eyes upon the pasta on her plate. Maybe he was a friend of Sarah's. Maybe he was jealous. Maybe he simply took pleasure in stirring it. But to face him out, force him to make overtly manifest his dislike, or disapproval, of her, would be to risk her dignity. She'd never quite achieved the techniques of successful assertiveness, came closer, in those circumstances, to making a red-faced, spluttering fool of herself. Instead, she said, in the most pleasantly conversational tone that she could muster, 'Have you known Theo long?'

'We were at university together. We met up again when he joined the firm. Though we never really lost touch. We had friends in common. A friend, particularly. She died some years ago. It was a dreadful shock. Well, obviously, Theo was considerably more affected than me. I'm not sure that he ever did get over it.'

Suddenly she was no longer aware of her surroundings: their fellow diners, the waiters' cries, the clatter from the kitchen. 'What do you mean,' she said, 'obviously Theo was more affected?'

'Pudding?' he said, as the waiter hovered. 'No? Just coffee? Well, it had been in the nature of what I believe is known as a grand passion. You know?' he said once again, his expression suggesting that any such knowledge would lie completely beyond her ken, that her capacity would extend no further than participating in squalid affairs.

He said, 'That's why we were all so pleased when Sarah came along.'

There should be an island in the lagoon reserved for people like him, she thought, those who derived pleasure from the discomfiture of others.

'And it didn't hurt his career prospects either,' he said.

'What do you mean?' she asked, although she really didn't want to know.

He paused for optimum impact and then he said, 'Sarah's the chairman's daughter. Didn't you know? Not a bad move for someone as ambitious as Theo.'

She was conscious of her heart's erratic rhythm, concentrated on the rapid disposal of her coffee so that this nightmare meal could be concluded, scalded her tongue in the process.

When the bill arrived, he slapped down his credit card and said, 'Would you excuse me? Nature calls. I shan't be a moment and then I'll get you back to your hotel.'

'No,' she said. 'If you don't mind, I'd prefer to walk a bit first. On my own.' She felt that she couldn't abide his poisonous presence for a moment longer.

'If you're sure?' he called after her. 'Don't go talking to any strange Italians.'

She left the restaurant, almost running, such was her desire to place the greatest amount of distance between them. Her head was whirling. The same two phrases kept repeating themselves: 'a grand passion' and 'the chairman's daughter'. She'd crossed a bridge and turned two corners before she realized that her surroundings looked unfamiliar. She paused and then, disobeying Duncan Fry's instruction, asked a passer-by for directions. Unfortunately, this gentleman, though he listened to her with perfect civility, seemed to have no comprehension of her English, and even less of her halting Italian. 'Vaporetto?' she said feebly, trying vainly to remember the name of the stop at which they'd disembarked.

'Ah!' he said. 'Vaporetto!' And unleashed a torrent of Italian, of which she understood only the words *sinistra* and *destra*. Obediently, although a trifle sceptical, she followed his pointing finger, crossed another bridge and found herself entering what appeared to be a maze of ill-lit alleys. No other footstep was to be heard, except the ringing echo of her own heels on the pavement. A great dark windowless church loomed up in front of her. She saw, in the glimmer of the lamplight, an inscription in an unrecognizable script above its huge carved door. And then the alley debouched into a deserted square and there was a sign on the wall, next to a plaque depicting some holocaust horror that said Campo di Ghetto Nuovo and she realized then that she had walked in completely the wrong direction.

There was a Museo Israelitico and a bookshop and a kosher bakery, but they were, all of them, shuttered and dark. She tried to consult her map but the light was too dim to make it out properly. She seemed to have a choice of equally eerie *sottoporteghe* to lead her out of the square. She chose the nearest. A cat streaked across her path and she froze. Walls seemed to loom inwards towards her, and though they were studded with windows showing chinks of light around their shutters, still there was no evidence of another human soul abroad. It was quite unnerving. At any moment she expected to see a homicidal dwarf in a red coat leaping from boat to boat along the canal in murderous pursuit.

Instinct propelled her eventually towards a major canal and a vaporetto stop which was called, quite logically, Ghetto. She boarded the first boat that came along, assuming that, like the Tube, you could always get off somewhere and change. But it soon became apparent that this particular vessel was the one that did the most circular of circular tours – via Trieste, probably, that there was no name at any of the stops that seemed remotely familiar, and that she dared not disembark in case she found herself even further disorientated. She sat, dejectedly, as the boat sailed through the unprepossessing landscape that was the underside of all that Venetian beauty: docks, boatyards, a railway station, mortified by her own stupidity. And then her spirits rose as she spied the dome of the Salute, but at that moment an official-looking person who'd boarded the boat at the previous stop seemed to be demanding to see her ticket and, upon sight of it, launched into a tirade. A fellow-passenger with a smattering of English explained: her *carta* was invalid for this particular journey; she must pay a spot fine of thirty thousand *lire* to the inspector here. She counted it out resignedly from her wallet as she saw a name that she recognized, San Zaccaria, and prepared to disembark.

Even then there remained a fairly long walk to the hotel. A blister on her heel rubbed excruciatingly against the inside of her shoe. She put one limping foot before the other, doggedly following the signs: *per Rialto*.

A message awaited her at the reception desk. Transcribed into curly foreign script, it said: *Change of plan. I have to fly to Zurich tomorrow. Safe journey home. Talk to you soonest. Theo.*

191

The young night manager, who had a medieval scholar's face but only a meagre command of English, smiled and said, 'Is good?'

'Is just brilliant,' she replied. 'Is what we call, in English, the end of a perfect day.'

Chapter Seventeen

After Joe left, Maisie found the unaccustomed quiet almost uncanny, could scarcely remember that it wasn't so long ago since quiet had been the normal level of sound.

She'd let herself into Clare's house and saw the note that was propped against the sitting-room clock. It wasn't in an envelope and she'd read it before she realized what it was. *Sorry Ma*, it said, *about the gate-crashers and the hassle. Gone to stay with some mates for a bit. It'll be cool. See ya soon. J.* She supposed that it would be politic of him to stay away until the dust had settled. She hadn't been certain that Clare needed to know about the party but Lizzie had said, 'Too damn right she needs to know. What if the politzei decide to bang a charge on her? It's her property, after all. And don't try to make excuses for laughing boy. It was a thoroughly sneaky thing to do.'

So she supposed he was for the high jump when his mother came back.

It was a phrase that Bob often used: the high jump. 'Crikey!' he'd say, catching sight of the clock face as they lay snuggled together, like interlocking pieces of a puzzle, on the little bed in Rita's back room. 'I'm late. I'll be for the high jump.'

(It was slang, she believed, for death by hanging, but now it seemed newly appropriate, a suitable addition to all those other jargon phrases employed by air-crews: baling out, ditching, going for a Burton.)

And she'd try to assist him: knotting his tie, passing him his jacket, searching out his shoes from wherever he'd kicked them earlier in his urgency to be naked with her.

And all the time he'd be attempting to snatch kisses until she pushed him away, positioning his cap at the correct angle, cramming the remains of the sandwiches she'd made for him into his pocket. (She'd forfeit her entire butter ration for the month; he was always hungry and she wasn't, except for him.) 'Go. Now,' she'd say, 'before they put you on a charge.' It would have been foolish to jeopardize what little time they had together.

Afterwards she'd straighten the bed and fold up the towel with which she'd covered the sheets and carry it home to be washed. 'Why do you need a towel with you?' Mother had asked suspiciously. 'The one on the roller in the washroom at work is always filthy,' she'd said. Mother could identify and sympathize with that; she had always been fanatical about other people's germs.

'You've clicked, haven't you?' Rita had said one morning at work. 'Come on, you can't fool your auntie Rita.' Maisie had kept her head down over her machine and her eyes fixed on regulation khaki but later, in the canteen, when they were eating what Rita called dogs' knackers' rissoles and listening to *Workers' Playtime*, she returned to the subject: 'Is he nice-looking? Is he a good kisser? Have you had a cuddle on the back row yet? If so, describe it to us in detail. I've forgotten what it feels like.'

A tarty girl called Mavis who was sitting opposite overheard their conversation and said, 'Has he had his leg over, Maisie? Or are you still keeping your hand on your halfpenny?'

'We can do without your crude remarks,' Rita said, pausing in her preparations to relight the dog-end of a Gold Flake, 'Miss Dirty Mouth.'

She was very pretty though, Maisie thought. Like Hedy Lamarr.

'Hedy Lamarr? Only if Hedy Lamarr has a tidemark a yard wide round her neck.'

Tidemark or no, she had all the men after her, though Rita said it was for one thing and one thing only. Anyway, Rita said, anybody could get a chap if she put her mind to it. All that was needed was the appropriate technique. 'With blokes,' she said, 'it's all kidology.'

But, though Rita was undoubtedly infinitely experienced in the ways of men, this time she had it all wrong. Kidology was a concept that had no place in the relationship between herself and Robert Worthington. She loved him and he, amazingly, almost unbelievably, loved her. He was her lover and her friend. Until he came along she hadn't been aware that it was possible for these two separate entities to reside in the same skin.

'I'd like to see you again,' he'd said when he awoke the night they'd met in the shelter. At some point during sleep he had moved so that his shoulder was pressed against her face and she was aware that the impression of his stripes was scored deeply into the flesh of her cheek. But that hadn't deterred him. He'd been quite shy, anxious to convince her that he wasn't the sort to indulge in casual pick-ups. 'I d-don't make a habit of asking girls out the minute I meet them . . .' He stammered when he was nervous. She found it endearing. 'It's just that . . . I might never see you again.'

They both knew, had known almost from the moment they set eyes on each other. The notion of cheapness didn't come into it, nor impropriety; they simply acknowledged their destiny.

Sex was a mutual discovery. 'Have you ever?' 'No. Have you?' 'Well, the chaps think I have but I haven't. Are you sure about it? Quite sure?' 'Oh yes, quite, quite sure. Absolutely certain.'

Even so, the strength of her response astonished her. She'd wondered, as she pushed away the groping hands of the young men before him, if she was one of those women they called frigid. He, most assuredly, convinced her otherwise.

Location had been the problem. Fortunately Rita divined their dilemma and offered them her back room. 'If it was anybody but you, kid . . .' she had said. And then: 'Go on. Fill your boots.

195

Why not? But not our bed, mind. I'm funny about that. There's a put-you-up you can have in the scullery.'

Love among the cooking pots. And the washboard and the mangle. Rita would unwind the turban within which her hair was confined during working hours, let her chestnut waves fall free à la Veronica Lake and go down to the Railwayman's Arms for a glass of stout with her mother-in-law: 'At least you won't have that to contend with, Maisie,' she said. 'Thank your stars.'

It was Bob who would have the mother-in-law problem. She stalled for as long as possible. Her excuses wore thin. Other girls' beaux, their intendeds, even their casual flings were, in these free and easy times, brought home for Sunday tea. June and Patricia Maxwell had a succession of swains eating the raspberry sponge sandwiches that Mrs Maxwell conjured out of powdered egg and some ersatz form of jam with pips in it that resembled balsa wood.

'Are you ashamed of me?' Bob said, at length.

'No. No!' she had cried, horrified that he, who had been made to feel ashamed so often before, should imagine that she, of all people, would feel that way. 'I love you,' she'd said. 'I'm as proud as punch.'

'Well then?' he'd said. So there was really no option but to tell him.

He'd held her, very still and very tightly, after she'd related the bleak facts, how Mother was . . . peculiar. How she, Maisie, could no longer delude herself that what she'd thought of as mere idiosyncrasy had now developed into something more sinister. Men no longer looked at Mother admiringly for the simple reason that her looks were no longer admirable. Her face was the same sweet oval shape and her eyes as darkly blue but she appeared, sometimes, quite askew. Sometimes she looked worse than askew.

She'd never really believed, despite her disinclination to tempt fate, that he'd fail her, that his response to this information would be to give her the cold shoulder. And he didn't disappoint her expectations. He continued to hold her close and he said, 'I can

196

help you with her. I've got very broad shoulders, in case you hadn't noticed.'

There wasn't an inch of him that she hadn't lovingly committed to memory, not a mark or a mole, nor a curve nor a contour; his body was as familiar to her – and infinitely more pleasing – than her own. But when it came to it, to bringing about their meeting, she procrastinated. Broad-shouldered he might be and brave and willing to take on the problems that came with loving her, but once they were acquainted, he and Mother, then this lovely secret life that she enjoyed with him would be finished. So, still, whenever she was preparing herself to meet him, always with an excitement that bordered on the delirious, she'd let Mother's monologue of complaint – 'You're not off *again*? You're never in. Night after night' – wash over her and field her attempts at inquisition – 'Where are you off to? What are you getting up to?' – before leaving the house with the excuse that she was doing overtime, scarcely caring whether she was believed or not.

She'd start running as soon as she got off the bus, as did he, from the opposite direction. They'd collide, breathless, holding on to each other for support, gulping air until they'd recovered sufficiently to essay that first kiss – as thrilling, each time, as their very first kiss – and they'd kiss all the way along Rita's front path and through the hall and up the stairs and into the scullery.

It was north-facing, the scullery, chilly even in the summer. But it wasn't the cold that caused her to tremble, rather that she shivered with anticipation.

He'd joke, as he covered her with kisses, allege that she'd led him astray, that, until her own appetite had awakened his, he'd been an innocent.

She was three years his senior. 'Does it matter?' she'd asked worriedly.

He'd taken her hand and played 'This little piggy' with her fingers. 'It might do,' he said, 'when I'm a hundred and you're a hundred and three.'

After the war was over.

Men of his squadron went out and didn't come back. She found herself thinking guiltily: if they die, then surely that must lengthen the odds for him. 'Don't worry,' he'd say. 'I've always been a lucky beggar. Ask anyone. Ask Tonks, or McIver.'

They were his pals, fellow air-crew. Once he took her for a drink in a public house and introduced her to them. She was shy but they were genial young fellows and put her at her ease. Perhaps they became a little over-excited in drink, but who could blame them? Afterwards he'd said proudly, 'They remarked what a nice girl you were, and good-looking.'

And it was true. She realized that, in the benign glow of his affection, she had become so. People noticed. Rita said, 'You're blossoming. Well they do say it's better than a beauty treatment.'

When they were apart she spent most of her time listening for the drone of planes, could identify, before anyone else, which was what, wondered, whenever the sound was that of the big, heavy, four-engined Halifax, whether he was aboard, isolated in his turret, so very vulnerable to the searchlight's beam, the bursting shell, the hostile gun heading inexorably in his direction. She'd close her eyes and pray, cross her fingers, make pacts with the devil, fix her concentration totally on willing his safe return. 'You've just sewn two legs together, you crate egg,' Rita said.

She'd attempt to pull herself together, to be more conscientious. She was paid well and they'd need as much money as they could lay their hands on if he were to pursue his plans to study. After the war. After they were married.

Because they *were* to be married. She was over twenty-one and no one could stop her. Mother would have to like it or – as Rita said – do the other.

One day he told her that there was talk of a posting. Perhaps North Africa. She couldn't bear to think about it. A friend of his had been found to have perforated eardrums and been grounded. She added to her prayers the request that this might happen to him. Or any other, relatively minor, physical dysfunction causing him to fail his medical. 'Don't worry so much,' he'd said. 'There's not long to go now anyway.' They were only allowed to fly many operations at a time in case they became bomb-happy.

She tried to be unworried, for his sake, but the phrase that kept coming into her head was 'borrowed time'.

The Maxwells had an egg-timer filled with sand. Mrs Maxwell kept it beside the stove, though her husband would roar: 'What damn use is that thing when there aren't any eggs?' (Although, occasionally, back-door deliveries were made and next morning June and Patricia were to be observed cracking open the speckled shells of new-laid eggs with their apostle spoons.)

Maisie would wait for her toast to brown and turn this timer upside down, watching the sand trickle slowly to its base. They said that luck was like that: that it drained away.

A fly buzzed frantically in the window. She swatted it absently, wondering if it realized that its continuing existence depended entirely upon her whim. The power that we have, she thought, each over the other. Once, when Mother had soiled herself for the third time in succession, and Maisie hadn't slept for two nights running, she'd taken all the pills she had and crushed them into a powder until there was enough to provide the basis of a cocktail from which neither of them would wake. And then she'd heard that cracked old voice singing a song that used to be sung to her as a child: 'You are my sunshine, my only sunshine. You make me happy when skies are grey . . .'

She'd tipped the lethal mixture down the sink. They might have been good parents, Rose and Alfred, had not life intervened.

The doorbell rang and she bequeathed whatever was left of its circumscribed life to the agitated fly and went to answer it. A distraught Clare held out Joe's note. Could Maisie provide any explanation? She knew from Lizzie all about the party and the police, and she had rung up every 'mate' of his with whom she was acquainted, but no one knew anything of his whereabouts.

Maisie said cautiously, 'Perhaps he went to stay with the girl.'

'The girl?'

'Mickey, her name was.'

'It's usually a case of *cherchez la femme*,' Lizzie said. She'd arrived just as Clare was leaving. 'Calm down,' she said. 'I've just seen him.'

'Where?'

'He's up a tree in those woods beside the motorway. You know, where they plan to build that new spur? I was giving Michael a lift, his car's in dock. Anyway, we noticed this commotion with bulldozers and so on and a lot of young scruffs being hauled from their perches and, lo and behold, who should be among them but the lad himself.'

'Is he still up there?'

'As far as I know.'

'Come back with me,' Clare begged, making for the gate. 'Shall we take my car?'

'Not if we want to get there before a week on Wednesday,' Lizzie replied.

Two persons drove away and, an hour or so later, the same two persons returned. They went straight into the house and closed the door behind them. Maisie gathered from Clare's grim expression that their quest had been unsuccessful.

In fact, he came back the next day while his mother was at work, presumably of his own accord. Timmy leapt down from the gatepost and gave him a hero's welcome. He bent to stroke the cat and Maisie, trundling her binbag to the pavement for collection, almost fell over him.

'Hi there,' he said.

His brutal haircut had grown out unevenly in strange tufts. He was clad in several layers of clothing, all equally dirty and dishevelled. There was a rip in his jeans that ran the length of one leg and an ugly graze down the side of his face. 'Bastards!' he said, fingering it gently. 'One of them hit Mickey.'

'Who?' she said.

'Bailiffs. The Filth. The government's private army. They're on a loser though. They can pull us down and smack us around all they like but there'll always be more to take our place.'

She didn't doubt it; what she did doubt was whether, given the inequality of resources, such effort was worthwhile. But she confined herself to saying, 'Would you like a bath?'

Clare's bathroom, newly decorated, ought not to be defiled by the mess that the soaking away of such extremes of dirt as this would create.

He picked up his rucksack. 'Thanks, Maisie,' he said. 'You're a pal.'

'I'll make you something to eat.'

She scrambled him all the eggs she possessed and he fell on them like one famished. They'd lived on Big Macs apparently, brought by well-wishers and placed in baskets and buckets which were then hauled up into their arboreal eyries.

She said, 'How on earth do you sleep in a tree?'

'No probs,' he said, 'if you have a hammock. Otherwise you don't. You just get terminal displacement of the lower vertebrae. I reckon I may have slipped a disc.'

She recalled the briefly broken ankle that he'd claimed at the time of their first meeting; exaggeration seemed to come to him as naturally as breathing. She said, 'You won't be able to dance, then?'

'Oh, I dunno . . .' he said, following the direction of her gaze to where his sequinned suit hung over the back of a chair.

'Is it finished?'

'Almost. But never mind that,' she said. 'Your mother has been very worried.'

'Oh yeah? Thought she'd have been too taken up with Mr Smooth to notice whether I was there or not.'

'I don't think you're being very fair,' she said. 'She did her utmost to make arrangements for your welfare before she left.'

'My welfare doesn't need any arranging,' he said coldly.

She said, 'Don't you feel that you've let her down?'

He picked up his fork, the better to gesticulate. 'Look, Mais,'

201

he said, 'it's changed since your day. You lot *had* parents. For all your life. The same ones. With our generation, parents swap and change around so much . . . well, we'd rather rely on each other, you know, our mates.'

And, of course, it couldn't be denied that young men had always needed the comradeship of other young men. 'Pals,' they'd been called in her father's day; they'd formed battalions to go off to the war, supported each other throughout the horrors: divided up the pack of a sick friend between themselves, helped to carry him along for the duration of a march, risked life and limb to drag him, mortally wounded, into the nearest shell-hole. She remembered Bob's friends, the men of his crew, Johnny and Tonks and McIver, thought of the special relationship that such a degree of dependency produced. It didn't seem to her that the word 'friend' could be used in the same breath to describe those with whom Joe consorted.

December 12th, 1941.
It's even colder today. Your breath freezes on the air and every night is bright moonlight. They call it a bomber's moon . . .

How she hated that phrase. Whenever she heard it she felt as though icy water was trickling down the back of her neck. She longed for murk, for a low-lying pall of cloud to obscure every source of illumination, for weather conditions so bad that take-off would be impossible. But still they continued: the clear, starlit, moonlit nights.

At six-thirty that evening she and Rita clocked off, wound their mufflers round their necks and linked each other down the icy pavement. They were on their way to the Lyceum to see Marlene Dietrich in a film called *Flame of New Orleans*. Rita said, 'I hope you've cleared it with Mona Lott?'

That was Mother. Rita knew that Mother was over-possessive, kicked up a fuss whenever Maisie asserted her right to independence, but nothing more than that.

'You want to give her what for,' Rita said. 'Trying to rule your life. At your age! You want to tell her straight, put your foot down with a firm hand ... Speaking of which,' she said, 'give us yours. My glove's got a great hole in it.'

Hands clasped, she pushed both of them deep into her coat pocket and pulled up her collar. 'There'll be more runny noses than standing pricks tonight,' she said.

And then the siren went. 'Hurry up,' she said, 'get your skates on. We'll make it if we run. I'm not getting stuck in that flaming shelter again.'

The surface of the street glittered in the merciless moonlight; there seemed to be no shadow deep enough to afford shelter. Maisie was suddenly seized with a shudder that seemed not to be due to the plummeting temperatures. If that ever happened to Mother she'd say: 'A goose just walked over my grave.'

They could hear the ack-ack guns starting up, saw the searchlights cutting swathes through the sky. 'Come on!' Rita shouted, running ahead. 'What's up?'

It was his number that was up. She knew it, as she stood exposed in the moonlight's glare, as certainly as if she'd already taken delivery of the telegram.

They were all gone: Tonks and McIver and Johnny and Bob, shot down over the cold North Sea beneath the moon's bright impartial gaze. They'd sent the telegram to Rita's flat because, although he'd named Maisie as his next of kin (having no other), she dared not risk communication arriving at her own address.

Missing, it said, *presumed killed*. Rita was weeping as she handed it over but Maisie couldn't cry, not for a long time, try as she might. Perhaps because she couldn't take it in: that they would never again lie together, murmuring endearments, surrounded by Rita's dripping smalls, her frying pan, her zinc bath; that never again would her heart somersault as she turned a corner and saw him running towards her. It could not be, not when her cheek still bore the imprint of his last kiss. It seemed inconceivable that he'd never kiss her again.

Dry grief; it was unhealthy. Rita tried to coax the tears with sympathy, with tenderness and, eventually, when this approach failed, with a deliberate brusqueness: 'Life goes on, kid. Whether we like it or not, life goes on.'

And it wasn't long before she discovered that that was true, though not exactly in the way that Rita meant. The first time that her monthly period failed to occur passed almost unnoticed: she had no attention to spare for anything other than the gnawing misery that accompanied her sleep, invaded her dreams, woke with her every morning; it wasn't until a second month had passed without its usual accompaniment of blood that it dawned on her that she might be pregnant.

She'd waited to be horrified, remembering how, a few months earlier, June Maxwell had been discovered by her mother mixing up concoctions at the sink. She remembered the subsequent commotion, silenced only when Mr Maxwell came in, wanting to know what all the palaver was in aid of. She remembered overhearing prodigious vomitings, and then, one afternoon, a little, dirty-looking woman had come to the back door and soon after that June Maxwell was her old insouciant self again: bleaching her hair and swinging her key, as her father – fortunately, still in the dark – was wont to put it.

It was a terrible thing, to be pregnant and unmarried. Small wonder that June Maxwell glowed with relief, sang *The Boogie-Woogie Bugle Boy of Company B* at the top of her voice and gave so much cheek to her father that he threatened to tan her arse, as big as she was.

It was a terrible thing. But it was a wonderful thing too. It meant that Bob Worthington, foundling, antecedents unknown, Bob Worthington, blown to his component pieces, sunk fathoms deep in the ocean, unburied, could not be wiped from memory as if he had never existed.

It was this knowledge that enabled her to confront the doctor in his surgery and stare down his obvious disapproval. 'Oh dear,' he said, having examined her and confirmed that she was the possessor of a fructified womb. 'This is a sorry state of affairs, isn't it?'

She refused to bow her head, to be humbled. 'I'm entitled to extra rations, aren't I?' she said. He was talking about mother-and-baby homes. She thought of Babs Poole who had never been the same after they'd taken her child from her and put it in the orphanage.

'No thank you,' she said. 'We'll manage.' She wasn't going to allow a second-generation Worthington to start life in the orphanage.

Of course it was only a matter of time before Mother noticed: either her increasing girth or the lack of any laundering of sanitary pads. She might never have got round to telling her about Bob, but this was different. On the day when she discovered that her work-trousers would no longer meet, she fastened them with a safety-pin from Mother's work-box and that night, while they were eating the remains of a stew, made from the prime quality tinned beef that had come in one of Lottie's parcels, she said, trying to control the clatter that her knife and fork were making within her trembling grasp, 'Mother, I'm going to have a baby.'

'Stark raving mad' was a phrase used so very casually to describe the slightest deviation from the norm; 'I'm going stark raving mad,' Rita would say, if she forgot her tea-money or couldn't call to mind the name of an actor who'd starred in some old film.

Mother went authentically stark raving mad. First she threw everything that was close to hand at Maisie's head. Fortunately the accuracy of her aim did not match the power of her pitching: her plate bounced off the wall, the remains of the stew trickling towards the skirting-board; three pieces of cutlery flew, in succession, past Maisie's ear and gouged channels in the panel of the door, a glass smashed into a dozen pieces on the oilcloth. And then, these projectiles having failed to connect with their intended target, she stood up and began to belabour Maisie about the head and shoulders. When Maisie managed to escape to the kitchenette, she then set about trying to rip the tablecloth to shreds. Being a sturdily constructed sort of tablecloth, it withstood all her efforts so she was eventually obliged to fetch the scissors to it, ripping through its lace inserts and its embroidered edges with grunts of satisfaction and yelps of triumph.

Then, quite suddenly, calmness prevailed. She put down the scissors very precisely on the edge of the table and began to fold the tattered cloth neatly, edge to edge. 'You'll have to get rid of it,' she said. 'Do you know how?'

Maisie cried out that she didn't and she wouldn't, that other girls managed to bring up their babies. (Though she knew only of one: a girl at the factory who was always trying to wheedle coupons off everybody, and anyway she pretended the baby was her mother's.)

'You'll have to,' Mother said flatly. Later she'd carry the table-cloth over to the machine and mend it so carefully that you'd hardly know that it had been taken apart.

'Otherwise,' Mother said, 'it'll be born an imbecile.'

The words of protest tumbled from Maisie's lips. They came in no particular order, were not entirely coherent. 'Bob,' she said, 'handsome ... clever ... how can you *say* such a thing? ... nothing wrong ... why do you always make out there's something *wrong*? Bob ... was going to marry me.'

Mother didn't seem to be interested in Bob. 'Or deformed,' she said. 'Is that what you want?'

'But why?' Maisie cried. 'Why?' in the same way that she'd voiced the query when chastised for going to the pantomime, when advised to avoid Babs Poole, when warned about love, about boys, about the outside world in its entirety.

'Because,' Mother said, retrieving the cutlery from the floor, scraping the stew from the wallpaper, 'your father caught a disease and he passed it to me and I passed it on to you and any baby you have will be crippled, or crazy. Or born in little pieces.'

There'd been a long silence after that, broken only by the sound of a knife scraping stew from a plate, the ticking of a clock and the Maxwells' wireless, featuring Sandy Macpherson at the theatre organ. Maisie extricated herself and her swelling abdomen from the lee of the dresser and went into the bedroom – latest in such a long line of bedrooms that she'd shared with her mother – and lay, face down, on top of the bed. She realized that she'd always known, even before she was capable of understanding, that some festering secret set them apart, drove them from the farm, propelled them from rented room to rented room and cautioned them against entering into anything more than the most cursory of relationships with other people.

After a time she undressed and got into bed. Later, Mother did too. Before she turned off the light, she said, 'That little woman, Betty Glenister, that came to June Maxwell. She's the one.'

And then she pulled the switch cord and turned on her side and pretended to be asleep.

April 22nd, 1942.

I can't stop crying. Nurse Pym hugs me and wipes my eyes. She says, 'Go on, lass, cry, tha'll pee less.' She comes from up in the Dales not far from where I was born and she has a really pronounced country accent just as I did when I first came here.

I feel quite insubstantial, as though I could float upwards from this bed and look down on myself. Rita came with a Picturegoer and a bunch of daffodils. She chatted about work and then, as she was buttoning her coat and getting up to go, she mouthed: 'It's for the best, kid.'

She thinks I did a wicked thing. So do Sister Norton and some of the other nurses. They are very brisk and disapproving in their dealings with me. They think I let that horrible dirty little woman help me out of what they call my 'predicament'. As if I'd have let her anywhere near me. What happened was that I got up from my dinner last Wednesday in the canteen at work and went to the toilet

207

and suddenly there was this awful pain and blood everywhere and I think I must have fainted because the next thing I knew I was here in hospital and I asked somebody was it the baby and they just said, 'Hush.' And then they wheeled me away and put a thing in my arm and when I woke up I knew it was gone. 'Why?' I asked Nurse Pym. 'When I didn't do anything? I didn't do anything, you know.'

'Course you didn't, lovey,' she said, straightening the bedclothes. 'It's just nature's way.'

Afterwards I plucked up my courage and asked her. I said, 'Did you see my baby? Was there anything wrong with it? Was it deformed?'

She was disposing of wads of gauze in an enamel bucket and she straightened up and said, 'Deformed? Whatever makes you think that? He was a perfect little boy, just too tiny to live, that's all.'

'Are you sure?' I said, catching her eye to see if I could tell if she was lying. But there was no guile at all in her expression. 'Perfect,' she repeated. 'In every way.'

Chapter Eighteen

Pauline received her appointment from the hospital. She brought in the letter to show to Clare, wearing such a doleful expression that you'd have thought it said 'Report to barracks for immediate embarkation to the Front' rather than 'Ward G5, bringing with you an early-morning specimen of urine.'

She said, 'D'you think I could put it off, postpone it, like?'

'Only if you want to be shoved to the back of the queue and get your next appointment three years hence.'

'It's our Kerry, see,' said Pauline.

'Is there still a problem?' Clare asked absently; she was trying to concentrate upon the matter in hand, her boss having saved up a pile of the most technical of research papers for copy-editing. 'Venice, eh?' he'd said, with mock geniality. 'All right for some. Well I'm afraid that now it's back to planet Earth.'

'She's still bunking off school,' Pauline said. 'She's got one more chance and then she's going to be excluded. Kids!' Pauline said. 'Who'd 'ave 'em?'

Now there was a sentiment, Clare thought, with which she was in wholehearted agreement.

They were not speaking, she and Gwyn. She'd demanded that he should prostrate himself at her feet, perform penitential tasks, beseech her forgiveness. Failing that, an apology would do. 'Well I apologize for the broken chair and the burn mark on the coffee table,' he'd said, 'and I'll pay for the damage, but none of the rest of it was down to me. I mean, I wasn't to know, was I, that

209

that lot would turn up and somebody'd bring along the draw and some other pillock would ring the Bill?'

'What about perching up a tree and refusing to come down?' she'd said. 'I suppose that wasn't your fault either?'

'That,' he said, 'was a matter of principle.'

His principles, she'd told him, seemed to be something of a moveable feast. And, to add insult to injury, while he was engaged in flouting the law, he'd somehow found the time to acquire a tattoo. 'A tattoo!' she'd told Lizzie. 'At the top of his arm. A spider's web. God only knows who did it or what risks he's run. He *said* it was in a proper shop and the equipment was sterilized, but . . .'

'It could have been worse,' Lizzie had said, in a feeble attempt at consolation, 'it could have been love and hate on alternate fingers.'

Lizzie wasn't all that interested anyway. She had other things on her mind. She and Michael had decided to set up home together again. 'A bit previous, aren't you?' Clare had remarked waspishly. 'I thought the whole idea was to take it exceedingly slowly. According to what you said, you should just about be holding hands by now.'

She was jealous, of course, because Lizzie and Michael were making the sort of commitment that she could only fantasize about in terms of herself and Theo.

Ever since she'd got back she'd been nerving herself for some kind of confrontation. Now Pauline interrupted this new train of thought to say, as she turned to the appropriate page of the *Sun*, 'What's your sign?'

'Cancer.'

'Fancy! Same as me.'

And she proceeded to read out some rigmarole to do with discretion being the better part of valour except that, being a tabloid pronouncement, it was expressed rather less subtly.

The portents were inauspicious. Pauline certainly didn't seem to be having much luck with her love-life either.

There was a timid tap at the back door and Pauline went to answer it. 'Hello there, stranger,' Clare heard her say. 'Not seen you for a good bit.'

It was Maisie. She began by apologizing for disturbing them, for her presumption at knocking on the door. Before she could reach the point of apologizing for her very existence, Clare cut her short, asked how she might help.

'Do you happen to have a copy of the *Yellow Pages*?'

'Sure.'

Maisie began, rather uncertainly, to turn them. After a bit – and chiefly to curtail Pauline's account of how their Kerry had stopped out all night, staying with her friend Lisa, as it happened, but not having the forethought to let anybody know, and Terry hadn't staggered in till next morning either; sometimes she wondered why she bothered – Clare said helpfully, 'What exactly are you looking for?'

'One of those cattery places. It's for Timmy.'

Clare found her the relevant entries. 'Are you going on holiday?' she asked.

'No,' Maisie said. 'I'm going into hospital.'

'Snap!' Pauline said, wringing out her wash-leather – the cleaning of windows rather than the recounting of domestic problems being the proper purpose of her visit. 'What you in for? Gynae, me. I go in a week Monday. I'm having kittens just thinking about it. I hate hospitals,' she said, as though, dyed-in-the-wool hypochondriacs excepted, there might be those who actually liked them.

'I've to have an operation,' Maisie replied, peering closely at advertisements for Feline Friends and The Cat Basket and Pussies Galore.

'Me too,' said Pauline. 'Don't worry, love, we'll have a laugh. Blimey!' she said, struck suddenly by an intriguing thought. 'It'll not be one of them mixed wards, will it? Oh I say, we *will* have some fun.'

Clare gently took the *Yellow Pages* from Maisie's near-sighted

211

gaze and copied out the addresses and telephone numbers of the catteries. 'Will you need a lift?' she asked. Timmy was enormous, requiring not so much a cat basket as a forklift truck.

'She's a right funnyossity, that one,' Pauline said, after Maisie had left, expressing gratitude and depositing, as Clare noticed later, a pound coin by the side of the phone. 'I know she's clocking on,' Pauline said, and then added with a most unexpected perspicacity, 'but she seems dead young. In a way.'

It was the kind of youthfulness occasionally met with in those who'd been institutionalized all their lives, as though the touch of ordinary experience with its burden of disillusionment had passed them by. And there was a wariness too, as though trusting too readily would be considered a very risky proposition.

And without trust, any relationship was bound to founder. Clare's natural inclination might be to procrastinate but she knew that she required, now, some token of his intention, of his good faith, otherwise the needle-jabs of doubt, Venice-bred, would intensify to the point where the most unselfconscious of their pleasures was tainted.

She hadn't seen him for a week. She tried not to imagine – but failed – a fervent reunion, gifts exchanged (what Venetian beads had he bought for his wife, while Duncan Fry was busy pouring poison into her ear?); she imagined excited children, friends invited round for a leisurely meal, while he refilled glasses and offered some amusing and expurgated account of his trip.

Which was the more agonizing, she wondered: the jealousy of the wife or that of the mistress? She supposed it depended upon the role you occupied at the time.

Gwyn vaulted the railings from Maisie's side and came up the path. She saw that he was carrying, over his arm and very carefully, what looked like a suit of clothes. As he drew nearer she saw that it *was* a suit, the sort that bullfighters wore: encrusted with sequins and beads. She couldn't look at it for very long without being dazzled.

212

'Great, isn't it?' he said, stroking its garish adornments quite tenderly.

'Who does it belong to?' she asked. It didn't look the sort of thing that would be worn by any of the raggle-taggle company of eco-warriors or itinerants who appeared to comprise his social circle these days.

'It's mine,' he said. 'Maisie made it for me.'

'Whatever for?'

'It's almost an exact copy of the costumes they wear for the finale of *You Gotta Dance*,' he said proudly.

'But why should you want one? Gwyn,' she said, 'this tap-dancing: it's all very well as a hobby, but I really do think that you ought to get it into perspective.'

As always, she could have bitten her tongue the minute she'd spoken. He walked past her and into the house, not even deigning to acknowledge her comment.

Relationships, she thought: my forte.

She gathered her courage the next morning and rang Theo at work. 'What a pleasant surprise,' he said suavely, as though nothing could have pleased him more than to receive a telephone call from her, however inopportune the circumstances.

She said, 'We need to talk.'

She knew that, generally, it was what women said and men shied away from hearing. It was for this reason that she had a couple of gins while she was waiting for him to arrive the following evening. A stutteringly repetitive jungle rhythm pounded above her head with a force and intensity that made the ceiling light tremble and rotate. It ceased abruptly and Gwyn came thudding down the stairs. He'd done something weird to his hair with gel and it stuck out from his skull in an arrangement of quiffs and spikes and elflocks; she was reminded of an engraving of a village idiot she'd once seen in some old-fashioned book.

'Can you lend us a tenner?' he said. 'Pay you back out of next week's allowance.'

'Whatever happened to your gardening money?' she asked.

'Oh if there's going to be an inquest, forget it.'

'Gwyn,' she said, 'I mean Joe,' as she furnished him with the requested amount of currency, 'you don't *have* to go out every time Theo's expected.'

'No?'

He pulled on a battered jacket that she'd never seen before. She wondered if he and his gang of tree-squatters had exchanged garments, much as footballers swapped shirts after the game was over. If so, he'd definitely got the worst of the bargain.

'No.'

Although tonight she was rather glad that he wouldn't be in.

Theo was late, extremely late. So she had another gin, larger than the first two and was, consequently, a trifle unsteady on her feet when she opened the door to him.

'Squiffy! Tut-tut,' he said, putting out a hand to steady her. Then he said, 'I'm sorry, I'd have been here an hour ago but I was delayed at the last minute.'

'Oh? By whom?' she said. 'Was it the chairman?'

'No,' he replied, taken aback.

'Or should I say your father-in-law?'

Relationships were not her forte and neither was sarcasm. Aware that her attempts usually misfired, she tended to avoid using it. Therefore, never previously having been at the receiving end of it from her direction, he seemed quite shocked.

'Why didn't you tell me?' she said.

He sat down, somewhat stiffly, on the edge of the sofa, began to pluck at the creases in his trousers. 'I didn't realize it was relevant,' he said.

'Why didn't you say,' she enquired of him heatedly, 'that afternoon when he arrived, why didn't you say "my father-in-law"? Obviously it was because you didn't want me to know. I had to find it out from Duncan Fry. Horrible man,' she added as a coda, forgetting, in her annoyance, that criticism of another person's friends is usually construed as being grievously insulting.

'What difference does it make?' he asked. And she was almost persuaded that his bewilderment was genuine. The difference that it made being exclusively pertinent to her own concerns (her own self-interest, if she was honest) meant that she could hardly make it explicit. She tried a more subtle approach, trusting that he would make the connection himself without the need for her to spell it out: 'He said you were very ambitious.'

But he only replied, calmly, 'I suppose that, compared with him, I am. Look, what is this all about?'

'I was subjected to an evening of snide comments,' she said. 'Either he's very jealous of you or else he's in love with you—'

At this, he began to laugh. 'Duncan?' he said. 'Oh, I'm not to his taste at all. Firstly, I'm not gay and secondly, he prefers them younger.'

'Anyway,' she said, rather sullenly, 'whatever. The fact remains that he was being perfectly foul.'

He shifted impatiently in his seat. 'Don't you think you're over-reacting a bit?' he said. 'Duncan has a big mouth and a tendency to mischievousness, but there's no real harm in him.'

They sat in silence for a while. She wondered how he could not be aware that Duncan Fry was an obnoxious creep. The only alternative explanation, that he'd reacted that way because he genuinely considered her behaviour to be morally indefensible, was too disquieting to contemplate.

Theo reached for his cigarette packet and then thought better of it. He said, 'Is that what you wanted to talk about?'

'Among other things.'

The gin had loosened her tongue in a way that made her seem aggressive, which was not how she had intended it to be at all. She poured him a drink, but allowed her own glass to remain empty and attempted to moderate her tone. 'It's just,' she said, 'that I don't know where I stand.'

He examined his gin and tonic closely as though it was a concept that lay entirely outside his experience before saying, 'You're wondering if I'm just stringing you along, is that it?'

'It has been known.'

He caught her eye. He said, 'Can't you trust your own judgement?'

'It's never been very reliable to date. I'm not much good at distinguishing between people, understanding their motives . . .'

'And mine may be bad, is that what you're saying?'

Suddenly he was no longer the man with whom she'd recognized instant affinity; he was the other one: the stranger whose inner life was closely guarded. After all, what did she know about him, even in terms of hard fact: a Home Counties upbringing, father – now deceased – a solicitor, one sister, education: minor public school followed by Cambridge, hobbies: music, travel, adultery . . . ?

Eventually he said, rather pompously, 'If bad is hurting people, intentionally, then I hope not.'

'But in a situation like this, someone is bound to get hurt, whether you mean to or not.'

He said, 'Are you trying to tell me something? Is this the big renunciation, or what?'

She shook her head vehemently.

'Well then,' he said, 'it's just as I said in the beginning: I wanted to be with you. So much. It's not a feeling that happens often . . .'

After a moment, and against her better judgement, she said, 'Your friend, Duncan Fry, told me about a previous relationship of yours, a "grand passion" was actually the phrase that he used.'

He looked, instantly, very angry indeed. He said, 'Duncan had no business to tell you that.'

'Why not?'

'Because it's private. And because it has no bearing whatsoever on anything.'

But she knew that that was a fallacy, that everything had a bearing on everything else.

She said, 'Is it too private for me to know about it?'

This time he succumbed to temptation, took a cigarette from his packet and lit it, coughed a bit and then said, 'Other people's old love affairs are about as interesting as other people's dreams.'

'Not to me,' she said. 'Not when the other person is you.'

He was weighing it up in his mind, regarding her narrowly. At length, he said, 'It was a long time ago. I fell in love with somebody. Well, it was a long time ago that I first fell in love with her. It was never going to work – I loved her more than she was ever going to be able to love me, but I couldn't read the signs, or wouldn't, even when she eventually married someone else. I couldn't make the break, not completely. I'd leave, but I'd keep coming back. It seemed as though she was offering me just enough hope to feed on – and I think, although she didn't love me in the same way, she wasn't averse to having an adoring admirer. She had only to raise her little finger . . .'

There was blood in his veins after all. Emotion, or perhaps it was embarrassment, had reddened his complexion. 'I was what you call a complete fool,' he said, 'for a very long time.'

'How long?'

'Years.'

He tapped the end of his cigarette rhythmically against the edge of the ashtray. It was the only sound in that quiet room. She was trying to imagine him, seemingly so dominant, so controlled, being strung along by this *belle dame sans merci*. 'What happened?' she asked. All that imaginary pack of previous girlfriends resolved themselves into one entity and that one more threatening than multitudes.

He said, in a very level tone, as though recounting something of minimal importance, 'She was killed in a car crash. Near Junction 11 on the M1. An articulated lorry jack-knifed, crossing the central reservation. She didn't stand a chance. She was dead by the time they cut her free.'

He paused for a moment and then swallowed his drink at one gulp. He said, 'She was driving to meet me. We'd booked in at a hotel. I was still trying to persuade her to leave her husband. Well, that was certainly the way it worked out. Two kids left motherless as well.'

Cruelly, as if on cue, a police car came hurtling down the road, its siren screaming.

'That's terrible,' she said. The words seemed scarcely adequate, but then the repertoire of acceptable consolatory phrases constituted a very slim dictionary.

She said carefully, 'If she hadn't – if that hadn't happened, would you still . . . ?'

'Who knows?'

She moistened her lips. 'What did she look like?' she asked. She was mad with curiosity but thought that her question might be considered to border on the unforgivably crass.

'Tall,' he said. 'Very striking. Dark eyes. Why?'

She thought of the Byzantine madonna in the church on Torcello. 'Beautiful?' she asked, unnecessarily.

'I thought so.'

'Not like me?'

'No,' he said, and then corrected himself immediately. 'I don't mean that you're not beautiful. I mean that we're talking two totally different physical types . . .'

Weren't people supposed to go for the same sort of partners, unconsciously replicating some early influential image? She said, 'What was her name?' Without a name, she had no real existence, this long-ago and best beloved.

'Elaine.'

Elaine, the lily maid of Astolat, who had loved Lancelot *with that love which was her doom.* But Elaine's love had not been returned, *that* was her doom. It would have been more appropriate if Theo's lover had been called Guinevere. She voiced her thought: 'It should have been Guinevere.'

He raised an eyebrow.

'She was Lancelot's forbidden passion. Elaine was the girl who loved him in vain.'

'And what happened to her?' he said. 'I only remember *The Lady of Shalott.*'

'*He loved her with all love except the love of man and woman when they love the best.*'

They'd done it for A Level.

218

'She pined away and died.'

They listened to the police siren's diminishing blare, neither of them knowing how to return to the normality, the safer territory, of ordinary conversation.

'Does Sarah know?' she asked suddenly.

He shook his head.

She ploughed on, throwing tact and caution to the winds: 'Was it after that you got married?'

'Yes.'

The cigarette had burned down, unnoticed; its heat singed his finger. He winced and extinguished it.

'And did you feel the same way about her?'

'No.'

'Well then why?'

He answered her impatiently as though she'd asked the dumbest question imaginable. 'Because I swore to myself that I'd never go through that again: waiting for phones to ring, last minute cancellations, never knowing if she meant what she said, never knowing from one minute to the next if and when we could be together: when the kids grew up, maybe? When *he* died? The years going by. Raging jealousy. Loneliness. Constant turmoil . . .'

She said, 'And then you met Sarah.'

'. . . and then I met Sarah and everything was easy and right and uncomplicated.'

'But you didn't love her?'

'Oh don't be childish,' he said fiercely. 'Of course I loved her—'

'But not like you loved Elaine?'

He stood up and began to move restlessly around the room, picking up an ornament here and there, inspecting it from every angle, replacing it gently. He said, 'I love my children. And my old mum too. The difference is in sort, not intensity.'

'And me?' she said, croakingly, going desperately for broke. 'How do you love me?'

He stared bleakly at his reflection in the mirror. He said, 'You

219

know how I feel about you. I feel about you the way I never intended to feel about anyone ever again. But, if you want the truth and nothing but, I also believe that passion is not sustainable. Maybe even with Elaine it had become something else – habit. I think if you're lucky it turns into something sufficiently ... *consoling* to make up for the loss.'

'Like marriage?' she said, just as bleakly.

'Like marriage,' he repeated.

And of course he already had one of those which was, presumably, perfectly satisfactory.

Chapter Nineteen

Joe's suit was the business, it was brilliant; it couldn't have been better if he'd ordered it specially from the theatrical costumier's. She was touched by the effusiveness of his gratitude, though she hadn't expected him to turn up the day after he'd collected it, flourishing a couple of theatre tickets.

'To say thanks. Wednesday night. So get your glad rags on.'

'But I go into hospital on Friday,' she said.

'All the more reason for a good night out then,' he replied.

'I don't think so . . .'

'It's *You Gotta Dance*,' he cried. 'Touring. Tickets are like gold dust. I only got these because my mate at the class, his mother works in the box-office.'

'Isn't there somebody else you would like to take?'

'Maisie,' he said sternly, 'when was the last time you had a night out? During the war? Now stop arguing. You'll enjoy it.'

He was more persistent than the Morecambe people. And he wasn't so far out in his estimate of the day when she'd acknowledged that she must exclude herself from what was generally known as 'normal' life.

She'd heard that today's youth were wont to experience terminal embarrassment if obliged to endure – and to be seen to be enduring – the company of anyone older, but if this was so, he concealed it most effectively, even waving to attract the attention of someone he knew on the other side of the road as they walked to the bus stop.

They'll assume I'm his grandmother, Maisie thought. Except that he squired her more solicitously, she suspected, than was the case, in these alienated days, with most youths and their elderly relatives.

First there was to be a meal. He'd warned her to leave room for it. He'd said, 'Don't go pigging out on Wednesday, will you? We'll eat beforehand.' And though her customary evening meal, consisting as it did of a cup of tea and a Marie biscuit, could scarcely be categorized as 'pigging out', she decided to forgo it anyway. It occurred to her, as she tried on her best frock which was alarmingly loose, that cups of tea and Marie biscuits had become the norm, formed the staples of her diet now that she was no longer obliged to cater for two.

She'd noticed the place in the shopping precinct that called itself a Pizza Hut but she'd never been inside, believing that, even if she'd wanted to, her age would have excluded her, almost as though the rules that barred the under-age drinker from public houses worked the other way round in these establishments: the pizza parlours and hamburger joints and fried chicken emporia.

'I'd have taken you somewhere posh,' he said, 'but the show starts at half-seven and most of them are hardly open by then. And besides,' he added with engaging frankness, as they sat down at a plastic-covered table, 'the tickets swallowed up most of my dosh.'

'Well,' she said, trying to make sense of a menu that listed totally unrecognizable fare, 'let this be my treat then.'

'Nah,' he said. 'No way. Fair's fair.' And proceeded to explain to her the difference between Margaritas and Pepperonis, to describe the taste of anchovies, mozzarella cheese and peppers and other such delicacies with which her palate was unacquainted. 'Have you never had a pizza before?' he asked, amazed.

The pictures; alcohol; a boyfriend: 'Have you never?' they'd said. Well she had, eventually. And now she was about to try a pizza.

She hadn't bargained on it being so overwhelmingly large, too large for her to make more than the smallest inroads upon its perimeter. 'Aren't you going to eat it all?' he asked after a while, as he saw her struggling. He'd polished his own off in the time it had taken her to pick up her knife and fork and make an incision.

She handed it over gladly. No doubt tap-dancing burned off a great many calories. And he seemed to be tap-dancing for all he was worth these days. What the Lizzie person had called his disreputable retinue had become conspicuous by its absence. Mickey too.

She asked about her. 'Such a pretty girl,' she said. Though she hoped, privately, that Mickey was a thing of the past. She was trouble, anyone could see that.

He made wings of his arms, lacing his fingers together behind his neck where tendrils of the hair that had been so brutally shorn were once again beginning to curl. 'She's gone roadie-ing for an all-girl group,' he said. 'Tutu, they're called. They're crap. We were getting fed up with each other anyway. I don't like bossy women.'

He had a very large ice cream and the remains of her much smaller one. He said that he was only just beginning to get his appetite back after the dire culinary regime that had prevailed at his school. 'A dietician would have condemned it outright,' he declared. 'And we were *paying* to be poisoned. It was just disgusting lumpy stodge, day in, day out: potatoes like bullets and rice like shot-blaster's grit and everlasting Spotted Dick. Except they had an Irish cook, so everyone called it Spotted Mick. That was about the level of the humour at that place. It was pathetic.'

'Never mind,' she said, 'perhaps your new school will be better.'

He wiped a moustache of cappuccino froth from his own fledgling version as she watched the blinds coming down over his eyes. 'Yeah,' he said. 'Right.'

'You'll need qualifications, won't you?' she said. As far as she could tell there was a qualification for just about everything these days, and not a job to be had unless you could produce one of them.

'You see,' she said, 'I had to leave school at fourteen. I never had the opportunity . . .'

'That must have been a real bummer,' he said. The tone of his voice and the expression on his face contradicted each other; no doubt he'd have been all in favour of the school-leaving age reverting to fourteen. 'We'd better move,' he said, before she could get into her preaching stride concerning the benefits of continuing education, 'or else we'll be late.'

Theatres no longer smelled of plush and dust and lingering whiffs of town gas; they smelled these days of synthetic carpets and air-freshener, but the sense of excited anticipation was the same, the conversation in the auditorium building up to a crescendo before suddenly diminishing at the raising of the safety curtain, the cessation of all the shifting and chewing and crackling and seat-banging as the lights were gradually dimmed.

She'd expected something along the lines of the Rogers and Astaire films that he watched so avidly, something glamorous, featuring tail-suits and satin frocks and sweet melodies, was amazed when a line of beefy young men attired in what appeared to be workmen's overalls and hob-nailed boots raced on to the stage and began to pound its surface as though desirous of reducing it to matchwood.

But once she'd got over the initial shock she was captivated. What was forfeited in elegance was more than made up for in terms of exuberance and gymnastic spectacle and sheer fizzing energy. She could feel the vibration from Joe's feet as he attempted to imitate their intricate routines. Her own feet were moving too, as were, probably, the feet of the entire audience, in involuntary syncopation.

'I was always stage-struck,' Nancy used to say. 'My ma used to clean down the Hackney Empire and take me with her ever since I was a baby. I never wanted to do anything else.'

And neither did Joe. It was obvious. His face shone, his fingers

224

beat a tattoo on the arms of his seat. He applauded until his palms stung.

Afterwards, when the cast, clad at last in their shimmering suits, could not be prevailed upon to return for yet one more encore, as he danced down the steps, he said, 'Let's go for a drink.'

And he'd pushed through the doors of the Frog and Firkin before she had a chance to protest, to say: 'Surely you're not old enough?' When she did, he looked at her blankly, as well he might, in view of the fact that the majority of the pub's clientèle appeared to be no older than himself.

'What are you having, Maisie?'

Her legs were wobbling a bit. She sat down before she lost her balance. She said, 'Do they have that Bailey's Irish Cream here? I like that.'

'*Do* you?' he said doubtfully. And then, 'Well I suppose somebody must,' and went to the bar. She watched him, wondering how it could be that she sensed between them, despite the sixty years of experience – or lack of it – that divided them, a compatibility that transcended the obvious impediments. Affinity, it was, she supposed.

He brought her back her drink, sniffing at it dubiously. 'It must be like drinking custard,' he said. He drank direct from a bottle of beer which had a slice of lime stuck into its neck, crossed his legs extravagantly, the heel of his boot resting on his knee. She saw that he'd worn what were presumably his best, unripped jeans in honour of the occasion.

He looked at her quickly and away again. 'Can you keep a secret?' he said.

She nodded. Oh, indubitably. If she had any talent at all it was for keeping a secret.

'They're auditioning next week at the Empire for *Feets Don't Fail Me*. I'm giving it a go. I think I'm good enough now. It's a musical,' he explained. 'They're opening here. With luck it'll transfer.'

'To the West End?'

'Uh-huh.'

How, she wondered, would that tie in with new schools and qualifications? He lit a cigarette, drawing its essence deep into his lungs. 'Well you'll not last very long behind the footlights if you carry on with *that*,' she said crossly. It was the only form of rebuke available to her; to express disapproval would be over-stepping the mark. Besides which, it would also be hypocritical because there was a part of her that applauded his nerve; you always admired in others what was signally lacking in yourself.

She hadn't been into hospital since she lost the child. And since Timmy's arrival, she hadn't been away from the house. He knew that there was dirty work afoot. She tried to entice him out from under the sink, but he remained obdurate to all her bribery. Under the sink there was an ancient tin of rat poison, souvenir of the pre-Timmy days when they'd had an invasion of mice. Looking at it, she was reminded of Mother saying that she'd prefer to take poison rather than go back home where her shame was common knowledge.

'Come on, Timmy,' called Maisie, advancing with a saucerful of milk. Timmy scorned it. He'd probably do his business in there as a gesture of protest. She picked up the rat poison tin and took it outside and put it into the bin. 'Life is sweet,' Mrs Mendelssohn used to say, pressing upon her a morsel of cake, heavy with dates and honey. 'Come! Eat!' And the sweetness in her mouth had made whatever it was that was hurting hurt less. 'Life is sweet,' Mrs M would say. 'And God is good.'

In the end, Joe fished the cat out, his arms being longer than hers. They thought he'd struggle and claw but he came quietly, merely staring at Joe in the way that a condemned man would regard his executioner. When placed on the floor he began to butt the boy's ankles with his head. He did this with such vigour that eventually, and inadvertently, he performed a complete somersault and righted himself, blinking.

'Fang the acrobat,' Joe said, caressing him roughly. 'He could be in Billy Smart's Circus. Or maybe Billy-Not-So-Smart's Circus.'

'Joe,' Maisie said, 'if anything should happen to me, will you look after him?'

'Oh come on!' he said. 'Morbid city!'

'But will you?'

'Yeah, OK.'

'Promise me?'

'Promise! Cross my heart and hope to die.'

But that was a phrase she found exceedingly sinister, ever since Nancy.

There were other provisions that ought to be made. After Clare had driven her to the cattery and the most poignant of farewells had taken place, Maisie asked if she might be dropped off in the town centre. She had another errand to perform, involving Stoneman, Stoneman and Finch, Solicitors and Commissioners for Oaths.

May 9th, 1945.

Everyone was going wild last night. Rita and I went into town to join in the fun. A couple of aircraftsmen, 'Erks', my Bob used to call them, attached us to the end of the line of a conga that wound itself all the way from the war memorial, across the road, round the corner of the Home and Colonial and back again. Some girls had joined a group of sailors who were splashing about in the fountains and some others, wearing their boys' army caps, had linked arms and were doing The Lambeth Walk, *singing the words at the top of their voices, so loud that you could hear them above the rest of the hubbub.*

Rita pointed out a soldier who was cheering and throwing his hat into the air. 'He's nice,' she said. He saw that she was looking at him and shouted across, 'Hello, girls! Are you going to come and help me celebrate?' He had the most lovely cheery smile. Rita nudged me. She said, 'It's you he's got his eye on. Why don't you?'

I said, 'I don't think so.' I always say that when she tries to match me up with some fellow. And she always says, 'You can't pine for ever, sweetheart. He wouldn't have wanted you to.'

When I got home, Mother was on her knees in front of the kitchen cupboards. 'I'm tidying them out,' she said, looking up. 'What's all that noise in aid of?' she said. 'Is it a procession?' I nodded. I'd told her three times already that the war was over, but the first time she just stared right through me and then she started to cry and begged me not to say that word: 'Don't say that word, Maisie, not ever again.'

Later on, when I went to get plates for our supper, I found that the cupboard was full of underwear. She'd put all the plates and the cutlery in the dressing-table drawer.

There's a new doctor's surgery opened up in Talbot Road. I noticed the shingle on the gate post. He's private, I believe, so it wouldn't be like having to tell Dr Morrison. I've walked past the house a few times but the truth is that, although I want to find out, I'm too scared.

Stoneman, Stoneman and Finch was the firm that had supervised the purchasing of their house after the war when her grand-parents' estate had finally been settled. She remembered Rita coming with her to view the property, Rita picking her way across the litter-strewn floors in her smart new duster coat and her wedge-heeled shoes. Her Geoff had come through Burma rela-tively unscathed and now they were set on emigrating to Canada.

'You'll have to come over and visit us,' Rita had said, gingerly fingering a pair of grimy nets which began to disintegrate at her touch.

Maisie had nodded and smiled.

'We'll keep in touch, won't we, kid?'

And they did. Letters at first, and cards, and then just cards at Christmas. They still arrived, the number of signatories to the greeting increasing as time went on: *Rita and Geoff, Rita and Geoff and Colin, Rita and Geoff and Colin and Susan and Graham* . . .

'This is going to be a job and a half,' Rita had said, back then, standing amid a shaft of sunlight that striped the floor which was covered in innumerable decaying layers of oilcloth. 'You'll have to get yourself a big strong fellow to give you a hand.' Then, eyes narrowed above a plume of exhaled smoke from her Craven A, she'd said, 'Don't you miss it? Sex, I mean?'

It was not so much sex that Maisie missed, as sex-with-Bob. And anyway sex with anyone else was not now a feasible proposition.

'I take cold showers,' she said jokingly to Rita. Although, considering the state of the geyser in the bathroom, this might be a distinct possibility.

Now, forty-five years on, she concluded her business with the younger Mr Stoneman, who had not been born when she first entered into conflict with the geyser, and went to Marks and Spencer where she bought herself two nightdresses suitable for public scrutiny.

She hadn't bargained on them having to be appropriate for male scrutiny. She'd read about mixed wards, naturally, remembered Pauline's remark on the subject, but was still quite unprepared to find herself in the next bed to a wild-eyed, muttering creature who, though whittled by age to the bone, was undoubtedly of the masculine gender. A nurse bent over him. 'Got a nice neighbour now, Harry.'

Harry – Mr Purves – contented himself with muttering and banging his locker during the daylight hours, but in the middle of Maisie's first night he clambered out of his bed and trudged, unseen by the staff, to the toilet, his pyjama bottoms collapsing around his ankles with every step. Upon his return (and having failed to pull them up again), he attempted to climb into the bed of the woman opposite.

The night staff were distinctly unamused. One of them said crossly, 'You're nothing but an old nuisance, Harry. You're going to have to have your sides up now.' His response was to shake them frantically for the rest of the night, thereby abolishing even the faintest hope of sleep.

The nurse explained to a new colleague, 'Everything's in chaos with the reorganization. We've got all sorts in here. *She*,' and she indicated Maisie's bed, 'ought to be in L7 but they've only got six beds left. God knows what'll happen on Monday when they start switching them over from Gynae to the Patterson Wing.'

The interminable dragging of the hours as she lay in her unyielding hospital bed lent themselves to nothing but introspection; she couldn't concentrate on her library book and the occupants of the other hard beds, while not obviously deranged, looked too ill to be capable of conversation. Mr Purves had been removed and a woman was now in his place, a large fat inert woman, festooned all about with tubes and drips and catheters, whose laboured breathing would, every so often, momentarily cease, causing Maisie great anguish, not knowing, each time, whether or not she should call for assistance.

The clock on the wall was afflicted with a similar malfunction: its hands jerked irregularly around the dial, only occasionally providing one with an approximation to the correct time. More reliable were the trolleys bearing pills and food: 'Special Diet. High Protein.' 'You've been neglecting yourself,' the staff nurse said. And Maisie was obliged to concede that a regimen of tea and Marie biscuits was perhaps something less than nutritionally sound.

'I don't want to see a scrap of food left on that plate,' the staff nurse said, 'when I come back to give you your iron injection.'

Or your suppository, or your sleeping tablet. She almost looked forward to them; they provided a break in the monotony.

She didn't look forward to visiting time, not daring to hope that there'd be anybody making for *her* bed. Although Clare had said, as she drove to the cattery, 'I'll pop in and see you, see if there's anything you need.'

She looked at other people's visitors, all those nexts of kin. The nurse who'd filled in the form when she was admitted had asked her who hers was and she'd had to tell her that there wasn't anyone.

'Nobody?' the nurse had said sceptically.

'Not that I know of.'

And then it dawned on her that Miss Miles probably fulfilled that function. She provided the nurse with her name, reflecting wryly that it had come to something when you had to admit that your next of kin was the state.

'Oh God,' the nurses said, as the next admission was made, 'not another one from the Gerry ward!'

This gentleman was less obviously decrepit than the unlamented Mr Purves but even more of a trial to them. Throughout the weekend he persisted in emptying his bowels without feeling the need to vacate his bed. She heard the staff chastising him: 'Call for the commode, George. You're doing this quite deliberately.' Maisie's bed being nearest to the nursing station, she overheard their private comments: 'Dirty old bastard. If that isn't an argument for euthanasia, I don't know what is.'

On Monday morning, having voided the contents of his lower intestine into his pyjamas once already, he delivered himself of a wavering cry: 'Nurse, I need the commode!' Running feet propelled the contraption towards him, ran back to acquire the compressed paper insert, but before the twain could be introduced to one another he had leapt from his bed, squatted upon a seat which opened on to nothing but the floor, and relieved himself, mightily.

The foul deed having been discovered and the chair wheeled away to the accompaniment of vociferous expressions of disgust, a symmetrical semi-circular configuration of torpedo-shaped turds was revealed, all pointing very precisely up to the ceiling, a kind of ordurous Stonehenge in miniature.

Consequently Maisie was relieved when, some time later, she discovered that she was to be transferred to another ward. The entire hospital appeared to be in transit. Patient-laden trolleys hurtled through the corridors. 'It's like the Wacky Races,' the nurse said, as they almost collided with another one. Maisie enquired tentatively why they simply weren't following the sign which pointed to the Cardio-Thoracic Unit instead of heading off in another direction entirely. 'Cardio-Thoracic?' the nurse said. 'It's out of commission. One half's being closed down and the other's got a bug.'

Eventually they came to a halt outside Ward M3. The escorting nurse met another at the door. 'One for Mr Haydn-Jones,' the first one said. 'Just *don't* tell me you've let the bed.'

'No,' said the other nurse. 'Still room for one more on top. Though I've almost lost track of what we *have* got in here. Did you know the Patterson Wing's not ready? There's Gynaes scattered all over the place.'

At least it appeared to be a single-sex ward. Presuming that she would be safe from bed-hopping predators, Maisie opened her book, a Barbara Pym, relying upon it to transport her into a cosily ordered world of villages and vicarages, but she hadn't got past the second paragraph before there was the sound of badly fitting mules flip-flopping across the floor and this sound seemed vaguely familiar; she'd raised her head even before their owner said, 'Well, fancy meeting you. Where are you meant to be? I've been shunted round three wards already. And I'm sure I shouldn't be in a geriatric ward. No offence.'

Pauline – for it was she – sat down on Maisie's bed. 'Just been for a smoke,' she said, unnecessarily, as the acrid smell clung to her frayed towelling robe and the Snoopy nightshirt beneath it. 'They've just told me they're not doing the op now till tomorrow and I won't have enough cigs to keep me going till then. I'll go spare. You wouldn't happen . . . ? No! I'll have to wait for our Carol coming in. *If* she comes in. No use relying on Terry. He hates hospitals, same as me. It gives you the creeps,' she said, looking around her at their fellow inmates, all of whom appeared to be under the influence of sedative drugs. 'The Dead Zone. At least Gynae might have been a bit more lively. It's not as if you're ill as such, just more like waiting to have bits you don't need any longer taken away.'

The clock struck three. It was, in fact, a quarter past one.

'Bloody hell!' Pauline exclaimed, looking out of the window opposite, 'I can see the mortuary from here. I hope you're not superstitious.' She took a folded copy of the *Daily Star* from her pocket and unfolded it. 'What's your sign?' she said.

'My sign?'

'Yeah. Your star sign.'

'I don't know.'

'You don't know?' Pauline said incredulously. 'Well when were you born?'

'January 8th.'

'You're Capricorn,' Pauline said, 'like our Michelle. "Fight the urge,"' she read, '"to act impulsively. Your patience will soon be rewarded." Mine says: "Make sure your affairs are in order as others may not be reliable." That sounds good, doesn't it, just before they're going to cut you open?'

She flicked back the top of her cigarette packet, surveyed its contents and closed it again with a sigh. 'Come with us to the day-room?' she said. 'There's a big telly in there. We can watch *Neighbours*.'

But when they got there they found that the men had commandeered it for the purpose of viewing a golf tournament and showed no inclination whatsoever to give way to any chivalrous impulses.

'Bloody men,' Pauline said, without waiting until they were out of earshot. 'It's down to men that I'm here now.'

Me too, Maisie thought, me too.

Clare came that evening. She brought flowers and a couple of paperbacks. One of them was *Rebecca*. 'I know you like her books,' she said shyly.

Maisie had read *Rebecca* several times already but was extremely touched, having supposed that the offer to visit had been merely lip-service. Clare enquired as to her comfort, her health and the projected date of her appointment with the surgeon's knife; Maisie enquired about Joe. 'He's gone off clubbing, I think,' Clare said.

Maisie, who thought she'd said 'cubbing', unsurprisingly looked mystified.

'You know, *clubs*?' Clare said. 'They dance themselves to a standstill and blow whistles and get perforated eardrums from the noise and have epileptic fits induced by the flashing lights – and that's the least of it. You hear such dreadful things,' Clare said, 'but short of locking them up until they're thirty . . .'

And then the conversation faltered until Clare, glancing across the room, said, 'I say, is that Pauline?'

Her bed was surrounded but her voice was unmistakable.

There were three girls and a small boy displaying all the ominous signs of boredom that is about to develop into disruption and a woman who bore a faint resemblance to Pauline. 'Our Carol?' whispered Clare. Maisie nodded.

This was Our Carol's second visit of the day. She had arrived during the afternoon with just two girls and a boy in tow. Maisie, ever polite, had tried to concentrate on her book in order to block out their conversation but both Pauline and her sister were strangers to the notion of keeping their voices down. She heard Carol saying indignantly, 'Don't blame me. It's not my fault she's out of control.'

Kerry, it transpired, had stayed out again all night. Pauline was extremely agitated, Carol more sanguine. She said, 'She's probably staying with that mate of hers. She'll turn up.'

Afterwards, and fortified with several of the cigarettes from the packet that Carol – who'd got her priorities right in one area at least – had brought in, Pauline came over to Maisie's bed and expressed her concern. You never knew these days. Kerry was still only a kid really and terrible things happened to kids: they were abducted, murdered; they locked themselves inadvertently into abandoned fridges or fell down the shafts of disused mineworkings.

And there were even direr possibilities: perhaps she had taken to sniffing with the glueys who hung round the Spring Park estate; perhaps she had choked to death and would be found on some scrubby piece of waste land, sprawled among the used johnnies and the dog-shit and the empty cans of Evostik. Or perhaps she'd boarded the train for Euston, propelled by one of those silly adolescent whims and would be met by a man with a kind face who'd offer her a bed for the night and in no time at all she'd be part of the meat rack at King's Cross. Or – worst of all – the Herbert Morrison Heights pushers had got to her: she was shooting up in an empty flat, dirty needles and a tarnished spoon and a guttering candle on the bare floorboards, contaminated junk and deadly viruses coursing through her veins.

Eventually she ran out of tabloid-fuelled horror scenarios and said, 'Trouble is, she won't do as Terry says.'

But when Carol returned later she had the miscreant practically by the ear. 'In!' she said, and 'Sit!' as though attempting to train an undisciplined dog.

Kerry sidled in, shuffled, came reluctantly, crabwise, but eventually she sat. 'So where were you,' Pauline said, 'last night?'

And then Clare had come in and Maisie had lost track of what was going on until shouting from the vicinity of the opposite bed obliged them to pay attention.

Kerry, it seemed, had been discovered back at her own house and Pauline had wanted to know the reason why. The girl had said blankly, 'I just got bored of their Dean winding me up.'

'Liar!'

'It's not a lie. He's a pig.'

'Don't you be calling my Dean a pig, you little swine,' Carol said.

'Well why did you go without telling your auntie Carol?'

'Because she wants a bloody good hiding,' said Carol. 'And if she were mine, she'd get it.'

'I'm not asking you.'

Their conversation was increasing in volume, its tone becoming more strident. Other patients and their visitors stopped talking in order to eavesdrop more thoroughly. Pauline called across to them, generally, 'What's your problem?'

'Oh dear,' Clare said.

'Well? I'm still waiting for an answer. What were you doing last night?'

Kerry said sullenly, 'That's for me to know and you to find out.' Whereupon Pauline reached over and smacked her across the face.

Shock rendered the girl speechless for a moment and then she began to yell. Pauline had to shout to make herself heard: 'You're nothing but trouble: bunking off school, stopping out all night, giving cheek. No wonder Terry loses his temper with you.'

Kerry stopped crying quite abruptly. 'You're just jealous,' she said, 'because he likes me better than he likes you.'

And her pert little fourteen-year-old face could not have conveyed a more knowing disdain if she'd had a lifetime of experience.

Chapter Twenty

'How,' said Lizzie, 'do these women end up with these awful men?'

She could have been talking about Clare, or even herself, but actually she meant Pauline.

'It's not the awful man,' Clare said. 'It's the awful daughter.'

'Undoubtedly *fathered* by some awful man,' said Lizzie. 'Poor cow. Pauline, I mean. I suppose I ought to go and see her.'

'You just want to be in on any further dramatic developments,' Clare said sourly.

'What's the matter?' Lizzie asked. 'Still got the post-Venetian blues?'

When told of Duncan Fry, Lizzie had not been similarly horrified. She'd said, 'Every man has at least one awful friend who hates the idea of any female muscling in on their territory. Wives are OK, they can be kind of neutralized and pushed into the background. Honestly, Clare, you come across sometimes as if you'd spent most of your life in a cave on the Albanian coast.'

Clare said portentously, 'By their friends shall ye know them.' And Lizzie, as expected, said, 'Bollocks.'

And then she said, 'Oh just *look* at *that*,' and exhibited signs of orgasm as she surveyed a picture of some tropical island: impossibly blue sky, green sea, yellow beach.

They were sitting in Lizzie's flat, surrounded by holiday brochures. And perhaps this contributed to Clare's acerbity. 'I don't know what you've got to whinge about,' Lizzie said, 'you've only just got back from glamorous nights in a gondola, for God's sake.'

Lizzie and her husband were planning a late summer holiday. Exotic locations, imaginatively photographed, stared up at them from every surface. Theo too, and his wife and children, had a holiday booked. In the Seychelles.

'Perhaps we ought really to make do with a weekend in a caravan on the coast,' Lizzie said, flicking through the delights waiting to be discovered on the Costa Smeralda. 'There are whispers at Michael's firm about a take-over, and we all know what that could mean.'

The motives of Michael Twist in his desire to effect reconciliation suddenly became abundantly clear.

But first, before any such holiday could be embarked upon, there was their joint birthday party to be organized. Lizzie had decided, on surveying Clare's by now attractive garden, that they should hold it there, and now they were engaged in running through a list of their friends and acquaintances, exclusive and mutual, in order to compose a guest list. By far the larger number of names was contributed by Lizzie. Whenever Clare put forward a tentative suggestion, Lizzie would say, 'Oh God, not those two: Mr and Mrs Perfect,' or, sarcastically, 'Oh yes, why not? The most fascinating couple on the face of the earth,' or, 'Come on! This is meant to be a party, not a wake.'

Eventually Clare said, 'Oh please yourself,' and flounced off to the bus stop, her car having broken down and been towed into the garage where, no doubt, they would discover that it required some ruinously expensive repair.

There were other people at the bus stop, waiting meekly for what seemed an exceptionally long time for the bus to arrive. She remembered how Huw had rescued her from bus stops, remembered how, huddled in her parka, she'd look up to see his purple and white Triumph Herald slowing down. It was quite customary in those days for benevolent motorists to offer lifts to students; the difference was that Huw had stopped specifically for her.

'He's fifteen years older than you and he's still married,' Lizzie had said, 'and there's something indescribably yucky about student–lecturer liaisons.'

'If it's indescribable then don't try to describe it,' said Clare who had been a rather pedantic young girl.

Student–lecturer liaisons might or might not have been yucky; they were certainly frowned upon by the authorities. They'd had to observe a certain decorum until she'd graduated and then, a week after his divorce came through, he'd married her.

She'd been flattered, and charmed, and thought that he, a man thus far apparently incapable of sustaining a long-term relationship, had at last found his salvation. But she'd come on the scene too late. He was, by then, inveterate, incapable of preventing himself from falling into customary response mode to the stimulus of the next pretty face.

And now Huw was dead and the First Man to Really Matter since he'd left her seemed to be sounding the death knell to any hopes she might have had of occupying more than a part-time and/or impermanent role.

As she walked down the road towards her house, she heard noises issuing from the one next door. For a second she froze. But the noises combined together to form a recognizable tune; surely, she thought, burglars didn't break, enter and play music? Though one never knew, these days. Perhaps Maisie had squatters. Arming herself with the poker, and amazed at her courage, she crept round the back of the house, bending double beneath the windows that overlooked the garden, straightening up cautiously to look in at the kitchen where she saw Gwyn, wearing his silly suit, tap-dancing.

She rapped on the glass but he had his back to her and the tape-deck was going full-blast. She watched him for a while. He was really rather good. And he could have been less wholesomely occupied.

239

'What are you doing in here?' she asked, when he eventually noticed her and opened the door. 'And what have you got on your hair? You look like a South American gigolo.'

He gazed at her for a moment and then he said, 'Is there any way I could look that just might happen to suit you? I wish you'd stop being such a pain.'

He had never before been quite so overtly rude. She said, 'So these are the sort of manners that your fancy education has produced?'

'I don't know about that. It produces a bunch of snarling fascists though, and snobs, and prize-winning plonkers. Which is why I wanted to leave.'

And then, relenting, he said, 'Maisie lent me her keys so I could get some practice in.'

'But practice for *what*?' she said.

He raised a hand and ruffled his patent-leather hair. 'I was going to keep it as a surprise . . .'

The tape continued to blare out a tune in ragtime as he told her about the audition. Suddenly she felt that she couldn't embark upon the usual debate that drained her of so much emotional energy and never resulted in any sort of satisfactory resolution. She was, at that precise moment, sick of trying to be a good mother. You clutched them to your breast and watched over their childhood illnesses, you warmed the scarves that you wound round their necks and had their feet measured by trained shoe-shop assistants; you encouraged their interests, bought them tele-scopes and chemistry sets and guitars; you ferried them to scout huts and stood cheering on touch-lines in sub-zero temperatures; you arranged, at the appropriate time, for music lessons and swimming lessons and braces on their teeth; you emptied the coffers so that they would receive an education superior to that provided by the run-down state equivalent; you tried your best to protect, nurture and guide, and the upshot was that they did exactly as they pleased and for all the influence you wielded you might as well have put them into Barnardo's at birth.

She left the inevitable bloody conflict for another day and made her way home. He needed a man's hand. But whose? She had no father, brother, brother-in-law or grandparent and she couldn't manufacture some authoritative male figure whose opinion would carry weight. It hardly seemed feasible to imagine Theo fulfilling that role.

She'd brought work home and began to psych herself up to get on with it. Flicking back, for reference, through an earlier issue of the *Journal*, her eye alighted upon a diary entry. Normally she never bothered to read the diary of events, which was compiled by a girl who was a martyr both to hay fever and caddish men and who, if she cornered you in the loo, insisted on giving you a blow-by-blow account of her various doomed love affairs, to the accompaniment of a barrage of sneezing.

A name jumped off the page: it was Kriess-Rettingen and they were launching a new form of hormone replacement therapy. And the time and date of this launch was the following morning.

Theo hadn't mentioned it. Mind you, Theo seldom spoke of the products which he helped to sell. Perhaps employees of pharmaceutical companies took an oath of allegiance, a vow of silence, the record of these concerns being hardly spotless, what with faulty research procedures, premature distribution, flash lawyers employed in hand-washing exercises, and disempowered members of Joe Public left with crippling neuroses or truncated limbs.

She supposed that if there had been an invitation then her boss had snapped it up. When she got to work the next day his secretary was waiting for her with the news that he'd rung in sick. 'He's come down with this virus,' the girl said. 'Actually it was his wife who rang. She said he daren't leave the bathroom . . .'

It must be serious, Clare thought, if he was willing to forgo the chance to get his snout in the trough; the hospitality provided by Kriess-Rettingen was usually lavish.

'She told me he said to tell you that you'll have to go in his place.'

She found the idea of encountering Theo in his official capacity without any prior briefing a little unnerving. And besides she looked a fright.

'I'll have to go home first and change.'

She took a taxi. They hadn't gone more than a few hundred yards when they ran straight into a snarl-up of gigantic proportions. 'Lorry,' said the cab driver, 'shed its load somewhere up ahead.' After ten minutes he told her she might be better off walking. She took his advice, but an Olympic sprinter couldn't have covered the distance there and back in time. Grimly, she retraced her steps, turned in the direction of the hotel.

The International was the epitome of plushness. A top-hatted commissionaire and several liveried porters sprang towards her as she mounted the steps, directed her to the Jubilee Suite which was occupied by a crush of people making a great deal of noise. She turned towards the cloakroom. Late already, she might as well go the whole hog. In fact, she thought as she entered its marbled opulence, why didn't she just turn tail and go home? Who'd know?

Her boss would know, would make it his business to know, would nag her about it until the end of time. If she saw Duncan Fry, though, she'd go home, whatever the consequences.

That decided, she approached the mirrored wash-basins in the hope of making herself more presentable. A woman came out of one of the cubicles, a good-looking woman, impeccably groomed, wearing a most covetable blue silk dress. Lizzie, looking at her sideways, would have said, 'She didn't get that off the market.'

The woman smiled pleasantly, washed her hands at an adjoining basin, combed her stylishly coiffured golden hair. The comparison was odious. Clare rammed her comb back into her bag and hauled up the zip on her skirt so violently that it broke.

'Shit!' she said, not entirely involuntarily. The flawlessness of the woman's appearance impelled her to some kind of demonstration of ugliness, if only to relieve her feelings.

But the woman made a sympathetic face and said, as Clare

struggled to reconnect the zip's teeth, 'Perhaps if I were to hold it at the bottom while you pull?'

She seemed to be a nice woman, despite being so good-looking and well-dressed and physically superior in every way. Clare accepted her offer and the woman held the bottom of the placket taut while she endeavoured to align the constituent parts of the zip. And then they changed over. But still it wouldn't budge.

'There's usually an attendant in here,' the woman said. (And of course she'd be a habituée.) 'She does minor running repairs. She'd have been able to sew it together for you, at least.'

She began to delve into her handbag which bore the distinctive Hermès insignia. Clare's, the one that she used for work, over-stuffed and cracking at the seams, stood next to it on the shelf, abjectly, like the poor relation that it was.

'I've a safety-pin,' the woman said. 'If that would help?'

Clare held her waistband together while the woman pinned. 'It'll do until you get home,' she said, and smiled. They both did. And then the woman snapped her bag shut and left and Clare reflected that life was full of such collisions: you met someone in a cloakroom, or a waiting-room, or a railway carriage, and you warmed to them during the course of this brief impingement, and then a name would be called, a destination reached, and that would be the end of that.

She went into the conference suite, returned the greetings of two or three acquaintances and then made her way to an incon-spicuous end-of-row seat in the lecture room. Gradually everyone streamed in. They always had the spouting before the refresh-ments, otherwise people just stuffed their faces and disappeared. She couldn't see Theo. Nor, thankfully, was there any sign of Duncan Fry.

Several expensively suited men got up to speak. Statistics flowed from them in a numerical cascade, case histories were recited. Women privileged to swallow these neat pink tablets each embed-ded in its individual bubble-wrap had unanimously reported not only an end to the drearier symptoms attendant upon the menopause, but also an upsurge in libido, energy, enthusiasm and general joie de vivre. This, quite apart from the fact that they would not, in the fullness of time, be cluttering up hospital beds with their fractured hips and their myocardial infarctions.

Clare yawned. Undoubtedly, even as she absorbed this information, someone somewhere else would be intent on proving otherwise: an increased incidence of breast cancer and stroke, a catalogue of unacceptable side-effects.

The presentation concluded, there was a rather unedifying dash to the buffet. Medical journalists, representatives of health organizations and other assorted hangers-on demolished food and quaffed drink as if the words cholesterol and cirrhosis were not part of their vocabulary. A woman Clare knew, a free-lancer who contributed to various medical journals, hailed her. She was an old hand at the business. She raised her glass and said, 'Last year when they brought out that new one-dose thrush pessary we had a rather better vintage, I believe. And I don't know when this smoked salmon last saw Scotland. I suppose they must be drawing in their horns after that tranquillizer pay-out, such as it was . . .'

And then she heard a familiar voice and she turned round, feeling her heart jump, as it always did, and he was standing there, a little way off, beside the buffet table, filling a plate with sandwiches and vol-au-vents, and the woman at his side – a slim, good-looking woman with shining blonde hair – was laughing and protesting: 'Steady on, darling! What do you think I am: a Strasbourg goose?'

His eyes met hers above the woman's head as she bent to pick up her glass. Had they been cartoon characters then the balloons issuing from their mouths would have been crammed with asterisks and exclamation marks. She tried to melt into the wallpaper. But the blonde-haired woman turned back from the table with her plate and her glass and she saw Clare and said, 'Hello again,' and then, more quietly, privately, 'Is everything still holding together?'

Not quietly enough. Theo caught the remark. He looked from

one to the other of them. She wondered if, like her, his knees had begun to wobble, if the sweat was trickling freely from under his armpits.

'Just what you would call girl talk,' the woman said.

'Have you two met?'

'Only informally,' she said. 'In the ladies' cloakroom, actually.'

And he said, without betraying the slightest hint of discomposure, 'Mrs Williams and I are old friends. Clare,' he said, 'this is my wife, Sarah.'

She wanted to faint. She said desperately, as she felt the woman's cool hand within her own perspiring palm, 'It's good to meet you but I'm running late. I have to go.' The words ran into each other, formed one long breathless sentence. She was conscious of his steady gaze, of a difference so profound in the way that they were handling this most unwelcome of encounters, that they might not have shared membership of the same species. Cold-blooded, was the description that sprang to mind. She walked tremblingly towards the door, began to run as soon as she was outside, kept on running, down the stairs, through the swing doors, past the hat-touching commissionaire; it wasn't until she'd reached the bus stop that she realized she was still clutching her glass. The queue stared at her curiously. Defiantly, she raised it to her lips and drained the drop that remained. The journalist had been right: it wasn't a patch on last year's.

He turned up, unbidden, that evening. He had scarcely crossed the threshold when she launched into him: 'Why on earth didn't you tell me about the function?' and he replied, 'Well I didn't expect you to be there . . .'

'But surely you must have realized there was the possibility . . .'

'If you must know, I didn't expect Sarah to come either. She doesn't usually.'

'I had to stand there with her safety-pin in my skirt . . .'

She could have added: and her looking a million dollars and me like someone let out into the community.

245

She put the kettle on, spooned instant coffee into mugs. Normally, for him, she took pains: Blue Mountain and the percolator.

'She's nice.'

'You sound surprised,' he said. 'What did you expect: two heads?'

'What I didn't expect was for you to come over so cool. People win awards for acting that's far less convincing than that.'

'What did you want me to do: ignore you totally?'

'How do you think I *felt*?'

'The same as I did, I expect. Awkward. Embarrassed . . .'

She stirred her coffee with noisy vigour and flung the spoon into the sink. 'Then you concealed it remarkably well,' she said. 'Just as though you were perfectly *au fait* with situations like that.'

Just as though it had happened before was what she thought but didn't say.

Gwyn came into the kitchen, saw him, said, 'Oh!' and went out again.

She wished he wouldn't always make it so obvious that Theo's company was undesired. Granted there was bound to be some awkwardness between one who had been thrown up over and one who'd done the throwing up, but surely some sort of civilized interaction was possible.

'I come,' Theo said, 'I go.'

'He's not exactly in favour at the moment,' she said, by way of excuse.

She knew that instead of dwelling on that morning's contretemps, she ought to be addressing the far more important issue of Gwyn's future, that she ought to be seeking Theo's advice: My son, who has probably as many GCSEs at high grades as anybody else in the land, has decided to throw away the possibility of an education for the sake of a chance of what might be no more than a week or two's engagement in the musical theatre. What do you suggest I should do?

But she couldn't get Sarah's face out of her head. She said, 'She seemed so nice, nice-looking, friendly. I felt *terrible*.'

'And if she'd been a dog and unfriendly, you wouldn't?'

'No, not to the same extent.'

'Curious logic,' he said.

'And is she as nice as she looks?'

'Yes,' he said, 'she is.'

'Then why?'

He said, 'You don't choose who you fall in love with.'

'Perhaps not, but you can choose to *continue* falling in love.'

He said, 'You're the literary one – what's that quote – something about nothing either good or bad, but thinking makes it so?'

She thought it was *Hamlet*; she'd have to ask Lizzie. But she didn't need to consult her on the subject of moral absolutes.

'*Having* fallen in love,' he was saying, 'as I see it, we can only try to think in terms of . . . damage limitation . . . try to work something out that causes the least possible hurt to everyone involved.'

Or, she thought, we could go along with Duncan Fry's implication, and do the right thing.

Chapter Twenty-One

They took Pauline down for her operation early on Tuesday morning. She was silent, for once; terror, presumably, having paralysed her vocal cords. Maisie gave her an encouraging wave. She was being chivvied by a student nurse into eating her lunch. She'd just finished chewing valiantly on the last piece of gristle when she looked up to see, as if in reward for her effort, Joe pushing through the swing doors and walking down the ward, glancing with alarmed lack of recognition to the right and the left as though, since he saw her last, she might have undergone wholesale metamorphosis. 'I'm here,' she called joyfully.

He wore a raincoat, buttoned up to the neck, the sort usually associated with dirty old men. When he reached her bed, he looked furtively around him before unbuttoning this unflattering garment to reveal his suit of lights in all its splendour.

'Well, go on,' he said, 'ask me!'

She said, 'I don't think I need to ask.'

'I got it,' he crowed. 'I've just come from the theatre.'

Where Nancy had kicked her legs and turned somersaults and known with such radiant certainty that she would some day become a star.

'There were hundreds up for it,' he said, 'a queue right round the theatre, practically into the next *postal* district . . . But I got it. Rehearsals start August and we open in October. What do you think about that?'

She knew that she ought not to be thrilled, that he was a young man who should have his sights set sensibly on examinations and a steady career, but she *was* thrilled, thrilled to bits. He took his tap shoes from the pocket of the macintosh and changed into them. 'I'll show you a bit of the routine,' he said, 'that I did.'

And for a moment or two the ward came alive as he tapped and whirled and spun, an explosion of energy and light, shimmering and glinting amid the arid, antiseptic surfaces that surrounded them; an impromptu cabaret that might even have penetrated the tranquillizer-drowsy brains of his audience.

He concluded this performance with a sliding bow in acknowledgement of the applause of the two student nurses who appeared to be in sole charge of the ward, then sat down and unwrapped the Mars bar which he'd brought in for her and absent-mindedly began to eat it. 'You *will* be better by opening?' he said indistinctly. 'When do you actually have this operation?'

'Soon.'

Her blood count was improving and she was gaining weight. 'You're highly privileged,' the staff nurse had said. 'Normally we send patients home until they're fit for surgery.' Maisie supposed that she owed her continuing occupation of one of the NHS's precious through-put beds to the fact that they didn't trust her to obey their dietary instructions if left to her own devices.

Joe changed back into his boots and donned his raincoat. 'Gotta go,' he said. 'Er . . . Maisie,' he said, as he turned to leave, running his hand through the strange tufty hair which had been sleeked back for the occasion so that he resembled a cross between a hedgehog and a Maltese pimp, 'thanks a heap. For the suit and the practising and that.' And then his hand must have touched the chocolate wrapper that he'd stuffed into his pocket because he clapped the other one to his forehead. 'Oh God,' he said, 'I ate your Mars bar. I'll bring you another one the next time I come.'

'Just bring yourself,' she said, though she could hardly believe that hospital visiting would loom large on his agenda.

'By the way,' she said, 'does your mother know yet?'

249

He shook his head and rolled his eyes as if in anticipation of the *Götterdämmerung* that awaited him.

She said, unnecessarily, 'She won't be happy about it.'

'No,' he said, 'I don't suppose she will. But it's not her life, is it? It's mine.'

Mr Haydn-Jones, the same pin-striped suit and gold-rimmed half-spectacles but different cufflinks, leaned forward and talked to her as though addressing a half-wit. 'Miss Carruthers,' he said, consulting his notes, 'you remember I told you when I saw you last about the weak place in your artery?'

She said coldly, 'Yes, I remember. An aortic aneurism.'

'Quite so,' he said, somewhat taken aback. 'Now, you wouldn't object, would you, if some of my gentlemen were to take a look at you?'

And then, without waiting for her reply, he beckoned across half a dozen students and proceeded to conduct a question and answer session while they, in turn, prodded her in the affected region.

Then they retreated, talking quietly among themselves, confident, probably, that her seventy-seven-year-old hearing, combined with the sedative she'd been given to prepare her for some fresh assault that was planned on her person for that afternoon, would render their conversation unintelligible.

But it was her sight that was poor; there was nothing wrong with her ears and the pill she'd had produced only an intermittent stupor, and parts of what they were saying were perfectly audible.

'I remember this patient's mother being admitted,' said Mr Haydn-Jones. 'She presented with evidence of a syphilitic infection of long standing. And now, interestingly, we see one of the classic tertiary symptoms of that disease: an aneurism . . .'

'But her Wassermann was negative,' said one of the students.

'That's not so very uncommon. Which is why, if there's sufficient evidence, a test of the cerebrospinal fluid is indicated. I've ordered one for this afternoon. With regard to the mother, penicillin therapy was administered, but a subsequent scan showed Alzheimer's and the autopsy confirmed it. Symptoms, gentlemen?' he said.

One of them said, 'What rotten bad luck.' Another began to recite: 'Alzheimer's disease: disorganization of the structure of the brain: masses of neurofilaments and tubules in disarray. Also senile plaques. Accumulation of amyloid in nerve tissues and blood vessels. Main symptoms: irreversible memory loss, deficit in judgemental skills, inability to abstract, sometimes hypersexuality, and then apathy, withdrawal, incontinence . . .'

'Good, good, Chalmers,' said Mr Haydn-Jones.

Mother, Maisie thought, her neurotubules all in disarray, chewing at the rubber bands dropped by the postman, crying out in terror, calling: 'Maisie, Maisie, remember your promise!' And she would remember how she'd promised that, no matter what, she'd never disclose to anybody else the terrible information which Mother had vouchsafed.

'So we're talking here possible congenital—?' one of the students, brasher than his fellows, said in a cocksure sort of way. The consultant gave him a level stare before saying, 'The risk to the foetus in cases of early maternal infection, if untreated, is in the region of eighty to ninety per cent, but . . .'

And then Maisie drifted off. When she awoke Mr Haydn-Jones was pointing out the date of her birth, occurring as it did bang in the middle of the First World War, saying that VD was rife then, though the authorities tried to play it down.

The First World War, Maisie thought sleepily, and Pa, dying of the Spanish flu. Millions of people had died of it, her mother had said: the hale and the hearty as often as those like her father whose health had been damaged anyway as a result of that war.

'. . . those were the days prior to any really effective cure. Most affected foetuses would either spontaneously abort, be stillborn or else die in infancy. The fact that this patient is still with us . . . at seventy-seven . . . suggests to me that either she was extremely fortunate or else whatever treatment she received was prolonged enough to be effective.'

The black hospital and the doctor with the mutton-chop whiskers and the white-faced women in their iron beds and the one with her nose eaten away . . .

'But surely,' one of the medical students was saying as the entourage left the ward, 'wouldn't the army have informed wives as a matter of course: if not on moral grounds, then at least to prevent the spread of infection?'

Maisie could have enlightened him, could have told him how an afflicted soldier would be sent down the line to the base hospital at Le Havre, how his pay would be stopped, together with his family allowance. She could have told him that, during the early years of that war, wives were indeed informed of their husbands' illness, and that some men preferred to shoot themselves rather than face such an ignominious return.

But – and she could have told him this too – it was sometimes the case that soldiers went home on leave before they were even aware that they were playing host to that once-deadly spirochaete.

So many of life's little ironies could be attributed to the simple fact of bad timing.

When Maisie saw Miss Miles entering the ward she pulled the covers up to her chin and closed her eyes, as though, by doing so, she might make herself invisible.

But Miss Miles acknowledged her only briefly and in passing and went across to where Pauline was having a drain removed from her wound, and making what the unsympathetic staff nurse, who was carrying out this procedure, called a real song and dance about it.

Of course, Maisie realized, 'my' social worker was bound to be somebody else's as well.

Pauline had an infection. Almost everyone did. You'd be safer, one of the young doctors had said, having your operation at home on the rug in front of the fire. Pauline, running a temperature, had

252

fanned herself vigorously. 'Oh bloody hell,' she'd said. 'I'm having hot flushes!', and had listened, a touch sceptically, to the gynaecological registrar's explanation that although her womb had been consigned to the hospital incinerator, her ovaries were still intact and therefore her production of the requisite reproductive hormones continued unabated.

'If I'd known I'd feel like this,' she'd called across to Maisie the evening after she came round from the anaesthetic, 'I'd have taken me chances with the big C.' There was some disgusting-looking yellow-brown fluid in a bottle under her bed and she had a catheter too, draining her bladder into another one. Worst of all, until she was capable of making it unaided to the loo, she couldn't have a cigarette. To go from forty a day to nil in the space of twenty-four hours was more than humankind could bear. She was practically climbing the walls, she told Maisie, and her nerves were in shreds.

Terry hadn't been in either, to check whether she was alive or dead. Tears had been shed. 'Come on, Pauline, this isn't like you,' the staff nurse had said, just as if she could have the faintest inkling, Maisie thought, of what Pauline was like.

'Mrs Shaughnessy?' said Miss Miles, drawing up a chair. 'How are you feeling now?'

'As though I've been kicked down three flights of steps by a rugby prop-forward wearing hob-nailed boots,' Pauline said. 'How do you think?'

'Rosemary Miles,' said the owner of that name, producing proof of her identity. 'Do you remember: we met when you had that spot of trouble with your husband, the one who . . . ?'

'Got banged up,' Pauline finished for her, unnecessarily loudly. She looked across at Maisie and winked.

'Mrs Shaughnessy,' said Miss Miles, 'I'm afraid we have a bit of a problem concerning your daughter Melissa.'

Pauline said, 'I haven't got a daughter called Melissa,' and Miss Miles, looking puzzled, reached into a folder, consulted a piece of paper and then said, 'I'm sorry. Kerry, is it? Kerry McMahon.'

And then she said, 'I think we'd better pull these curtains, don't you?'

The chintz curtains were not soundproof; you couldn't help but hear. Maisie could have lifted down her earphones and listened in to the hospital radio; it was surely to her eternal shame that she didn't.

Miss Miles was talking about moral danger, a state of affairs directly linked to the fact that Kerry had been picked up by the police the night before at five-past twelve in the bus station. Her explanation was that her step-father had taken her to the seaside and then abandoned her to find her own way home and the bus that she'd caught had arrived too late to connect with the local service.

At this point Maisie heard Pauline interject: 'He's not her step-father.'

'But he does live with you, as your common-law husband,' Miss Miles said, and there was the rustling of papers as she, presumably, consulted her files, 'Mr Terence Malone?'

There was a pause and then a change of tone on Miss Miles's part to that kind of coaxing intimacy intended to encourage the sharing of confidences. 'Mrs Shaughnessy,' she said, 'is Kerry usually a truthful girl?'

Pauline was undoubtedly feeling very poorly. She hadn't lost her spark though. She said, 'Do pigs fly?' And then there was the sound of a match being struck and a drift of smoke rose above the curtain. She must have persuaded one of the students to bring her in some cigarettes; the staff nurse would have a fit. 'All kids tell porkies,' Pauline said.

'Kerry has made a very serious allegation concerning Mr Malone,' said Miss Miles. 'The police will be interviewing her again today and depending on the outcome, charges may be brought.'

Pauline gabbled: 'Kerry says all sorts, she says things just to get attention. She makes up stories . . .'

'I'm sure that this must be most distressing for you, but we

254

are led to believe that offences of the same nature have been occurring for some time ... so in view of the fact that you are in hospital and your sister seems unable to exert the necessary degree of control, we're applying for a Place of Safety order on Kerry's behalf ... At the moment she's being looked after in The Dell, a children's home in Staincross—'

Pauline's shout brought the staff nurse, the student, the ward-manager and everybody else within earshot running: 'What gives you the fucking right to take my child anywhere?'

There were ructions then all right. Eventually the staff nurse suggested that the only way in which order might be restored was if Miss Miles were to depart. 'If there's any way in which I can help,' she said, retreating through the curtain. Pauline was heard to reply that the only way she could help was by pissing off out of her sight.

June 25th, 1993.

I have my operation tomorrow. I'm first on the list after lunch. There's a special man coming in to do it, an expert in the field.

My back still feels sore where they did the lumbar puncture. A junior sort of doctor did it, but Mr Haydn-Jones was on his ward-round so he dropped by to supervise. He was talking quite loudly, as usual, and the nurse kept shooting him meaningful glances, but I believe he thinks that I'm deaf and daft as well as old because he scarcely dropped his voice as he said to the young man, 'I put this to you: you know that this woman is carrying a child that has probably inherited a potentially fatal disease ...'

The young doctor said, 'What?' as he was pushing what felt like the thickest, bluntest needle in the world into my back, 'This woman?'

'No, of course not,' Mr Haydn-Jones said irritably, 'a woman. You know that there is no cure and that the child will be born weak and sickly and will certainly become totally deaf by the time it reaches adulthood. Knowing this, do you advise termination?'

The young man said yes, in a weary sort of way, as though this particular hypothetical dilemma had been presented to him often before.

'Then,' said Mr Haydn-Jones smugly, 'you have just consigned Beethoven to oblivion.'

'Or, on the other hand,' the young man said, 'I have just consigned a total moron to oblivion.'

Mr Haydn-Jones said, 'Quite so.' I don't think that young man has done his career much good.

Sometimes I think back and I wish I'd been braver. I wish I'd had the courage to go to the doctor years ago and find out the truth, one way or the other. I was always terrified of ending up like Mother, but when I read about it, it said that that didn't always follow. So I clung to that hope.

If I come out of this intact, I'm going to put whatever time I may have left to good use. Goodness knows, I sacrificed enough of it.

The first operation after lunch was always wheeled down to theatre too soon and had to wait in a little ante-room, holding a nurse's hand, for longer than was strictly desirable. The staff stood around, chatting about their holidays: past, future and projected. A couple of them had skiing trips planned for the end of the year. 'Ooh,' somebody else said, 'Christmas in a chalet, gallons of *glüwein* and all that après-ski. Hold me back!'

Maisie thought of the Christmas at the farm when they'd had the heavy snowfall. She remembered Mother warming her scarf on the fireguard and then wrapping her up and allowing her outside to pull a wooden sled across the hard-packed snow. She remembered blood-red berries in the hedgerow and there being one goose short and how Grandpa had laughed when she enquired of him whether it had gone to heaven. 'Oh, a far better place than that, little bairn,' he'd said, and urged her to mop up the rich aromatic juices that they'd drained from the roasted bird with a crust of Grandma's bread.

After that, Christmases had dwindled until they became quite unremarkable. Though her mother still insisted on warming her scarf before she put it on to go out; it was one of her most pervasive childhood memories: the harsh smell of scorching wool that accompanied her even on the mildest of spring days.

They were waiting for Mr Davies, the expert in the field, who'd been delayed by a tail-back on the motorway. She could hear the unmistakable braying of Mr Haydn-Jones as he conversed with some other masked and gowned figures. 'Negative, yes,' he was saying. 'Ironic really: the mother tests positive and yet develops the dementia characteristic of Alzheimer's, and the daughter presents with the classic aneurism and tests negative. Ain't nature strange?'

'So it's just an ordinary aneurism, then?' the other person said.

'They're all just ordinary aneurisms, Chalmers,' Mr Haydn-Jones replied. 'But if you're talking in terms of etiology then, yes.'

'I've been reading, sir, some of the latest genetic research on Alzheimer's,' Chalmers – obviously the class swot – was saying. 'Apparently several studies have shown linkage to DNA segments on chromosome 21 . . .'

And Maisie, dutifully counting backwards from ten, could only think, with a mirth born of utter resignation: if the left doesn't get you, the right one will.

She was dreaming. About that long-ago Christmas. The snow was on the ground and there were berries as red as fresh blood in the hedgerows and Mother and Pa were standing at the gate that led into the Top Field. They were laughing together but their clothes seemed thin, suitable only for summer weather, so she warmed her scarf at the fireguard until the steam rose from its damp fibres and there was the smell of scorching in the air and she ran outside and wound it about them until they were bound together.

They opened the gate and they each took one of her hands and she walked between them. A red sun smouldered in the white sky but she knew that, once through the trees, it would climb in

257

splendour, that the corn would sprout from the hard rutted earth, springing so tall that she would have to be lifted on to Pa's shoulders, and she knew that the sun would always be golden and the sky blue and nothing black or ugly would ever appear on the horizon again.

Together they walked through the wood and into an utter radiance of sunlight and she realized, with a jolt that felt something like the perception of familiarity, that Mrs Mendelssohn had only got it half-right when she said that life was sweet; death was sweet too.

Though *she* wasn't ready for it. Not quite yet.

Chapter Twenty-Two

Clare was not one of life's natural born hostesses. She preferred other people's parties, if at all. Swept along, originally, in the wake of Lizzie's planning fervour, she was now experiencing grave misgivings. 'You'll come, won't you?' she implored Gwyn, although she had given up on the idea of him politely handing round canapés and engaging their guests in small talk, and simply desired the moral support of his presence. 'You could invite a few of your friends,' she said recklessly. 'It's going to be fancy dress.' He stared at her astonished, that she could be so deluded as to suppose that a bunch of wrinklies prancing around as Napoleon and Cleopatra could be considered an inducement. She thought she heard him say: 'Sad!' She did hear him say, 'Sorry, it's the Reading Festival that weekend. I told you.'

'You didn't.'

He said she must have Alzheimer's because the arrangements had been made ages ago. He and Toby Jamieson were taking a tent. Nervously, she rang up the unknown mother of the known-only-by-hearsay Toby Jamieson who confirmed that this was so. 'Are you happy about it?' Clare enquired.

'Why ever not?' said Toby Jamieson's mother, somewhat reprovingly.

'Do we *have* to go through with this?' she said, as the day of the party approached. 'Do you *have* to keep on whingeing?' Lizzie said. 'It isn't as if you need to do anything, apart from providing the venue. We've got the booze organized, the offy's lending us the glasses and, let's face it, most of the catering's coming courtesy of Marks and Sparks. Surely buttering the odd bit of French bread and cutting up a quiche isn't beyond your capabilities?'

'It isn't that. I think I may be developing social phobia.'

'What the hell is social phobia? Something invented by psychotherapists that requires their hideously expensive services to cure it?'

It's when you're filled with gloom at the thought of a troop of strangers and slight acquaintances marching across your doorstep, Clare thought; it's when there is every possibility that the only person you really want to socialize with won't be there.

'By the way,' Lizzie said, 'I had a phone call from Pauline, wanting to know if there was any work. She was laying this long tale of woe on me. Apparently the boyfriend has done a bunk, the police want to question him about this under-age sex business, the daughter's been taken into care and Pauline's skint. She sounded desperate so I said she could help out on Saturday. It's worth a few bob.'

'But shouldn't she be taking it easy after an operation like that?'

'Oh, just to collect glasses and pass the odd plate and so on,' Lizzie said. 'No lifting or anything. I felt so sorry for the poor cow.'

'You could have just given her the money,' Clare said. 'It would have been far nobler.'

'Absolutely not. Firstly, it would be insulting and secondly, it would suggest that money can be acquired without effort,' Lizzie said sternly.

She still took the *Guardian*, but it wouldn't be too long, Clare thought, before she cancelled it in favour of the *Daily Mail*.

She blitzed the house, she cut kilometres of French bread and prepared dips and filled vol-au-vent cases with interesting culinary combinations and laid out the borrowed glasses in long gleaming rows on a starched tablecloth. She arranged flowers in vases and nuts in dishes, and tried to prevent herself from compulsively plumping cushions and adjusting curtains while she awaited the arrival of their guests. She was dressed as a pierrette. The costume involved a frilled ruff. Gwyn, before he left, had said, 'No, don't tell me! Dog Toby!' And she wasn't entirely sure that he'd been joking.

The bell rang and she adopted a welcoming smile, but it was only Pauline come to don her pinny and stand (or sit, actually, given the delicacy of her condition) beside the buffet table, recycling glasses and replenishing plates.

She looked rough. Her natural black had grown back through the blonde of her hair, giving it a curious badger-like appearance; there were dark purple shadows beneath her eyes and she seemed to have acquired a whole network of new lines on her face.

She was considerably less vocal too. When Clare enquired after her health, and whether she had been able to rest as ordered, she merely shrugged and said, 'Our Carol's been giving us a hand but you know what it's like with three kids.'

She'd almost forgotten herself and said four.

Lizzie and Michael arrived: he decked out in Norfolk jacket, deer-stalker and leather gaiters and carrying, beneath his arm, what she hoped was an imitation shot-gun, she clad in a diaphanous flapper-style dress that was cut away at intervals to reveal a flesh-coloured body-stocking. Festooned around the nipple area were silk sprays of oak leaves and nosegays of bluebells, and sewn in a triangular pattern, coinciding with the pubic region, were tufts of campion and trailing forget-me-nots.

Clare stared, nonplussed. Lizzie said, 'Lady Chatterley, of course. What did you think? I told you that Michael was coming as a gamekeeper.'

Clare said, 'I thought you said *goal*keeper.'

'Michael,' Lizzie said, 'get those conservatory chairs on to the terrace. Otherwise we won't be able to fit people in.'

He leaned his gun against the door and touched his forelock.

261

'Right, your ladyship,' he said. There was evidence of a certain taciturnity on his part as he trundled the furniture into the garden. Perhaps, Clare thought, he was simply acting in character, but she doubted it.

Guests began to arrive. She was kept busy for a while performing introductions: vicars to tarts, Indian rajahs to elephant men, Snoopy to Baron von Richthofen. She counted three Scarlett O'Haras, two Long John Silvers, several Helens of Troy and braces of the inevitable Laurels and Hardys.

Lizzie had brought her CDs. She looked scathingly at Clare's collection. Most of these people might be middle-aged in terms of years, but they were essentially hip, *au fait*, conversant with where it was coming from, in every form and direction. They wouldn't want to drink and talk to a background of – what, Leonard Cohen?

Leonard Cohen was very fashionable again, actually, Clare had protested, but was nevertheless overruled in favour of Björk and Blur and Radiohead.

They couldn't have chosen a better evening for the party: the weather was warm and windless. The french windows were opened wide. People lingered only briefly indoors before proceeding into the garden. A few of the less self-conscious began to dance on the terrace, that curious amalgam of every dance-style of the Sixties and Seventies typical of the middle-aged.

'I've invited a couple of nice men for you,' Lizzie said, 'nice unmarried men.'

They did indeed seem very nice. There was a pagliaccio, otherwise known as Alan. This disguise was most appropriate in that Alan was just surfacing from a painful divorce. 'We match,' he said hopefully, indicating their costumes. And there was Rob, a widower with a young son and sad eyes and nice legs, displayed to their best advantage in his doublet and hose. She recognized in them that same eagerness to please, that thinly veiled social desperation, indicative of those thrown, unwillingly, once again in at the deep end of the partner-seeking pool. She'd been there herself. All the time that she was talking to them her eyes kept wandering towards the house as though, if she looked long and hard enough, she could make him appear.

A pale, gibbous moon rose, drink flowed, Pauline refuelled the buffet table and the bar, more people cast off their inhibitions and danced, to Oasis and Erasure and a Motown tape that Clare recognized as her own. Perhaps Motown was fashionable again too.

She found herself deep in a conversation concerning horticulture with two of Lizzie's colleagues, Biggles and Ginger, who really were a male couple in ordinary life, and were in the throes of landscaping their own garden. They were discussing ericaceous compost and raised beds when Lizzie, passing by with a fearsome-looking knife in order to cut their joint birthday cake, hissed, 'I go out of my way to find you suitable heterosexual men and you spend all night talking to the other sort.'

Evening merged imperceptibly into night, one of those clear, starlit nights when the light never quite dies. Only a few tired-looking remnants of food remained on the table, row upon row of empty bottles flanked the sink. The music changed to something slow and moody. Couples danced closer. He won't come, she thought bleakly. She wandered among the throng, brushing centurions' tunics and milkmaids' skirts, stepping now and then upon a Roman-sandalled or Turkish-slippered foot, colliding with a braided sleeve that was bent to raise a glass. She overheard snatches of conversation: '. . . opted out, oh absolutely, one can't experiment with one's own children . . . The Maldives, actually, we thought we've sacrificed enough years to buckets and spades and the Isle of Wight . . . There's this marvellous place where they sell off designer stuff at rock-bottom prices . . . It can't be true, you're pulling my wire? I saw them together only last week . . . Gemini, actually, but that's not what counts, it's what you've got rising . . .'

She felt invisible.

As she came downstairs after visiting the loo (why did men –

some men – always manage to miss their aim?) she heard the doorbell ring. Somebody answered it in the giggly effusive manner of the thoroughly well-oiled and although by then she was almost out of earshot, the response that she heard faintly sent her running.

He stood in the doorway. He was carrying an overnight bag. The world was bright again. Was there to be the added bonus of a night together? 'This is Theo,' she said proudly. 'Hello, Theo,' said the door-opener, a tipsy woman, who propped herself against him. 'I knew you'd be spoken for.'

Clare thought: if only you knew.

'Happy birthday.'

He kissed her and handed her a small, gift-wrapped parcel. 'It's not an exact match,' he said, 'but probably as close as you'll get, short of going back to Venice.'

She unwrapped it. It contained a bracelet set with semi-precious stones: jade and soapstone, chrysoprase and carnelian, and it complemented exactly the earrings that he'd bought her and which she would have been wearing tonight except that they'd been replaced by Gwyn's birthday present earrings.

'They're hand-made,' her son had said proudly, as she opened the box. He'd bought them from one of his erstwhile associates, one of the raggle-taggle gypsies – oh, who manufactured jewellery for sale at fairs wherever the caravan (or, in his case, ex-corporation bus) came to rest.

They were fashioned crudely, in the shape of stars, and studded with beads in rather garish colours; she thought that they were the most beautiful earrings she was ever likely to possess.

She embraced Theo. She was beyond caution. But his response was guarded. He said, 'I don't think you're going to like what I have to say.'

'Go on,' she said resignedly.

'Oh it's not that desperate,' he said, watching her face drop. 'It's just that I'm on a plane back to Switzerland at one o'clock tomorrow morning. There's a crisis. Duncan's going too, so I've

264

arranged for him to pick me up from here. I hope you don't mind?'

She swallowed her disappointment. Better to have him briefly than not at all. And, among this crowd, it would be easy to avoid the odious Duncan. 'Come and dance,' she said. They'd never danced together before but it was obvious that their rhythms would correspond.

They had set candles in coloured glass lanterns on the terrace, at the edge of the lawn, in the branches of the poplar tree, and green and gold reflections glimmered, attracting a cluster of mesmerized insects towards their beam. A woman screamed in startlement as a large furry moth brushed her arm with its wing. Someone had – by mistake, surely? – put on her Leonard Cohen record and *So Long, Marianne* floated out into the night. It wasn't really dance music, but you could cling together to anything. They swayed, enfolded; occasionally she raised her face to his, ghostly in the gloaming, to exchange a moth's-wing kiss. She was reminded of the time they'd first met, when the anticipation of a kiss was enough; it was all the times and all the boys and the young men and older men that she'd ever desired all rolled into this dream of a night, with its sky of blue velvet shot through with starlight and the consoling closeness of his warmth and the wafting of mingled fragrances: jasmine, nicotiana, white roses.

I am happy, she thought, as they held each other, scarcely moving, softly singing to each other the words of the songs, *The Sisters of Mercy*, *Memories*, *Ain't No Cure for Love*, at this moment, I am perfectly, unequivocally, happy.

And then there was the waft of another fragrance and it didn't emanate from the jasmine or the nicotiana or even the white roses; it was the unmistakable aroma that issues from the lighting up of an illegal substance. She disengaged herself from him. 'Ask Pauline to give you a drink,' she said. 'Not the plonk on the bar. There's some Chablis in an ice bucket underneath.' And she went, fuming, to seek out Lizzie from her dope-smoking lair.

She was draped across the rattan sofa in the conservatory, her eyes closed, a big stupid grin on her face, humming along to *Famous Blue Raincoat*. Most of her forget-me-nots had become dislodged from her private parts.

Clare shook her savagely. There was a whole group of them reclining in various stuporous poses all over the place.

'Hi, Clare,' she said. 'What's the word?'

'For God's sake, Lizzie!'

'Good stuff,' Lizzie said. 'Lebanese Red. Over there.'

They'd switched off the lights and the room was lit only by the glow of a lantern, but she could see the glimmer of the toke as it was passed back and forth. Somebody had brought in a tape-deck and *Nights in White Satin* built up to a crescendo.

'Lizzie, what are you thinking of? It was bad enough when Gwyn's friends brought their stuff along . . .'

'Ah,' Lizzie said placidly, 'but we're grown-ups.'

'That's debatable. Anyway, get them out of here. Now!'

Lizzie raised one heavy eyelid. She said, 'Up your Chinese mini-kilt! Who used to say that?'

She was hurrying back through the hall when the front door opened and in came Gwyn, cautiously, rucksack first. She came to an abrupt halt. 'What are you doing back here? I wasn't expecting you until Monday.'

'Obviously,' he said and began to sniff the air, following his nose to the source of the smell, glancing into the darkened conservatory. When he withdrew his head, it was to direct at her a look that succeeded, quite brilliantly, in mingling disgust, outrage and extreme sanctimoniousness.

'They're all totally monged out in there.'

'I know. I was just going to get Theo to get rid of them.'

'I'll get rid of them,' he said, and switched on all the lights and yelled, 'Shift!' at the top of his voice. 'God,' he said, 'this is so pathetic!'

People rose slowly to their feet. Befuddlement held sway. Michael Twist's moleskin trousers had slipped below his paunch; he hitched them up, exposing the lard-white flesh of his belly in the process. A woman dressed as Bo-Peep got her crook jammed between two chair legs, extricated it clumsily. Batman and Robin linked each other for support.

Only Lizzie seemed unbudgeable. Gwyn poked her gingerly with the end of a rolled-up copy of *Mojo* that he'd brought in with him. She stirred briefly, sighed quite contentedly.

'Why *are* you back so early?' Clare asked him as, one by one, her guests, adjusting their dress, straightening their spectacles and blinking like moles newly surfaced, wended their intoxicated way into the garden.

'Oh,' he said, 'bit of bother. It's cool.'

A further bit of bother was something she was happy to pass up but, as the Rolling Stones track that had succeeded Leonard Cohen warned her at that precise moment: 'You can't always get what you want.'

She stepped into the garden, saw Theo at the far end in conversation with three other people, one of whom was the decidedly uninvited guest, Mr Fry. She was steeling herself to join them when her attention was diverted. Beside the buffet table, a scruffy man, with several days' growth of beard, who appeared the worse for drink, was engaged in what could only be described as a slanging match with Pauline. Clare overheard part of this interchange: 'So why did you dump our Kerry, leave her to find her way back on her own?'

'I didn't leave her. I told her to wait for me outside the pub. She was kicking up shit because I wouldn't buy her this necklace-thing she'd seen. When I come out she'd gone. She got back, didn't she? She had her ticket to get back. You know Kerry. You can't do nothing with her.'

'You did though, didn't you? You did things with her.'

He lurched a little. He said, 'What you on about?'

He coughed. Phlegm rattled in his lungs. And then he spat into her beautiful white nicotiana. 'You don't want to believe what that little cow tells you. She can lie faster than she can walk.'

And all the time the volume was rising, the postures growing more aggressive.

This, Clare presumed, must be the errant boyfriend. She went back into the conservatory which was occupied now only by Gwyn and the softly snoring Lizzie. She said, 'That chap of Pauline's has showed up. Apparently he's wanted by the law for questioning. It looks like turning nasty. I'm going to ring the police.'

He grabbed her arm. 'Are you mad?' he said, and began throwing open the windows.

'Why are you doing that? What's wrong?'

He began to search through the ashtrays. 'Is there any air-freshener?' he said.

'In the utility-room, under the sink. Why?'

'You filthy bastard,' she heard Pauline yell. Her hand moved towards the phone. He grabbed it before she could lift the receiver. 'Don't be an idiot,' he said. 'If the pigs arrive, we'll be done this time for sure.'

Outside, things were building up into a full-scale fracas. They were squaring up to one another. Apparently he had come for money. 'Just till Friday,' she heard him say wheedlingly, 'just till I get me Giro.' This request had been enough to send Pauline stratospheric. She shook her fist. 'You scumbag,' she shouted. 'I hope your prick drops off.' He called her a fucking cunt. She returned the compliment. The assembled guests, dwindled considerably since Gwyn's cleansing of the conservatory, gathered, at a discreet distance, to watch this altercation. She ran down to the bottom of the garden. Theo and Duncan Fry and their companions were drinking Chablis and discussing some film that had been on television the previous night. 'Of course,' she heard Duncan Fry saying, 'he's as camp as a row of tents. And looks it. Why they insist on casting him as a lusty hetero all the time is beyond me—' And then he saw her and smiled and said, 'Why hello, Little-Miss-End-of-the-Pier.'

She ignored him. 'Can't you *do* something?' she begged of Theo.

He looked across to where Pauline and her boyfriend were making ever more threatening lunges towards one another as though he'd only just noticed this performance or else, assuming that it was part of the night's entertainment and finding it not to his taste, preferred to ignore it.

'What would you like me to do?' he asked, in a measured tone that contrasted oddly with the frantic obscenities that were being exchanged in his immediate vicinity.

'Well – separate them,' she said. Distantly, she saw Pauline fetching the man a great clout around the ear. Luckily for him, it didn't quite connect.

'Good grief,' Duncan Fry said. 'You didn't tell me, Theo, that there was going to be cabaret.'

Theo raised his glass to his lips. 'It is most unwise,' he said, 'to intervene between man and wife. Usually they both turn on you.'

'But they're not man and wife,' she said. 'And Pauline had a hysterectomy not long ago.'

Pauline shrieked. 'Now you was asking for that smack,' she heard the man say. 'Don't say you wasn't.'

She ran back towards the house, intending to ring the police, pot or no pot. One or two of the less feeble men had started to move towards the now darkly struggling mass that was Pauline and her boyfriend. Suddenly Gwyn appeared, outlined in the french windows, an aerosol can in his hand.

It all happened so quickly: there was a bright flash in the gloom as Pauline picked up the birthday cake knife and flailed it and the sound of a can hitting the floor as Gwyn sprang down the steps and hurled himself between them, and a yell and a long-drawn-out exhalation of breath. And then Duncan Fry, unhurriedly, it seemed, strolled across, disarmed the one, felled the other with what, she believed, was called a clean left hook, and bent down to look at Gwyn. There was blood everywhere, she saw when she reached the terrace, such an incredible amount of blood.

*   *   *

Somebody rang the police, a neighbour, no doubt, perhaps the same one who'd summoned them to Gwyn's party. They found the boyfriend, heavily bruised, crouching in the bushes in the front garden of number thirty-nine. One of them called up an ambulance while the others trod heavily through the garden and the house. By unhappy coincidence they were the same policemen who had been called to the scene when the place had been invaded by previous pot-smoking partygoers. Their noses twitched in the conservatory which reeked of insect-repellent, Gwyn having picked up the wrong aerosol.

'Plague of mosquitoes?' one of them asked pleasantly. The other said, 'We'll be back for a word with you, son,' and nodded at Gwyn, who was sitting on the sofa clutching the tourniqueted towel round his forearm, next to Lizzie who hadn't woken despite all the commotion.

Afterwards, in the ambulance, he was almost incoherent with rage. 'Shit!' he kept saying. 'I'm being hassled on account of a bunch of monged-out wrinklies. Shit!'

She'd envisaged major surgery, if not amputation, but although the wound had bled with such alarming profusion, it was only superficial, requiring nothing more than a few stitches. Pauline had been using the knife for gesticulatory purposes rather than with murderous intent. Still, Theo had been proved right: outsiders involving themselves in domestic disputes invariably came off worst.

The policemen had asked for witness statements, but there had been a great melting away of people at the sound of the siren, Theo and Duncan Fry included, she discovered, discretion obviously having been perceived as being much the better part of valour.

Gwyn had always been prone to exaggerating the slightest of accidents: a graze might require a blood transfusion, a scratch could lead to lockjaw; subjected to the real thing, he proved remarkably stoical. 'God!' she said, hugging him, 'you could have been really *hurt*.'

He submitted, momentarily, to this embrace and then shrugged her off. 'Mind my arm!' he said. He was still only a kid, after all.

Maybe violence was contagious. When they got back, Lizzie was slumbering still and – even more irritatingly – so was Michael Twist, his mouth open, his chin slumped on to his red-spotted neckerchief. She fished out his replica shotgun from under the sofa where he'd deposited it – and the police, thankfully, had failed to notice it, and pointed it at him, the barrel gently nuzzling his chin. 'Wake up!' she yelled, and was immensely gratified to witness his sudden and panic-stricken arousal.

It was a good feeling, being in control; she thought perhaps she ought to try it more often.

'You do understand,' Theo said, telephoning from Switzerland the following day, 'why I had to disappear like that? Apart from the fact that I had to get to the airport?'

'Perfectly.'

'It might have been rather awkward: witness statements and so forth.'

'You don't have to worry,' she said. 'They accepted that what happened was an accident.'

'How is Gwyn?'

'Well, thanks to your friend, he's OK. He only needed a few stitches.'

It grated, oh how it grated: having to accept that Duncan Fry had been the one to demonstrate the necessary machismo.

'A bit over the top, don't you think?' Theo said. 'He's nursing bruised knuckles today, I can tell you.'

She said, 'He did what was necessary. He intervened.'

As Gwyn had done: rashly, perhaps, and with unnecessary flamboyance but, all the same, prompted by an instinctive desire to do the right thing. She kept seeing Theo in her mind's eye, standing at the bottom of the garden, elegantly smoking a cigarette and keeping a low profile. She had wanted *him* to act the hero, to behave instinctively. But Theo was a pragmatist. What was it he'd said: something about things being neither good nor bad but thinking made them so? She could understand, in view of his history, why he held back, weighed the pros and cons, calculated the outcome; she knew whence derived his tolerance of moral ambiguity; she just wished that she could have met him before that protective coating had been acquired.

Chapter Twenty-Three

Maisie sent a postcard from her every port of call: views of the Golden Gate Bridge, the Hollywood sign, Yosemite National Park, the Grand Canyon. The accompanying messages conveyed a childlike wonderment as they described the extravagant splendour of the scenery, the cosmopolitan crush of the cities, the vastness of the scale upon which everything – roads, cars, apartments, *meals* – seemed to be constructed, the *kindness* of everyone: Lottie and Eva, Lottie's family, a friend called Rita who'd flown from Canada especially to see her, bus-boys and taxi-drivers and waitresses in wayside diners. *It's just grand*, Maisie wrote. *I'm being treated like a queen.*

Clare pinned them up on the notice-board in her kitchen: vivid reminders of brighter skies and broader horizons.

'It's absolutely the last thing I'd have expected her to do,' she told Lizzie who was, rudely, detaching the cards in order to read them. 'The minute she came out of that convalescent place, she announced that she was going to the States to visit her friends.'

'I should have such friends who would underwrite that sort of trip,' Lizzie said. 'Nice work if you can get it.'

Her own holiday had not come up to scratch. Or perhaps that was an unfortunate way of putting it. Michael had consumed suspect shellfish in some quaint harbourside taverna, and suffered for it; she had attracted the attention of every blood-seeking mosquito in the vicinity of the coast and spent the best part of a week in torments of itching.

'She's due back on Wednesday,' Clare said. 'I said I'd pick her up from the airport.'

'How very noble of you,' Lizzie remarked. 'I'm sure you'll get your reward in heaven.'

Wednesday was one of those days, from the failure of the alarm clock to go off, to the car refusing to start until the nth attempt, to being coned off on the motorway.

She sat drumming her fingers on the steering wheel as the minutes ticked by, trying to force the traffic to move by an effort of will. Maisie would be starting to panic. Old people did. Clare had been astounded that she could undertake international travel at her age with such apparent insouciance, and had said so. Maisie had paused in her packing. 'You only get one life,' she'd said. 'I let mine be ruined for all sorts of reasons: being a coward, not standing up for myself, letting bad luck get in the way. If I'd any advice to give anybody, I'd say, "Make the most of every single minute of it."'

And then she'd blushed and looked away, because, of course, the giving of advice might be construed as presumptuous, and left Clare seething with curiosity as to the precise way in which Maisie considered her life to be ruined.

When she finally got to the airport she sprinted for her life, reaching the meeting point in the arrivals lounge with minutes to spare, only to find that the flight had been delayed. There was time for two cups of coffee and a browse through the bookshop before it was finally announced.

Maisie came slowly, chatting quite vivaciously to a young man who was pushing her luggage-laden trolley as well as his own. She thanked him, her face lighting up as she caught sight of Clare. 'No need to ask if you've had a good time,' Clare said as she approached. They stood at a distance from one another, rather awkwardly, each too shy to attempt a kiss or an embrace, each recognizing the other's shyness. Maisie said, 'I've had the time of my life,' and then opened her duty-free carrier bag to reveal a long package of cigarettes. 'I got them for

Joe,' she said, 'on the way out. I know you'll say I shouldn't have done . . .'

Actually he'd given up on health grounds, but she didn't tell Maisie that. 'It'll be better,' she said, 'if you wait here with the luggage and I'll bring the car as close as I can.'

'Yes, dear,' Maisie said obediently. She wore a scarf patterned with stars and stripes and there was an AIDS awareness ribbon pinned to her coat. 'I've got you some other little things,' she said, 'but better wait till we get back. There were these cowboy boots in Santa Fe. Joe was always saying he wanted cowboy boots. I do hope they fit . . .'

'I shan't be long,' Clare said.

And Maisie settled back into her seat with the ease of an airport habituée. 'Take your time,' she said. 'There's no hurry.'

And it was as well that she'd said that because when Clare went back to the car-park she found that some idiot had hemmed her in and the said idiot didn't return for a good ten minutes and by the time annoyance had been expressed and excuses offered and the car finally shifted, another five minutes had elapsed. She was fuming by the time she got back to the terminal building. She dashed across the lounge. Maisie appeared to be asleep, her head, fallen sideways, resting on her shoulder. Clare shook her gently; she looked so peaceful, it seemed a pity to wake her. 'Maisie,' she said softly. 'Time to go!' It was only when Maisie's hand, dislodged by the shaking from where it had been resting in her lap, touched her own and she recognized a torpor emanating from it, that she realized that she had already gone, that Maisie had completed more than one journey.

Clare inherited the cat. Collecting him from the cattery, she walked past cage after cage of sleek aristocratic creatures until she came to the one that housed Timmy. He regarded her gravely for some considerable time. 'Well,' she said uncertainly, 'aren't you a handsome fellow?' Actually she thought the scars on his muzzle gave him a cock-eyed look. At last, just as she was about

275

to turn away, he stretched his neck and rubbed the side of his face against her hand.

And then he bit her, quite badly. Blood flowed from the wound and she was advised to have a precautionary tetanus injection. Lizzie said, 'I know what I'd do with him and it wouldn't be to sit him on a silk cushion with a saucer of cream.'

But after that initial assault he was completely docile. It was as though he'd needed to put his mark on her.

Gwyn, of course, had been popular with him from the start. Really, though it was she who fed him and de-fleaed him and took him to the vet, he was Gwyn's cat.

Gwyn's cat, Gwyn's house. They were astonished when, summoned by letter to the offices of Messrs Stoneman, Stoneman and Finch, shortly after Maisie's death, they were informed that twenty-one, Dearborn Avenue, being the former residence of the deceased, had been willed to one Gwyn Joseph Williams.

Clare had blushed crimson; Gwyn had turned pale. This cast of complexion, together with his eyes, which were extremely bloodshot, gave him a faint resemblance to a silent-film vampire. She'd have suspected him of smoking pot, except that, coming home early from work the previous day, she had heard sounds of weeping issuing from his bedroom. She'd wondered if he wept not just for Maisie but perhaps, belatedly, for his father too, for the abandonment and loss that had occurred so prematurely.

She left him in peace to cry himself out; she'd learned that much.

The funeral had been a modest affair, the mourners consisting of herself and Miss Miles, two ladies from the library and one from the corner shop, and Gwyn. 'Are you sure you really want to go?' she'd asked him. 'You kept me from Dad's funeral,' he'd said by way of answer, and most unfairly, she'd thought, as her intention at the time had only been to spare him embarrassment and pain. So she'd fished out of his wardrobe the nearest approximation to sober clothing that she could find (she'd wondered, for one ghastly moment, if he'd intended to wear his sequinned suit) and together they went to the crematorium where the vicar intoned a few banal sentiments concerning the life of Miss Margaret Alice Carruthers before consigning her mortal remains to the fire.

And then Clare accompanied Miss Miles back to Maisie's house to ensure that everything was secure. They walked through the rooms, checking doors and windows. Everything, as always, was spick and span. 'She must have been a strong woman,' Miss Miles said, drawing back the living-room curtains which had been closed as a mark of respect while the hearse made its slow departure. 'You know, the majority of people, just as soon as their elderly relatives look like being even slightly bothersome, they're holding up their hands and demanding home helps and nursing-homes and round the clock care, while Maisie here looked after her severely demented mother, virtually single-handed, for all those years. It was no mean achievement. At least,' Miss Miles said, 'she had a good death.'

She'd sailed through the operation, made a complete recovery, had, it seemed, been granted a new lease of life. But perhaps the excitement had been too much, because her heart had given out. That was probably not what was written on the death certificate but it was how Miss Miles described it: 'Her heart gave out.'

Though not before she'd acted out of the goodness of it.

'But why Gwyn?' Clare had said bewilderedly in the offices of Stoneman, Stoneman and Finch. 'We'd known her scarcely any time at all. Surely, if she had anything to leave, it should have gone to her American friends? Or the one in Canada?'

Though, judging by what Maisie had said, her transatlantic friends were well-to-do. Certainly they'd sent the largest and most luxuriant of wreaths to the funeral.

Mr Stoneman the Younger couldn't comment on Maisie's reasons for disposing of her assets in this way (her assets being, in fact, few: just the house and its contents and a small insurance policy which would cover the cost of the funeral), but he did have some more information for them. The will contained a certain proviso: viz. that any moneys accruing to Gwyn Joseph Williams after the sale of the assets were to be held in trust until he was a) twenty-five and b) had completed his Advanced Level examinations.

Clare sat next to Gwyn, unfamiliar in his funeral suit, across the desk from the younger Mr Stoneman and she thought: Maisie, you are, *were*, brilliant!

The news caused Gwyn to regress, initially, into a state of infantilism. 'Crikey!' he said, and, 'Wow!' and began to bite the nails of both hands furiously. Clare imagined that racing through his mind would be images of cash-registers ringing up sales of must-haves: cars and guitars and CDs and concert tickets and Dexter Wong trousers and Timberland boots and Wannabe shoes, cartons of cigarettes, lorryloads of booze, cargo ships stuffed to the gunwales with ganja.

Later, when they were at home, toasting Maisie in something called *Méthode Champenoise* that she'd purchased for the occasion from Sainsbury's, he said, sneezing as the bubbles hit his sinuses, 'That gives me eight years to do my A Levels without forfeiting the money.'

Maisie's house was too dilapidated to fetch much of a price, even if the market had not been depressed, but the capital, earning interest, at whatever modest level, for eight years, would produce a final sum more than most twenty-five-year-olds could expect to collect. Perhaps, she thought, he'd have learned sense by then.

She hazarded a joke about him being able to keep her in her old age, to which he responded with a touching earnestness that he certainly wouldn't see her go short.

'You won't need to put up with some chap just for the sake of security,' he said.

'Is that what you believe: that I'm . . . ?' She was lost for words. 'Anyway,' she said, eventually, 'never mind that. What's more important is how this is going to affect *your* future.'

Rehearsals for the show had started on schedule. He'd returned each night bursting with information to impart: the brilliance of the choreography, the catchiness of the tunes, the conviction of the company that they had a sure-fire hit on their hands. 'They've got Laurie O'Connell for the lead,' he'd said. 'I mean, that practically ensures bums on seats.'

'Isn't Laurie O'Connell a singer?' she'd said, having a vague recollection of seeing the name on posters.

'Yeah.'

'Oh you mean it's dancing *and* singing?' she'd said. 'You mean *you* have to sing? I didn't know you could.'

But perhaps the despised Welsh genes had come in useful after all.

'Don't you have to be trained to sing at that level?'

She'd had a bizarre image of Gwyn, trilling scales at the piano, being tutored in this exercise by some ex-diva with a bust like Dame Clara Butt called Madame La Zonga, or whatever.

'I'm going to start classes. Did I tell you . . . ?'

There'd been nothing she could say that would dissuade him from his course. He was on cloud nine.

But since then Laurie O'Connell had come down with hepatitis and the opening had had to be postponed.

And now she had been provided with further ammunition.

'Wouldn't it make sense,' she said, 'to go back to school and get your exams out of the way *now*? There'll be other shows. And anyway you might change your mind . . .'

'I won't,' he said.

But he'd said that about studying medicine, about guitar-playing, about wanting to be an astronaut.

'Gwyn, you'll *need* those exams.'

'Why?' he said. 'So I can go to university and get a degree and then get a job I hate, just like you?'

She changed her tactic: 'So what if this career takes off? What if, in eight years' time, you're still singing and dancing? Where does that leave you in terms of your inheritance? Without it, that's where.'

'If that happens,' he said, 'then I won't need it, will I?'

He could outflank, outwit, outargue her, even at his tender age. She said wearily, 'Oh Joe – if I must call you that – how about just doing it for me?'

But he was old enough to know that that was the worst possible reason.

He still had the keys to Maisie's house. She told him that they should be returned to the solicitors forthwith, but he procrastinated. She knew that he wanted to let himself in and lord it around his property, shabby though it was. Timmy followed him inside, stood waiting expectantly beside his empty dish, emitting the occasional puzzled chirrup. Clare, who had gone after him, suspecting that, despite his rations being doled out next door, he might be tempted to return, picked him up and stood waiting while Joe opened a drawer to reveal a heap of steel hair-curlers, a pair of broken spectacles, pieces of string, out-of-date money-off vouchers, tablets long since dissolved into a scum of powder, farthings, threepenny bits, a watch stopped at five-past three on some forgotten afternoon.

A few cheap ornaments, utility furniture, crockery of the sort called Pink Dawn that Woolworth's used to sell, tablecloths gone mouldy at the creases, a Bakelite wireless set that, when plugged into the mains, broadcast from no discernible station, a fly paper hosting a few desiccated corpses that continued to twirl gently beneath the electric light bulb – 'Not exactly Blenheim, is it?' she said, transferring the cat, which was heavy, into the arms of the inheritor of these paltry possessions.

The valuers would come in and the house-clearance people, picking over Maisie's life like scavengers on a refuse tip.

'You never know,' he said, handling a chipped plate of garish design as tenderly as if his squint at its base might reveal it to be Clarice Cliff, 'some of this stuff might be antique.'

She let him dream on, knowing full well that Maisie's effects were not the sort that dealers would be fighting over, rather, you would have to pay them to take the stuff away.

280

Maisie's bed was made, the balding candlewick coverlet pulled up neat and tight and smooth. There was an item of furniture beside it which, Clare had discovered as a result of assiduous attention to the *Antiques Roadshow*, was used to house a chamber pot. 'Don't!' she said, as Joe went to open it, afraid that one of the same might be revealed, long overdue for emptying. However, rather than this indelicate article, the cupboard contained a stack of books of various sorts: exercise books, jotters, ledgers and, now and then, a volume bearing the official title of *Diary*.

He lifted them out and piled them on the bed. Each was labelled with a date, the earliest being 1925. He began to sort them into chronological order, counting aloud as he did so. There were sixty-eight of them, little thin books and big sturdy ones, red ones and green ones and ones with stiff marbled covers, ones whose pages could be separated only with difficulty and released a haze of mould spores and paper dust; there was one for every year until they reached 1992.

'Where's this year's?' cried Joe, scrabbling through them again. It was inconceivable that Maisie should suddenly have ceased to fill in her diary, that this last and perhaps best year of her life should be unrepresented.

They came upon it later, the final volume. It was with the rest of Maisie's belongings which had been unpacked by Miss Miles from her luggage.

'I never realized that people kept diaries all their lives,' Joe said.

'I don't suppose many do. If you're living your life, you don't usually have much opportunity to record it.'

She read the final paragraph on the last page of the most recent book: *Tomorrow, they're hosting a farewell party for me. I've had such a wonderful time. It's a marvellous place, America. No wonder emigrants flocked here. What is it it says on the Statue of Liberty: 'Give me your poor, your huddled masses . . .'? After the wars or the poverty or the persecution that they'd suffered, it must have seemed like the land of their dreams.*

'We'd better leave them for the valuation people,' she said, in her best mothers-should-set-a-good-example voice.

'Oh right. I expect they'll sell them at Sotheby's for a record-breaking sum,' Joe said. 'Honestly! I mean, what are they going to do with them?'

Consign them to some unidentified refuse bin, she supposed. Or incinerator. Maisie's life reduced to ash, on every count. The temptation to salvage them was irresistible. She rationalized her action: the house and everything in it belonged to Joe. If sold, the proceeds would come to him anyway. A sale being highly unlikely in this case, failure to remove them could, theoretically, be construed as a loss-making exercise. She carried them home and that night, in bed, she flicked through them at random, found herself reading the entry for April 22nd, 1942. It said: *I've lost the baby. Everything of Bob is gone now. Except my memory of him. I won't let that go. Ever.*

I can't stop crying. Nurse Pym hugs me and wipes my eyes . . .

She read on, avidly, backwards and forwards, reading about the day that Maisie's mother, having heard the declaration of war on the wireless, took a copy of the *News Chronicle* and stuck dress-making pins into a photograph of Mr Chamberlain, before closing her mind totally to the fact that there was a war on, reading about Bob, during the Blitz, helping to dig survivors from the rubble and discovering a woman with a baby in her arms who had taken refuge in a disused chimney, upright still, both of them stone dead, reading about Maisie's black hospital, which had been built originally for the forcible internment of disease-ridden prostitutes, and the one in Le Havre to which her unfortunate father was dispatched when they discovered the nature of his malady. She fell asleep, the diary still in her hand. She dreamed, not of Theo, as was so often the case, but of dead babies and doodlebugs.

'Well, it's not exactly *The Country Diary of an Edwardian Lady*, is it?' Lizzie said. 'I don't think you'd be able to flog the T-shirt franchise or the duvet-cover concession.'

'It's fascinating,' Clare said vehemently. 'Sixty-nine years of recording the minute events of daily life.'

She kept going back to the diaries whenever she had a spare moment. An unknown Maisie, different altogether from the shy scuttling creature in the old felt beret and unravelling cardigan who had apologized so profusely for being alive, spoke clearly from the pages. Her descriptions were so precise that characters came alive: Nancy in her red tap shoes, thumbing her nose at Solly Rubin from the wings; Eva polishing her violin tenderly, lifting it to her shoulder and playing the Mendelssohn *Concerto* with a passion that foretold tragedy; Bob, loading up an ambulance with sandbags and gleefully taking the opportunity to drive through the streets like the clappers, the bell clanging furiously, as people assumed that he was delivering casualties to hospital; the day that *Workers' Playtime* was broadcast from Maisie's factory and sluttish Mavis boasted of having it off behind the ladies' lav with a Famous Radio Personality who proved to be wearing a truss.

'But she didn't *do* anything,' Lizzie said. 'She didn't get elected to parliament or sail round the world single-handed or paint pictures or meet famous people. It's not a *Country Diary* and it's not Bloomsbury either – it's not even Auden's *Shilling Life . . .*'

More like a penny life, Clare thought, an old penny, one that had lain for years in Maisie's drawer, covered in lint and dust and powdered aspirin. She thought of Maisie faithfully recording the small domestic details, in the same tone as the larger events, as her life gradually became more and more circumscribed; Maisie, the innocent victim of two world wars, whose talents and appetite for life had been crushed by what she erroneously believed to be her shame, subordinated to what she thought of as her duty. At least the diaries had given her a voice.

And perhaps it was a voice that ought to be heard, to command a wider audience. Clare's editorial fingers itched to lay professional hands upon it, to cut and shape and refine it, a task delightfully different from the dry statistics and cold facts that comprised her normal daily routine. She'd already begun to make a few tentative pencil marks on the first few pages of the 1925 diary when Theo rang to apologize for the fact that things prevented him from coming round this evening as he'd planned. Had she not been so absorbed, her disappointment would have been keener. These diaries were, in their way, social histories. In microcosm, perhaps, but she'd read somewhere that there was a market for this kind of thing.

'What about Thursday?' Theo was saying. 'I think I could manage Thursday.'

'Mmm hmm,' she said. She'd tried to harden her heart against him, but every time she heard his voice her resolve faltered. Great renunciations were the stuff of fiction. Perhaps, she thought, I'll have to wait until they develop a morning-after pill for the heart. Perhaps Theo's company will produce it. She thought: timing is everything, really. Undoubtedly, if they'd discovered penicillin prior to 1915, then Maisie's life would have been markedly different.

'Have I called at an inconvenient moment?' Theo was saying.

'No,' she said, 'not at all. It's just that I've had this idea . . .'